X

WITH AN EXTREME BURNING

WITH AN EXTREME BURNING

Bill Pronzini

Carroll & Graf Publishers, Inc.
New York

PRO
CI

Copyright © 1994 by Bill Pronzini

First Carroll & Graf edition 1994

Carroll & Graf Publishers, Inc.
260 Fifth Avenue
New York, NY 10001

Library of Congress Cataloging-in-Publication Data

Pronzini, Bill.
    With an extreme burning / Bill Pronzini.—1st Carroll & Graf ed.
        p.   cm.
    ISBN 0-7867-0139-0 : $19.95 ($28.00 Can.)
    I. Title
PS3566.R67W58   1994
813'.54—dc20   94-22393
                                                                    CIP

Manufactured in the United States of America

The Lord shall smite thee with a consumption, and with a fever, and with an inflammation, and with an extreme burning, and with the sword, and with blasting, and with mildew; and they shall pursue thee until thou perish. . . . And thy life shall hang in doubt before thee; and thou shalt fear day and night, and shalt have none assurance of thy life.

—Deuteronomy 28: 22, 66

WITH AN EXTREME BURNING

PART ONE
Slow Burn

ONE

He awoke at his usual time, seven-thirty, and as usual in the first groggy seconds he reached out for Katy on her side of the bed. Then he remembered. Even before his fingers touched the cool, empty sheets, he remembered.

His grief was easing now, after more than three weeks; he felt one small twist of pain, nothing more. He rolled onto his back, opened his eyes. Sunlight in the room, slants and patches of it. The quality of light told him it was going to be hot again today. What day was it? Saturday. Another long weekend. Almost the end of August, though. Next weekend was Labor Day, and right after that fall classes started ... first week of September this year. Easier, then—a little easier. Not so much time alone. He had better see Elliot Messner right away, before it was too late to take on an extra class or two, maybe teach a couple of rudimentary history courses in the university's extension program to fill up weeknights or Saturdays. Work and plenty of it was what he needed, at least for this semester, until more time built up between himself and the accident.

He lay listening to the quiet. There were usually birds in the big heritage oak outside the bedroom, that damned mockingbird that was worse than an alarm clock sometimes, but not today. The silence beyond the open window had a flat, padded quality. He could smell the heat gathering, absorbing the early-morning coolness; smell dust and the dry brown grass on the hillside above. For some reason, the smells made him remember an exchange during the excessive heat of early July. Katy: "Dix, I'm worried about fire this year. It's so *dry* up on that hill.'' Him: ''The grass has been mowed, there's no real danger. Why worry about things that aren't likely to happen?''

Like accidents and fire.

Like dying in flames so hot they reduced five and a half feet of flesh, skin, and bones into an unrecognizable four-foot lump of charcoal—

There was a curtain in his mind, as thick as metal, forged over the past three weeks; he yanked it down now, locked it tight. Abruptly he swung himself out of bed. In the bathroom he used the toilet and then put on his swim trunks and robe. Downstairs to the kitchen. Grind some beans, start the Mr. Coffee. And then down to the bottom level, out onto the rear terrace.

Mist in the valley below, a thin, floating strip of it that would be gone in another hour or so. At this hour and from this height, the town had a somnolent look except for the broken ant-stream of cars on the freeway that cut through the south end. Los Alegres. Population: 32,000 and growing, thanks to tract-home developers consuming east-side farmland at alarming rates. He'd been born and raised here, spent nearly all of his life here. Just seven of his forty-one years away, beginning with his army service in North Carolina during the 'Nam years. (Some people seemed puzzled when he told them he'd never left U.S. soil, much less fought in Asian jungles; it was as if they thought every male who had been drafted in those ugly days had been immediately shipped overseas, leaving the homefront military bases entirely in the hands of over-aged officers and National Guard weekenders.) Then four years at UC Irvine, earning his master's with a thesis on post–Civil War Reconstruction in the border states. And when it came time to choose a teaching post, straight back to Los Alegres to accept a position on the faculty at Balboa State. Just a country boy at heart, Katy would say, forgetting that Los Alegres was little more than an hour from San Francisco and hadn't been ''country'' in thirty years. My roots go deep, he would say. Trite but essentially true. Katy's had gone just as deep: She'd been born and raised here, too, and never left for more than a few months at a time. Never would, now.

When they'd bought this house eight years before, just affordable on their combined teaching salaries thanks to the $50,000 cash bond her father had left them, it was an ascension in more ways than one. High on the hillside above the town and the valley: trees that had sprung tall from their deep roots. For him, a symbol that he'd Made

It. One acre of the Ridge, one acre of the American dream—and to go with it, a full tenured professorship, *A Darkness at Antietam* accepted for publication, a happy marriage. No children, because Katy couldn't carry to term, but that was a small regret. Now eight years had passed, eight rapid years. And even before the accident, it had all gone just a little stale.

Teaching didn't fulfill him quite as much as it had when he was younger. Living on the Ridge didn't seem to mean as much. *A Darkness at Antietam* was still his only published, only completed novel; he couldn't seem to get a second one to jell properly. The marriage to Katy had not been quite as good either. Nothing either of them could pin down; they'd tried once last year, when Katy decided to quit full-time counseling and teach part-time—one of those let's-get-it-all-out-in-the-open-so-we-can-fix-it discussions. The problems were just too nonspecific. A vague restlessness on both sides, small dissatisfactions, little frictions that couldn't be identified much less resolved. It was a case of two people married for seventeen years, entering middle age, comfortable with each other, still able to communicate verbally and sexually (although even sex had grown somewhat mechanical), yet discontented, bored. Tolerably bored, to be sure, but bored nonetheless. Maybe it was like that for most long-married couples, he'd thought. Midlife crisis in tandem. But he was sure they'd weather it somehow. Work through it. Divorce was never discussed, never a consideration. Kathleen and Dixon Mallory were fated to celebrate their silver wedding anniversary, possibly their golden as well; to grow old together up here on the Ridge. He'd never had any doubt of that. Never a moment's doubt.

Until the two highway patrol officers showed up at ten-forty P.M. on Friday, August 6.

Until they told them in their bleak, clumsy fashion that Katy was dead.

He turned away from the view, went to the back part of the terrace. He pushed the button to roll back the automatic pool cover, then shed his robe and dove in cleanly. The water was cool but not cold, just the right temperature for swimming laps. He swam fifty without stopping, counting each one off in his mind, using both crawl and backstroke. When he was done, his arms and legs ached but he was not badly winded. Getting proficient at this. One hundred and fifty laps per day now, in three sessions. Helped him get through the daylight hours, helped him sleep at night. He rubbed himself dry with one of the pool towels, noticing without satisfaction that his paunch was almost gone. Nearly fifteen pounds overweight on Friday, August 6. Twenty-two days later he was almost as trim as he'd been in his army days. Katy had been after him to eat less, exercise more; it had taken her dying to get him to do it.

Showered and shaved and dressed, he was pouring coffee in the kitchen when the telephone rang. It kept on ringing: He'd left the damn answering machine off again.

There was no one he cared to talk to. And condolence-bearers and misguided samaritans bent on easing his sorrow by inviting him to lunch, dinner, or some little get-together depressed him. He'd tried to make it clear at the funeral, politely but firmly, that for the time being he didn't want visitors or callers; he wanted to deal with his grief in his own way. Most of his family and friends respected that, but a few were tenacious because they thought they knew better than he did what was good for him. Mrs. Tarcher, down the hill, for one. Jerry Whittington. His sister Claudia . . .

Still ringing. Let it ring, he thought. But he was one of the breed who is constitutionally incapable of ignoring a ringing phone, and the noise was becoming an irritant. "All right," he said aloud, *"okay."* He went to pick up the receiver. "Yes? Hello?"

Somebody breathed at him. That was all.

Oh Christ. This bastard again.

He said hello twice more; the line stayed open on the other end, the breathing slow and steady, just loud enough to be audible. "Let me tell you something," Dix said. It was an effort to control his anger, keep it out of his voice. "You're committing a crime, do you know that? You can go to jail. Understand? Jail."

Inhale. Exhale. Inhale. Exhale.

Dix hung up. Gently, curbing an impulse to jam the receiver back into its cradle.

Disturbed personality, probably sociopathic. Read in the *Herald* about the accident, was getting his kicks by tormenting the recently bereaved husband. It had started too soon afterward, the day after the funeral, for it to be a random thing, coincidental. There was no other purpose to it that he could see, this continued calling; four times now that he knew about, when he'd picked up the phone, and God knew how many hang-ups when the machine had been on. It certainly wasn't sexual. He'd never heard of gay men playing sick telephone games, and it was not that sort of breathing anyway. What was it that Burke, up at the university, had called this type of head case in that psych book of his? Tormentors, that was it. One of the chapters had been titled "The Age of the Tormentor."

Well, if it happened one more time, he'd get the number changed and keep the new one unlisted. Enough was enough. He had already suffered more torment than any man ought to have to endure.

Elliot invited him to his home in Brookside Park for drinks that evening. He didn't want to accept, but he couldn't think of a way to refuse gracefully. He was asking for a favor, and Elliot meant well, and there was a certain amount of protocol that had to be observed when you were dealing with your department chair. At least Elliot didn't offer any advice on how to cope with his loss or his life; judiciously refrained from mentioning Katy or the accident. Besides, he liked the man. They weren't exactly friends—too many attitude and lifestyle differences—but they were friendly, and Elliot could be stimulating company when he was in an expansive mood. So Dix said yes, he'd come, and five o'clock would be fine.

He spent most of the morning in the garage, working on the white oak sideboard. He'd always liked to noodle with wood, and a few years ago he had decided to take up furniture-making. He'd made the mahogany armoire that was in the bedroom and then started on the sideboard for the dining room. Six months of intensive work. But the sideboard hadn't been turning out the way he'd envisioned it, and finally he'd lost interest and abandoned it. It had sat in a corner of the garage, hidden away under a tarp, until two weeks ago. He'd been out there looking for something to occupy his time, and found and uncovered it, and saw immediately where he'd gone wrong in its original design. He'd worked on the sideboard every day since, sometimes for five and six hours at a time. It was nearly finished. Laboring with wood was the only activity he'd been able to sit still for. He couldn't write, or read, for more than a few minutes; his normal powers of concentration were nil. When he was working with table saw and jigsaw and planer and sander, he could shut his mind down. His hands became independent entities, performing their appointed tasks with skill and precision. They didn't even seem part of him at times.

Shortly before noon he ran out of fine-grade sandpaper for the mortise and tenon joints he was fitting. He didn't mind; it gave him

something else to do. He got into the Buick and drove downtown to
Ace Hardware.

There was not much traffic on Main Street—officially Los Alegres
Boulevard for the past twenty-odd years, but only newcomers and
visitors called it anything but Main Street. Not many residents traded
downtown these days; most preferred the air-conditioned malls on
the east and north sides. There were more antique shops and trendy
restaurants on Main than anything else, and they catered to the tourists who came to gawk at the Italianate Victorian buildings—wood,
brick, and ironfront, most of which were well over a century old—
and to walk along or ride on the river. Dix shopped here because he
always had and because he preferred the old to the new in most
ways and things. Katy had told him once that he was inclined to be
stuffy on the subject of the past. His standard comeback was that
he'd made his living for nearly twenty years on the study and analysis
of American history and was entitled to wallow in the past if he felt
like it. Besides, he said, dead people were a hell of a lot more
interesting than most live ones he knew.

Not so funny, that remark, even then. Unfunny now.

He lingered in Ace, though he bought nothing more than a new
supply of sandpaper. Outside again, he was approaching the Buick
when a woman's voice called his name. He relaxed when he saw
that it was Cecca. Francesca Bellini, Cecca to her friends. Pronounced "Cheka," like the old Russian secret police—an Italian
diminutive that had survived the transition from girlhood to adult-
hood. One of Katy's closest friends, one of his favorite people.

"Dix, hi," she said. She caught both his hands in her small ones.
"I thought it was you."

"Out on an errand," he said.

"That's good. That you're getting out, I mean."

"About time I did."

"It's good to hear you say that. Good to see you. You know, I
almost called you on Thursday. I was showing a house on the Ridge
and I thought, well, maybe you wouldn't mind if I stopped by for a
minute or two."

"I wouldn't have minded. Thursday was one of my better days."

"Then I'm sorry I didn't call."

Her eyes probed his face, as if trying to read it by the lines and
creases. She had wonderful eyes—round, luminous, so black they
were like polished opals. Her own face was unlined, even though

they were the same age. He'd thought, when they were both seventeen, that she resembled a pocket-size version of Annette Funicello, and for most of that year he'd been passionately in love with her. Chet Bracco would no doubt have broken his jaw if he'd tried to do anything about it. Chet and Cecca: They were planning marriage even then.

"Dix," she said, and stopped, and then said, "I wish I knew how to say how sorry I am."

"You've already said it. And I really am okay, or will be pretty soon. As soon as school starts."

She squeezed his hands. "I'm on my way to the Mill to meet Eileen—lunch at Romeo's. Why don't you join us?"

He wasn't ready for that. Eileen Harrell was a determinedly cheerful woman, another of Katy's close friends, and the restaurant would be crowded ... no, not yet. "Raincheck, okay? I've got a nearly finished sideboard waiting for me."

"You're working on that again?"

"Yes."

"I'm glad. That armoire you made is lovely."

He smiled and nodded.

"Well," Cecca said, "I'd better run. Let's not be strangers."

"We won't be."

Another squeeze, and she was hurrying away from him. He watched her until she crossed the street to the Mill's entrance. He thought again, as he had several times over the past four years, that Chet Bracco was a damn fool for cheating on a woman like Cecca and then walking out on her. The thought stirred a vague anger, and this surprised him. Maybe he *was* starting to come out of it, to feel again. Old feelings, old sympathies, for others besides Katy and himself.

Even with the doors up and the fan going, it was stifling inside the garage. Ten minutes at his workbench and he was soaked in sweat, his mouth and throat parched. A cold beer, he thought. Maybe something to eat, too; he was almost hungry. Another hour or two out here, as long as he could stand the heat, and then his afternoon fifty in the pool. By then it ought to be time to get ready for his evening with Elliot.

He was taking a bottle of Miller Draft out of the refrigerator when the telephone bell went off.

He'd forgotten again to put on the machine. Two rings, four rings, six rings ... and his feet carried him across to the counter and the phone.

"Hello?"

Breathing.

The tormentor again. Twice in one day—escalating it.

You weren't supposed to provoke people like this; you were supposed to be calm, rational, so they wouldn't think they were getting to you. But he'd had enough. Too much. "Listen, damn you, don't you understand that I lost my wife recently? Don't you have an inkling of what that's like? Don't you have any decent human feelings? If you don't stop bothering me, you'll regret it. I mean that. Stop bothering me!"

He would have hung up then, banged the receiver down. Almost did. He was just starting to take it away from his ear when the voice jumped out at him.

"Don't hang up."

The words were sharp, commanding, but the voice had an unnatural quality, as if it were being electronically altered or filtered. It made Dix's scalp crawl.

"So you can talk after all," he said. "All right. You want to say something to me finally? Go ahead, say it."

"I want to tell you about your wife."

"... What?"

"Your wife. I want to tell you about her."

"You don't know anything about my wife."

"I know something you don't know."

"The hell you do."

"Oh yes," the voice said. "She was having an affair. A very torrid affair. For a little more than three months before she died."

"That's a goddamn lie!"

"It started on May second, at two o'clock in the afternoon, at La Quinta Inn in Brookside Park. After that, usually twice a week. Monday and Friday afternoons, when you thought she was studying with Louise Kanvitz. That is what she told you, isn't it?"

Dix's larynx seemed to have undergone a temporary paralysis. He made an inarticulate sound.

"The usual meeting place was a motel. Not always the La Quinta; different ones in different locations. Once in a field off Lone Mountain Road. And more than once in her car, in the backseat, dog-fashion.''

You son of a bitch! he thought. But he couldn't say the words; he was like a mute trying desperately to speak.

''Shall I tell you some of the other ways she liked to do it? No, I'm sure you already know most of them. I will tell you who her partner was. You'd like to know that, wouldn't you?''

Lies, lies!

''I was her partner,'' the tormentor said. ''I'm the man who was fucking your wife.''

The verbal paralysis left him all at once. Words came spewing out like vomit. ''You sick lying bastard how can you do this to me what kind of man are you—!''

He was shouting into a dead phone.

TWO

Cecca said, "*Condoms.* And not just one—a whole package."

"What kind?" Eileen asked curiously. "Not french ticklers?"

"Eileen, for God's sake. Not so loud."

"Oh, nobody's paying any attention to us. It's too noisy in here anyway."

Which was true enough. Romeo's at noon on a summer Saturday was always noisy. Poor acoustics and babbling tourists. Still, Eileen's voice carried. And usually at the wrong times, when she was making one of her more uninhibited comments. I should have waited to talk about this, Cecca thought. Someplace private. But it was too late now.

Eileen said, "It could have been worse, you know. It could've been drugs you found."

"I know that. Amy's always been dead set against drugs; I count both of us lucky on that score. But condoms . . . I didn't think I had that to worry about either."

"Mothers always want to believe their daughters are virgins."

"Naive, huh?"

"The protective instinct. Was the package opened?"

"No. Why do you ask that?"

"Maybe Amy's carrying it just in case. Maybe she hasn't had occasion to use one of the things yet."

"That's possible," Cecca admitted. "She hasn't had a steady boy-friend in months."

"Planning ahead. Very mature, if you ask me."

13

"Yes, but my God. She's only seventeen."

"Uh-huh. How old were you and Chet when you started doing it?"

"What does that have to do with this situation?"

"Seventeen, right?"

"We're talking about Amy, not me."

"Kids are sexually active a lot younger these days. You know that." Eileen devoured part of her bacon cheeseburger. Chewing, she said, "I can guarantee that neither of my kids is a virgin. I wouldn't be surprised if Bobby started when he was twelve or thirteen. He's a handsome little devil, if I do say so myself."

"Boys," Cecca said, "you have boys, not girls. It's not the same thing. Girls get pregnant."

"Not if they carry condoms in their purses."

"Eileen, this isn't funny. Not to me, it isn't."

"I know, honey."

Eileen reached across the table and patted her hand. The gesture was maternal and her expression was serious, but even at her gloomiest, Eileen seemed to be on the verge of a wink or a chuckle, if not one of her bawdy laughs. It wasn't that she was frivolous or insensitive; it was just that she looked at the world with a positive, sometimes wryly humorous eye. Her self-assessment, which she was fond of quoting to people she'd just met, was that she was "a big brassy blonde who loves life and doesn't give a hoot who knows it." Even a sudden disaster like poor Katy's death hadn't dampened her spirits for long, although she'd cried as hard as Cecca had when they first heard about it.

"What would you do if you were me? Ignore what I found, or talk to Amy about it?"

"Probably ignore it."

"You wouldn't want to know if your daughter was sexually active?"

"I don't think so."

"Ignorance is bliss?"

"Her right to privacy, too, even if she is under age."

Cecca picked at the remains of her Cobb salad. "I keep telling myself the same thing. But I still want to know."

"So what's stopping you from asking?"

"Amy's finally quit blaming me for the divorce; we have a good relationship again. I don't want to do anything to rock the boat."

"You mean she might think you were snooping."

"I wasn't snooping. I really did bump her purse off the table by accident. But what if she doesn't believe it?"

"Mmm," Eileen said reflectively. She finished the last of her burger, licked her fingers, wiped a spot of grease off her chin, and permitted herself a ladylike burp. "Have you ever talked to her about the birds and the bees?"

"Once seriously, when she was thirteen. I've tried since, but . . ."

"Awkward?"

"Awkward."

"You used the mother-to-daughter approach, right?"

"What other approach is there?"

"Woman to woman. Casual, chatty, the way you and I talk. If she's been doing the deed, and you don't make her feel threatened about it, she'll either tell you straight out or let something slip. At least you'll know how she feels about sex at this stage of her life. And you won't have to mention the condoms at all. She'll tell *you* about carrying them, if she wants you to know."

Sometimes Eileen amazed her. She could be so cavalier, downright flighty at times; and then she'd come up with a perfectly wise, practical suggestion like this. Funny how someone could be your close friend for thirty years and you still didn't have a clue as to how her mind worked.

Eileen said, "Good idea?"

"A lot better than any I could come up with."

"You know, maybe I missed my calling. Maybe instead of a nurse I should have become a family counselor. Or a sex therapist, like Dr. Ruth. What do you think?"

"I think I'm going to buy your lunch."

"Ah! The exact amount of my consultation fee. It also entitles you to an extra ten minutes, so let's move right along to *your* sex life. How're things with you and Jerry?"

"Jerry and I are just friends, you know that."

"Meaning you still haven't slept with him."

"No, I haven't."

"Going to?"

"I don't know. Probably not."

"Doesn't make your toes tingle? He's a real hunk."

"Let's drop that subject, okay?"

"Uh-oh. Do I detect a hint of sexual frustration?"

"No, you don't."

"That's what it sounds like to me. How long has it been, anyway, since you got laid?"

"Eileen . . ."

"Come on, how long?"

"I don't keep track of things like that," Cecca said, which was a flat-out lie. It had been thirteen months, give or take a few days. One night with Owen Gregory. On a sudden whim or temporary brain lock . . . whatever you wanted to call it. After she and Owen had been to a party at Eileen and Ted's, as a matter of fact, and she'd drunk a little too much wine. It hadn't been very good. In fact, it hadn't been good at all. One-night stands weren't for her; she'd felt cheap afterward and still wasn't quite at ease in Owen's presence, even though he'd been a gentleman about the whole thing. She was a woman who needed a strong emotional attachment before she was comfortable in a sexual relationship. And since Chet, there simply hadn't been anybody. She wasn't even sure she wanted there to be anybody again. Once burned, twice shy.

Still, Eileen was right: She *was* a little frustrated. You didn't lose your sex drive when you got divorced and then turned forty. And with all the things that had been wrong with her marriage to Chet, sex hadn't been one of them. Lord, no. In fact, if it hadn't been so damned good, she might have left him before he decided to leave her—and wasn't *that* a sad, pathetic comment on the life and mindset of Francesca Bellini?

A busboy took their plates away. On his heels was the waiter with a dessert tray. Eileen said, "Oh, no, not for me," and then allowed herself to be seduced into ordering a piece of Chocolate Decadence. "My friend and I will split it," she said, and smiled at Cecca, who thought fondly: No, we won't. You'll eat the whole thing, you pig.

When the waiter was gone, Cecca said, "Oh, I didn't tell you who I saw earlier" to forestall any more of Eileen's probing sex questions.

"Who?"

"Dix."

"You stop by his house, or what?"

"No, he was coming out of the hardware store."

"How did he look?"

"Pretty well, considering. He's lost some weight."

"I'd be surprised if he hadn't. Poor Dix."

"I think he's going to be all right."

"I hope so. I worry about him, rattling around in that big house all alone."

"It was what he wanted."

"What people say at funerals isn't necessarily what they mean."

"Dix meant it. He has a right to grieve in his own way."

"Well, sure he does. But I still think a person needs friends at a time like this, not isolation. If I lost Ted the way he lost Katy, I'd want a houseful of people around me every minute."

"I suppose I would, too," Cecca agreed. "If it hadn't been for you and Katy when Chet walked out, I don't know what I might have done."

"So is Dix ready to start letting us back into his life?"

"Soon, I think. He as much as said so."

"Encouraging," Eileen said. "When are you seeing him again?"

"I don't know, I hadn't thought about it."

"Don't wait around. Invite him to dinner tomorrow night."

"That's too soon."

"No it isn't. He's alone, you're alone. Two needy people. Make your move before somebody else does."

The waiter brought Eileen's Chocolate Decadence and two forks. She plunged into it greedily. Cecca didn't touch the second fork; she was frowning.

"You think I'm needy?" she said.

"Aren't you, honey?"

"No. And even if I were, even if I were interested in Dix Mallory that way, which I'm not, Katy's been gone only three weeks. Three weeks, Eileen!"

"The living go on living. You're not attracted to Dix?"

"Not the way you mean, no."

"Well, he's always been attracted to you. The way he looks at you sometimes ... I'd say he's very interested. He never made a pass at you?"

"Dix? Don't be silly."

"Well, why not? He's a man, and men are horny beasts, thank God."

"He worshipped Katy. He wouldn't have cheated on her."

"It's too bad Katy didn't feel the same way."

"Oh God," Cecca said.

"I know, I know, she was like a sister to me, too. But I swear she had a lover."

"You don't *know* that she did."

"Well, you don't always have to have proof positive. She was getting it from somebody besides Dix, all right."

"I don't see how you can be so catty about her."

"I'm not being catty. I'm the brutally frank type, honey, you ought to know that by now. I say what I think."

"But after the horrible way she died . . ."

"Sure, it was horrible. But quick in an accident is a lot better than slow with cancer, no matter how awful the accident."

"Even at forty? I suppose so."

"You bet it is. Besides," Eileen said philosophically, "accidents happen. Most of the time we're lucky enough to survive them, like when the ceiling panel collapsed at the hospital and almost squashed me. Or that time up in Oregon—all three of us could have been highway statistics that night. Poor Katy's luck just ran out."

"Can we please change the subject? My lunch is starting to curdle."

"When you've been a nurse as long as I have," Eileen said, "nothing bothers your digestion. Or your appetite. You sure you don't want some of this cake? There's only one thing I can think of that tastes better than Chocolate Decadence, and Ted's not here."

Cecca sighed and watched her vacuum up the cake. And thought about Dix. Attracted to her? Maybe, in the same platonic way she was attracted to him. Nothing serious, just an easy, good-humored friendship. Nothing sexual. She liked the way he looked, and his intellect, and his gentleness, and his smile—but that was all. Eileen was crazy if she thought there could be a romance between them. Still, she had to admit that he appealed to her more than Jerry or Owen, and she'd gone to bed with Owen. There was no harm in inviting him to dinner, seeing him socially. Not dates, exactly, just two friends getting together. Not even Katy could have found fault with that.

Katy, she thought. My best friend Katy. Dead three weeks, burned to death at the bottom of a ravine, and here I sit, planning casual get-togethers with her husband. I'm as bad as Eileen. Worse, because I'm not as honest.

God, what predators we humans are.

When they stepped out of the Mill's air-conditioned coolness, heat closed around them like sticky wool. Splinters of sun-glare pricked at Cecca's eyes; she put on her dark glasses. The light change bothered Eileen even more, made her grumble as she donned her own shades.

"Why did we have to have a heat wave *now*?" she said. "It'll be even hotter up at the lake."

"Not in the water, it won't. What time are you leaving tomorrow?"

"Ted says we'll be on the road by seven, but if we're off by eight, I'll be happy."

"Coming back Monday or Tuesday?"

"Labor Day, dammit, fighting traffic all the way. I've got to be at the hospital at eight A.M. on Tuesday. Still—seven glorious days of R and R."

"I envy you. I'd settle for a two-day vacation right now."

"Honey, are you sure you can't get away for that long? There's plenty of room at the cabin; the boys can double up."

"I'd love to, I really would, but I've got showings scheduled for next week and there's a good chance the couple from Walnut Creek will decide to make an offer on the Morrison property. I really need at least one commission soon. Otherwise I don't buy any new fall clothes or you any more lunches."

"Well, if things happen fast and you have the time, just come ahead. No need to call first."

"I will."

"Give my love to Dix when you see him," Eileen said, and winked, and went off toward the public parking lot behind the Mill, her ample hips grinding inside those hideous paisley stretch pants she insisted on wearing.

Cecca drove to Better Lands to check her voice mail. The Agbergs, the Walnut Creek couple, were still debating, evidently—not that she'd expected otherwise. They were a methodical pair; it might take a week or two before they made up their minds. There were no other messages and not much going on at the office. Tom Birnam, boss and friend, told her there'd been only half a dozen calls and one showing all day. Saturdays were usually a busy time and she'd been a little sorry to have this one off. End-of-summer doldrums ... but she knew that wasn't it. This damn recession was hurting everybody. She'd had just two sales in the past fifteen months, and it was the sheerest luck that one of those had been on the Ridge. One of the other agents hadn't had a sale of any kind in ten months.

And what made the pill even more bitter was the fact that Los Alegres had once been and should still be a real estate agent's paradise. Home prices had climbed radically in the greater Bay Area in recent years, but most houses here were still affordable and a good value for the money. Small-town America was dying, thanks to global shrinkage, overpopulation, technology, a dozen other factors. You couldn't find many towns in California these days, particularly close to a major urban center like San Francisco, that had a hundred-and-fifty-year history, an untricked-up, old-fashioned ambiance, community pride, good schools, a jobless rate of four percent (half the state average), no serious drug or gang problems, at least not yet, and therefore a relatively crime-free environment, *and* a commute to the city of not much more than an hour. Escapees from Oakland and Berkeley and San Francisco ought to be flocking here, engaging in bidding wars for prime home sites. Would be, once the economy perked up. *If* it perked up in the foreseeable future.

She stopped at Safeway for a few things, so it was almost three when she turned onto Shady Court. She'd always loved this one-block cul-de-sac; it was the prettiest little street on the west side. Tall elms lined both sides, their branches interlocked overhead to form a tunnel of summer shade. Well-maintained old houses of mixed architectural styles: Spanish, Victorian, neo-colonial, 1920s frame. Shady Court had such traditional charm that Hollywood location scouts, like bugs with highly sensitized antennae, had scoped it out and offered enough money to make the residents give in and allow their homes to be used as backdrops for (at last count) three TV commercials and scenes in two films. Cecca had voted against the intrusion of cameras and outsiders the last time, but as the newest resident, she was outvoted. In fact, she'd been the only dissenter.

She had adored Shady Court as far back as she could remember. Her parents' Christmas-tree farm had been a nice enough place to grow up, but it was too far out in the country to suit her; she preferred town and its attractions. When she was at Los Alegres High, eight blocks to the north, she had driven by the Court often on her way to and from school and had told her friends, "I'm going to live there someday." They'd laughed at her. Well, it had taken her twenty years and an ugly divorce, but here she was. Thank you, Chet, she thought wryly and not for the first time. Walking out on Amy and me was a lousy thing to do, but at least you were decent about the settlement. Half the joint savings, Chet agreeing to give her seventy-five percent of the proceeds on the sale of their Cherry Street house in exchange for title to the Mendocino beach cottage, this place coming on the market at just the right time and at just the right price ... sometimes in the midst of chaos there is an island of good.

Amy's little Honda, that her granddad had bought her over Cecca's protests last Christmas, was neither parked out front nor in the driveway. Off somewhere with her friends; she finished work at Hallam's Bookshop at one on Saturdays. Cecca felt a small disappointment. Eileen had psyched her up and she thought she knew now how to approach Amy on the subject of sex, if not the subject of the condoms. You had to walk such a fine line with the girl sometimes. Most of her hostility was gone, but it still flared up now and then, when Amy felt she was being threatened in some way. "If you and Dad had stayed married, it wouldn't be like this." Insecurity. Distrust. Thank you again, Chet Bracco, you deceitful jerk. At least Amy's hostility had extended to her father as well, and in fact seemed to be lingering there, where it belonged. Cecca couldn't have stood it if she had somehow been twisted around in her daughter's mind so that she became the villain.

Some leaves were down already, she noticed as she dragged the groceries out. Elm and magnolia both. Still August, hundred-degree temperatures, and the trees were showing fall color and losing leaves. Easterners were wrong about California not having seasons, but there was no getting around the fact that the seasons were erratic.

It was relatively cool on the porch. She thought she would sit out there for a while and wait for Amy to come home. The porch was her favorite part of the house—a half wraparound that extended to the back on the south side, with rounded pillar supports and intricate filigree work, wide enough for plenty of furniture and plants without crowding. The house, a two-story frame, had been built in 1926, when life was much slower paced and people had time to sit and relax on porches like this. The fact that modern architects wouldn't even think of putting such a porch on a new house was a sad commentary on present-day lifestyles. Houses weren't built to last like this one either. Nearly seventy years old and in sound condition; its succession of owners had treated it well. The people she'd bought it from had painted it four years before, in rich browns and tans, and done the interior with such style and taste that she hadn't had to alter much of it at all. Eight large rooms, two and a half baths, a detached garage ... too much house, really, for just Amy and her.

Just her in another year, she thought. Amy seemed determined to
move out next summer, take an apartment with a couple of girlfriends
who were also planning to attend UC Berkeley. Eighteen and caught
up in the wild Berkeley scene . . . every small-town mother's nightmare. She wouldn't listen to Cecca's touting of Balboa State. She
wanted to be out on her own, she said, and she had the grades to
get into UC, and UC's journalism program was so much better than
Balboa State's—a point Cecca could hardly argue. Amy wanted to
be an investigative reporter, either TV or newspaper/magazine, but
preferably TV. She would probably succeed at one level or another;
she had the talent and the determination. But she was still so young,
prone to letting her emotions rule her common sense. And now this
thing with the condoms. Good or bad, wise or foolish—Cecca
couldn't decide which.

There was one message on the answering machine, for Amy. Cecca
put the groceries away, drank a glass of ice water, and went upstairs
to change into shorts and a thin blouse, no panties or bra. One good
thing about having small breasts: When you turned forty, you didn't
have to worry about sagging, flopping, rounded shoulders, or the
need for sweaty uplift on hot days. Downstairs again, heading for
the porch—and the telephone rang.

Her first thought was that it might be the Agbergs; she'd given
them her home as well as her office number. She did a quick about-
face, hurried into the kitchen to pick up.

"Hello? This is Francesca."

Silence. A steady, rhythmic breathing.

Him again.

How many times now? Five, six? Never said anything, just
breathed. Something to be grateful for, that, since twice it had been
Amy who answered. But Cecca was not going to tolerate any more
of it. The man at the telephone company had told her to buy a big
whistle and to put it up close to the mouthpiece and blow on it as
hard as she could; sometimes that hurt their eardrums enough to
make them think twice about calling again. She opened the drawer
under the counter, found the whistle she'd picked up at K-mart, lifted
it out.

"Don't hang up."

Male voice, but weirdly distorted, unreal.

Oh, God, she thought, now it starts. The filth, the profanities. She put the whistle in her mouth, thinking: No, you don't, I won't listen to *that,* not in my own kitchen.

But she didn't blow it because when he spoke again it wasn't sexual obscenities she heard. It was something worse—something much more chilling.

"Do you know where Amy is, Francesca?" he said. "Do you have any idea what's happening to that little bitch of yours this very minute?"

THREE

He didn't believe it about Katy.

Not for a minute.

A vile lie, part of the tormentor's sleazy bag of tricks. Vicious goddamn sociopath. Out there somewhere, enjoying himself, laughing behind his anonymity.

No, he didn't believe it, none of it.

Then why couldn't he stop thinking about it?

He walked; he couldn't seem to stop walking, either. The restlessness had driven him out of the house, into the Buick, up here to the university. Familiar surroundings, and a place where he could have people near him and still be alone. Not too many people; he couldn't have stood crowds. A few conscientious summer-school students, a smattering of teachers, custodial people, campus security ... just enough to give him a feeling of human connection without intrusion.

She was having an affair. A very torrid affair. For a little more than three months before she died.

I'd have known, he thought. Wouldn't I have known, after seventeen years of marriage?

It started on May second, at two o'clock in the afternoon, at La Quinta Inn in Brookside Park.

Specific place. Clever touch; it gave the lie weight and substance. But it could be checked, proven false.

After that, usually twice a week. Monday and Friday afternoons, when you thought she was studying with Louise Kanvitz. That is what she told you, isn't it?

Even easier to check. The tormentor didn't care, that was the point. He wants me to check, because checking means doubt, and doubt means he's got me hooked.

Once in a field off Lone Mountain Road.

Another clever touch. Lone Mountain Road was the scene of the accident. Got that out of the paper. But what was she doing up there, alone, at nine o'clock on a Friday evening? Nothing off Lone Mountain Road except a few scattered dairy ranches. Hilly area, mostly cattle graze with patches of woods, hairpin turns in the road like the one she'd missed, deep ravines like the one her Dodge had crashed into. Isolated . . . known as a lover's lane. But there was nothing in that; the possibility had never even occurred to him. The highway patrol: Why was she up there, Mr. Mallory? Do you have friends on Lone Mountain Road? No, no friends. She said she was going for a drive; she liked to drive when she was nervous or out of sorts or blue, it relaxed her. Was she nervous or out of sorts or blue tonight, Mr. Mallory? Twitchy—that was the word she used. She was feeling twitchy and thought she'd go for a drive. What time did she leave? About six. Mmm, two and a half hours before the accident—did she usually stay out for such a long time? Not usually, no . . .

And more than once in her car, in the backseat, dog-fashion.

Bullshit. But she'd been fond of that position. "Do me from behind, sweetie, you know I love it that way." Dammit, no. A devilishly lucky guess, that was all it was.

I was her partner.

No.

I'm the man who was fucking your wife. . . .

He walked. Balboa was one of the newer state schools, built in the mid-sixties for a limited enrollment; now the student roster was upward of seven thousand, with another three thousand in the extension and graduate programs. A dozen new buildings had been added, from a huge library to prefab overflow classrooms and offices, and until the massive state education cutbacks, a new gymnasium had been planned for the following year. Commuter school, limited student housing, but the campus already covered more than fifty acres. Gray concrete buildings for the most part, institutional modern, purely functional—ugly. But the unlovely architecture was offset by parklike landscaping that included hundreds of shade trees. Good place to walk even on hot days. Relaxing.

But not today.

Down past the library, over by the Foundation Center and the Student Health Center, detour past the Hall of Sciences, veer left toward Guiterrez Hall, where he taught most of his classes and where his office was. Hurting inside. And disliking himself for that small nagging worm of doubt that seemed to have burrowed deep into his mind.

Three months. A long time. There would have been little indicators to arouse his suspicions, but there hadn't been. Had there? Very little physical contact between them in those three months. Not tonight, dear, I'm really not in the mood. Once that he could remember; maybe twice. Part of the vague dissatisfaction they both felt: cooling passions. That was what he'd thought, when he thought about it at all.

Another thing: She'd been withdrawn. Spent more time away from home than usual, and when she did stay in she'd preferred to be alone in the back bedroom she'd converted into a studio, working on one of her paintings.

Katy, he thought, I was faithful to you the whole time we were married. Seventeen years. Mind-sin now and then, sure, I'm no better than Jimmy Carter or anybody else, but I never did anything about it. Never even came close. Wouldn't have hurt you that way, didn't think you'd hurt me that way either. Trust.

I'm the man who was fucking your wife.

It never happened. Not even once, let alone twice a week for more than three months. Couldn't have with somebody like that. Out of all the men in Los Alegres, not a vicious sociopath. But Katy might have had no idea of what he was because he'd kept it hidden, seemed outwardly normal. And if he was good-looking? And sympathetic, patient, reasonably intelligent, accomplished at seduction? And if the circumstances and the timing were just right?

Dix was at the student union now. Closed on weekends, nobody around except for a young man in cutoff jeans reading on one of the outside benches. The angle of the sun was such that it turned the windows into mirrors: He saw himself walking past. The reflection was shimmery, oddly indistinct, as if all his molecules and atoms had begun to separate. *Star Trek* image: Beam me up, Scotty. He looked away, quickening his pace.

Three months, three months . . . if it was true, then it hadn't just been a fling, it had been serious or had serious undertones. On Katy's part, at least. How long would it have gone on if the accident hadn't happened? A while, maybe, but not indefinitely. He may not have known Katy as well as he'd thought, but he'd known her that well: She hadn't been duplicitous by nature, hadn't gotten off on illicit intrigue. She had to have been under tremendous pressure. Caught and unable to make up her mind which way to go—

Driven to a third alternative?

Too much guilt, too much pressure? And suppose her lover had let his mask slip and she'd seen him as he really was?

Dix stopped walking.

What if it hadn't been an accident at all?

What if she had missed that turn on Lone Mountain Road on purpose?

The Brookside Park La Quinta Inn was just off the freeway, less than four miles from the university. Big place, three separate buildings, over a hundred rooms; visiting football teams put up there in the fall. Crowded on this late-summer Saturday: most of the parking slots were filled and twenty or thirty adults and children were making noise in the motel pool. Dix parked behind one of the shuttle vans near the lobby entrance. And sat there watching people go in and out.

I don't want to do this, he thought.

But he was there now, and the need to know was stronger than his fear of the truth. Get it over with. He prodded himself out of the car, across to the entrance.

Inside, the air-conditioning had been turned up high; the cold air was a shock. There were two clerks behind the desk, a middle-aged man and a young woman, both wearing La Quinta blazers. They were attending to three customers, one of whom was talking loudly about a restaurant that specialized in mesquite-grilled steaks. Dix hesitated, then sat down on a piece of lobby furniture. He couldn't do this with other people nearby.

It was five minutes before the customers left and the male clerk disappeared through a doorway behind the desk. Dix stood, went quickly to where the young woman was tapping at a computer terminal. Her professional smile wavered slightly when she glanced up at him. He thought: I must look like the wrath of God.

"May I help you, sir?"

"I hope so. I'm trying to find out . . ."

"Yes?"

The rest of the words wouldn't come. He reached for his wallet, fumbled it open to the photograph of Katy. It was a color portrait photo taken by Owen Gregory as part of a Christmas-gift package two years ago. Quite a good likeness not only in the physical sense but in that it captured Katy's vivacity, even hinted at her puckish sense of humor; Owen was the best professional photographer in Los Alegres. Dix held the wallet out so the young woman could see Katy's image.

"Do you recognize this woman?"

The clerk squinted close, lifted her head again. Her smile had gone. "No, I'm sorry, I don't know her."

"Never saw her before? You're certain?"

"Well, you know, I see a lot of people . . ."

"She may have stayed here more than once. Several times, in fact, beginning about three months ago. Weekdays, afternoon check-in . . . Monday, Friday . . ."

"Then I really can't help you, sir," the clerk said. "I don't work weekdays. Just Saturday and Sunday."

"Oh. Oh, I see." Sweat seeped out of him despite the air-conditioned coolness. He brushed a drop of it off his nose. "I guess I'll have to come back on Monday then . . . a weekday."

"Well . . ."

The male clerk came out through the doorway. The bar tag over one pocket of his blazer said that he was an assistant manager. His disapproving expression said that he'd been listening and didn't like what he'd heard.

"I'm sorry, sir," he said, "but we don't give out information about our guests." He turned reproachful eyes on the young woman. "Joyce knows that, don't you, Joyce?"

Dix said, "I don't mean to cause any problems, it's just that I . . . my wife . . . I'm trying to find out if she stayed here . . ."

"Under no circumstances, sir. That's our policy."

The young woman, Joyce, was looking at him in a new way. A look that said she'd figured out what this was all about. A look that was half sympathetic and half pitying.

Dix turned and fled.

He was almost an hour late arriving at Elliot's. He wasn't sure why he bothered to keep the appointment at all, his present state being what it was; the prospect of polite chitchat was distasteful. But he was a man who honored his commitments, and he was already in Brookside Park, and Elliot's home was close by. One drink, he thought, quick discussion about his expanded teaching schedule, then he'd make excuses and leave.

He had trouble finding the house—another reason he was so late. He'd been there twice before, but Elliot's street, Raven's Court, was one of dozens of short, twisty cul-de-sacs that made a maze of the sprawling development. Brookside Park had been built a few years before Balboa State and had grown proportionately, if indiscriminately, from an unincorporated country tract spread out along the freeway into a full-fledged town with a population larger than Los Alegres's. The ranch-style houses and tree-lined streets looked alike to an outsider. Several of his fellow professors—those with enough tenure to afford the relative luxury—lived there because of its proximity to the university.

Elliot's front lawn had sprouted a Better Lands Realty FOR SALE sign, new since Dix's last visit. He parked in front of it, looked at himself in the rearview mirror. Gaunt and dull-eyed, but otherwise not too bad. His hair was mussed and damp with sweat; he ran a comb through it before he went up and rang the bell.

Elliot didn't seem annoyed by his tardiness. He said mildly, "I'd about given up on you, my friend."

"Sorry I'm so late . . ."

"Don't apologize. You all right? You look wobbly."

"Nerves. And this damned heat."

"Come in, sit down. I'll get you a drink."

The drink was gin and tonic, not too strong. Dix drank half of it in one swallow. "Oh, I needed this."

"I don't doubt it."

They settled in what had once been the living room and was now Elliot's study. Books and papers covered most of the furniture, were scattered in little piles on the floor: Neatness was not one of his virtues. The only uncluttered surface was a prominent wall shelf on which Elliot's own books were displayed. He took the university system's publish-or-perish edict seriously; he had published a dozen volumes in the past twenty years, most with university and regional presses, two with small New York publishers. The centerpiece of the display was the book he considered to be his magnum opus, an eight-hundred-page combination biography of the crusading San Francisco newspaperman Fremont Older and history of California journalism. Not a modest man, Elliot Messner.

Dix moved a stack of pamphlets to make room for himself on the couch. Elliot occupied his huge cracked leather armchair. It needed to be huge because he was a big man, three or four inches over six feet, weight about two-twenty. Shaggy hair and a thick beard, both flame-red, coupled with his size and rough I'll-say-what-I-please manner gave him the aspect of one of the rugged-individualist pioneers of the last century. The image may have been calculated to reflect his academic specialty, California and Pacific Coast history, but Dix didn't think so; Elliot had his faults, but role-playing wasn't one of them. He was two years older than Dix, divorced, and if you believed campus rumors, not averse to laying women teachers, TAs, and regular students whenever the opportunity arose. If this was true, at least he was discreet about it. He didn't flaunt his conquests the way some men did.

Dix said, "I didn't know you were selling your house."

"Trying to. Not much interest so far."

"How long have you had it on the market?"

"Six weeks. If the Democrats don't turn the economy around, I may never sell the damn place. It's not a financial decision, in case you're wondering. I'm just tired of living in a frigging tract. I never did like it here, you know. It was Grace's idea to buy in Brookside Park. Hell, I should have realized then that the marriage was doomed."

"Where will you go when it does sell?"

Elliot shrugged. "Out in the country someplace. Not too far away; I hate commuting. A farm, if I can find one that's affordable. I always did want to own a farm. Grow my own fruit and vegetables." He laughed his seal-bark laugh. "Chop the heads off my own chickens for recreation."

Dix finished his drink. Elliot did the same and got immediately to his feet. "We can both use another one," he said, and took the glasses away before Dix could protest.

When he came back with the refills, he asked, "Feel like talking about it?"

"About what?"

"What it is that's got you all worked up."

"I'm not . . . it's just the heat, that's all."

"Bullshit," Elliot said. "It's more than that. More than what happened to Katy. Looks to me like you've had a shock of some kind."

"No . . . all right, yes."

"I'm a good listener," Elliot said.

"I know you are."

"But? Tell me it's none of my business and I'll drop it."

Dix hesitated. He didn't want to talk about it. Talking about it seemed disloyal, to give the doubts weight, the accusations merit. And yet the need to unburden himself was strong. He said at length, without making a conscious decision, "I've been getting . . . phone calls."

"Oh?"

"The anonymous kind. Half a dozen since just after the funeral. Heavy breathing, crank stuff—somebody who read about the accident in the newspaper. They didn't bother me much until today."

"What happened today?"

Dix told him about the call earlier. But not the details, and he didn't voice his doubts. "'Lies," he said, "evil lies."

Elliot was shaking his head. "Any idea who he is?"

"No."

"Well, it's likely he's someone you know."

"Why do you say that?"

"The altered voice, for one thing. Why bother to disguise his voice unless he's afraid you might recognize it."

"Christ," Dix said. He hadn't thought of that before.

"Another thing. If he's a stranger, he'd have to be one hell of a diligent researcher. And that's not the pattern in these crank-call cases."

"So many private details, you mean."

"More than he could've gotten out of the paper."

"It's hard to imagine anyone I know personally doing a thing like this."

"Doesn't have to be a friend or acquaintance. Man who works in a store you trade in, for instance—knows who you are, knows people who know you and can provide the details."

"That's possible. But why *me*?"

"Random selection. Or he was triggered by news of the accident. He might even be a former student of yours."

Dix hadn't thought of that, either. He nodded slowly.

Elliot said, "Failing course grade, low grade on a term paper or thesis, some other slight real or imagined . . . things like that prey on young minds. Hell, you've been a teacher as long as I have. You know how much hostility some of the little shits can generate."

"All too well."

"Even with the voice filter, could you tell his age?"

"No."

"But you're sure he's a man?"

"Positive. Women don't play sick games like that."

"Not usually. But it has been known to happen."

Dix finished his second gin and tonic. Even though Elliot had made the drinks light, he could feel the effects of the alcohol. When Elliot asked him if he wanted a third, he said, "No, I'd better not. The last thing I need is a DUI arrest on the way home."

Elliot rummaged on the table beside his chair, came up with a package of Pall Malls. "Mind if I smoke?" he asked perfunctorily, and when Dix shook his head, he said, "I've *got* to quit one of these days," and lighted up. He didn't mean it about quitting; he said the same thing every other time he had a cigarette, had been saying it as long as Dix had known him. He had cut back to a pack a day in the past year, but the faculty betting was that he would never go all the way.

"I wish I could offer you some sage advice on handling this guy," he said, "but I can't. I don't know what I'd do if I were in your shoes. Change my telephone number, I suppose, and hope for the best."

"That's what I intend to do," Dix said.

"In any case, he'll go away eventually. They always do. Meanwhile . . . it's his shit and you don't have to wallow in it. Right?"

"Right."

"So. On to a more pleasant topic. I spoke to Lawrence Hampton after you called this morning. Under the circumstances, he's willing to let you take his four-five-three for this semester."

"He is? That's good of him."

History 453 was the Age of Jackson, 1815–1850. Expansion and sectional change, economic sectionalism and national politics, the rise of Jacksonian democracy, and social and political reform in the U.S. from the Peace of Ghent to the Compromise of 1850. It was supposed to be a department course, with rotating instructors, but Hampton's specialty was pre–Civil War U.S. history and he'd taught 453 for the past several years by tacit agreement.

"Three classes, six hours a week," Elliot said. "Not much, really, but there'll be refamiliarization and preparation to keep you busy over the next few weeks."

"It'll help. Anything in the extension program?"

"One Saturday class, ten A.M. to noon. Twentieth-Century California History. Starts mid-September."

"That's one of yours," Dix said.

"It is, and I'll be glad to get shut of it. Open up my Saturdays for a change."

"If you're sure you don't mind ..."

"Absolutely," Elliot said. "But there is a contingency: You have to take it for three semesters, not just one. Give me a full year of free Saturdays. Fair enough?"

"More than fair. Thanks, Elliot."

"Least I can do. You'll need to get together with Lawrence before classes start next week; he has some material for you. I told him you'd call."

"As soon as I get home."

He was aware of the emptiness of the house the instant he walked in. The heavy silence seemed to gather around him, to take on a weight he could feel. Could he go on living here alone? It was a question he'd asked himself before and he still wasn't certain of the answer. On the one hand, it was the only place other than his parents' home that he'd ever felt comfortable living in. Too large for one person, one man alone—but so was Elliot's house, so were a lot of other people's. Money wasn't a consideration, at least not right now; and the prospect of putting the house up for sale, dealing with potential buyers trooping through and pawing possessions he'd shared with Katy, and then having to pack up and move and reacclimate elsewhere filled him with distaste. On the other hand, he saw and felt Katy in every room, every stick of furniture, as if some part of her lived on here. Maybe that ghostly quality would fade in time and he would grow used to the emptiness and the silence. And maybe not. You couldn't tell after only three weeks. How could you make any kind of long-range decision after only three weeks?

The message light on the answering machine was blinking: two blinks, two messages. No, he thought, not tonight. He went into his study and looked up Lawrence Hampton's number in his Rolodex. Four rings, and Lawrence's machine answered. He left a message, thinking: What did we do in the days before all these technological gadgets? How did we ever manage to communicate with one another?

He built himself a gin and tonic, stronger than the ones Elliot had given him, and took the drink out to the balcony off the living room.

Almost dusk. He watched the last of the sunset colors fade and the sky turn a smoky lavender. Going to be hot again tomorrow. Streetlights and house lights came on, on the Ridge and across the valley and in scattered wink-points up on the eastern hills. In the new dark, crickets set up a throbbing racket. Somewhere a dog barked. In the east side rail yards a locomotive whistle sounded, thin and haunting, like a chord in a sad, lost melody.

And all at once the loneliness struck him, a sudden stabbing sensation so sharp that his flesh seemed to curl inward around it, as if it were a blade.

Katy, he thought. I'm so sorry, Katy.

Sorry she was gone, sorry for doubting her fidelity, sorry for thinking she might have taken her own life. Sorry for himself, his loss, his pain. Sorry that he had to keep on trying to find out if the accusations were true.

Sorry that he was the kind of man who always had to know.

FOUR

Six o'clock. And Amy still wasn't home yet.

Cecca was in the kitchen with Owen Gregory, making a fruit salad for supper, trying not to worry. It wasn't that late, still broad daylight—but her eyes kept straying to the wall clock. *Do you know where Amy is, Francesca? Do you have any idea what's happening to that little bitch of yours this very minute?* Subtle torture, without any foundation whatsoever. That was what these telephone freaks counted on, wasn't it? The victim torturing herself?

Amy said she'd be home around four. Why isn't she here yet?

Owen's presence should have helped keep her calm, but it was having the opposite effect. He'd stopped by at five-thirty, unannounced, to bring her the photos of the Andersen farm in Hamlin Valley, her newest listing. He did most of the brochure photography for Better Lands, and he'd done his usual expert job of making a property look better than it really was, focusing on the Andersen place's hilly backdrop and that impressive line of old eucalyptus that flanked the access drive. The color shots were crystal-clear, yet you couldn't tell that the house and barn were in poor repair. But he could have dropped the prints off at the office or waited to give them to her on Monday. They were an excuse, of course. To see her. To sit and make small talk and gaze at her with his big, sad, worshipful eyes.

Those eyes were what had led her to sleep with him that night last summer. It was flattering to be the object of someone's passion, even if it wasn't reciprocated; and she'd been tight and Amy had been staying at a friend's house, and it had been so long since she'd had sex, and when she looked into those worshipful eyes ... bad judgment, a foolish mistake. It had given Owen false hope that it could happen again, that there could be something serious between them. The morning after, she'd told him the truth in the gentlest possible terms: She cared for him but she didn't love him, they could go on being friends but nothing more. He'd said he understood, but it didn't keep him from pursuing her in his low-key way. She liked him, she really did. He was kind, gentle, attractive. But she felt more sorry for him than anything else. And he got on her nerves sometimes, like right now—

"Cecca."

She turned her head. He was sitting at the table, his long legs stretched out, rolling the bottle of Coors she'd given him between his hands. His dark hair was its usual mop, damp and lank now from the heat, a long wisp plastered over one eyebrow. The tail of his shirt was untucked. There was a grass stain on the knee of his cords. Thirty-seven going on twelve, she thought. It was a wonder he'd never married. God knew, he'd had opportunities; maternal women loved him to pieces. But he didn't want a mother figure. He wanted the ex-wife of Chet Bracco, and had even when she was married. Poor Owen, because the ex-wife of Chet Bracco wanted a man, not a little boy.

"What's the matter?" he asked her. "You keep looking at the clock."

"Just wondering where Amy is. She should be home by now."

"Where'd she go after work?"

"I'm not sure. Some errands, she said."

"Kids. I wouldn't want to be a teenager these days."

"Why do you say that?"

"Oh, you know, all the problems and pressures."

"What does that have to do with her being late?"

"Nothing. I was making an observation—"

"My daughter's a good girl, Owen."

"I know that. Lord, Cecca, I didn't mean to imply—"

"Damn!" The potato peeler she'd been using to core strawberries had slipped and nicked her finger. She sucked at the drop of blood that appeared.

Owen was on his feet, petting her arm. "Hurt yourself?"

"It's nothing," she said. "I'm sorry I snapped at you. I'm feeling a little prickly today."

"It's the heat."

"Yes. The heat. Owen . . . I'd ask you stay for supper, but—"

"No, that's all right. Date tonight?"

"No. I just don't feel up to company."

"I understand."

No, you don't, she thought. "All I want to do is eat and take a long, cool bath and zone out in front of the TV."

"Sounds good. I'll probably do the same."

She finished the strawberries, started to cut up a peach. Owen stood watching her, making no move to leave. Like an adoring puppy. Can't you take a hint, Owen? Go home!

Lights slid across the kitchen window as a car swung into the driveway. Amy's Honda—that little engine had a whiny rumble that was unmistakable.

"There she is," Owen said.

Cecca felt a greater relief than the situation called for. That damned telephone freak . . . if he knew how deep under her skin he'd gotten, he'd be thrilled. He'd probably come all over himself.

The back door banged and Amy slouched in carrying three bulging shopping bags. She looked wilted but pleased with herself. "Whew," she said, "what a day. Oh, hi, Owen."

"Hi yourself," Owen said, smiling.

Amy dumped the bags on the kitchen table, dragged open the refrigerator. "Iced tea, good." She took the pitcher out.

Cecca said, "Where have you been?" The words came out sharper than she'd intended.

"Oh God," Amy said, "you're pissed."

"I'm not. I expected you hours ago, that's all."

"Well, it was crowded at the malls."

"Is that where you've been?"

"Shopping. Me and Kimberley."

"Kimberley and I," Cecca said automatically.

"I know that." Impish grin. "I'm a journalism major, remember?"

"Just the two of you? Shopping?"

"Isn't that what I just said?"

"Amy . . ."

"School's about to start. Foxy new outfits this fall."

Cecca tried to lighten her voice as she said, "Looks like you bought every one in stock," but the words sounded forced even to her.

"Dad gave me a hundred dollars to match the hundred you said I could spend. I paid for the rest with my own money, don't worry."

"When did your dad give you a hundred dollars?"

"When I saw him last week."

"You didn't ask him for it?"

"No, I didn't ask him. He gave it to me."

"Why didn't you tell me?"

"I didn't think it was exactly cosmic news," Amy said. "Why're you making such a big deal out of nothing?"

"I'm not making . . ." Cecca let the rest of the sentence die. She *was* making a big deal out of nothing. And Owen, standing there with his big ears flapping, was not helping matters. She said, "Owen, if you don't mind?"

"Sure," he said, "I'm out of here." He came over and kissed her cheek. Then he said to Amy, "See you later, foxy."

She wrinkled her nose at him.

The silence following Owen's departure had a strained quality. Amy poured a glass of iced tea, drank half of it. "Fruit salad," she said then. "Is that all we're having?"

"Too hot to cook."

"I guess. I'm going up and take a shower, if that's okay with you."

"Amy, don't be angry. It's been a long day. . . ."

"For me too. What time are we eating?"

"I don't know, seven or seven-thirty."

"I'm picking Kim up at seven-thirty."

"Going out again tonight?"

"It's Saturday night, Mom. Just because you don't go out doesn't mean I have to stay home, too."

"That's a cheap shot. I stay home by choice."

"And I go out by choice, okay?"

"You have a date?"

"I told you, I'm picking Kim up. We're going to a movie."

"Just the two of you?"

"What *is* it with you, Mom? You know I'm not seeing anybody right now. Not since Davey and I broke up."

"You've had plenty of dates since then—"

"Dates, sure, big deal."

"There's nobody you're interested in?"

"No. Who would I be interested in?"

"I don't know. That's why I asked."

"Well, there's nobody."

"There must be dozens of boys who are interested in you."

"Boys," Amy said, "my God. I'm tired of *boys.*"

"Now, what does that mean?"

"It means I'm tired of boys, that's what it means."

"You're not seeing somebody older—?"

"I'm not seeing *anybody,* for God's sake! How many times do you want me to tell you that?"

"Then why are you carrying condoms in your purse?"

The question surprised her as much as it did her daughter. She hadn't intended to ask it, it had just come spitting out. Amy was staring at her openmouthed, color staining her cheeks—embarrassed and angry. She had Chet's dark good looks and smoky eyes, and at moments like this she looked just like him. Acted like him, too: flew off the handle, became aggressively defensive. The time Cecca had caught Chet with the waitress from LeGrande's . . . his expression of flustered outrage had been the same as Amy's was now.

"You've been in my purse. How could you *do* that?"

"No, I haven't. You left it on the dining room table the other afternoon, right on the edge. I brushed against it accidentally and things spilled out when it fell."

"Oh, sure, right. Accidentally."

"I'm not lying to you. Now don't you lie to me. Why're you carrying condoms around with you?"

"What's the next question? Am I still a virgin?"

"That isn't the point—"

"Isn't it? Sure it is. But I'm not going to tell you. What I carry in my purse is my business and what I do with my body is my business. Okay? All right? And don't you ever go through my personal stuff again. Don't you *ever!*"

"Listen to me—"

"No," Amy said, and grabbed up her shopping bags and stormed out of the kitchen.

Cecca sat at the table. She'd handled things badly; Eileen would probably say she couldn't have handled them any worse. It had taken so long to mend the painful rift that the divorce had caused, and now she'd let that damned phone call rip it open again. Why hadn't she just told Amy the truth instead of letting herself slide into the mother-from-hell role?

Too late to tell her now? Maybe not. She took another minute to compose herself and then went upstairs to Amy's room. The door was shut; she knocked and tried the knob. It wasn't locked.

Amy was in her bra and panties. The shopping bags and their contents were all over the room, as if she'd hurled them around in a demonstration of her anger. Glaring, she said, "Now what? You want to search my room, too?"

"No. I want to apologize."

"Oh, you do? Isn't it a little late for that?"

"I don't mean about your purse. That really was an accident; I wasn't snooping. And you're right, your personal life is your own and you're entitled to your privacy. If you want to tell me about the condoms, fine, but I won't ask you again. Is that fair?"

". . . I guess." But Amy wasn't mollified. When she felt wronged she had a tendency to nurse her anger. Just like her father in that respect, too.

Cecca said, "I shouldn't have snapped at you. I'm sorry for that, too. But I had a reason."

"What reason?"

"Another one of those calls this afternoon. Only this time he said something that upset me. Something ugly."

"What did he say?"

Cecca told her.

"God, what a dickhead creep," Amy said. She plunked herself down on the edge of her bed. "But you should have known it was just crap."

"I can't help worrying. I love you, you know that. The thought of anything happening to you . . ."

"Nothing's going to happen to me. I mean, he *wanted* you to worry. That's how those weirdos get off."

"I know that."

"So don't let him get to you, okay? If he calls again, which he probably will."

"If he does and you answer, don't say anything to him."

"Why not? I'd like to tell him some things."

"We talked about this before. Talking back will only provoke him. Promise me you'll just hang up."

Amy scowled. But then she said, "All right. It's no big deal anyway. He'll go away eventually. Chris Ullman's mother had an obscene caller last year and he said all kinds of crazy things to her.
And he went away after a few weeks. This one will, too."

Will he? Cecca thought as she returned to the kitchen. Yes, probably. Except that he's not a random caller. He knows my name, he
knows Amy's name, he knows where we live.

What if he's more than just a telephone freak?

What if he's some kind of psycho?

They went to the new Tom Cruise movie. Kimberley wanted to
see it, she was a big Tom Cruise fan, and there wasn't anything else
playing that excited Amy much. It was all right. Funny in parts; once
Amy even laughed out loud. Lots of sex. But every other word was
"fuck" or "shit," like a lot of movies you went to, and it got to
be pretty monotonous and silly. People didn't really talk like that,
and if they did, who wanted to listen to them? It just wasn't very
intelligent. Kids' stuff. She wasn't a kid anymore, even if Mom
insisted on treating her like one sometimes. Like tonight. Big scene
in the kitchen with Owen there, and then going ballistic about the
rubbers. And all because the creep on the phone had upset her and
she'd been worried. There wasn't anything to worry about, for God's
sake. Besides, she could take care of herself. The divorce had turned
her into an adult a long time ago, more than three years ago. The
divorce, and then Davey Penner.

After the movie Amy wanted to go to Big Red's for something to
eat, but Kimberley didn't. Kim thought she was getting fat. She
wasn't, she was positively anorexic, but that was the way she was.
So they drove around instead. Cruising (Tom Cruising, Kim said,
ha-ha), which was technically illegal in Los Alegres, but the cops
didn't hassle you as long as you didn't ride in packs. Amy didn't
mind. She liked to drive. In fact, she loved it. The Honda handled
like a dream. Not much power, but she wasn't into fast driving like
some of her friends were. That was kids' stuff, too. Adults, if they
had any brains, didn't drive like maniacs and endanger other people's lives.

They went over to the east side once, to see if anything was going
on at Sonny's Pizza Shack (nothing was), but mostly they cruised
the full two-mile length of the Main Street. Not much was happening
there either. Kimberley thought Brian might be out cruising, too, but

he wasn't. Amy knew it wouldn't have mattered much if he had been, even if Kim didn't know it, but there wasn't anything else to do and she didn't mind playing the game. Let Kim go on thinking she and Brian were going to get back together if it made her happy. Everybody knew they weren't. Not with Brian making it with Tara Sims. If you could believe the skinny—and Amy believed it—Tara did things with guys that Kimberley never even dreamed of.

"That Tom Cruise," Kim said for about the hundredth time. "Man, what a hunk."

Amy didn't think he was much of a hunk at all. But she didn't say anything.

"I'll bet he's hung like a horse."

Who cares? Amy thought. "Probably," she said.

"If I ever saw it, I'd probably die. Right on the spot."

"Probably."

"Wouldn't you? I mean, Tom Cruise's dick!"

Silly, Amy thought.

"The only one I've ever seen is Brian's," Kimberley said. "It was kind of disappointing, you know? Not nearly as big as I thought it would be."

"Mmm."

"What about Davey's? You never said what it was like."

"I don't want to talk about Davey."

"Come on, Amy, tell me. Was it big?"

Amy sighed. "Huge," she said.

"Didn't it hurt a lot?"

The radio was playing a rap song. Ice-T or somebody. Amy reached out and fiddled with the dial and got an oldies station.

"Why'd you do that?" Kim asked. "I like rap."

"I don't."

"Well, excuse me."

"Oh God, Kim, don't you get pissy."

"I'm not pissy. You're the one who's pissy. The way you've been lately, it's been like going around with my *mother*."

"Thanks a lot."

"Well? You don't want to talk about anything, you don't want to do anything, you just want to mope around, looking deep."

"I haven't been moping around."

"Well, you *have* been deep. Half buried."

"I've got things on my mind."

"Like what?"

"Like things, different things."

"Davey?"

"Davey and I are history."

"Then what? Some other guy?"

"No."

"I'll bet it is. Some other guy, right?"

"No."

"What's his name?"

"Oh, balls, Kim."

"Come on, what's his name?"

"Wouldn't you like to know?" And wouldn't you just *crap* if I told you?

"Steve Payton? I saw you talking to him at Safeway the other day."

"Steve Payton's a nerd."

"Then what were you talking to him about?"

"Ice cream, if you have to know. Tom and Jerry's versus Häagen-Dazs. Big deal."

"Uh-huh."

"Think what you want. I don't care what you think."

"So who is he, really?" Kimberley asked.

"Who?"

"Your mystery lover."

"I don't have a mystery lover."

"But you'd like to, right?"

Maybe, Amy thought. Maybe I would.

"Well?"

"Look," Amy said abruptly, "there's Brian!"

"Oh, shit, where?"

"In that Ford that just passed. In the backseat."

"Turn around, quick!"

Amy drove around the block instead of making an illegal U-turn; she wanted the Ford to get far ahead of them so it would take time to catch up to it. Brian wasn't in it; Brian was probably parked somewhere by now, screwing Tara Sims's brains out with his not-nearly-as-big-as-Kim-thought dick. But for a while, at least, she wouldn't have to fend off any more of Kimberley's questions.

She wasn't about to tell Kim about *him,* not now and probably not ever.

Kim would think she was crazy.

Maybe she was.

She worried her lower lip, wondering again if she could be wrong about the way he felt about her. No, she was sure she wasn't. The looks he gave her, the smiles, the occasional wink . . . and the warmth in his voice when he was alone with her . . . and the time he'd held her hand for a few seconds and it had been like electricity shooting up her arm . . it was body heat, pure and simple. She'd sent out signals, too, in spite of herself at first and then, lately, on purpose. So what if he was old enough to be her father? What difference did that make anyway, people's ages? The important thing was how they felt about each other. He didn't treat her like a kid, either; he treated her like a woman. *Thought* of her as a woman. That was plain, too, in everything he said and did, in every look and smile.

Of course, he hadn't tried to hit on her yet. Not yet. And he'd have to be the one because she wasn't that bold, or that sure of herself. What if she made the first move and she was wrong after all and he blew her off cold? He might even tell Mom. God, she'd die of mortification.

Would he come on to her?

The idea thrilled and frightened her at the same time. What would she do if he did? Say yes right away? Play hard to get? Lose her nerve and blow *him* off cold? Did she even want him to make a move? Because if he did, and she melted, it meant going all the way. All the way.

Her thoughts shifted to the package of rubbers in her purse. She'd got them from the machine in the women's rest room at Big Red's, right after the last time with Davey. The first three times he'd had rubbers, so there was no problem, but not that last time. She hadn't wanted to let him then, but he'd kept playing with her, getting her hotter and hotter, and finally she'd given in. I won't come inside you, he'd promised. Hah. Boys were such liars. So then she'd had to worry about AIDS and getting pregnant and she'd vowed it would never happen again without protection and then they'd had that big fight about Davey doing coke and broke up. Four months ago, and the package of rubbers was still unopened. She wasn't going to do it with just anybody, no matter what Mom might think. It had to be somebody she cared about, somebody who cared about her.

Him?

"There's the Ford!" Kimberley shouted. "Pull up alongside, I want to see if Brian's with that bitch Tara."

Silly. So silly.

Kids' stuff.

FIVE

Early Sunday morning Dix spent an hour going through what was left of Katy's things.

He had already boxed up her clothing, cosmetics, items like that; the cartons were in the garage, waiting for him to summon the wherewithal to call Goodwill or one of the homeless shelters. But he hadn't been able to bring himself to pack the remainder of her belongings. For that matter, to even go into her office and studio. The packing had to be done sooner or later—but not today. Today, all he was doing was looking.

The room was cluttered with canvases, finished and unfinished. All were oils; she'd been studying watercolors with Louise Kanvitz, Los Alegres's resident art expert, but none that she'd done had been worth bringing home to show him, she'd said. And all were the quirky abstracts that several knowledgeable people besides Louise praised as showing genuine talent. It had been Louise's lofty assessment, in fact, that had led Katy to trade full-time high-school counseling for part-time teaching so she could devote more hours to her painting. He'd been supportive. Would have been even without Louise and the showing at Louise's Bright Winds Gallery last December and the three paintings she'd sold for Katy at $350 each. The drop in household income hadn't been a problem, not with a moderate mortgage and few other debts. He'd been proud of her, and willing to do anything within reason to make her happy. Anything within reason to shore up the unstable foundation of their marriage.

In one corner was her desk, with its littered surfaces and bulging drawers. He started to it first, changed his mind, and went to the closet instead. It wasn't the storage boxes or the painting supplies or the old ledgers that drew him; it was her treasure box. That had been her name for it, the hammered copper box where she kept all the little mementoes that she'd accumulated over the years. She had shown it to him once, a long time ago, but she hadn't let him look inside. He had never tried to look on his own. He'd respected her privacy, just as she had respected his.

He opened the treasure box first. Photographs, dozens of them: Katy when she was a toddler, a little girl in her father's arms, a teenager in her prom dress, a student at Balboa State, the two of them at a community dance, on Tom Birnam's sailboat in San Francisco Bay, in atrocious Heckel and Jeckel costumes at a Halloween party, in other places and in the company of other friends and relatives. The joke engagement ring he'd presented to her—a pot-metal thing bought at Woolworth's—when she'd accepted his proposal, in lieu of the diamond to come. A sappy and mildly obscene Valentine's Day card he'd given her so many years ago he'd totally forgotten it. A tiny gold nugget she'd found on a pack-trip in the Sierras. A McGovern for President button. The plastic penis, Eileen Harrell's birthday gift one year, that hopped around like a toad when you wound it up and that had sent Katy into hysterics the first time she tried it. Other things, some he recognized and some he didn't, that had been significant to her but that meant little or nothing to him.

The desk next. Drawers, cubbyholes, accordion files; canceled checks, paid bills—by mutual consent she had done most of the bill-paying—and correspondence. Then the boxes in the closet: old tax records, old Christmas and holiday cards, and little else. He even poked through the cartons of paint supplies and the two sketchpads, one filled, one partially filled, of her charcoal drawings of places, objects, people.

Memories, little surprises and curiosities—nothing else.

Nothing incriminating.

Well, what the hell had he expected to find? A diary full of steamy references to a lover? A packet of compromising letters? Nude photos, for Christ's sake?

He felt relieved, yet vaguely disappointed and angry at himself for being disappointed. Not finding proof of infidelity should have helped put the doubts to rest, but it hadn't; they still lingered, like splinters under the surface of his mind. Maybe at some level he *wanted* to believe Katy was guilty, that her death had been a kind of divine punishment; at least that would give it some meaning, some justification however frail and hateful. Down deep he was angry at her, too. For dying, for leaving him alone.

His head ached. And he still felt foggy—fuzzy-skulled, Katy had termed it—from the Nembutal he'd taken the previous night. He always had that next-day reaction to sleeping pills, but it was either take one or spend the whole night lying awake, thinking too much. Maybe a swim would help clear his head. He hadn't done his fifty morning laps yet.

Outside, on the terrace, he could hear church bells in the distance. Old St. Thomas, down on Park Street, where he'd once been an altar boy. Where Katy's funeral services had been held. She hadn't been particularly religious, but she had gone to services on Good Friday and Easter Sunday and Christmas Eve, and it had been her wish to have a Catholic funeral and to be buried in consecrated ground. None of that for him, though. Lapsed Catholic. Lost his faith somewhere along the way. He hadn't even felt comfortable at the service, sitting and kneeling in the front pew, fingering Katy's rosary and Bible, listening to the priest talk about God the Father and Christ the first fruits and life everlasting, and thinking only: She's gone, she's gone, I'll never see her again in this life or any other.

Now, listening to the tolling of the bells, he found himself remembering his childhood, all those Sunday mornings when he'd had to get up at five A.M., in the cold dark, so his father could drive him to St. Thomas's in time for six o'clock Mass. Putting on the black and white cassock and the surplice. Preparing the Eucharist, the bread and wine that were the body and soul of Jesus Christ. The liturgy was still in Latin in those days: the robed priest with his back to the laity, chanting *Dominus vobiscum,* and then replying along with the congregation, *Et cum spiritu tuo.* The opening words of the Lord's Prayer in Latin, indelible even after all these years: *Pater noster, qui es in caelis; sanctificeteur nomen tuum; adveniat regnum tuum; fiat voluntas tua sicut in caelo et in terra.* Fingering his own beads while he pondered the fifteen meditations on the mysteries in the lives of Jesus and Mary; while he recited an Ave Maria in English: "Hail Mary full of grace . . . blessed art thou amongst women . . . Holy Mary, Mother of God, pray for us sinners now and at the hour of our death, amen." Those words were indelible, too, and yet he hadn't

been able to speak them at the funeral service. *Kyrie eleison*. She's
gone, she's gone. . . .

It would have been, would be, so much easier if he still believed.
And what made it even harder was that he wasn't sure why he didn't,
or just what it was that made him lose his faith.

He was in the garage, working on the sideboard, when he heard
the car come up the hill and swing into his driveway. Now, who
was that? Cecca? Yesterday he'd as much as invited her to stop by
whenever she felt like it. He put down the router he'd been using,
went out through the side door.

Not Cecca—Jerry Whittington. Dix felt a small letdown. Jerry was
a good guy and he meant well, but he had a tendency, like Eileen
Harrell, to be pushily cheerful, as if he thought it was his mission
in life to infect others with his viral sunniness. They had been friends
for over three years, since just after Jerry moved to Los Alegres
from Washington State, and his upbeat disposition had been easy
enough to take before the accident. The past three weeks, though,
Jerry had made a crusade out of trying to cheer him up, drag him
back into their circle of mutual friends and activities. Mostly Dix
resented the hands-on intrusion. He knew the dangers of prolonged,
solitary grieving and he had no intention of succumbing to them.
He needed time, that was all. He just couldn't seem to make Jerry
understand that.

" 'Morning,'' Jerry said. "Hey, what're you doing in those
clothes? It's ten o'clock.''

"Working in the garage.''

"Well, hurry up and change. We've got an eleven o'clock tee
time.''

"Golf? I'm not up to a round of golf.''

Jerry had a way of squinting lopsidedly when he was bemused.
"Why'd you change your mind?''

"I didn't. What made you think I wanted to play?''

"Didn't you get my message?''

"What message?''

"The one I left on your machine. Yesterday afternoon.''

"No. I was out most of yesterday and I haven't gone near the
phone since.''

"Oh. Damn. I thought it'd be a good idea for you to get out, get some fresh air and a little exercise. When you didn't call back, I went ahead and set up a foursome with Tom and George.''

"Jerry, I'm sorry. But I just don't feel up to it.''

"Do you a world of good.''

"I don't think so, not today.''

Jerry gave him a long, probing look. He was a couple of years Dix's junior, trim and sinewy from all the golf and tennis he played. Electric-blue eyes and craggy blond good looks that kept him well supplied with female companionship. You might take him, as Dix had the first time they'd met, for someone in an outdoor trade: builder, engineer. In fact he was a CPA. And a good one; he'd saved the Mallory's several hundred dollars in taxes last year. He was divorced and lived alone. The divorce, which must have been painful because he wouldn't talk much about it, was the reason he'd moved to California. The reason he'd picked Los Alegres, he claimed, was that it was a town with fewer CPAs per its population than any other he'd found. Jerry was nothing if not practical.

"You holding up all right?'' he asked.

"More or less. Don't I look it?''

"A little ragged around the edges.''

"I didn't sleep too well last night.''

"Any particular reason? I mean . . . well . . .''

"I know what you mean.'' He had no intention of telling Jerry about the tormentor; theirs was not the serious, confiding kind of friendship. For that matter, he wouldn't have felt comfortable confiding in any of his male friends. Maybe that was why he'd blurted it out to Elliot last night: Elliot invited confidence. Today, though, he wished he hadn't. Talking about it hadn't done him any good, had it? "No, no particular reason,'' he said. "Just a bad night.''

"You eating regularly? Look a little thin.''

"Thin, hell. I'm as fit as you are. I told you how I got rid of the pot belly I was growing.''

"Hundred laps a day in the pool, right.''

"Hundred and fifty.''

"I'm impressed. If this country ever forms a Senior Olympics swim team, I'll write you a letter of recommendation.''

"Thanks a bunch.''

"But you still need to get out into the world again, see your friends, take up the old pursuits. Sure I can't talk you into at least nine holes today?''

"I'd rather not, Jerry. Maybe next weekend."

"Next weekend you've got another date."

"Oh? What's that?"

"My place, Saturday afternoon anytime after four. I'm hosting a pre-Labor Day barbecue. Sound good?"

"Well . . ."

"Eight or ten friends, that's all. Cecca, Owen, Tom and Beth, George and Laura, Sid and Helen, probably Margaret Allen. I wanted Ted and Eileen to come, too, but they won't be back."

"Back?"

"From Blue Lake. You did know they were going away?"

"No. No, I didn't."

"Left this morning. Coming back next Monday."

"Uh-huh."

"Day before you start teaching again, right? School starts on the seventh?"

"Early this year, yes."

"How do you feel about getting back into the classroom?"

"Good. I'm looking forward to it."

"That's the attitude. College kids are full of life. Stimulating to be around."

"Very."

"So you'll come next Saturday?"

"If I feel up to it, I will."

"Anytime after four, like I said. If you're not there by five, I'll come up here and haul you down bodily. I mean it, Dix. Ropes and handcuffs if necessary."

Dix managed a smile. "All right, you talked me into it."

"Good man. Well, I'd better get a move on. If you feel like company later on, drive over to the club. We should be done hacking divots by two. Late lunch, drinks, whatever."

"Maybe I'll do that," Dix lied.

When Jerry was gone, he returned to the sideboard. Another two or three days and he would have it fitted, bonded, sanded, and ready for primer sealing and then staining. It had become important to finish it as soon as possible, but at the same time to make it as perfect as he was capable. When he was done and satisfied with it, it would mark both an ending and a beginning: Then, finally, he felt he would be through grieving and ready to start living again.

Heat and hunger drove him into the house at twelve-thirty. He made himself a tuna salad sandwich, opened a beer, ate sitting at the kitchen table and with some appetite. As he carried his empty plate to the sink, he noticed the blinking light on the answering machine. Three blinks now—three messages. He hesitated, then leaned over and pressed the playback button.

The first message was the one from Jerry about the golf date. The second was from a school acquaintance of Katy's who lived in San Francisco and who said she'd just heard about the accident and oh, Dix, dear Dix, she was so dreadfully sorry, if there was anything she could do, wouldn't he please call her back right away. Dix had met her once, years before, and could barely remember what she looked like. He didn't bother to write down the number.

The third message—

"Go look in your mailbox," the tormentor's voice said.

That was all.

Now what? Come onto the property, put something in the mailbox? Christ. Virtually no risk of anybody seeing him if he skulked up Rosemont in the middle of the night. Trees and shrubs screened off the nearest neighbors, and the mailbox was down at the foot of the drive, invisible from up here unless you were standing out on the parking area in front of the garage.

What, though? Written calumny? Lies cut and pasted out of newspapers and magazines?

Dix went out and down the drive, forcing himself to walk at a normal pace. The mailbox was the rural kind, mounted on a pole. He dropped the front lid, bent to look inside.

A little box, about six inches square. Plain white, sealed with filament tape.

He removed it gingerly, held it for a few seconds—it hardly had any weight—and then shook it. Faint rattling. Unease began to build in him. Throw it in the garbage, he thought, don't open it. Instead, his legs carried him straight uphill and into the house. He slit the tape with a knife, lifted off the lid.

The box was stuffed with cotton, a thick wad of it. When he pinched up the wad between thumb and forefinger, something fell out and clattered on the drainboard. Its twin dangled from the cotton, glinting in the sunlight that burned down through the kitchen skylights.

Earrings.

White jade teardrop earrings with a tiny sapphire set into each hammered gold clip. One-of-a-kind pair, made to order by a jeweler in Santa Rosa four years ago.

Earrings Katy had been wearing the night she died.

SIX

It was five-thirty when Cecca drove up Rosemont Lane and turned into the Mallory driveway. She hesitated as she got out into the thinning afternoon heat, wondering again if she should have called first. But Dix's message had been as urgent-sounding as it was succinct: "I need to see you right away. Call or come up to the house—please, Cecca. I'll be home all day." He hadn't left the time of his call; it could have been anytime after noon, when she and Amy had left for the tree farm. Monthly Sunday meal with her folks—"dinner," Ma called it, even though they sat down at the table promptly at two o'clock. Ritual, but usually a pleasant one. Not so pleasant today though. The heat, and Pop's wearying new litany of complaints: getting old, useless, couldn't use his hands because of the arthritis, couldn't even get an erection anymore (this in front of Amy, who'd thought it was funny), might as well die and get it over with. And he was only sixty-eight! And now this urgent message from Dix, with the distraught edge to his voice. She couldn't imagine what had prompted it. Something else for her to worry about, no doubt, whatever it was. Sometimes she felt like an emotional sponge, soaking up other people's problems as readily as she soaked up her own, absorbing and then squeezing them out as if they *were* her own. "Why do you care so much about other people?" Chet had asked her once, seriously—a legitimate question coming from him, because the only person he cared about was himself. "I was born with a Mother Teresa gene," she'd said. It was as good an answer as any.

She rang the doorbell three times without getting a response. She

57

went to the garage; he wasn't there, but his Buick was. Out by the pool? She made her way down the side steps and around onto the rear terrace.

She heard him before she saw him. He was in the pool, swimming laps in a kind of frenzy: head down, eyes shut, arms and legs pummeling the water into a froth. Not really swimming, she thought as she watched him; it was as though he were trying to rid himself of some inner turmoil. It added to her feeling of concern. The man struggling in the pool wasn't the Dix Mallory she knew—the gentle, controlled one. Even Katy's death hadn't altered those qualities; he'd been the same man at the funeral and downtown yesterday. What could have happened to change him so radically in twenty-four hours?

He didn't realize she was there until she moved to the pool's edge and shouted his name. Then he stopped beating the water, caught the lip, and lifted himself out. He stood beside her, dripping, round-shouldered with fatigue, working to get his breathing under control.

"Amy and I were out at the farm," she said. "Didn't get home until a little while ago."

"Thanks for coming."

He reached for the towel draped over one of the outdoor chairs. Cecca could see the strained muscles rippling in his arms and legs as he dried himself. And noticed, in spite of herself, how trim he looked in his swimsuit, the flatness of his belly.

"How long have you been in the pool?" she asked.

"A while. Too long, probably."

"You look exhausted."

"That was the idea."

"Dix, what is it? What's happened?"

"In the house. I've got something to show you."

He led her inside. Upstairs in the living room he said, "I'll go put on some clothes. Make yourself a drink if you want one."

"No. Unless you do . . ."

"I'd better not."

Waiting for him, she prowled the room. It was the first time she'd been there since the accident, and it felt odd. Katy's house, Katy's pride and joy—a legacy now. Blue and white decor, lots of crystal and cut-glass accessories, all chosen by Katy to her tastes. Her paintings on the walls, the huge dominating one she'd called "Blue Time": rectangles and rhomboids in various shades of blue, splotches of white, three little dollops of yellow. Abstract Expressionism. She'd thought Jackson Pollock was the greatest of all American painters. Yet her own work was more in the style of Mark Rothko, whom she'd also admired—simple, sensuous color shapes rather than explosions of color. Rothko had once said that his paintings were façades, telling little but just enough about his perception of the world and his own life. "It's the same thing with my paintings," Katy had been fond of saying. "Façades, little snippets of the real Katy Mallory." And when someone had asked her what the snippets were, a wink, a grin, and: "That's for *you* to figure out, sweetie."

Cecca had always liked this room, the house, but today it depressed her. Her mood, coupled with Dix's. She sat down on the blue brocade couch. She was staring out through the tall windows, watching a small plane circle for a landing at Los Alegres Airport across the valley, when Dix came down from the bedroom.

He'd put on slacks and a pullover, run a comb through his brown hair. His shoulders still wore their burden of fatigue. His jaw was set tight; she could see ridges of muscles at the corners of his mouth. He looked grim. Worse than he had the day after the accident. He had something in one hand, but his fingers were closed tight around it and she couldn't quite tell what it was. A box of some kind?

He said as he sat down across from her, "There's something I have to know, Cecca. I need you to tell me the truth—the complete and honest truth. Will you do that?"

"If I can. Of course."

"Was Katy having an affair before she died?"

". . . An affair? Dix, what on earth?"

"Was she?"

"I don't think so, no."

"You don't think so? You're not sure?"

"She never said anything to me about an affair."

"You were her best friend."

"Yes, but she didn't confide everything to me."

"To Eileen, then?"

"No. There was a private side to Katy, you know that. Parts of herself that she never shared with anyone . . . any of her friends, I mean."

"Not with me either. I thought I knew her so well, but now . . ." He shook his head. "She could've kept it a secret," he said. It wasn't a question.

"She could have, but that doesn't mean she did."

"Did you suspect she was cheating? Any suspicion at all?"

"No."

"Something she said you could interpret that way now?"

"No. Not to me."

"Eileen? Somebody else?"

"Oh, she said something once that Eileen . . . well . . ."

"What was it?"

"I don't remember exactly. I didn't believe it—you know how Eileen exaggerates—so I didn't pay much attention."

"Try to remember."

"It . . . something about having too much excitement in her life. It could have meant anything. Or nothing."

"When was this?"

"A couple of months ago."

"And Eileen thought it meant Katy was having an affair."

"She took it that way, yes, but—"

"She tried her damnedest to find out, I'll bet."

"Without any success. Katy laughed it off."

"But she didn't deny it?"

"For heaven's sake, Dix, what's this all about? Why do you think Katy had a lover?"

"A man told me she did," Dix said. "In detail. Plenty of graphic goddamn detail."

"What man? Who'd do an ugly thing like that?"

"I don't know."

"You don't *know* who told you?"

"A voice on the phone. An anonymous caller who claimed to be Katy's lover. At first I took it for a filthy lie—"

"Oh my God," Cecca said.

"What's wrong?"

"Anonymous caller, you said. Only that one call?"

"No, several. They started right after the funeral. Just breathing, then he'd hang up."

"When did—" The words caught in her throat. She coughed to loosen the constriction. "When did he tell you all that about Katy? What day?"

"Yesterday."

"Yesterday. Was that the first time he spoke to you?"

"Yes, why?"

"Unnatural voice, like a computer's?"

He sat forward jerkily. "Jesus . . . not you, too?"

"For about the same length of time. Nothing but breathing until yesterday afternoon."

"What did he say to you?"

She told him.

He said, "But there was nothing to it, nothing wrong with Amy."

"No. But I was half frantic until she came home. Dix . . . do you think he's dangerous?"

No response. He was looking at her, but there was a remoteness in his eyes, as if he were seeing something—or somebody—else.

"Dangerous," she said again. "More than just a telephone freak."

"I don't know," Dix said slowly. "In any case, he may not be a liar where Katy is concerned."

"You don't believe he really was her lover?"

"I didn't until this morning."

"What happened this morning?"

"He left a message on my machine, telling me to go look in the mailbox. I found this. He must have put it there sometime during the night."

He opened his fisted hand, extending it so she could see that what he'd been gripping was a small white jewelry box. She took it, lifted the lid.

Frowning, she said, "Katy's favorite earrings."

"Made especially for her. No other pair like them."

"But how could he—?"

"She was wearing them the night she died."

"She . . . oh no, you must be mistaken."

"I wish I were," he said. "She had them on when she left here that night."

Cecca shook her head: confusion, dismay.

"They should be lumps of metal, melted and fused by the heat of the fire. The only way he could've gotten them is if he were with her before the accident."

"She could have lost them—"

"Both? And he just happened to find them? No, Katy must have given them to him for some reason. Or else he took them from her."

"Even if that's true, it doesn't have to mean they were lovers. There could be another explanation."

"The only one I can think of is a hell of a lot worse."

"What . . . ?"

"That her death wasn't an accident."

She stared at him. "What do you— Suicide?"

"That's the first thing that occurred to me. An affair that had gotten out of hand, guilt, depression . . . I thought it might be possible."

"But now you don't."

"Now I don't. There was that private part of her, yes, but I can't make myself believe it was that bleak. She loved life too much to give it up voluntarily. She was full of life. You agree with that, don't you?"

"Yes." She made herself take a long, slow breath before she spoke again. "You mean murder, then. You think Katy could have been murdered."

"I didn't say that's what I thought. I said it's a possibility that occurred to me. I shouldn't have mentioned it."

"Dix, you're scaring me."

"I'm sorry, I didn't mean to." He moved over beside her, took her hand. "I think we'd better just drop this before our imaginations run away with us."

"Random violence, is that it? Katy being in the wrong place at the wrong time?" She was trying to talk herself out of crediting it, even a little, by dealing with it directly. But the questions served only to open up her fear. "Or . . . somebody stalking her? The same man who . . . the man on the phone . . . if you're right about Katy, then he could be—"

"No, Cecca."

"He could be after us, too. You, me, Amy."

"That's what I meant by letting imagination—"

"But why us? Why would anybody want to hurt *us*?"

"We don't know that anybody does."

"Those calls, the things he said—"

"—Could be nothing more than a sick game. There are all kinds of psychoses. He doesn't have to be violent."

"Katy . . . the earrings . . ."

"He knew her, he got them from her—all right. But her death is still an accident as far as we know. The highway patrol, the county sheriff, were satisfied of that; we have to be, too. Dammit, I could kick myself for opening up this can of worms."

"What're you saying? Just forget it?"

"That part of it, yes."

Inside her now was a visceral sense of something unseen and terrible lying in wait for her—the kind of nameless terror she'd had as a little girl. Bogeyman in the closet, monster under the stairs. "I don't know if I can," she said.

"You have to. We both have to. Wild speculations aren't doing either of us any good."

"We can't just sit back and pretend none of this is happening."

"I know that. We need to focus on identifying the tormentor, putting a stop to his damn games."

"Tormentor," she said. "That's the right name for him."

Dix said, "Options. All right, we can go to the telephone company. They can trace one of his calls if they're set up for it and he stays on the line long enough. But I don't think that would work. He's too smart to fall into that kind of trap. Chances are, he makes his damn calls from a public phone anyway."

"The police?"

"I doubt if there's much they can do without some idea of who he is. We'll have to try to find that out ourselves."

"Us? How?"

"I've got some ideas. Are you willing?"

"Do I have a choice?"

"I don't see one for either of us. Except a stopgap measure: have our home phone numbers changed."

"What good will that do? He could still call me at the office. Besides, a third of my business calls come to me at home. A realtor can't afford an unlisted number."

"I see your point. But I'm still going to have mine changed. If nothing else, it may help narrow the field a little."

"I don't understand. Narrow the field?"

"If he gets hold of the new unlisted number, keeps calling, it'll tell us he's someone we know."

"Someone we know," Cecca said.

"Not a friend—a casual acquaintance, a clerk or gas station attendant, somebody who took a disliking to us for some reason."

"How would a clerk or a gas station attendant get your new unlisted number?"

Dix made no reply.

"It would have to be somebody we know fairly well in that case, wouldn't it?"

"Not necessarily."

"But probably. And I don't want to believe that anymore than I want to believe Katy's death wasn't an accident."

An afternoon breeze had come up; Cecca could feel it wafting in through the open balcony doors, carrying the scents of pine and dry grass. Outside the windows, a hawk wheeled down and sat fluffing its wings on the electrical wires strung from the house to the pole on Rosemont. From one of the neighboring yards she heard the shrieks and laughter of children in the midst of a swim party. Normal Sunday afternoon in late summer. Small town, small-town life: familiar, comfortable. Nonthreatening. Safe. The conversation they'd just had, the revelations that had made it necessary, seemed unreal . . . no, surreal, like a scene in a murky avant-garde play.

How can this be happening? she thought. I don't understand how a thing like this can happen to us.

She said abruptly, "I'd like that drink now."

"I can use one, too. Bourbon, Scotch, gin, vodka?"

"Scotch. A double, on the rocks."

He let go of her hand—she was surprised to discover that he'd still been holding it—and stood and went into the kitchen. She sat there staring out at the valley. Then, slowly, her head moved and her gaze shifted until she was looking again at Katy's "Blue Time" painting.

Façade, she thought, little snippets of the real Katy Mallory. What had lain behind the façade, what did the little snippets mean? Smile, wink—that's for *you* to figure out, sweetie.

I thought I had. I thought I knew her pretty well.

Maybe I didn't know her at all.

And what if Katy weren't the only one in Los Alegres she thought she knew well who was hiding behind a façade? Darkness concealed by a smile. Evil covered by a mask of normalcy. But no façade is perfect; that was one of the first lessons you learned in the real estate business. There are always little flaws, little indications of what lies hidden, if you look for them closely enough. The naked truth is there to be figured out, sweetie, if you can stand to face it. It's all there behind the façade.

SEVEN

It was cool and shady on the cabin's enclosed sun porch. Cool and shady most of the day, a fact that had always amused Eileen. A sun porch was supposed to be sunny, right? Or else it would be called a *shade* porch. But the angle at which the cabin had been built, the thick growth of pine and redbud that flanked it down to the water's edge, kept the sun's rays from hitting the windows there until late afternoon. This was one of the things she'd always loved about the cabin, coming up to the lake. She could sit here most of the day in perfect lazy comfort if she felt like it—and she often did. She had no use for direct sunlight; she burned easily, she had a light sensitivity that affected her vision, and she began to sweat like a pig as soon as the temperature climbed above eighty. Early evening was her time to stir her stumps. And the hour before sundown was the best time of all. Cool then, with the night sounds just starting, the lake changing color under a sky that darkened slowly into a velvety black . . . oh, yes.

From where she was sitting in the big rattan easy chair next to the window, she had a clear view of the lake and the stubby pier directly below. Bobby and Kevin were in the water just off the forward edge of the pier, playing some kind of game with a beach ball. The noise they were making drifted up to her, brought a smile to her mouth. Teenagers. So damn much energy. She'd gone for a quick swim herself earlier, or, rather, a dunking because it had lasted for all of thirty seconds. The lake was just too cold in the morning. Maybe she'd go in again before her evening walk; the water would be warm then from the day's drippy heat. But probably she wouldn't. Swimming was too much like work. Let the boys exercise all they wanted. Ted, too. A leisurely sunset stroll—and a good-night screw if she and Ted were both in the mood—was more than enough physical exertion for her. Vacation days, as far as she was concerned, were for reading the new Danielle Steel, stuffing herself until she got sleepy, and then going in and taking a nap. With minor variations over seven glorious days.

She snagged the last of the English muffin with cream cheese from the plate beside her, popped it into her mouth. Her gaze fell on her thighs as she chewed. White and chubby; the fat cells rippled when she moved, like little winking eyes. *I really ought to go on a diet,* she thought. She knew she was only kidding herself. Diets were a torment, and she was not into self-abuse these days. Besides, she was forty-one and entitled to be middle-aged pudgy, and Ted liked her just the way she was. "Lying on you is like lying on a cloud," he'd said a couple of months ago after they'd finished making love. She'd thought he was being smart-ass and smacked him one, but he'd been *serious.* Men. Alien creatures. Not that she'd trade her three, not for any amount of money.

She peered out over the flat surface of the lake. No sign of Ted yet. He'd gotten up at the crack of dawn and carted his fishing gear down to the skiff and rowed off happily to murder some poor catfish or lake bass or whatever. Fishing . . . now, there was a nasty sport for you. Not as nasty as slaughtering deer or elk for fun, but nasty just the same. Hauling those poor creatures out of the water at the end of a hook, watching them wiggle desperately to get free while they strangled on air, cutting or ripping the barb out of their mouths while they were still flopping . . . ugh! She'd gone with Ted once and that had been one time too many. Not only hadn't she been able to clean the fish he'd brought home since, she couldn't even bring herself to eat one. If he'd caught anything this morning, he and the boys would devour the remains at supper and welcome to it. She'd have a hamburger smothered in sauteed mushrooms.

The thought of a hamburger made her mouth water. *Pig,* she thought, and got up and went to see what the refrigerator had to offer. They'd stopped in Ukiah on the way yesterday and loaded up on groceries. Another bagel with cream cheese? No, something sweet . . . peanut butter and strawberry jam sandwich. Yum. Eat your heart out, Jenny Craig. Chuckling, she took out the jar of Jif, the jar of Smucker's, and went for the loaf of white bread.

The telephone rang.

If that's the hospital, she thought, I'm not going back, not for *any* emergency. This is my vacation, dammit. Even resident nurses are entitled to vacations.

But it wasn't the hospital. It was Cecca.

Eileen was surprised and pleased. "Make my day," she said, "and tell me you can get away after all. Did you close the deal on the Morrison house?"

"No, not yet. That isn't why I called."

"Well, it can't be just to chat."

"No. I saw Dix last night."

"Took my advice and invited him to dinner? Good!"

"He called and said he wanted to see me."

"Even better. How'd it go?"

"Eileen, it wasn't social."

The way Cecca said that put Eileen on alert. When you'd been a person's close friend for more than half your lives, you developed antennae. "There's something wrong," she said. "Tell mama."

"Those crank calls I've been getting? Well, Dix has been getting them, too—from the same man."

"Dix? Heavy breathing calls from a *man*?"

"They're not sexual. Not the way you mean."

"What are they, then?"

"Something a lot sicker."

Eileen listened breathlessly as Cecca explained about the calls she and Dix had received on Saturday. Hers was bad enough, but the one to Dix . . . good God!

"He claimed *he* was the one Katy was having an affair with?" she said. "But why in heaven's name would he tell Dix about it? What does he want?"

"To gloat, maybe. I don't know."

"Well, he's got to be a head case, no matter what. You and Dix believe it's true?"

"It could be," Cecca said. "All the details . . . it could be."

"Lord. I've thought all along Katy had a lover, you know that, but a man with a bunch of his wires loose . . . *brrr*. That's not her fault, though. You can't always tell a book by its cover." She shivered despite the day's gathering heat. "You think he's dangerous?"

"We don't know. He could be."

"Well, have you gone to the police?"

"Last night. We went together and made a report."

"Who did you see? Chief Rennick?"

"No, a lieutenant named St. John. He's been on the force here only about a year and a half. He was sympathetic enough, but he said what we expected to hear: There's nothing the police can do without some idea of who the man is and what he's after."

Eileen began slathering a piece of bread with peanut butter. When she was upset she craved food. Some people wrapped themselves in their security blankets; she ate hers.

"What're you going to do?" she asked.

"Try to find out who he is."

"How? A stranger, a disguised voice on the phone—"

"He may not be a stranger," Cecca said.

"Someone you *know*? But then ... if you know him, so do I. Oh, brother!"

"I hate the idea, too. But it could be."

"I guess it could. Damn, I wish Katy hadn't been so secretive! If she'd dropped just a *hint* of who she was seeing ..."

"But she didn't."

"No. Not that night I told you about, in June, and not afterward. Every time I tried to bring it up, she changed the subject."

"What exactly did she say that made you suspect she was having an affair?"

"It wasn't so much what she said, it was how she said it and how she acted."

"Tell me again. In detail."

"All right," Eileen said. Strawberry jam on top of the peanut butter, big gooey globs of it that reminded her of clotted blood. She took a bite of it anyway. Another bite before she spoke again, with her mouth half full and peanut butter sticking to the roof. "It was a Friday night. The first Friday in the month, I think. Ted's bowling night, and the boys were off somewhere." She finally managed to swallow. "You were having dinner with Jerry at River House. That Friday."

"I remember."

"Well, I was feeling lonesome, so I called Katy and she came over. We got into the wine. A chardonnay that Owen recommended to Ted. At first we just talked, I don't remember what about. Talked and drank. Then we started reminiscing, you know how you do on about four glasses of wine. The trip the three of us took up the Oregon coast after you and Chet split up, what a good time we had. Well, except for Pelican Bay.''

Eileen stuffed the rest of the bread and Jif and Smucker's into her mouth. Cecca said her name twice before she could get the mass— *mess*—chewed and swallowed. ''I'm here,'' she said, and wiped a smear of jam off her chin before she went on. ''I said we should do something like that again. Take a trip together, just the three of us, let our hair down the way we did in Oregon. Put some excitement back in our lives. Katy agreed it was a good idea, but not right away—next year sometime. Why wait? I said. All three of us had been bitching about how bored we were, hadn't we? She said, well, she didn't feel bored anymore, she was really getting into her painting. I said painting isn't exactly exciting and she said she had enough excitement in her life right now, more than she had any right to have. There was something about the way she said it . . . I don't know, but I said, Oh really? Don't tell me you've gone and taken a lover behind my back?''

''And she reacted to that?''

''Reacted is right. Jerked as if I'd slapped her, spilled her wine.''

''Then what?'' Cecca asked.

''She covered up fast. You know how good Katy was at covering even when she was flustered.''

''What did she say? What did you say?''

Eileen's memory had flowered; she'd always had the capacity for near-total recall. The conversation with Katy was already replaying in her mind, as clearly as if she were listening to a tape of it.

''Katy, my God, you are *having an affair!''*

''I am not! What makes you think that?''

''Well, the look on your face . . .''

''Oh, crap. You surprised me, that's all.''

''Oh come on, honey. You are, aren't you.''

''I just told you I'm not.''

''You can tell me. I'm your best friend.''

''And you can't keep a secret for ten minutes.''

''I'd keep this one.''

''Sure you would. You'd be on the phone to Cecca as soon as I walked out the door. You'd probably have her paged at River House.''

"*You're really not?*"

"*I'm really not.*"

"*But you would if the right man came along? The right man, the right circumstances, spice up your life a little?*"

"*I don't know. Would you?*"

"*I've thought about it. He'd have to have a big dick.*"

"*That doesn't matter, and you know it.*"

"*It does when you're married to Theodore J. Harrell. Ted's not exactly hung like a horse. Or a Shetland pony, for that matter.*"

"*Count your blessings. If he was, you'd be walking funny.*"

"*Katy, let's suppose you* are *having an affair—*"

"*I'm not. How many times do I have to say it?*"

"*But suppose you were. Because you were bored and looking for some excitement . . . whatever reason. Who would you be having it with?*"

"*What kind of question is that?*"

"*A man you've known for a long time—a friend? Like Tom Birnam or Jerry Whittington or George Flores—*"

"*Sweetie, you're being ridiculous. Don't start jumping to wild conclusions.*"

"*I'm not, I'm only asking.*"

"*Well, the answer is no.*"

"*Too close to home?*"

"*Yes. Too close to home.*"

"*But it wouldn't be somebody you just picked up, in a bar or someplace. I mean, the AIDS thing—*"

"*No. Can we just drop this?*"

"*I don't want to drop it. I find it fascinating.*"

"*Well, I don't.*"

"*It couldn't be a stranger, could it? It couldn't for me. I'd have to have* some *feelings for the guy before I could go to bed with him. Be able to talk to him about things that mattered, before and after. Feel comfortable with him.*"

"*. . . Okay, yes, for me, too.*"

"*So it wouldn't be just sex, the big O. There'd have to be some real emotion, too.*"

"*If you're talking about love . . .*"

"*I don't mean love. I mean feelings.*"

"*Feelings.*"

"*You'd have to like him. Not love but like.*"

"*I suppose so. Is there any more wine in that bottle?*"

"*Help yourself. What if it grew into more, though—got really intense?*"

"*Intense? What're you talking about now?*"

"*Same subject. Your affair.*"

"*Eileen, if you don't stop . . .*"

"*All right, your hypothetical affair. What if it turned into something more than sex, deeper than just liking?*"

"*That wouldn't happen.*"

"*Are you sure it couldn't?*"

"*I wouldn't let it.*"

"*Suppose it was heading that way. What would you do?*"

"*Break it off.*"

"*Just like that? Sorry, it's been nice, good-bye?*"

"*Not quite that coldly, but . . . yes.*"

"*So you'd never leave Dix? No matter what?*"

"*I don't think I could, no.*"

"*That doesn't sound very definite.*"

"*Bad phrasing. No, I wouldn't leave Dix. Never, no matter what.*"

"*You love him that much?*"

"*That much. Always have, always will.*"

"*Suppose he finds out about the affair?*"

"*There's nothing for him to find out, Eileen.*"

"*If there was. Would he leave you?*"

"*No. Never.*"

"*He might. Men are unpredictable sometimes.*"

"*Not Dix.*"

"*He'd just forgive you and go on as if nothing happened?*"

"*Sooner or later. But it would never come to that.*"

"*No? Why not?*"

"*Because he'd never find out. I wouldn't let him find out.*"

"*Famous last words. Skeletons have a way of falling out of closets, honey, you know that.*"

"*I'd do anything to keep that from happening. Anything. And if you start spreading this nonsense around town, start a lot of nasty rumors, our friendship is kaput. I mean that. I'll never speak to you again.*"

"*Oh, lighten up, will you? We're just playing a game here.*"

"*Some game.*"

"*How long would you let it go on?*"

". . . What?"

"The affair. A few weeks, a few months, a year or more?"

"Oh, God. No, not that long."

"Six months?"

"No."

"How long, then? Maximum?"

"Three months, okay? Are you satisfied now?"

"Three months. I guess you could get a lot of screwing in in three months. How many times a week would you do it with him, anyway? Two, three, four?"

"Shit, Eileen—!"

"How often do you and Dix do it? Three or four times a month? That seems to be the general marital frequency for people our age. Sometimes I think that's the real reason we have affairs, men and women both—not so much because we want to try out another body, but because we want more nookie than we're getting from our spouses. What do you think?"

"I think you're a motor-mouth when you drink too much. I think you're driving me to distraction with all this talk. I think I'm going home."

And she'd done just that. Stood up and put on her coat and walked out without even saying good-bye.

Eileen related the gist of this to Cecca, who said, "I still don't see anything to make you so certain she was lying."

"You weren't there, honey. You would if you'd been there."

"And she wouldn't talk about it after that?"

"Froze me out completely. Closed issue, she said."

"That's it, then," Cecca said. "If you think of anything else, anything at all, call me. Okay?"

"Maybe I'd better just come home."

"Oh, Eileen, no. You've been there only one day."

"There might be something I can do. . . ."

"There isn't. What could you do that Dix and I can't? You stay right where you are."

"How can I relax with *this* going on?"

"You'll find a way. I'll let you know if there's anything to report. Just do me one favor—don't tell anyone else about this."

"Not even Ted?"

"Ted, yes, if you swear him to secrecy. But not Laura, Beth, any of our friends."

"Honey, one of them might know something . . ."

"Then Dix and I will find it out. Please, Eileen? The worst thing right now is for too many people to know, rumors to start flying."

Motor-mouth Eileen. Can't keep a secret for ten minutes. Well, it was true, wasn't it? Biggest gossip-monger in Los Alegres . . . no wonder Katy hadn't confided in her. She sighed. "Ted and nobody else. I swear. But you have to promise me you'll call the minute you find out anything or anything else happens."

"I promise."

As soon as she put the receiver down, her eye fell on the jars and the loaf of bread on the table. I don't want any more of that, she thought, and immediately made herself another sandwich, thicker than the last one, so that some of the jam squeezed out when she bit into it and plopped on the floor. She left it there, the hell with it. She was too upset for housekeeping chores.

There was something Cecca hadn't told her, she was sure of it. Some even more startling piece of information. Didn't trust her with it, which meant that it must be really explosive stuff. She couldn't imagine what it was. Her fault for being the way she was—though she had every intention of keeping her promise not to blab to anyone but Ted. But still she felt left out. Of all times to be away on vacation! Maybe she *should* go home, Ted and the boys could fend for themselves . . . no, that was silly and selfish. Cecca was right, there wasn't anything she could do. Except fret, and she could do that right here at Blue Lake.

She finished the sandwich and went into the bathroom to wash her hands. She felt bloated and a little sick to her stomach from all the food. But her mind was active, and as she dried her hands something began to scratch at her memory like a cat trying to get through a door. Something about Katy . . . something she'd done or said. Not that half-drunk June Friday; later, quite a bit later. It hadn't had anything to do with a lover, but . . . what the devil was it?

There was a banging out in the kitchen. Footsteps. Ted's voice: "Eileen, where are you? Come take a look at what the old man caught this morning."

She'd remember it sooner or later. That was the good thing about a memory like hers—she always remembered what she wanted to sooner or later. She put the towel down and hurried out to tell Ted about the awful phone calls and Katy's affair with a maniac.

EIGHT

Lone Mountain Road was narrow and not in the best of repair. Edges had crumbled away in places, making it even narrower; if two cars met at these places, one would have to back up or down to let the other pass. The road corkscrewed its way up into the hills for more than six miles, finally deadending just beyond the gate to the Chenelli ranch near the top of a piece of high ground some obscure local wag had christened Lone Mountain. Once you were on the road, there was no way to get off except to turn around and drive back down to the intersection with East Valley Road. It had been built in the twenties by the county to accommodate the ranchers whose property flanked it. The only other people who used it, as far as Dix knew, were kids on beer parties and lovers looking for a private place to park and screw.

It seemed incredible, now, that he hadn't questioned Katy's presence up there on the night of August 6. Just assumed she'd taken Lone Mountain Road on a whim, as part of her pattern of aimless driving. Blind trust. Now, though, his faith had been badly shaken. Women alone don't drive out to a remote lover's lane for no good reason; they drive there to meet a man, a lover. Park and screw. Forty-one years old and humping in the backseat of a car like a teenager.

Why?

And how did he get her earrings that night?

There were plenty of places to park off the road. Little clusters of oak and madrone, cowpaths that skirted hummocks and the boulder-

75

size rocks littering the hillsides. Occasionally county sheriff's deputies cruised up there, when one of the beer parties got too noisy or out of hand and a rancher called in a complaint. But for the most part nobody bothered the lovers in their parked cars. None of the ranchers gave much of a damn, and why should they? A minor trespassing offense meant nothing as long as their fences weren't knocked down or their cows harmed or spooked.

This is a waste of time, Dix thought. I shouldn't have come up here. I don't want to look at the place where she died.

His hands were sweaty on the Buick's steering wheel. But he didn't brake or turn around; he continued to drive slowly uphill, through the monotonous series of twists and turns. He had gone about three miles now and there were no dropoffs or dangerous curves at the lower elevations. Just the scattered trees, the rocky fields of summer-cured brown grass, the placidly grazing cattle—Friesians, black with white harnesses, and brown and white Guernseys. And ranch buildings clustered here and there in distant hollows.

He had the window rolled down and the air was breezeless, sticky with early-afternoon heat. Dry grass and manure smells clogged his nostrils. When he glanced up at the rearview mirror he saw the valley spread out behind him, watery with heat haze. If a wind came up later, fire danger in the general area would be high. Especially in the hills to the north, behind the university, where there were more homes and fewer cattle to help keep the grass cropped low.

Four miles by the odometer. The highway patrolmen hadn't told him the exact location of the accident, just that it was "near the top of Lone Mountain Road." Getting close; the pitch of the road had grown steeper, twisting through cutbanks, along sere shoulders. His back had begun to ache from the stiffness of his posture. He bent forward, squinting against the sun-glare.

Another half-mile, the road climbing at a sharper grade. The terrain on the south side had begun to fall away—gradually in some places, more steeply in others. Around a curve, through a stand of trees. A brush-choked ravine opened up below on his right. Another curve—

And there it was.

Sheer, rocky slope, at least twenty degrees down and a hundred yards long, from the road to the ravine. Gouges in the earth, dislodged rocks, burned grass, shards of glass and pieces of metal agleam in the sun—a trail of destruction that ended in a huge blackened section of the ravine and the higher ground on both sides of it.

Dix's stomach churned. He drove past the place where she'd gone off the road, up to where there was a flat parking area half-hidden beneath a clump of oaks. For half a minute he sat there, gathering himself. Then he got out and walked back down to where it had happened.

It registered on his mind that the burned area could have been much larger, that the fire from the wrecked Dodge might have spread over hundreds of acres if Harold Zachary, the rancher who owned this property, hadn't been home and heard the crash. He'd notified the county fire department and they'd gotten equipment out as quickly as they could. The Dodge had been an inferno by the time the firemen arrived. *I don't think she suffered, Mr. Mallory. Chances are she was ... already gone before the gas tank exploded.* At least that. *It's all any of us can ask for at the end. To go fast, without suffering.* Yes, but that hadn't made it any easier then and still didn't now.

They had winched up the burned-out hulk of the car, trucked it away, but the spot where it had landed and the fire had first raged stood out plainly. A blackened pit at the bottom of the ravine. In spite of himself, he imagined the stench that must have been in the air that night, and the sensory perception made his gorge rise. He turned away, stood with his back to the scarred slope.

After a time he grew aware of the road surface. No skid marks. The highway patrolmen hadn't mentioned that fact to him; neither had the account in the *Herald*. The road was straight here, too—a seventy-five-yard stretch from the oaks above to the curve below. Her car had gone over midway down.

The absence of skid marks didn't have to mean anything significant. Dark that night, no moon, clouds, and she might have been driving too fast or been preoccupied and not paying enough attention to the road. Wheels slid off the edge, she overcorrected or didn't correct in time ... that was the way accidents happen. Still, there should be *some* tire skin on the road, shouldn't there? Or some crumbling along the asphalt edge. There were no marks on the slope close to the road either; the first deep gouges in the grass were at least fifteen yards down—as if the Dodge had sailed off at some speed and landed hard, nose to the ground. As if she had driven off at an accelerated speed, on purpose—

No, he thought, Cecca and I settled that issue. It wasn't suicide. Katy did not commit suicide.

And the highway patrol hadn't questioned the circumstances, had they? Trained investigators, weren't they? Yes, but every accident scene is different and it had been night and they had no real reason to suspect foul play and even trained observers overlooked things, made mistakes. . . .

How did he get her earrings?

It keeps coming back to that. She wouldn't have given them to him, not those earrings, not under any circumstances. They were her favorites; she wore them all the time; she'd be afraid her husband would notice they were missing.

Took them from her. He must have.

Before he killed her?

Up here alone with her, hit her, knocked her out, put her under the wheel, wedged the accelerator down with the emergency brake on, jerked the brake off so the car would shoot downhill and off the road?

Monstrous . . . senseless . . .

Before he *murdered* her?

Harold Zachary's ranch buildings were old, weathered, in need of paint—a reflection of the difficult times rather than neglect, because the grounds were orderly and the fences in good repair. The woman who answered the door at the house said she was Mrs. Zachary and her husband was probably in the dairy barn. Dix found him there, working from a toolbox on one of the automatic milking machines.

Zachary was a spare man, with a wild shock of ginger-colored hair and sweat glistening in deep creases on his neck. Not unfriendly, and sympathetic enough when Dix introduced himself, but wary at first. "Don't know what I can do for you, Mr. Mallory. The accident happened on my property, but that's a county road out there. Just not my responsibility."

"I know. That's not why I'm here."

"Then?"

"I can't help but wonder why my wife was up here that night. As far as I know, she didn't know anybody who lives off Lone Mountain Road."

"Can't help you there either."

"There was no one else around that night, no other car, when you reached the scene?"

"Didn't see anybody, no."

"How soon did you get there after the crash?"

"Few minutes. Not more than ten," Zachary said. "Knew it was bad as soon as I heard the explosion and saw the flames. Told my wife to call nine-eleven, and lit out in my truck." His eyes shifted away from Dix's. "Wasn't nothing I could do for her. Wish to God there had been."

"Thank you. The *Herald* printed a photo of my wife. Did you see it?"

"I saw it."

"Did you recognize her?"

"I never knew your wife, Mr. Mallory."

"No, I mean had you ever seen her before?"

"I see people every time I go into town. Can't remember them all."

"Not in town," Dix said, "up here. On Lone Mountain Road."

"Hard to tell from a newspaper photograph."

"Does that mean you might have?"

"Might have. Once."

Dix took Owen's portrait photo of Katy from his wallet. "This is a much better likeness of her," he said.

Zachary studied it for a few seconds. Returned it without saying anything. His mouth had a pinched whiteness at the corners.

"Mr. Zachary?"

"Couldn't tell much about her car that night, by the time I got there. The fire. Paper said it was a Dodge."

"That's right. Three-year-old Dart."

"What color?"

"Burgundy. Dark red."

"Personalized license plate?"

"KATYDID. Her name was Katy."

"All right," Zachary said. He still wasn't meeting Dix's eyes.

"You did see her, didn't you."

"Once. Just once."

"When? How long ago?"

"Can't say exactly. Three, four weeks before."

"Before the accident?"

"Yeah."

"Driving on Lone Mountain Road?"

"No," Zachary said. "Parked."

"Alone? Or with somebody?"

"Alone. Waiting for somebody, she said."

"You spoke to her, then."

"Middle of the afternoon, sitting there all by herself. My property. I was on my way to town, so I stopped, asked her what she was doing there." He paused. "Thought maybe she needed some help."

No, you didn't. That's not what you thought at all. "And she said she was waiting for somebody."

"That's right."

"Did she say who?"

"No."

"Or why?"

"No."

"What else did she say?"

"I told her she was on private property and she said she was sorry and she'd leave as soon as her friend showed up. I said all right. Seemed like a nice lady. Polite. None of my business, really."

"Did you pass anybody on the way down—the person she was meeting?"

"Not that I recall."

"Where was it she was parked?"

"Right up the road from where the accident happened. Patch of old oaks. Kids sometimes—" He bit off the rest of it, shifted his feet and tried to hide his discomfort by bending and picking up a pair of Channellocks. But Dix knew what he had been about to say.

"I won't take up any more of your time, Mr. Zachary. Thanks for talking to me."

"Shouldn't have, maybe."

"No, I appreciate it. I needed to know."

He started away, and behind him Zachary said, "Mr. Mallory? Don't mean much, I guess, but . . . I'm sorry."

Dix nodded and went on without looking back. Hearing Harold Zachary's pity was hard enough; he did not want to see any more of it written on the rancher's face.

He drove straight to the university, to keep his two o'clock appointment with Lawrence Hampton at Guiterrez Hall. He didn't relish the meeting; he wished as he walked across campus from the faculty parking lot that he hadn't agreed to it this morning when Hampton returned his call. But he'd felt that it was important to maintain a tight grip on the normal patterns of his life, and it had seemed best to get the meeting over and done with as quickly as possible.

Hampton was a decent sort but inclined to be pedantic. He lectured his fellow professors as if they were his students; the joke in the department was that there were two ways to teach and interpret U.S. history, the accepted way and the Hampton way. In Lawrence's stuffy office—he considered air-conditioning to be unhealthy—Dix endured an hour-long discourse on Jacksonian democracy and economic sectionalism. Complete with graphs and charts and pages of detailed notes to support the not very original Hampton theories.

On the way out of the building he passed Elliot Messner's office. Elliot wasn't there, which was a relief; he might have wanted to talk, ask if there had been any more phone calls. Dix wasn't up to that. He still regretted opening up to Elliot on Saturday. And after what he'd learned today, the suspicions that were building in him, the only person he could or would confide in now was Cecca—and her only up to a point because he didn't want to panic her. Until he had a better idea of what had happened on the night of August 6, and why, there was not even much point in relaying his suspicions to Lieutenant St. John. Or the highway patrol, or the county sheriff's department. Without some kind of evidence, he had no leverage to convince any of them to reopen an investigation into Katy's death.

He drove straight home from the university. As soon as he walked into the kitchen he was aware of the message light flashing—twice—on the answering machine. The telephone company hadn't been able to get somebody out today; tomorrow morning between eight and noon, they'd told him. He stood watching the red light blink. One of the calls would have been from the tormentor; he had no doubt of that. And the message? Something about Katy's earrings, probably. Words he didn't want to hear.

He ran the tape back to the beginning without listening to either message. And felt better for having won even a tiny victory in this ongoing war of nerves.

NINE

Bright Winds Gallery was on the second floor of the Mill, the riverfront complex that also housed Romeo's. The cavernous building had once been a feed mill, Kraft Bros. Feed & Grain, in the days when Los Alegres was an agricultural and poultry-producing center and goods were regularly shipped downriver by barge to San Francisco. When the town began to lose its agricultural identity in the sixties, the descendants of the Kraft brothers had gone bankrupt. A local developer had bought the old mill in the early seventies and converted it into a unique kind of shopping mall on two levels—boutiques, craft shops, galleries, eating and drinking establishments. To Cecca's surprise, Los Alegresans had taken to it as readily as tourists, mainly because the developer had been smart enough to preserve much of the original interior: exposed piping, pieces of milling equipment, the rough-wood and cement floors. He'd also added other historical artifacts and numerous old photos of the town dating back as far as 1870. With this kind of ambiance, the Mill had soon become *the* place to go with friends or to take out-of-town visitors.

Rents there weren't cheap as a result. Cecca knew what Louise Kanvitz was paying per month for the small space that contained her gallery, and it was exorbitant. How Louise had managed to meet it continually for a dozen years was a mystery. She certainly didn't do a large volume of business; the three paintings she had sold for Katy last Christmas had been one of her larger transactions for the year, or so she'd told Katy. Cecca suspected she had silent backing, though

83

who the backer might be was another mystery. Louise had never married (rumor had it that she was lesbian), lived alone, seemed to have few friends; and while she owned a small critical reputation in the Bay Area, her own paintings—odd, nonrepresentational water colors, mostly—were not commercially successful. She didn't make much from her teaching either. Yet she drove a newish BMW, dressed well, and never seemed to lack for ready cash.

She was with a customer when Cecca entered the gallery. Or at least she was answering questions from a matronly woman about a hideous free-form iron sculpture of an animal displayed on a cube pedestal. She glanced at Cecca but didn't acknowledge her, although they knew each other slightly. Waiting, Cecca wandered through the cramped space, looking at the paintings, sculptures, pottery urns and vases, Miwok beadwork, and other items for sale. As art, they struck her as eccentric and of no real distinction. But she was hardly a connoisseur, and her tastes ran along conventional lines.

Two of Katy's abstracts were hung side by side on one wall. Minor pieces, not nearly as well done as "Blue Time" or the three that had sold at Christmas. Still, Cecca wasn't surprised when she saw the yellow and red Sold tags hanging from the frames of each; given the ghoulish nature of people and all the publicity surrounding the accident, somebody had been bound to want them. What did surprise her—and make her angry—was the new price stickers next to the tags. One thousand dollars apiece! Each had been marked at two hundred dollars while Katy was alive; Louise had jacked the prices up an outrageous five hundred percent. Exploitative commercialism at its nastiest. And who in God's name would pay one thousand dollars for inferior work by an unknown artist, even a recently deceased one?

"Hello, Francesca. What brings you to Bright Winds?"

Louise had come up beside her; Cecca realized that the matronly woman was gone. She made an effort to keep her anger in check as she faced the older woman. "My brother's birthday is coming up," she said. "I thought I might get him a piece of local art this year."

"Did you have anything in particular in mind?"

"Not really. A painting, perhaps."

"Both of those have been sold."

"So I see. A thousand dollars each—my, my. They were marked at two hundred last month."

Louise stood stiffly silent, the way a person does when making a careful choice of words. She was about fifty, small and thin and bony, hair and eyes the unappealing reddish-brown color of kidney beans. The eyes had a chilly quality, as if she were looking at you through a thin glaze of ice. It was a full fifteen seconds before she spoke again.

"Katy Mallory was a talented abstractionist," she said. "These are her last two major works. In my judgment, they're now worth more than the original asking price."

"Now that she's dead, you mean."

"Bluntly, yes."

Cecca curbed a sharp response and said instead, "Your judgment must be right, since you've already sold them. Both to the same buyer?"

"Yes."

"Who would that be, if you don't mind my asking?"

"But I do mind."

"Oh? Is it a secret?"

"Hardly that. I make it a policy never to discuss my customers or my business transactions. You don't reveal who bought a particular piece of property and how much was paid, do you?"

"Sometimes. If the person involved is a friend."

"I'd rather not make an exception."

"All right. Tell me, though—did whoever it was buy Katy's watercolor, too? I don't see it here anywhere."

"Watercolor?"

"The one she painted under your tutelage. She told me about it," Cecca lied. "A representational landscape, wasn't it?"

"You must be mistaken. As far as I know, Katy never painted any kind of watercolor."

"Then why would she tell me she had?"

"I'm sure I don't know."

"She *did* study with you, didn't she? Monday and Friday afternoons, starting in May?"

"Yes, she studied with me."

"Every week?"

"Every week. Faithfully."

"But not watercolors."

"She wanted to branch out into other forms of expression. I encouraged her to concentrate on perfecting what she did best, to explore the subtleties of Abstract Expressionism."

"But she didn't paint any more abstracts," Cecca said. "You said those two on the wall there were her last works."

"Her last *finished* works. She experimented with different canvases, different approaches. They didn't please either of us."

"Do you still have them?"

"No. I destroyed them after her death."

"Because they weren't salable?"

"Because they were unfinished and inferior." Louise's eyes were colder now, darker. Glare ice, black ice. "Is there any particular type of painting your brother prefers? Abstracts, still-lifes, landscapes, seascapes?"

"Something representational," Cecca said, to prolong the conversation. "Watercolors, preferably."

"I have a good modern by a Bodega artist, Janet Rice. Reasonably priced. Over here ..."

Cecca followed her to another wall. The watercolor was a vineyard scene, pale and blurry at the edges. Vastly overpriced at $150. She pretended to study it.

"I've had it for a while," Louise said. "I don't think Ms. Rice would mind if I let you have it for one twenty-five."

"Let me think about it. Do you have any others?"

"Watercolors? No, not right now."

Cecca straightened. "You know, it's odd, really."

"What is?"

"That Katy told me she'd done a watercolor, when she hadn't. Why do you suppose she'd tell a fib like that?"

"I've already told you, I don't know."

"You did say she studied with you every week for the three months before she died? Twice a week, never missed a day?"

"Just what are you getting at, Francesca?"

"I think Katy was having an affair," Cecca said.

She was looking for a reaction, and she got one, small but unmistakable: involuntary twitch in one cheek, slight sideshift in Louise's cold gaze before it steadied again. The older woman said flatly, "What makes you think that?"

"I was Katy's closest friend. There were signs."

"Did she tell you she was having an affair?"

"No, she didn't. Did she confide in *you*, by any chance?"

"Hardly. Ours was a pupil-teacher relationship."

"So you wouldn't have lied for her."

"Lied?"

"About her spending Monday and Friday afternoons with you."

"Are you accusing me of lying?"

"I'm just wondering."

"Well, you can stop wondering. What business is it of yours, anyway, if Katy had a lover?"

"Her husband is my friend, too, and I don't want to see him hurt. If I know the truth, I can talk to the man she was seeing, make sure he keeps quiet about it."

"You're the one who'll hurt Dix Mallory if you keep prying. Why don't you just mind your own business? Katy's gone, it doesn't matter any longer what she was or was not doing. Let her rest in peace. Let sleeping dogs lie."

Four clichés in a row, Cecca thought. Very good, Louise. Very earnest and sincere. So why don't I believe you? Why do I think you're covering up?

"*Are* you interested in the Rice for your brother?" Louise asked. "Or was that just an excuse to come in and pump me about Katy?"

"I don't like the Rice. In fact, I don't like much of anything you're trying to sell."

The words sounded lame and defensive to Cecca even as she spoke them. But when Louise, purse-mouthed, turned her back and walked away without responding, she had no choice but to let them stand as an exit line.

On her way downstairs she worried that she'd mishandled the situation by making an enemy of the woman. Any other approach, though, would have netted her even less information. Katy *had* said she was studying watercolors with Louise as recently as a week or so before the accident; that made it definite Louise had lied. Why? Keeping a promise she'd made to Katy? Or did it have something to do with those last two marked-up abstracts, with the person who'd bought them?

One other thing Cecca was certain of: Louise Kanvitz not only knew about the affair, she knew the identity of Katy's lover.

When she got back to Better Lands she checked her voice-mail first thing. Still no word from the Agbergs. The only message was from Elliot Messner in Brookside Park, returning her call of this morning. She tapped out his number.

"Elliot, it's Francesca Bellini."

"Francesca, hello. Don't tell me you've found a buyer for this pile of mine?"

"I wish I had. No, that's not why I called earlier."

"Oh? Change your mind about my invitation to dinner?"

"Not that either, I'm afraid."

He sighed elaborately. "If you have any more bad news," he said, "don't tell me. I've been in a wrist-slitting mood all day."

"It may be good news, actually. I have a new listing that you might be interested in. A small farm in Hamlin Valley—eighteen acres, house, barn, chicken coop and run. The buildings need repair work, quite a bit in the case of the barn, but I think they're all structurally sound. And you won't find a more attractive setting anywhere in the area."

"What's the asking price?"

"Three twenty-five."

"Firm?"

"It is now, but it's a brand-new listing."

"So you think it might be on the market for a while?"

"There's no predicting that. This *is* a depressed market, though."

"Don't I know it," Elliot said. "Realistically I won't get more than two fifty for this place, right?"

"Honest answer? Probably not."

"I don't want to have to finance much on whatever I buy—if anything at all. Even if this Hamlin Valley place is what I'm looking for and I could get it for under three hundred ... I don't know. Maybe it's too soon."

"If you think so," Cecca said. "On the other hand, it couldn't hurt to take a look at it. See if it *is* the sort of property you're looking for and what you can expect within your price range."

"That makes sense. All right, when can I have a squint?"

"Anytime you like."

"Not today. And I'm tied up on university business in the morning. . . . How about three tomorrow afternoon?"

"Fine. I'll swing by and pick you up."

"I look forward to it," he said, and paused and then said, "Have you ever had the Thirty-five-cent Peasant Pot Roast?"

"The . . . what?"

"Thirty-five-cent Peasant Pot Roast. Otherwise known as the Best Thirty-five-cent Meal in North Beach."

"Elliot, I don't know what you—"

"There used to be a restaurant in San Francisco, in the gaslight era, called Brenti's La Gianduja. End of Stockton Street at Washington Square in North Beach. One of the city's best turn-of-the-century eateries. Their customers' favorite entree was the Peasant Pot Roast."

Uh-huh, she thought, now I get it. "And you happen to have the recipe."

"I not only have it, I make it splendidly, if I do say so myself. I also have some homemade grappa to go with it. Brenti's always served their pot roast with grappa, you see."

Cecca was silent.

"Francesca? What do you say? The Best Thirty-five-cent Meal in North Beach, tomorrow night after we look at the Hamlin Valley farm?"

"I'm busy tomorrow night," she lied.

"I have an open calendar ahead."

"I don't think so, Elliot. I appreciate the offer, but ... I'm just not in the market right now. For pot roast or anything else. Can you accept that?"

"Oh, sure," he said cheerfully. "But you really don't know what you're missing."

Meaning him as well as the pot roast, of course. "Well," she said. "Tomorrow at three, then."

"Tomorrow at three. And don't blame me for trying, okay? Consider it a compliment."

There was a sigh in her as she put the receiver down. And a groan, and a shriek. Why did every other man she knew or met, unmarried *and* married, keep trying to hit on her? She was available, yes, and reasonably attractive, but good Lord! Owen, Jerry, Leo Franklin at the bank, Harvey Samuels at the tennis club, Fred Alt at Garstein Electric, now Elliot Messner ... none of them interesting to her, particularly, and all of them sniffing after her like dogs in heat.

She thought cynically: Maybe it's because I'm a bitch. Look who does interest me, the only one. Look who *I'm* sniffing after.

Jerry said, "I'm worried about Dix."

"Why? What makes you say that?"

"Well, I went to see him yesterday. Figured enough time had passed. I tried to get him down to the club for a round of golf. He wouldn't budge."

"He's probably not ready for recreational activities."

"I suppose that's it. But he didn't look good; he's lost a lot of weight. On purpose, he says, but I don't know. He didn't act like himself either. It's been nearly a month since the accident. He shouldn't still be hiding from the world."

"I don't think he's hiding," she said. "I saw him, too, the other day. He didn't seem sickly to me. Or deeply depressed."

"Well, you've known him a lot longer than I have." Jerry tasted his Cutty Sark on the rocks. "I invited him to the cookout next Saturday."

"Is he coming?"

"Said he would if he felt up to it. I'll nudge him again; you might do the same. He needs to spend time with people who care about him, don't you think? Normal social activity in different surroundings?"

"Only if it's what he wants. It won't do him any good if he's pushed into it."

"I guess you're right."

Cecca stole a glance at her watch. Ten minutes to six. Still plenty of time; she wasn't due to meet Dix until seven. She sipped some of her own Scotch. Jerry had come by Better Lands just as she was about to leave, to invite her for an after-work drink. She'd tried putting him off, but he'd been insistent in his upbeat way; she hadn't wanted to hurt his feelings or to make an issue of it in front of Tom, and she *had* wanted a drink. So here they were at Romeo's upstairs bar-lounge, at a table by one of the windows overlooking the boat basin.

Jerry toyed with his glass, his head turned toward the window. The mellow-gold light slanting through the window sharpened and highlighted his features, his classic profile. Golden boy, she thought. He really was a handsome man, the more so because of the character lines in his face, the emotional depth in his blue eyes. But there just wasn't any chemistry between them, at least not on her part. He worked too hard at being charming and charismatic, was too superficially jolly. There was something in his makeup that wouldn't let you burrow underneath the surface to where the serious parts of him lay. A defense mechanism, maybe. He'd been badly hurt once; she sensed that in him. He wouldn't talk about his divorce, or much about his life before he moved to Los Alegres. "The past is dead," he would say, "it's the present that matters." Besides, it was the dark, quiet, brooding type that attracted her—Chet, Dix. In spite of herself, she glanced at her watch again.

Jerry's gaze returned to her. "Do you think he blames himself?" he asked.

"Who? Dix?"

"For the accident, Katy's death."

"Why on earth would he blame himself?"

"He might if they had an argument that night. If that was why she went out driving by herself."

"Dix never said anything about an argument."

"I know, but . . ."

"But what?"

"You were Katy's best friend, Cecca. Were they getting along?"

"Of course they were. What makes you think they weren't?"

"Well . . ." He looked uncomfortable now, and to mask it he gave her a quick bright smile and said, "Let's just forget it. How about another round?"

"No, one's my limit tonight. Jerry, what were you getting at?"

"Nothing. I shouldn't have opened my mouth."

"Do you know something about Dix and Katy?"

"No, no . . ."

"Something about Katy?"

She watched him fidget, his eyes not quite meeting hers. Then he said, "I don't like telling tales. Especially not unsubstantiated ones about friends."

"If you do know something—"

"But I don't. I don't *know* anything. Like I said, I shouldn't have opened my big mouth."

"You can't just leave me hanging like this."

"Cecca, Katy's gone. And Dix is still alive. I know how he'd feel if—I just know how he'd feel. I've been there."

Been there. The phrase made her wonder if Jerry's wife had been having an affair, too, if that was what had broken up his marriage. She asked, "How Dix would feel about what?"

"He's been through enough," Jerry said. "He doesn't need half-assed friends like me making things worse." Abruptly he signaled to the waitress. "Look, I know you want to get home, and I'd better do the same. Forget we had this conversation, okay? Please. I don't know anything you should know, believe me."

But he did. Or at least he suspected something. Heard rumors . . .

from Eileen's big mouth? Or was it more personal and direct—words spoken to him, a first-hand observation?

Eileen, Louise Kanvitz, Jerry—and how many others in Los Alegres? Well, the more there were, the better the chances that somebody besides Louise knew or suspected the identity of Katy's lover. It wouldn't, couldn't, remain a secret much longer.

TEN

The next few days were difficult for Dix. Half-knowledge, suspicion, frustration, a painfully emerging self-awareness, the waiting for something to happen—little bricks adding weight to an already oppressive burden. He'd told Cecca what he had learned from Harold Zachary, but he didn't share his fear that Katy had in fact been murdered. The weight of that brick alone kept him from sleeping much, and gave him little rest when he did sleep.

The new telephone number provided an excuse to call Jerry on Tuesday. He hinted around, tried to pry loose whatever it was Jerry knew; but Jerry wouldn't admit even as much to him as he had to Cecca. Just danced around, using good humor to fend off questions, as if he were on a mission to protect poor old Dix from any more adversity. Nobody else could or would tell him anything either. He considered confronting Louise Kanvitz himself, but he knew it would be wasted effort. If she hadn't opened up to Cecca, another woman, she sure as hell wouldn't open up to Katy's husband.

The phone did not ring once in three days. And the longer it remained silent, the more he kept listening for it. There were no more surprises in his mailbox; no surprises of any kind, for him or for Cecca. Cat and mouse. They agreed that it was only a matter of time until the harassments started again. And he thought privately that when they did, they would be worse than what had gone before.

He forced himself to work with Lawrence Hampton's History 453 notes, adapting them to his own style of teaching. He did some necessary reading for the coming semester—recent issues of histori-

cal journals and *American Heritage*—and managed to absorb most
of what he read. He worked on the sideboard. He swam, ate, tried
to fight off depression, and brooded too much when he couldn't.

Little bricks . . .

On Friday morning he finished the sideboard.

Most of Thursday evening he had devoted to the last fine-sanding
of the top and sides, paying particular attention to the inlaid design
he had built into the top, and then hand-wiped on three coats of
Watco Danish oil finish. When he came out on Friday to look at it,
the piece had a rich, warm luster that was close to being just right.
One more coat of satin? Or a coat of Varathane? He decided on the
Varathane; it would give the wood a smoother, shinier gloss. He
applied it without the latex gloves he'd used for the oil stain, taking
his time because this was the final step and because he had a desire
to feel the grain of the wood against his fingers.

When he was done he washed in the laundry sink, then ran the
garage doors up to get a look at his handiwork in natural light. He
stood looking at the sideboard for a long time with the sun warm
on his back. There was satisfaction in him, the craftsman's kind for
a job well done; even the critical creator's eye could find no real
flaws in the workmanship. Yet he felt no pleasure or pride in what
he saw, nor any in the accomplishment itself. The sideboard had
been and still was a symbol to bridge a gap, built for therapeutic
reasons. Not a piece of furniture to be used and enjoyed, but an
object meant to kick-start a new phase in a life that had been suddenly and violently reshaped.

But it was not the closure he had intended it to be. It had helped
him come to terms with the loss of Katy, a life without her. *Shall
the dead take thought for the dead to love them? What love was ever
as deep as the grave?* Swinburne. Truth in that, and irony, too:
Swinburne had been one of Katy's favorite poets, but not his. The
Englishman's work was too melancholy, too full of Victorian ex-
cesses for his taste. But he had more to deal with than the fact of
no more Katy. There could not be a full closure, any real peace,
until he came to terms with two other vital issues.

One was Katy's affair, and whatever dark reasons lay behind her
death.

The other was Dixon Mallory.

*   *   *

After lunch, a restlessness drove him out of the house and into the Buick. He had no idea where he was going—or at least no conscious idea—until he got there: Oak Grove Cemetery.

In his forty-one years he had visited Oak Grove just four times, and on each occasion it had been to watch a loved one being buried. First, when he was very young, his grandfather; then, two days before his seventeenth birthday, his mother; then, nine years ago, his father; and finally, Katy. The idea of visiting graves on holidays or birthdays, the so-called paying of respects, was repugnant to him. The idea of *graves* was repugnant to him. Repositories of bones were all they were, with labels to mark each pile as if it were an archaeological exhibit. Funerals were barbaric and so was the concept of placing a bloodless cadaver in a box and burying the box so flesh and wood could rot together in the cold dark. *The worms crawl in, the worms crawl out . . .* It was far more civilized, after you were dead, to have your remains reduced to ashes and the ashes scattered. It troubled him, vaguely, that no one in his family felt the same way, that not even Katy had felt the same way.

So why had he come to Oak Grove today? Not to have a little morbid chat with Katy, that was for sure. People who went to cemeteries to talk to the dear departed were self-delusional, and self-delusion was not one of his problems. If anything, the opposite was true—now. Why, then, so soon after he had been here to see her buried?

The cemetery was on the north edge of town, in what had once been open farmland; now it was hemmed in on all four sides by "country living" tract homes and condos. There were two halves to it, one nondenominational and the other Catholic. The older sections of both ran up hillsides thickly grown with heritage oaks, cypress, and eucalyptus. The newer sections were on flats and in hollows that contained fewer trees. Those sections reminded him of the Civil War burial grounds he and Katy had visited in the early eighties, when he was researching his novel. Maryland, Pennsylvania, Virginia; Antietam, South Mountain, Harpers Ferry, Gettysburg, Manassas Junction, Bull Run, Chancellorsville, Appomattox. The rolling green meadows and rows of white-markered graves at Gettysburg had impressed him the most, but he had found all the burial sites as fascinating as the actual battlefields. Katy had considered the paradox amusing. So had he, mildly, although he'd argued that his interest was scholarly and had nothing to do with the gravesites as gravesites.

He walked uphill into the Catholic half, to where tombstones and monuments jutted among shadows cast by the old trees. There the sites were larger, laid out in big squarish plots with raised cement borders, some family and some communal. Narrow roadways and paths, all unpaved, made an irregular grid pattern over the grounds. It had been so long since he'd seen his family's plot that he couldn't remember precisely where it was; it took him ten minutes to locate the stone border with the word *Mallory* etched into it.

All of his immediate family was here, except for Claudia. And Katy. Since it was his intention to be cremated, she'd seen no reason to be interred with his family. He had respected her wishes to be put into the ground with her family, the Duncans.

The black granite headstone that bore his father's name had a slight backward tilt. Otherwise the plot was in good order and mostly weed-free. Another paradox that Katy found amusing: He hated the concept of ground burial, he never visited his family's plot, and yet every year he plunked down a hundred dollars to the City Burial Commission for its care and maintenance. He supposed it was because the plot had meant something to his father. He was maintaining a tradition, then, and tradition was something he did believe in. It wouldn't have mattered to him, otherwise, if the plot nurtured a teeming jungle of weeds and grass. That was what he'd told Katy, anyway. Yet in an odd way it did matter. If he had come here today and found a jungle, it would have made him angry. And not because of the hundred-dollar annual fee.

He stood for a time looking down at the markers. He could barely remember his grandparents; they were vague recollections of dry, chapped hands and lilac perfume. His mother had died of cancer, a slow, eight-month deterioration that had left him with indelible visual, aural, and olfactory memories of hospital rooms, nurses, cries of pain, and half-heard whispers, the smells of medicine and body fluids and get-well flowers too-sweet and withering. But at least he had had time to prepare for her death, to say good-bye to her. His father had died of a heart attack, suddenly, two weeks after his doctor pronounced him the fittest sixty-four-year-old ex-construction worker and ex-tobacco abuser he'd ever examined. Out fishing for salmon one morning with a friend who owned a Bodega Bay charter boat, hooked onto a big King, laughed about it as he strained to pull the fish in—and in the next second he was gone. Dix had been at the university when notification came. It had been the same kind of numbing shock as the news of Katy's death. And the same long period of adjustment afterward. And the same lingering regret that he had not been able to say good-bye.

He turned away—not as easy a leavetaking as it should have been—and walked farther uphill. Cool under the trees; the intense heat of the past week had begun to ease, and there was a light breeze today. Quiet too. Nobody else in sight, just him alone among the acres of bones.

Stranger in a strange land, he thought. But not a stranger to myself, not anymore.

Most people never found out the truth about themselves. Didn't want to, took pains to keep it hidden. They were the lucky ones. He'd held his own self-knowledge at bay with Katy, his work, his daily routine, his friends and social activities, his half-formed and half-assed plans for the future. But Katy's death had shattered the thin wall of his defenses, and he had found himself standing naked among the rubble. You can't hide from yourself at a time like that. And never again afterward.

Last night he'd gone into his study to finish reading through Lawrence Hampton's History 453 syllabus. And after a while, distracted, he had noticed his shelf copy of *A Darkness at Antietam* and taken it down, the first he'd looked at it in a long time. In his hands it had felt strangely like a secondhand book, the pages no longer crisp, the binding just a little loose, the dust jacket curled at the edges, and its colors the slightest bit faded. And when he'd opened it and read passages and scenes at random, it had been painfully obvious to him why the novel had sold less than four thousand copies, why so many critics had given it unenthusiastic notices. He had set out to tell an intensely personal story of the bloodiest battle in the Civil War, the single most calamitous day of fighting in American history—September 17, 1862, on which the combined casualties of McClellan's Army of the Potomac and Lee's Army of Northern Virginia numbered 22,719 killed or wounded during twelve hours of what one Union soldier described as "a savage continual thunder." His research had been extensive, detailed; he had chosen and developed his primary characters—four Yankee and four Reb officers and enlisted men— with care and precision; he had taken pains to create those dozen hours faithfully in all their terrible drama. Four years he had spent on the novel, more than two in the actual writing. And when he was done he'd known, of course, that his book didn't approach the genius of *The Red Badge of Courage* or the epic caliber of *Andersonville* or *The Killer Angels*—he simply wasn't in a class with Kantor or Shaara, much less Crane—but he had nonetheless been convinced that he had written a major novel of the Civil War. He continued to believe that even after it failed both critically and commercially, or at least he'd pretended to himself that he believed it. Last night he had admitted the truth: What he'd actually written was a minor historical adventure, technically competent but without any real depth or insight or literary merit, publishable but forgettable.

He'd known then, too, that *A Darkness at Antietam* was an accurate measure of its author. Once he had considered himself an above-average teacher who remained on the faculty of a small, obscure state university because he could accomplish more in a relaxed and less competitive atmosphere. Once he had considered himself ambitious, a seedbank that would eventually produce more and better historical novels. Once he had considered himself a good husband and lover, who had given Katy the best of himself in all respects. Once he had considered Dixon Mallory a successful man, a happy and secure man. But the truth was—

Mediocre writer. Mediocre teacher at a mediocre school. Mediocre husband, mediocre lover. Mediocre accomplishments in a mediocre life.

Mediocre man.

Abruptly he stopped walking. He hadn't intended to seek out the Duncan family plot, but there it was at his feet. In fact he was standing in the same place he'd stood less than one month ago; he could almost hear the droning intonations of the priest, the sounds of weeping. He stared down at Katy's grave. You could still tell that it was a new grave, but now the clods of earth were dry and cracked from the heat, and the flowers that had been placed there were decaying corpses themselves.

I'm alone, he thought.

Goddamm it, I'm all alone.

Friends, sure, more than most men had. Claudia just an hour away in Healdsburg, the two of them closer than most siblings, talk to her any time about whatever was bothering him. People at the university, Elliot . . . there for him, too, if he needed them.

But you can't go to your friends, your sister, your colleagues, and say to them, "Listen, I've just realized some pretty basic things about myself. I'm mediocre, I've always been mediocre, and I can't stand the thought of being mediocre for the rest of my life. Can you help me out here? Can you tell me what to do?''

Alone.

Maybe that was why he'd been drawn here today. A need to touch the part of his past that represented stability and strength: his mother, his father, Katy. Find his courage through them. Pretty pathetic, if that was it. The answers weren't in the past or with the past. And sure as hell not among the bones of his dear departed. If he found them at all, it would be inside himself—and all by himself.

ELEVEN

He asked, "Have you read this, Amy?"

"Oh, the Gay Talese book."

"It looks interesting."

"It's okay, I guess."

"You prefer the political type of investigative reporting? Woodward and Bernstein?"

"Not really. No."

"But you didn't like *Thy Neighbor's Wife?*"

"It's not that I didn't like it, exactly."

"What then, exactly?"

"Well, you know, the subject matter."

"Sure, I understand. It's difficult to relate to a subject that you've had no experience with."

"I've had experience with it," Amy said bitterly.

"You have?"

"You know, my parents' divorce."

"Oh, right. I'm sorry, Amy."

"Well, I've learned how to deal with it."

"Of course you have."

"Anyhow, he's a good writer. Gay Talese."

"I think so, too. Should I buy the book?"

"Well, it's worth reading."

"A book about sex is always worth reading."

"If it's not just sleaze."

"Graphic in parts, is it?"

101

"Not as graphic as a lot of novels."

"Don't tell me you read sexy novels."

"Sometimes. Don't you?"

"I confess: now and then."

"Don't you think I'm old enough?"

"Do *you* think you're old enough?"

"Sure I do."

"Then so do I. You're a mature young woman. And sex is a very important part of life, isn't it."

"Yes."

"Very very important," he said.

He was leaning on the counter, casually, his face not more than eighteen inches from hers. Their eyes were locked. Amy couldn't have looked away if she'd wanted to, and she didn't want to. He had gorgeous eyes, with the longest, sexiest lashes. Looking into them, up close like this, made her weak.

"Aren't you going to let me have it?"

"Let you . . . what?"

"The book," he said, smiling. "I can't buy it if you don't ring it up."

"Oh . . . the book."

She had to force her gaze to the used copy of *Thy Neighbor's Wife;* and she was fumble-fingered when she opened it to look at the penciled price on the front endpaper. Her cheeks felt hot. He knows how I feel about him, she thought. He must know. Why else would he have started talking about sex?

It was quiet in the bookshop, so quiet she could hear the quick beat of her heart. There was nobody else there; Mr. Hallam had gone out a little while ago to run some errands. Just the two of them, alone together. It was the second time he'd come in this week, and on Monday she'd been alone in the shop, too. As if he'd been hanging around outside for just the right time to walk in.

"What's the damage, Amy?"

"Damage? Oh." She rang up the price; the computerized register added the sales tax automatically. "Eight sixty-three," she said.

He gave her a ten-dollar bill. His fingers brushed over her palm, seemed to linger there for an instant. It was like being touched with something electric. She could feel her nipples getting hard as she made change, as she put the dollar bill, the quarter, dime, and two pennies into his hand. Her turn to do the touching and lingering, with the same electric results. He noticed without seeming to notice. He was just so cool. Except for his eyes. There was nothing cool about his eyes.

"I won't need a sack," he said.

"You can have one if you want. We have lots of bags." The words just popped out of her mouth. God, what a stupid thing to say!

"Not necessary." He picked up the book, took a few steps away from the counter, stopped, and turned to face her again. "I just had a thought," he said.

"Um ... thought?"

"When I finish reading this, maybe we can discuss it—analyze it. Would you enjoy that?"

"Yes. I would."

"Just the two of us."

"Just the two of us. Where?"

"Oh, we'll find someplace quiet."

". . . All right."

"And we can talk about you. I'd like to know more about you, your plans, how you feel about different things."

"So would I. I mean, I'd like to know more about you, too."

"Well, then, we'll definitely do it. As soon as I finish reading the book."

"Are you a fast reader?" That just popped out, too.

He laughed. "Not too fast, not too slow. I like to savor things, the good things in life. Don't you?"

He didn't give her a chance to answer. He turned again and sauntered out.

There was a stool behind the counter; Amy sank down on it. Her nipples were still hard, her palms damp. The way she felt . . . it was like the first time she'd gone all the way with Davey, right before, while he was taking off her clothes. Pure body heat.

I really must be crazy, she thought.

She closed her eyes and imagined what it would be like making love with him, with a man instead of a boy.

It was a quarter after five when she turned her Honda onto Shady Court. Mom wasn't home yet; the driveway was empty. Amy parked in front in case she decided to go out again later on.

There was a package on the front porch. Wedged in between the screen door and the house door.

UPS, she thought, must be for Mom. She bent to pick it up, was surprised and pleased when she saw that it was addressed to Ms. Amy Bracco and Ms. Francesca Bellini. She didn't recognize the writing; it had been done with a black felt-tip pen in a funny kind of back-slanted block printing. There was no return address. And UPS hadn't brought it either. At least there was no UPS sticker on the brown wrapping paper.

A present for both of them? But from who ... whom? It was about the size of a dress box and it had been sealed with filament tape. Whatever was in it, it didn't weigh much: the package was so light, it might have been empty. Maybe it was a joke. Amy shook it up close to her ear. No, she could hear something moving around inside. A mystery. Good, she liked mysteries. Especially the kind you could solve in about three minutes.

She let herself in, took the package into the kitchen, and set it on the table. In the utility drawer by the sink was a pair of scissors. She was about to start cutting the filament tape when the phone rang.

She turned toward it, caught for an instant between the lure of the package and the summons of the bell. Then she remembered Mom's orders to let all calls go on the machine, because of the weirdo. She stayed where she was, waiting. The volume on the machine was turned up as far as it would go, so you could listen to anybody leaving a message. . . .

Dad. When she heard his voice she felt a mix of pleasure and anger, the same as always. More pleasure than anger now—she'd pretty much forgiven him for walking out on her and Mom—but forgiving wasn't forgetting. And loving your father didn't mean you had to like him one hundred percent either, not the way you had when you were a little girl.

He was calling for her, not Mom. She moved fast and got the receiver up before he finished with his message. "Daddy, hi, I'm here."

"Princess. Perfect timing."

"Did you say something about this weekend?"

"Wondering if you had any plans."

"No plans. Why?"

"Not going anywhere with your mother?"

"She has to work and so do I."

"Well, how'd you like to spend part of the holiday with us at the Dunes?"

"You and Megan?"

"Tony's coming, too."

Oh, God, Tony.

"He's driving up Saturday night," Dad said. "With his new girl-friend, so you don't have to worry about him putting any more moves on you."

"That'll make it pretty cramped."

"We'll manage. How about it, princess?"

"When are you leaving?"

"Tomorrow morning. You could drive here then, or come up to-night and stay over."

"Don't *you* have to work tomorrow?"

"Nope. Job site's shut down until Tuesday."

"I wish Hallam's was shut down, too, but it's not."

"Call in sick. Tell old man Hallam you've got the flu or something."

Mom was right: Same old Chet Bracco, no sense of responsibility. When he wanted something—or somebody—he told lies and made excuses so he could get it, and he thought everybody else should do the same. "I don't know," she said. "I don't think so. Besides, Mom wouldn't like it."

"Lot of things your mom doesn't like. Me included." He laughed. "We'd really like you to come, princess. I know how much you love the Dunes."

She did love the Dunes. The cottage was on a remote part of the Mendocino coast, near Manchester State Beach. Nothing much around it but sand dunes and ocean for miles and miles. Supposed to be part of a big development twenty years ago, like Sea Ranch; streets had been laid out, all paved, with names and signposts, but most of them didn't lead anywhere because the developer had gone broke after putting up just a few cottages. The Dunes was set off by itself, on high ground so you had a view of the ocean, with the nearest neighbor several hundred yards away. Funky and kind of eerie, especially in foggy or rainy weather. Not a place you wanted to live in year round—you'd be bored out of your skull after a while—but for a few days or even a week it was super fine. Walk on the beach, read, or just sit and think, and nobody around to hassle you.

She'd been six when Mom and Dad bought the cottage. They'd stayed up there four or five times a year back then, before Dad started messing with other women. Or anyway, before he quit trying to hide the fact that he was messing. Then they stopped going so often, and in the year or so before he moved out they hadn't gone at all. Sometimes she wished Mom hadn't let him keep the Dunes as part of the divorce settlement, even if it had helped buy them this house. Not only wasn't it *theirs* anymore, it wasn't *hers* either. Three times she'd gone with Dad since the divorce and it was as if she were a visitor, a person in a rented place. Megan was part of the problem, too. She didn't like Megan. Big phony blonde with tits out to there and the dirtiest laugh ... it didn't take a genius to figure what Dad saw in her. But God, she was such an airhead. All she talked about was clothes and food and what she liked on the tube, and all she'd done the one time the three of them went to the Dunes together was stare at a battery-operated TV she'd brought along so she wouldn't miss any of her soap operas or *Oprah* or silly sitcoms. Then there was Tony, her son by some guy in the navy. He was *such* an asshole. Five minutes after they met he'd started coming on to her. Another five minutes, if she hadn't blown him off cold, he'd have had his hand down her blouse. Four days at the Dunes would be good if it were just her and Dad. But with Megan and Tony and Tony's new bimbo ... a weekend from hell. The walls at the cottage weren't all that thick. She could just imagine the sounds at night. A regular symphony of moans and groans and grunts and squeaks ...

"Amy? You still there?"

"Yes, Dad. Just thinking."

"So how about it? You coming?"

No, she thought, and I'll be the only one who isn't. She stifled a giggle. "I'd better not. Mr. Hallam's counting on me, and with school starting on Tuesday ... Another time, okay?"

"Okay. But if you change your mind ..."

"Maybe you and I could go sometime," she said impulsively, "just the two of us."

"Sure we can."

But she could hear the faint hesitancy in his voice, and that was what made her say, "Like we used to when we were a family, before you left home."

"Yeah, well," he said, "I've got a new home now. Another family, too, maybe. Megan and me, we may get married one of these days. How about that?"

"Great." Shitty.

"Well . . . you take care, huh? Love you."

"Love you, too."

Amy put the receiver down. He doesn't want to be alone with me, she thought, at the Dunes or anywhere else. He doesn't know what to say to me when we're alone. He doesn't know me and I don't know him, not anymore.

What if I never did?

The thought depressed her. Better think about something else, something pleasant . . . *him*? No, not him. Whatever happened would happen, and fantasy-tripping wasn't going to make it happen any faster. All fantasy-tripping did was get you horny. The package. Maybe there was something in the package to cheer her up.

She picked up the scissors, cut the tape at both ends, and stripped off the brown wrapping paper. Inside was a gift box wrapped in fancy gold paper. No bow, and no card either. Probably a card inside, she thought. She pried one end of the gold paper loose, being careful not to rip it. It was expensive-looking and it could be used again.

Mom was home. She always came zooming into the driveway, gunning the wagon's engine like Richard Petty or somebody.

Amy thought: Oh, no, I've done all the work opening it, I get to look first. Quickly, she slit the Scotch tape on the other end with her fingernail and peeled off the gold paper. Then she lifted the lid on the box. Tissue paper, wads of it. Smiling, eager, she pulled it apart, spread it so she could see what was hidden inside—

She was staring into the box, not smiling anymore, when Mom came in. The sound of the back screen door banging made her jump. But it didn't make her stop staring.

"Amy? What's the matter?"

"Look."

Mom came over and looked. Amy heard her suck in her breath, make a noise like a dog growling.

"For God's sake! Where did you get this?"

"It was on the porch when I got home a few minutes ago. It was addressed to both of us, so I—"

"Your name, too? Where's the wrapping?"

"Right there on the chair . . ."

Mom found it, uncrumpled it so she could look at the block printing. Amy kept staring into the box; she couldn't seem to take her eyes off the three things in the nest of tissue paper. There were goose pimples all over her.

A white bra with embroidered rosettes, one cup almost completely burned away, the rest of it scorched and smoke-streaked.

A pair of blue monogrammed panties, torn, burned like the bra.

A photo of her and Mom in bikinis with their arms around each other, the edges curled and blackened, char marks reaching like ugly fingers over their bodies and faces.

"I don't recognize the printing," Mom said.

Amy shook her head. "Me neither."

"There was no card inside, no message?"

"No. Mom . . . *why?*"

"I don't know, baby."

"The weirdo?"

No answer.

"It must be," Amy said. "Who else would send us stuff like this? But then that means . . ."

She didn't finish the sentence. She didn't have to; Mom had to be thinking the same thing. For the first time in as long as she could remember, she was scared.

That bra with the embroidered rosettes . . . it was one of Mom's best. And the blue monogrammed panties . . . hers, her initials, AB, part of a set Dad and Megan had given her for Christmas last year. And the photo . . . taken two summers ago, at Eileen and Ted's cabin at Blue Lake, no other one like it, and she remembered putting it into the album herself—the family album that was upstairs on the shelf in Mom's closet.

Whoever he was, he'd been in the house.

He'd been in their *bedrooms. . . .*

TWELVE

Jerry's Saturday cookout was already under way when Dix arrived. Voices, a burst of laughter, rose from the backyard; he could smell charcoal smoke on the late-afternoon breeze. A fresh reluctance, almost an aversion, built in him as he opened the Buick's rear door and lifted out the bag with the three six-packs of beer—his contribution to the potluck affair. People, eight or ten of them. Friends, old friends, but still people to have to talk to, an entire evening of socializing to get through. He was not sure he was ready for this yet.

Not with the chance, however remote, that one of them might be the tormentor.

He stood for a little time with the beer cradled in one arm, listening to the party sounds. The heat wave was over now; the temperature hadn't gotten out of the seventies all day. Might even be cold once it got dark, if the wind picked up. He'd brought a sweater just in case.

Walnut Street intruded on his consciousness. Quiet residential street, one of the nicer ones, in the oldest section of town. Mixed architectural styles, everything from turn-of-the-century Victorians to modern three- and four-unit apartment houses. Shade trees lining this block and others, down the way three boys chucking a football back and forth, two dogs chasing each other, an old man dozing on a porch swing at the house next to Jerry's. The outside world had changed radically in the past thirty-odd years, Los Alegres had changed, but Walnut Street was still more or less the same. Take away the apartment houses, substitute Ford Galaxies and Chevy Impalas for the contemporary Detroit and Japanese products, and it

109

would look and feel exactly as it had in 1960, when he was a kid
riding over here on his Schwinn after school to play crazy eights
with Eddie Slayton, shoot hoops in Eddie's backyard. Eddie was
dead now . . . dead more than twenty years. Killed in Vietnam, blown
up by a goddamn land mine. Another one gone. But the street, the
town, the old way of life, were all still alive.

Weren't they?

I don't know anymore, he thought.

The feeling of aloneness was strong in him again.

The light wind gusted, brought a sharp whiff of the burning charcoal. It stirred him out of his frozen stance, prodded him along the
front drive and onto the path between the house and the detached
garage. The house was small, really a bungalow, built sometime in
the forties, but the front yard was good-sized, dominated by a flow-
ering magnolia tree, and the backyard was huge: lawn, patio area,
vegetable patch, walnut and kumquat trees. Jerry had a lease option
on it; he still wasn't sure if he wanted to stay there or move into
something smaller like a condo apartment, but the betting was that
he'd stay. Cecca had arranged the deal for him when he first came
to Los Alegres. That was how he'd met the members of their little
circle, through Cecca; how he'd become a part of it. . . .

Jerry?

Fun-loving, do-anything-for-you Jerry Whittington?

Newest member of the group, didn't talk much about his background or his divorce . . . what did anybody know about him, really?
Katy had always found him attractive—"deliciously good-looking,"
she'd said once. Katy and Jerry? That much was conceivable, but
the rest of it, the phone calls, the earrings, the burned things to Cecca
and Amy . . . cold-blooded murder? Even madmen had motives for
what they did, no matter how warped. It was inconceivable that Jerry
could so viciously hurt people who had befriended him, been good
to him.

The party voices grew louder. Dix's stomach muscles clenched,
his step faltered slightly, and then he was around behind the house
to where he could see the others. They were all on or near the patio,
standing or sitting on outdoor furniture, Jerry wearing a chef's apron
and poking at the briquettes blazing inside a brace of Webers. Dix's
gaze sought and found Cecca; she was talking to Owen, or rather
listening to something he was telling her. Everybody else was there,
too: Tom and Beth, George and Laura, Sid and Helen. And Margaret

Allen, Jerry's redheaded secretary/aassistant, who made no bones about the fact that she wouldn't mind sharing his bed as well as his office on a permanent basis.

Jerry saw him first and called, "Hey, Dix!" That started it; they all flocked around him, fussing, as if he were a long-lost relative or a celebrity. He endured it. Even managed to keep the pasted smile in place. He caught Cecca's eye; she seemed tense, too. She touched his arm and mouthed the words "I'm glad you came." He hadn't been sure he would when they talked last night; hadn't been sure he would until five minutes before he left the house today.

The fussing didn't last long. It would have turned awkward—almost did—and nobody wanted that. Sid Garstein gave him an out by offering to take the beer he'd brought and put it in the fridge. Dix said no, he'd do it, and kept smiling all the way into the house.

There was enough food in the kitchen to stock a homeless shelter. Thick T-bone steaks filling two big platters under Saran Wrap coverings. French bread, four different kinds of salad, corn on the cob and fresh fruit, and one of Beth's trufle dishes in the refrigerator. Plenty of beer, wine, hard liquor. Conspicuous consumption, he thought, while people starve on the streets. Residual liberal guilt. But what were you supposed to do? Stop enjoying yourself because others were hurting, give away what you had, what you'd worked hard for, and adopt the poverty lifestyle out of sympathy? He gave money to charity every Christmas; he did community work; he supported education and literacy programs, which were the only real hope for permanent social change. Wasn't that enough? Hell, maybe he should join the Peace Corps. He'd read about young retirees, men and women in their fifties, who were doing just that. Sold or leased their property holdings, put their personal belongings in storage, and went off to Africa or South America for two years or more. Giving something back, giving part of themselves. Could he do something like that? Was he that selfless?

No, he couldn't. No, he wasn't.

I got mine and fuck the world, wasn't that what it amounted to? Mr. Mediocrity.

He was thirsty; he opened a beer, swallowed four or five ounces before he came up for air. And when he lowered the can he saw that Tom Birnam had come in and was standing there grinning at him. "Better go easy on that stuff, boy. Dinner's an hour off yet."

"I'm not going to get drunk, Tom. This is only the second beer I've had all day."

"Sure, I just meant—"

"I know what you meant," Dix said. "I haven't been drowning my sorrows. I'm not a boozer, you ought to know that."

"I do know it. No offense meant, Dix."

Tom's grin was still fixed, like his own pasted smile a few minutes ago. Not natural, as if it were concealing something. Simple concern for an old friend's mental health, probably. Or—

Tom?

Paunchy, conservative, workaholic Tom Birnam?

He'd known Tom for more than thirty years, since . . . what, sixth grade? Not a mean bone in his body, everybody said, which wasn't quite true. He could be a ruthless businessman, and on occasion he exhibited a true I-got-mine-and-fuck-the-world mentality. He had a quick temper, too, but if it had ever exploded into violence, Dix wasn't aware of the circumstances. There was simply nothing in Tom's makeup to suggest a hidden psychosis, nothing in their relationship or in Tom's business or personal relationship with Cecca to foster a sick hatred. Besides, he was a faithful family man—the lust in his heart, he was fond of saying, was all for Beth. The idea of Katy taking him as her lover was ludicrous.

"—the party, what do you say?"

"What? Sorry, Tom, I was woolgathering."

"I said, let's go outside and join the party. It's stuffy in here."

"Yes," Dix said. His fingers, tight around the beer can, made indentations in the soft aluminum. "It is at that. A little stuffy in here."

Cecca saw Dix walk out of the house and glance her way. Come over here and rescue me, she thought, but he didn't. He stood for a moment, at loose ends, and then drifted to where Jerry and George were talking by the Webers. He didn't want to be partying any more than she did. Not after that damn package yesterday and what they both agreed it implied about the tormentor's identity. And especially not after the phone call that afternoon.

The call had almost made her stay home. But to what purpose? Amy had a date and refused to cancel it; it wouldn't have done either of them any good if she had. They weren't safe in the house. He'd already been *in* the house, for God's sake. Hadn't broken in, no, there wasn't the slightest sign anywhere of forced entry. Been invited in. Been given free run of the place, enough time alone to find out where she kept her bras, where Amy kept her panties, where the photograph album was tucked away in her bedroom closet. That ruled out delivery people or casual acquaintances. Amy swore she hadn't let Kimberley or any of her other friends wander around unsupervised. And that left only her own close male friends.

That left Owen and Jerry and Tom and George and Sid.

A betrayal by one of them, a man she had trusted completely, was almost impossible to credit. And yet, what other explanation was there? There had to be one ... but she was sick with the thought that there wasn't.

Should she tell Dix now about the call? Or should she wait until after the party? Better wait. It would only make the evening more difficult for him.

Owen's voice droned in her ear. "I just don't think it's possible," he was saying for the third or fourth time. Not to her, now, but to Laura and Margaret, who were standing next to her. "I mean, the whole concept is incredible."

"Well, isn't it almost the same thing the Christian Scientists believe?" Laura asked. "An offshoot of the power of self-healing?"

"I don't see it that way. There's a certain amount of evidence to support self-healing. But the power of positive *dreaming*? It's pure fantasy."

"The article said it's a matter of training the mind. Positive thinking while you're awake, positive dreaming while you're asleep."

"Yes, but bad dreams, nightmares, can be good for you. Freud proved that. You get rid of aggression, work out things that are troubling you. Even if you could program yourself to dream positively every night, there'd be no release for the negatives that pile up in your subconscious."

"The combination of positive thinking and positive dreaming eliminates the negatives over a period of time. See?"

"No, I don't see. The subconscious is a cesspool; you can't clean it out completely, because you're not always aware of what's growing in there. Dream your way to perfect mental health? I tell you, it's a crock—"

Shut up, Owen, she thought. You, too, Laura. Just shut up, all right?

In her mind's eye she kept seeing the contents of that gift box.

The burned bra, the burned panties, the burned photo. Burning . . . the way Katy had died. And the phone call this afternoon to confirm the connection, in case she'd missed it. To make his intent perfectly clear.

Soon, Francesca. But not too soon. The hottest fires burn slow. One fire burns out another's burning, one pain is lessen'd by another's anguish.

He'd murdered Katy; she no longer had any doubt of that. And he meant to kill her and Amy and probably Dix, too. By fire. Burn them all to a crisp.

Dix had tried to talk her out of the idea last night. An implied threat didn't mean an actual threat, he'd argued. And they still didn't *know* Katy had been murdered. The package could have been another move in the tormentor's sick, sly game. But he didn't believe that any more than she did. What was happening to them wasn't a game, had never been a game. It was something much more deadly. . . .

". . . Cecca? Are you all right?"

Owen's voice, no longer droning. Concerned. He was standing close to her now and he put his hand on her arm; involuntarily she shrank away from his touch.

The rebuff made him wince. "Are you ill?"

"No, I'm not ill. What makes you think that?"

"You're flushed and sweaty all of a sudden."

"He's right," Margaret said, "you are. Want to sit down?"

"No. It's . . . I feel fine, really."

"Don't tell me you're having hot flashes," Laura said. "Menopause at *your* age?"

"Not hardly."

Owen didn't want to hear that kind of talk; it made him uncomfortable. He said quickly, "Maybe you'd better sit down. I'll bring you some water—"

"I don't want any water."

"She's okay now," Laura said. "These things pass. Maybe it was the gin and tonic. You didn't make it too strong, did you, Owen?"

"No."

"How much gin did you put in?"

"A jigger and a half, that's all. Cecca, are you sure you don't feel feverish? You look like you're burning up . . ."

Shut up, shut up, shut up!

*   *   *

The burning charcoal in the Webers had a mesquite aroma now. And another, subtler scent that Dix couldn't identify. It was alder, he found out when he joined Jerry and George, because they were arguing about it.

"Alder is the wrong flavor for beef," George said. "It's for chicken or fish."

"Have you ever tried it mixed with mesquite?"

"Once. I had a rib-eye cooked that way."

"And you didn't care for the taste."

"No. The alder doesn't blend right with mesquite."

"Enhances it, if you ask me."

"Well, I'm a purist. What do you think, Dix?"

"I don't know. I've never cooked with alder."

"We'll take a vote after we eat," Jerry said. He punched Dix lightly on the shoulder. "Glad you decided to come. I'd just about given up on you."

"It was the threat of being handcuffed that did it."

Jerry laughed. George said, "Handcuffed?"

"Jerry said he'd put me in cuffs and haul me here bodily if I didn't show on my own."

"Oh."

Jerry winked at Dix. To George he said, "Tell me, counselor. If I'd gone ahead and done it, put the cuffs on Dix and dragged him down off the Ridge, would it have been a misdemeanor or a felony?"

"Felony."

"Kidnapping rap, if Dix pressed charges?"

"Not unless you tried to take him out of state."

"What would the charge be?"

"False imprisonment."

"Defined as?"

" 'The unlawful violation of the personal liberty of another,' " George said seriously. "Punishable by a fine or imprisonment for one year or both. Sections two-thirty-six and two-thirty-seven of the California Penal Code."

"Damn good thing for both of us, then," Jerry said, "that Dix came down on his own."

George nodded without smiling; he had no idea that Jerry was jerking his chain. He had been born without a sense of humor, not even trace elements of one. He took everything with utter seriousness, including the business of having fun. Not that he was a stick-in-the-mud; he liked to socialize, he was a good sport, and he fit in well with the group. Besides which, Laura had enough laughter in her for both of them. She needled him constantly about his sobersidedness with the same absence of malice as Jerry's kidding; theirs was probably the best marriage in the group. The joking didn't offend him. He'd learned tolerance along with patience and tenacity in the San Jose barrio where he'd grown up. Those qualities, along with hard work, had made his law practice a success. He had both Hispanic and Anglo clients, both Hispanic and Anglo respect.

George Flores? Harboring deep-seated resentments against a group of friends who were themselves ethnically diverse and who had never done him even a whisper of harm? Inconceivable.

A bray of laughter diverted Dix's attention to where Sid Garstein was overflowing a lawn chair under a kumquat tree, holding court for Tom and Beth. Madras shorts, a bright pink shirt, and floppy sandals gave him a clownish aspect. Typical Sid; even in his business dealings, as head of the largest electrical contracting firm in the county, he dressed garishly and in dubious taste. He didn't give a damn how he looked to others. "I'm not Joe Average, so why should I dress like him?" Sid, the frustrated stand-up comic: He knew more smutty stories than a convention of salesmen. Sid, the ass-patter and propositioner of his friends' wives. Occasionally one of them chewed him out, but mostly they tolerated it because it was meaningless byplay, not intended to be taken sincerely. Katy: "The truth is, he's afraid of women. If one of us ever said, 'Sure, Sid, let's go to bed,' he'd run like a scalded cat." Sid, the happy-go-lucky, childish bullshitter. Except that he was on the board of directors of the Los Alegres Boys and Girls Club, active in two antidrug programs and the county chapter of B'nai B'rith, and donated thousands of dollars each year to a variety of charities.

Sid Garstein?

Inconceivable.

Dix shifted his gaze again, to where Owen was still earnestly monopolizing Cecca's time. Owen was in love with her, had been for years. The hopeless, worshipful kind of love. He might take up with Cecca's best friend for revenge or spite, but neither of those applied to the situation. And Katy's feelings for Owen had always been maternal; if she'd found him physically attractive, she'd hidden it well. Owen: reserved, puppy-doggish, old-fashioned in attitudes and tastes; loved photography to the point of obsession, loved taking portraits of kids most of all. Still waters run deep, sure, and it was possible unrequited love for Cecca had turned to hate. But there was no earthly reason for him to want to harm Katy or Dix Mallory. None.

Owen Gregory?

Inconceivable.

These are my *friends*, he thought. Trivial in some ways, loaded with faults like everybody else in the world, but fundamentally good, decent men. Hateful and disloyal to even consider them.

But how can you know, really, what goes on inside another human being? I didn't know what went on inside the woman I loved and lived with for seventeen years. Didn't even know what went on inside myself until this week.

It could be one of them, all right.

It could be anybody.

In spite of her earlier resolve, she told Dix about the call as soon as they were alone together. She couldn't help herself. It was like a poisonous taste in her mouth that she had to spit out.

They were getting ready to eat. Jerry had put the steaks on; the aroma of barbecuing meat was strong on the cooling air. The smell made Cecca faintly nauseated. Her mind kept trying to associate it with human flesh cooking, Katy in her burning car. Most of the others were bustling around, setting up a buffet table on the patio, helping Jerry at the Webers, brokering drinks. Owen had gone off to the bathroom, thank God. He was driving her crazy with his solicitous hovering. She saw Dix by himself and went to him and drew him quickly onto the path between the house and the garage.

He said, "Christ," softly when she blurted out the tormentor's threat.

"That last part," she said, "about the lessen'd anguish. It sounds like some kind of quote."

"It is. From *Romeo and Juliet,* I think."

"*Romeo and Juliet*. Oh, fine."

"Did he say anything else?"

"Something about the package ... did Amy and I like our presents."

"Bastard. You did remember to switch tapes?"

"Tapes? What tapes?"

"In your answering machine. To preserve what he said."

"It wasn't a message. I talked to him."

"Talked to— I thought we agreed to let all calls go on tape. Why did you pick up?"

"I don't know. I was standing right there when the phone rang and I . . . habit, impulse, I don't know."

"You didn't provoke him, argue with him?"

"No. I didn't say anything, I just listened."

"You *did* record it?"

"I didn't have time. The cassette recorder was in my purse in the other room—"

"Cecca, what he said was the kind of evidence we need—"

"What good would it have done us? Don't you understand? He's planning to murder Amy and me. Unless we find out who he is, he'll kill us the way he killed Katy—"

"Keep your voice down, for God's sake. You're jumping to conclusions again."

"I'm not. Not this time. And you know it."

No answer.

"Dix, you know it. Stop pretending our lives aren't in danger!"

He ran a hand roughly over his face, pulled it down, and looked at it as if he expected to find it stained. "All right," he said.

"We've got to *do* something."

"What? What can we do?"

"Confront Louise Kanvitz, that's what."

"Beg her to tell the truth about Katy?"

"Pay her. She'd take money."

"Suppose she won't?"

"Force it out of her then."

"Threaten her? Beat her up?"

"If that's what it takes, yes!"

"We're not thugs, Cecca. Besides, she could have us arrested, put in jail—"

"I don't care about that. At least we'd have his name."

"If she really does know it."

"She knows. I tell you, she knows—"

"Who knows what?"

Owen's voice, startling them both. Owen had come around the corner and was standing there, head cocked quizzically, half smiling at them. Damn you, Owen! she thought fiercely. Are you the one? Is that why you won't leave me alone?

"Did I interrupt something?" he asked.

Dix said, "No, we were just chatting."

"Sounded pretty intense to me."

"It wasn't intense," Cecca said, "it was just a conversation. Can't I talk to somebody without you butting in?"

The words stunned him. She saw the hurt reshape his expression and didn't care; for all she knew he *was* the one. "Hey, I wasn't butting in," he said. His voice had stiffened a little. "I came looking for you because Beth asked me to. She wants some help in the kitchen."

"Tell her I'll be right there."

Owen glanced at Dix, gave Cecca a longer, hurt look, and went away without saying anything else.

Dix said slowly, "Maybe we'd better not stay for dinner. This isn't the place for either of us tonight."

"We can't leave now. How would it look to the rest of them?"

"You go, then. I'll make excuses—"

"No. We'll both stay. We'll get through this and then we'll go somewhere and talk, make a decision."

He nodded. "You'll be okay?"

"I won't lose it and start hurling accusations, if that's what you mean. You go ahead. I'll be along in a minute."

Alone on the path, she stood composing herself. She was on a ragged edge and it wasn't like her. She didn't fall apart in a crisis. Chet . . . yes, okay, she'd gone through a crumbly period when he walked out, but she'd still held herself and her life together, and come out of the divorce more or less whole. It was that this thing, this madness, was so foreign to anything in her experience. You couldn't adjust to it because it kept changing, shifting, so you couldn't get a grasp on any of it. The not knowing why, the gathering certainty that he was probably a man you knew well and liked and trusted . . . those were the things that made it so unbalancing.

But I can handle it, she thought. I am going to handle it. So is Dix. So is Amy. We'll be all right. We will.

It won't be us who ends up getting burned.

For a while Dix felt oddly detached, an almost schizoid detachment, as if only part of him were still there in Jerry's backyard. The other part . . . running around in a cage somewhere, rattling the bars, looking for a way out. Bits and pieces of conversation bounced off his mind without quite registering: food, baseball, taxes, local politics, jokes, old movies versus new movies, a kind of gibberish labeled the power of positive dreaming. He had no appetite, had to force down his first few bites of steak, but when dinner was over he saw with surprise that his plate was empty except for the steakbone and a few bites of pasta salad, as if somebody else had cleaned it for him when he wasn't looking. When Jerry asked him what he thought of the alder and mesquite combination, he said, "Wonderful, just wonderful," without realizing until minutes later what the question related to.

Cecca, he noticed, ate almost nothing. Otherwise she seemed to be holding up better than he was, making more of an effort to join in. Trying too hard, but nobody noticed because they were also trying too hard—to recapture the old, easy, relaxed camaraderie of good friends enjoying each other's company. It was not he who was preventing it from happening; it was the specter of Katy. The sudden death of one of the flock was a reminder, consciously or subconsciously, of their own mortality. For all but one of them, maybe.

They stayed outside after they finished eating and the remains were cleared away. They had more drinks, they talked, they watched the sun sink lower in the west and turn the sky a streaky gold, then a darkening pink. And a slow change came over Dix. The feelings of detachment and fragmentation went away; he grew sharply aware of what was being said and done around him, of what was in his own mind. Tension seemed to seep out of him, leaving a kind of shaky peace—the kind that follows a crisis point reached and overcome. Mr. Mediocrity was no longer looking for a way out.

The breeze had picked up, turned the coming night as chilly as he had anticipated earlier; they all put on sweaters and jackets. The last of the sunset colors disappeared into smoky gray, and when dusk became dark, the wind sharpened again. Somebody said, "Brr, it's *cold* out here." Jerry suggested they go inside, have some coffee, maybe a little dessert. Owen, still nursing his bruised feelings, said he'd pass, he had some film to develop and he'd better get on home. It was like a door being suddenly opened to reveal an escape route: The others made their own excuses as they trooped inside. Within ten minutes, despite Jerry's mild protests, the party was over—hours earlier than it would have been in the old days.

Dix's car was parked just ahead of Cecca's, so it was natural enough for him to walk her to the door of her station wagon. They were alone there, out of the earshot of any of the others. As she groped in her purse for her keys, he whispered, "You were right. We're not going to sit around and wait for something else to happen. We're going to put an end to it."

She looked up at him, her face silver and shadow in the early moonlight.

"Tomorrow morning we'll go see Louise Kanvitz and find out what she knows. One way or another."

THIRTEEN

It was going to be another beautiful night.

Eileen went out for her evening walk earlier than usual, right after they got back from Lakeport, leaving Ted and the boys to play Monopoly. This was their last night at the cabin—the end of another vacation, home tomorrow afternoon, school and dental office and hospital and the rest of the familiar grind on Tuesday—and she wanted to savor the sunset, the lake view, the coolness, the solitude.

She walked along the road toward the Milbank cabin several hundred yards to the east. It was the same route she'd followed every night the past week, had followed nearly every night up here since they'd bought the cabin twelve years ago: past the Milbanks', through the woods and along the water's edge, then up onto the promontory, where she would sit and watch the sky and the water until dusk began to settle. It was a ritual and a tradition. Her life was governed by rituals and traditions, not that she minded; it was comforting to do the same things over and over, year after year, things you enjoyed. Every summer, on their last night at the cabin, they drove into Lakeport and ate raviolis stuffed with cheese and Italian sausage, Oliveri's specialty of the house. Oh, lordy, those raviolis! They were to die for. She'd not only eaten her platter but half of Kevin's. He'd always been a light eater, Kevin, the only one in the family who was. Regressive gene, probably. Well, she and Ted and Bobby made up for him. Did they ever.

Nobody was home at the Milbanks'. Gone out for Sunday dinner, a later one; not everybody liked to stuff their faces as early as the

123

Harrell clan. Eileen walked on past, entered the thick growth of pines on the footpath that branched off the road. It was cool and darkish in there, with the branches thick-woven overhead. If this were Los Alegres, it would have made her uneasy to be in there alone at this hour; even fat women in their forties had to worry about rape these days. But not here in the country. Very little crime in the Blue Lake area, except for an occasional winter break-in like the one at the Scotts', their neighbors to the west, a couple of years ago. You were safe enough wandering around alone, although she wouldn't have tempted fate by going out walking after dark. Animals prowled at night, even if people didn't.

She wondered, as she made her way along the path, if Ted would want to make love tonight. She hoped so. That was another ritual: lovemaking on their last night, as long as they were both healthy and not fighting about something. And truth to tell, she was horny again. Must be the mountain air. Thursday night, the last time they'd had sex, had been very very good. A giggle rose up in her as she remembered its aftermath. In the moments following her orgasm she'd clutched at Ted and whispered, "You're a tiger, you are," and without missing a beat he'd panted, "What, you think I have a striped pecker?" The image that conjured up had struck her as hysterically funny. In her convulsions she'd almost rolled him off the bed onto the floor. He'd finally had to grab her and muffle her laughter against his chest to keep it from waking Bobby and Kevin. "You want the boys to think their mother's high on laughing gas?" he'd whispered, which only prolonged the spasms.

The pines thinned near the water and the ground, thick with ferns, rose in a long sweep to the promontory. There was dry grass up there now, but in the spring wildflowers bloomed in a riot of color: purple lupines, golden poppies, dark-red Indian paintbrush. A rocky projection, complete with a worn-smooth section that was just the right size for her broad heinie, provided a natural bench. She sank down on it, sighing, relieved to take the weight off her feet.

Now that the sun had ridden low in the west, the lake was silver-sheened. Half a dozen skiffs and powerboats moved over the surface, one of the inboards towing a pair of teenage water skiers trying to perform a crossover maneuver. The kids weren't very adept at it: One of them got his tow rope tangled in the other's and both of them went ass-over-teakettle into the boat's wake. Eileen smiled. Kevin and Bobby were *much* better water skiers. The Milbanks had a Chris-Craft and the boys had been out with them three or four times again this summer. I wish Ted weren't so stubbornly attached to that old outboard of his, she thought. A powerboat would be nice for the boys. Just a small one, with a sun awning in case she decided to go along for the ride. She'd have to talk to Ted about it again before next summer.

She watched the lower rim of the sun edge closer to the horizon. The sky was already taking on color—mostly different shades of red. That was one of the pleasurable things about sitting out there night after night: Each sunset was different, if only just a little. When she and Ted both retired and could spend the entire summer at the cabin, she'd have to see how many nights it took before there was a sunset rerun. Scores, she'd bet, if not hundreds.

She thought about Cecca and Dix and Katy. It was creepy to think that someone they all knew had not only been Katy's lover but a sleaze who made scary phone calls. Brrr. Cecca still hadn't had any idea who it was when they'd talked on Thursday evening, but at least there hadn't been any more calls or other surprises . . . so far. She'd racked her brain and finally remembered, just that morning, the thing that had been bugging her since Monday. It was something Katy had said to her just a few days before she died, something odd about Pelican Bay and a trophy she'd seen. Eileen had tried to get her to elaborate, but she'd closed up like a clam. "I'll let you know if it means what I think it means"—that was the last thing Katy had said about it. In light of what had happened since . . . well, there just might be a connection. As soon as she remembered, she'd tried to call Cecca and got her machine. And Cecca hadn't called back, or if she had, it was while the Harrell crew was inhaling raviolis in Lakeport. Probably better if they discussed it face-to-face anyway. Tomorrow night, if Cecca was available when they got back to Los Alegres.

In any case, it was going to be all right. You had to believe that. Whoever the asshole was, he'd be found out and that would be the end of it. Then maybe Cecca and Dix would get together. It would be the best thing in the world for both of them. They'd make a cute couple, too. When you got right down to it, they'd make a cuter couple than Cecca and Chet *or* Dix and Katy. Funny how things worked out sometimes, for some people. They had to suffer through the worst kind of tragedy in order to find a new and better happiness. That was soap-opera stuff, of course, the same sort that was on *All*

My Children, the day-shift nurses' favorite lunchtime program, but it was the truth nonetheless.

The sun was already half gone. For a couple of minutes there were wine-red streaks shooting out around it, then they bled away and so did all the other colors as the sun disappeared completely. Then there was nothing left but ashy gray and a thin band of yellow along the horizon. Shadows were gathering along the shoreline and in the patch of woods below. Almost dusk. And time to start back, like it or not.

Reluctantly Eileen got to her feet, stretched a kink out of her lower back, and picked her way down through the ferns to the footpath. She hurried through the woods, as she always did. There was nothing in any stretch of woods to make her tarry; trees didn't interest her in the least. Reagan had been a crappy president, but she'd never understood why people got so upset at his "Seen one tree, you've seen them all" line. She slowed to a leisurely pace again when she reached the road. More night shadows now, the sky darkening overhead. Dusk. Her second favorite time of day after sunset.

The Milbanks were home: lights on in their cabin, their car parked in front. She debated stopping long enough to say good-bye, see you next summer, but she didn't do it. Time enough for that in the morning.

She came around the slight bend in the road to where the lighted windows of their cabin became visible. It was almost dark now. Any second the outside lights—blue and white baby spots that Ted had mounted on the front and side walls—would come on; they were on a timer switch.

She walked even more slowly, savoring these last few minutes of her outing, the almost-night.

Out on the lake somewhere, a boat engine made a low, throaty whine. From another direction she heard faint snatches of music from a radio abruptly turned up loud, that rap crap the boys liked. An owl hooted and another one answered it. A mosquito buzzed her ear.

The night-lights came on, just briefly, almost a flicker—

And the cabin blew up.

It just ... it ... there was a terrific explosion that assaulted her eardrums, caused the roadbed to tremble under her feet ... the walls bulged and burst, the roof vanished in a huge spurt of flame and smoke ... it was as if a giant house-size match had been struck ...

Ted Kevin Bobby!

Stunned disbelief gave way to horror; her head seemed to fill and swell with it. Her legs wouldn't work, and then they would, and she was running frantically, into gusting waves of heat that robbed her lungs of air and set her gasping.

Drops of fire rained down around the raging shell of the cabin, landed on nearby trees and caused them to erupt in flashes of yellow-red. Roiling smoke choked the new darkness. The lake reflected the blaze so that it, too, seemed to be burning.

Ted what happened

Bobby Kevin

Oh my God no

Someone, she couldn't tell who, materialized ahead of her. Wasn't there, then was ... running out of the flames, away from the flames, except that he he

He was on fire, wearing spines of fire on his back, shoulders, arms, and he was

Screaming

No!

Running, stumbling, falling, getting up, racing toward the lake, trailing fire, and not for a second did he stop screaming.

She veered toward him on a converging path. The swelling pressure smothered thought, made her head feel loose and enormous, like a balloon at the end of a string.

He reached the beach before she did, plunged across it, hurled himself into the dark water. Thrashed around wildly, churning the water to froth. The cries stopped and the flames went out with a hiss she could hear above the pulse of the inferno. A cloud of steam rose like a bloody mist, stained crimson by the fireglow.

She staggered through the rocky sand and into the water, cold, and groped for him, touched his back, hot, hot. He was still moving but feebly now, facedown ... drowning. Her hands, strong hands, nurse's hands, caught hold of him and dragged him backward, out of the lake and onto the beach. She sank to her knees beside him, eased him onto his back—

Kevin

Her baby Kevin

His face oh Jesus his poor face

Raw blistered red and black the hair all burned off

But still alive breath bubbling in his throat

Kevin

He whimpered, the same sound he'd uttered in his crib when he was little, and she gathered him into her arms and held him gently, fiercely. The fire hammered and crackled behind her . . . Ted, Bobby . . . and a long way off there were people shouting. But it was Kevin she heard. He whimpered again and she began to rock him, to croon to him.

"Hush baby hush it's all right. Mama's here. Mama's here . . ."

The thing in her head, the horror in her head, swelled and swelled—

And then it burst.

PART TWO
Fast Burn

FOURTEEN

They said it was a freak accident.

They said there was no doubt of that.

They said the cabin had a propane water heater in a small windowless basement area and that the pilot light must have blown out somehow and the safety valve had been defective, allowing the gas to leak out. When that happened, the heavy propane spread out in a trapped layer across the floor. It was the timer mechanism for the exterior night-lights, which was also in the basement—a photoelectric sensor arcing through a relay switch when the timer activated it— that had caused the explosion. Propane was extremely volatile. Once enough of it seeped out, a single tiny spark was all it took for ignition. A tragic accident, the kind that happens now and then when people aren't careful.

"They're wrong," Dix said angrily. "Wrong as hell. It wasn't an accident, it was cold-blooded murder."

Police Lieutenant Adam St. John was silent. He had a lean, fox face that didn't reveal much of what he was thinking, and an irritatingly phlegmatic manner. He sat rolling an unlit cigarette between his fingers, alternately shifting his gaze between Dix and Cecca, sitting pale and tense beside him. He was trying to quit smoking, he'd told them last week. Toying with the cigarette was his way of easing himself out of the habit.

At length St. John slid his chair forward, laid the cigarette carefully on his desk blotter. He said, "Lake County has a highly competent team of arson investigators. They spent all morning going through what's left of the cabin, and the head of the team assured me there's been no mistake. It was a propane leak that caused the explosion.''

''I'm not disputing that,'' Dix said. He ran a hand over his face, felt stubble here and there; he'd shaved that afternoon but he hadn't done much of a job of it. His eyes felt gritty from lack of sleep. ''I know a little something about propane heaters; my father had a couple of different kinds. The pilot light could have been blown out deliberately and the safety valve tampered with to let the gas escape. There'd be no way for the arson investigators to determine that from the burned-out wreckage, would there?''

''No, I suppose there wouldn't.''

Cecca made a dry throat-clearing sound. ''Every year, on their last night at the lake, the Harrells drove to Lakeport for dinner at a restaurant called Oliveri's. It was a ritual; everyone knew about it. If you check, you'll find they did it again yesterday.''

''So it's your contention the alleged murderer drove to Blue Lake and tampered with the heater while they were away in Lakeport.''

''That's right.''

''Knew where to find the heater and what kind it was because he'd been there before, as an invited guest.''

''Yes.''

St. John was silent again. Late-afternoon sunshine slanted through the venetian blinds on his office window, laid bars of light across the surface of his desk. He rolled the cigarette along one of the bars, slowly, as if he were deriving some kind of sensual pleasure from the act.

Without looking up, he said, ''Why?''

''Why? Why what?''

''Why would he do it? A man who called himself a friend of the Harrells—why would he try to blow them up, all four of them?''

''For Christ's sake, if we knew that—''

''It's a fair question, Mr. Mallory. You're convinced that the same man who's been harassing you two is responsible for what happened at Blue Lake. All right, convince me. Show me some evidence that links the two.''

''We don't *have* any evidence.''

''Then what makes you so sure?''

''You think it's coincidence? My wife's death, the telephone calls, all the rest of it, and now the Harrells' cabin blows up—two more of our friends dead, two in the hospital. You think that's a *coincidence*?''

"Coincidences happen. Stranger ones than that."

"No. It wasn't an accident."

"Let's look at it this way," St. John said. "As far as you know, had either Eileen or Ted Harrell received harassing calls recently?"

"No, but—"

"Packages, any kind of implied threat?"

"No."

"Would you have known if they had?"

"I would have," Cecca said. "Eileen would've told me. She couldn't keep a thing like that to herself."

"You see my point, then? Why would the same person harass the two of you, threaten *you,* and then go after a family he hasn't bothered at all?"

"What if Eileen figured out who he is and made the mistake of contacting him, warning him to leave us alone?"

"Would she do something that foolish?"

"I don't know . . . she might. She can be unpredictable sometimes."

"What makes you think she might have identified the man?"

"She called yesterday when I was out, left a message on my answering machine. She said she'd remembered something Katy said to her and that it might be important."

"Did she say what that something was?"

"No. She doesn't like to talk to machines, so her messages are always brief."

"Did you call her back?"

"I tried to," Cecca said. "About four o'clock. There was no answer; they must have already left for Lakeport."

St. John shook his head. "I don't buy it. It's remotely possible Mrs. Harrell identified the man, tried to warn him off, and he decided to kill her and her entire family to keep them quiet. But do it by driving all the way to Lake County on the chance that they'll be out and then setting a deathtrap that's by no means guaranteed to work? Unh-unh. No. I can credit a deliberate tampering with the heater if he was in no hurry to kill one or all four of the Harrells: One method doesn't work, he tries another one. But a man bent on self-protection takes a hell of a lot more direct action.''

"Even if he happens to be a psychotic?" Dix said.

"Psychotics may not seem to behave rationally, but there's always a cunning internal logic to what they do, no matter how warped it might be. It makes sense to them. They operate in established patterns, with a specific purpose for each act. I don't see any kind of pattern where the Harrells are concerned.''

Cecca said, "Suppose that's just what he wants. For none of us to see a pattern.''

"I'm not sure I follow that.''

"He intended what happened at Blue Lake to look like an accident. That much seems obvious. He doesn't want it to appear connected to what he's been doing to us. Our version sounds paranoid to you, doesn't it? So you're not going to do much about it.''

"I never said I wasn't going to do anything, Ms. Bellini.''

"But not as much as you would if you were convinced a homicidal maniac was running around loose in Los Alegres.''

"My hands are tied, legally, without sufficient proof.''

"That's exactly my point. Your hands are tied, and so Dix and my daughter and I continue to be vulnerable. He can keep right on stalking us with impunity, take his time picking us off.''

"Are you saying he tried to blow up a family of four just to buy himself more time to go after you?''

"No, she's not,'' Dix said. "She's saying it's possible the Harrells were targets all along, that he's cunning enough—your word, Lieutenant—to use different methods for different victims. He seduced my wife before he killed her—''

"If he killed her.''

"He killed her, all right. He seduced my wife and he struck against the Harrells without warning and he's getting some kind of sick pleasure or whatever out of tormenting us.''

"That's a pretty elaborate methodology,'' St. John said.

"You don't believe it's possible?''

"I believe just about anything is possible these days. But that doesn't change the fact that you have no proof to back up any of these conjectures, nor can you give me a hint of a possible motive even though you both seem convinced the man is someone you know fairly well.''

How could you argue against that? They were like people from different cultures trying to find some common meeting ground: Cecca and him reacting with raw emotion to a menace they knew but couldn't prove was real, St. John desensitized and rigid and secure, adhering to the letter of the law like a Jesuit to the holy scriptures. You couldn't blame him for being what he was, a methodical and cautious man. But it was maddening nonetheless.

St. John was playing with that damn cigarette again, his gaze shifting back and forth between the two of them. A trick of his, Dix decided, to keep you quiet while he was thinking. It was another minute before he said, "Tell me again about this Kanvitz woman. She owns Bright Winds Gallery at the Mill?"

Dix nodded. "She helped cover up the fact that my wife was having an affair. Katy was supposed to be studying with her when she was meeting her lover."

"You're convinced of that, too?"

"Cecca is. She had words with Louise about it last week."

"She admitted it to you, Ms. Bellini?"

"No, she denied it. But it was plain she was lying."

"Why would she lie?"

"Well, not because she was trying to protect Katy's good name. She wasn't Katy's friend. She only pretended to be."

"Why do you say that?"

"A friend doesn't try to capitalize on personal tragedy. She raised the price on Katy's last two paintings from two hundred to a thousand dollars apiece. At best she's a flagrant exploiter. At worst—"

"At worst," Dix said, "she's a blackmailer."

St. John cocked an eyebrow.

Cecca said, "Both those paintings had Sold signs on them when I was there last week. She wouldn't tell me who'd bought them. It isn't likely she could have found a buyer—a legitimate buyer—at such overinflated prices."

"You think she sold them to Mrs. Mallory's lover?"

"In exchange for her silence, yes."

"He wouldn't give in to that kind of blackmail to cover up a simple affair," Dix said. "The only reason he'd pay is if he's guilty of something much worse."

St. John said, "That's quite a scenario you've worked out."

"It fits all the facts."

"Maybe. But again, where's your proof?"

"Louise is the proof. Make her admit it."

"*Make* her admit it? How do you propose we do that?"

"Blackmail is a crime, isn't it? Once she knows that we know—"

"Accuse her of it straight out?"

"Well, why not?"

"Suppose she's innocent. She'd have grounds for a lawsuit."

"Christ," Dix said, "are you saying she *shouldn't* be confronted?"

"I'm saying it's a good thing she's out of town for the holiday weekend so you couldn't already have made that mistake."

"If we don't confront her, who will? You?"

"I'll speak to her, yes."

"She won't admit it unless you put pressure on her."

"You just leave that to me, Mr. Mallory."

Yeah, Dix thought. "What else can you do to help us . . . legally?"

"Talk to Mrs. Harrell, of course, as soon as she's able to answer questions. Have lab tests run on the package wrappings and containers you and Ms. Bellini brought in. There may be fingerprints, some other kind of lead to the perpetrator."

There won't be.

"We'll also increase patrols in the neighborhoods where you live, day and night."

That won't stop him for a minute.

"And I'll try to get a court order to wiretap your home phones. There should be enough probable cause for Judge Canaday to agree to it."

Terrific. "Is that all?"

"Until we have more to go on, I'm afraid so. I could interview your friends, but I don't want to do that yet. The more people who know about this, the easier it is for word to get out—and once it does, it'll spread like wildfire. This kind of thing is media fodder. We'd have reporters up here from San Francisco, all sorts of wild speculation and rumor—a potential panic situation. None of us wants that. I'd advise you both to remain quiet, and to let us handle the matter from now on. Don't do anything without talking to me first, except to increase your normal safety precautions."

"You do believe us, don't you?" Cecca asked him. "That this isn't some paranoid fantasy?"

"Let's say I'm leaning your way."

Terrific, Dix thought again. He looked down at his fingers, knuckles white, gripping his knees. You lean and we're the ones who fall.

He had always hated the idea of vigilante justice; of citizens arming themselves "for protection," using that as an excuse to take the law into their own hands. Too many guns out there, he'd always argued, in the possession of frightened, irresponsible people who didn't know how to use them properly. Strong advocate of gun control all his adult life. Believed one of the nation's most insidious organizations, purveyors of lies and half-truths to disguise the fact that it was a tool of the weapons' manufacturers, was the frigging NRA.

Conservatives' definition of a liberal: Somebody who has never been mugged. Another definition: Somebody who has never been threatened with extinction by an unknown enemy for unknown reasons.

He wondered bitterly where he could go to buy a gun.

Neither of them said much on the ride from the police department to Shady Court. It was after six, and the downtown area was mostly deserted; there had been an informal small-boat regatta on the river earlier, speeches and kids' and adult entertainment, but the festivities were over and the participants already home or on their way. Cecca stared out at the familiar buildings old and new—and they seemed as strange to her now as they had on the ride over. Everything in and about Los Alegres seemed strange today, as if her lifelong perception of this town where she'd been born and where she'd lived for forty-one years had been illusion and she was suddenly seeing it through different eyes, as it really was.

Los Alegres was not the safe and secure community she'd imagined it to be, the relative crime-free zone, the haven in a state and country and a world that bulged with new and ugly menaces every year. There was greater malignity here than anywhere else. And more deception. She wasn't safe in the company of the people who lived here, or even in her own house. She was embattled and defenseless, a naked target. Where *was* she safe? Nowhere, unless she ran away and hid . . . she and Amy, like animals looking for a burrow. Who was she safe with? No one except her family and Dix. She glanced over at him, saw the hard set of his mouth, the dark eyes unblinkingly watching the road ahead—and felt a twinge of apprehension. She was not even a hundred percent sure she was safe with him. She didn't know Dix Mallory any better, really, than she knew anyone else in Los Alegres. They shared a casual past, and a present terror, but beyond that she had no idea of who and what he was behind his

public façade. Just faith in her judgment, faith in his basic goodness
. . . and faith didn't seem to be quite enough anymore.

Outside, the intersection of Main and Lawlor flashed past. Lawlor
was where the Harrells lived. Ted and Bobby . . . both dead in the
explosion. Like Katy, incinerated, reduced to lumps of charcoal.
Kevin had been stabilized at the scene and then flown by medevac
helicopter to the burn and trauma unit at Santa Rosa Memorial; he
was in critical condition with burns over sixty percent of his body.
And Eileen . . . oh, God, Eileen. She'd been outside when the cabin
exploded, they said, apparently just returning from her evening walk.
Saved Kevin's life by dragging him out of the lake, he'd run on fire
into the lake. Collapsed afterward, was in ICU at the hospital in
Lakeport suffering from severe psychological trauma.

Cecca thought again that it might not have happened if she'd tried
a second time to return Eileen's call last night; if they'd talked about
what it was Eileen had remembered. Slim chance, but now she'd
never know. Driving herself crazy with thoughts like that, useless
speculations and spasms of guilt. Should she have driven up to Lakeport even though Eileen was under sedation and not allowed visitors?
Beth Birnam and then Dix had counseled her against it. Eileen
wouldn't be kept there long; they'd fly her to Los Alegres Valley
Hospital as soon as they felt she was ready to be moved. Standard
procedure in trauma cases: Take the patient as close to home as
possible, where relatives and friends could make regular visits. There
was nothing she could do in Lakeport.

Nothing she could do here either. Except wait.

Beth had been the first to find out about it. Watching the late news
on the Santa Rosa channel and there it was, footage of the fire still
burning but contained, interviews with a county sheriff's deputy and
a volunteer fireman. She'd called Cecca, and Cecca had driven up
to the Ridge to tell Dix when she couldn't get through to him on
the phone. Calls to Eileen's brother in Fairfax and the hospital in
Lakeport and the Lake County sheriff's department. Fragments of
information pieced together over a period of hours, until they knew
the full story—or as much of it as was available. Back home to bed,
finally, but not to sleep. And then today . . . Owen stopping by, Beth,
Jerry, Dix to tell her the Lake County authorities were calling it an
accident and they'd better go and see St. John. . . .

She was exhausted, physically and emotionally. But the only way she was going to sleep tonight, she knew, was with the help of Scotch or Seconal. Or both.

Dix turned the car into Shady Court. Amy, she saw, had obeyed her instructions to move her Honda from the street into the driveway, back near the garage. She didn't want the Honda parked on the street any longer because it was too easy for somebody to tamper with it out there. It could be gotten at in the driveway, too, but not as easily. As Dix pulled up in front, Cecca wished again that there were room in the garage for at least the Honda. But it was cluttered with tools and yard maintenance equipment and painting supplies and all sorts of odds and ends left by the former owners. She'd intended to have it cleaned out, but she'd just never got around to it.

Dix had left the engine running. She said, "Don't you want to come in for a few minutes? We can both use a drink."

"I don't think so. I wouldn't be very good company right now."

"That doesn't matter. Neither will I."

He shook his head. "I just thought of something we can do that St. John can't object to."

"What?"

"Make some calls, find out where Tom, Sid, Jerry, Owen, and George were yesterday afternoon and evening. It's at least a six-hour round-trip between here and Blue Lake, and it had to have been made between, say, three and nine o'clock. Anyone who can account for that time is cleared. Anyone who can't . . ."

"We can't just come right out and ask."

"No. Do it as obliquely as possible. You could ask Beth about Tom, Laura about George, Helen about Sid."

"All right."

"I'll talk to Owen and Jerry," he said. "I'll call you later and we'll compare notes."

"I hope to God all of them have alibis. I still don't want to believe it's one of them."

"Neither do I."

She felt an impulse to lean over and kiss him, just briefly; put her arms around him, just briefly. But she couldn't quite bring herself to do it. A thin little smile was all she had to give him before she got out of the car.

There was a strangeness about the house, too. She felt it again as soon as she let herself in. Burglary victims used the word "violated," and now she knew exactly what they meant. The tormentor had walked here, touched her things and Amy's things . . . how many times? Touched their things while he thought of ways to kill them both . . .

She shut the door, harder than she'd intended, and double-locked it. Amy was in the living room, curled up on the couch with a book open on her lap, listening to a Billy Idol CD turned up too loud. She looked pale and withdrawn; she hadn't slept much either last night. Bobby Harrell had been her age, they'd grown up together, they'd been friends. But never anything more than that, thankfully, or Amy would be taking his death even harder than she was.

When Cecca entered the room, Amy used the CD remote to lower the volume. "There were a couple of calls."

"From?"

"Mrs. Garstein. Message on the machine."

"She didn't have any news?"

"No, there's nothing new."

"Who else? Owen, I'll bet."

"Yeah. I talked to him."

"What did he want this time?"

"Oh, you know, he's worried about us. He wanted to come over."

"You didn't tell him he could?"

"No. I said we didn't want company tonight."

Owen. Calling up, hanging around, fussing . . . part of the plan to torment her? And I let him into my bed, she thought, I let him into my body. . . .

"Mom? You okay?"

"Yes. Does it seem cold in here to you?"

"Not really. Where did you and Dix go?"

Cecca hesitated. "The police station."

"Why? What's going on? If it's something real bad, I have a right to know what it is."

Yes, you do, Cecca thought. She couldn't keep it from her, couldn't protect her that way. It was time Amy knew exactly what they were up against. "All right, baby," she said. "Let me make myself a drink and then we'll talk."

While she was in the kitchen, Amy shut off the CD player. The new silence beat against her eardrums, creating the same kind of pressure as the rock music. She sat on the couch with her drink, rested her free hand on Amy's arm.

And as she told her, looking into her daughter's wan face, she was aware of a small, mean emotion that seemed to have crawled out of the core of her. A mixture of relief and gratitude that made her hate herself because of what it revealed about Francesca Bellini.

She was relieved, grateful, that it was Ted and Bobby and Kevin Harrell who had been killed and burned, Eileen who lay shattered in the Lakeport hospital—them and not Amy, not her.

FIFTEEN

The first day of the fall semester was an ordeal.

In the past he had always enjoyed it—all the activity on campus, the new faces, the fresh challenge of trying to cram familiar historical material into young minds that might, in a scant few cases, find it as exciting as he did. The prospect of facing this one had almost led him to call in sick that morning. But the need to occupy his time and his mind had been greater than his reluctance, and so he'd driven up to the university just as if this were another normal fall opening. He didn't regret the decision as the day unfolded. But getting through each segment was still a trial.

Department faculty meeting first thing, at nine o'clock. Not much point to it, except that it allowed everybody to "get their game faces on," as Elliot liked to put it. It also allowed Elliot to deliver, for the benefit of new faculty members—an associate professor of medieval studies this year—and any administration spies, his "department chair's motivational speech." It was the same every semester; Dix could have recited parts of it verbatim: "History is holistic, involving humanity in all of its dimensions, interests, and activities, from the economic and political to the psychological and cultural. Therefore we're not only teaching our students history but encouraging them to reflect upon and analyze the interrelationship of ideas and material circumstances and of individual and group behavior as revealed in a wide range of human institutions and activities." And so on, mining the same vein of bullshit.

The meeting ended at nine-forty. Elliot caught up with him in the

143

hall outside the lounge. "We've got time before your ten o'clock," he said. "Let's have a quick chat in my office."

Elliot's office was as cluttered as his living room at home. Two shelves in his bookcase were devoted to extra copies of his own books, particularly the Fremont Older biography, in case any of his students or an enterprising faculty member wanted to purchase one for purposes of edification and/or brown-nosing. Once they were inside he shut the door, leaned a hip against a corner of his desk, and ran a hand through his shaggy hair.

"I wasn't sure you'd be here today," he said.

"Why wouldn't I be here?"

"What happened to the Harrell family at Blue Lake. Close friends of yours, weren't they?"

"Yes. How did you know that?"

"I knew Ted Harrell. He mentioned you a couple of times. Hell of a thing, a freak accident like that. He seemed like a decent guy."

"He was," Dix said. "I didn't know you knew him."

"Not socially. He was my dentist."

Dix nodded. He couldn't think of anything to say.

Elliot said, "I was watching you in the lounge. You holding up all right?"

"More or less. Do I look that bad?"

"Not bad, just off balance. Anybody would be under the circumstances. First your wife, then one of your best friends and his family . . . Christ, you've had a summer."

"If you're worried about my ability to teach, you needn't be. Teaching, hard work, is still what I need right now."

"Oh, hell, that isn't it. It's you I'm concerned about."

"I'm coping, Elliot, really."

Elliot fished a package of Pall Malls from his shirt pocket, set fire to one, and blew smoke toward the open window beside the desk. "How about those calls? Any more since we talked?"

"Calls? Oh . . . no."

"Changing your number took care of it, then."

"I guess it must have."

"The asshole hasn't harassed you in any other way?"

Dix felt edgy, uncomfortable. He had no desire to talk about this, any of this—to Elliot or to anyone except Cecca and St. John. He said, "No. None."

"Well, at least that's one cross you don't have to keep bearing."

Elliot blew more smoke, coughed, scowled at the cigarette. "I *hate* these things," he said, and crushed it out in his overflowing ashtray. "You think the patch works?"

"Patch? Oh, the nicotine patch."

"You know anybody who's quit with it?"

"Not personally. But it's supposed to be effective."

"Only trouble is, you need to see a doctor to get it."

"Is that a problem?"

"With me it is. I hate doctors, too." Elliot glanced at his watch. "Listen, Dix, I just wanted you to know you've got a friend if you need one. Sympathetic ear, somebody to get drunk with if you think that might help . . . whatever I can do."

"I appreciate that, Elliot."

"Don't just appreciate it. Take me up on the offer. Balboa may not be much of a university, but we take care of our own."

He had three classes that day; Tuesdays and Thursdays were the heaviest in his schedule. His ten o'clock was 453, The Age of Jackson. He got through that one quickly. Orientation lecture—what the students could expect to learn in the class, what was required of them, which textbooks they would need—and then an early dismissal. The new young faces that stared back at him were just that, faces; he didn't even try, as he usually did on the first day, to identify the few among them who were the most alert, the history majors and probable honor students, and to learn their names first.

An hour in his office afterward, trying to concentrate on his syllabus. The same old questions kept intruding: Who? Why? It wasn't Sid Garstein; Sid and Helen had spent all of Saturday with their daughter and her family in San Francisco. It apparently wasn't George Flores or Jerry Whittington; George had been with a client in Santa Rosa and Jerry had taken Margaret Allen on a wine-tasting tour of the Napa Valley. Only Owen Gregory and Tom Birnam had no one to vouch for their whereabouts. Owen claimed he'd spent Saturday alone working in his darkroom and watching tapes of old movies. Tom had spent the morning at Better Lands and then claimed to have driven down to the Black Point marina and taken his sailboat out on San Pablo Bay—alone. He hadn't gotten home until eight-thirty, late for dinner. A problem with one of the boat's sails was his explanation.

Owen or Tom, narrowed down to those two. Or was it? Dix kept worrying that he and Cecca were making a huge mistake in focusing on their close friends. The tormentor could be someone else they knew. Someone here at the university, for instance—

I knew Ted Harrell. He mentioned you a couple of times. Hell of a thing, a freak accident like that.

Elliot?

Strange guy in some ways. Loner, chased women, had a high opinion of himself, held attitudes that were just a little off center. Could he have seduced Katy? Maybe. Glib, good-looking in a bearish way—the combination of intelligence and animal maleness might have appealed to her. Did he know Cecca? Yes, probably; it was Better Lands that was selling his house for him, wasn't it? Had he ever been inside her house? Could have been invited at some point, for some reason.

But none of that meant a damned thing without a motive. What possible reason could Elliot Messner have to want to murder people he knew only casually? It kept coming back to motive in *every* case, though. Owen, Tom, Elliot, all the men he knew . . . there was simply no imaginable motive for any of them. And yet it was happening, so there had to be one.

Just before noon he walked over to the cafeteria on the Commons. He felt he should eat, even though he wasn't hungry, but he would have been better off staying in his office. Four professors, two TAs, and one of his spring-semester honor students took the opportunity to flood him with condolences on the loss of his wife. He fled back to Guiterrez Hall with his roast beef platter barely touched.

Civil War and Reconstruction at one o'clock, an aimless tramp around campus, and then American Social History at three. Brief orientation lectures and early dismissal in each of those classes, too. And finally back to his office to gather his papers and briefcase before leaving. He felt wilted, headachey, as if he'd been teaching or writing intensively for hours without a break. He couldn't go on like this day after day. The strain would—

His telephone jangled. St. John, he thought; word on Louise Kanvitz, maybe. He lifted the receiver, spoke his name.

The filtered voice of the tormentor said, "You're next, Dix."

The Agbergs, dressed as if they were on their way to a social event, showed up at Better Lands at nine-thirty that morning. Unexpectedly, surprising Cecca; she had all but written them off. They had checked and rechecked their finances, Mr. Agberg told her, weighed their present options against their future ones, and come to the conclusion that they could afford the Morrison property, that they liked Los Alegres better than Walnut Creek, and that he could commute to his job in San Francisco just as easily from here. They did want to look at the property one more time, though, before they made the final commitment to purchase. Just to make certain they hadn't forgotten or overlooked anything vital. "We're very methodical people," Mrs. Agberg said with some pride.

Really? Cecca thought. I never would have guessed.

She took them up to the Ridge and endured an hour and a half of poking and prodding and rehashing of various aspects of the contractor's and termite inspector's reports. If they change their minds after all of this, she thought, I will probably lose it and tell them what I think of dull, plodding people who get dressed up to go buy a house. But they didn't change their minds. At Better Lands they spent another half-hour reexamining the disclosure statement and counteroffer sheet and satisfying themselves that the Morrisons' counteroffer was absolutely firm and that the Morrisons wouldn't renege on paying for all termite damage repairs and a couple of minor structural repairs; then, finally, they affixed their signatures and Mr. Agberg wrote a check to cover the full amount of the down payment. By the time Cecca had answered a dozen "final" questions about close of escrow and other matters, and the Agbergs went on their merry way, it was after one and she was hungry and all but out of patience.

She went out for a tasteless sandwich. Ten minutes after she returned, a family named Hagopian walked in: father and mother in their late twenties, a little boy about five, a little girl about two. They were from Kansas and they were relocating in the area—Mr. Hagopian had gotten a job with a small manufacturing company in Los Alegres—and they were interested in buying a house, "something nice with at least three bedrooms and a large yard, good neighborhood, close to schools, for around $250,000." Better Lands had two possibles in that price range, one in an East Valley tract and the other Elliot Messner's house in Brookside Park. Cecca showed them the prospecti and photographs of both. They didn't care for the East Valley property; the well-landscaped Messner place elicited a much more positive response, even though it was listed at $279,000. Mrs. Hagopian said it looked "charming," a word Cecca wouldn't have applied to any structure in Brookside Park, including those that made up the Balboa State campus.

So she drove them up to Brookside Park, taking a route that brought them past Parkside Elementary School. They liked the school and they liked Brookside Park; their faces would have told Cecca that even if they hadn't said so. The house was deserted: Elliot was still at the university, which was probably just as well. She wondered, not for the first time today, how Dix was bearing up on his first day of school. She got the key out of the lockbox and took the Hagopians in, after warning them that the owner was a divorced man living alone and inclined to be a poor housekeeper.

She needn't have bothered with the warning. The clutter didn't faze the Hagopians; they were far more decisive and imaginative people than the Agbergs and they saw the house not as it was but as it could be if they owned it. The living room was large and had all the right elements ("Look at that fireplace, honey, it's enormous"), the three bedrooms were large, and the master had a walk-in closet that Mrs. Hagopian exclaimed over, the kitchen was perfect ("I just love island stoves, don't you?"), and the backyard so excited the little boy that he ran around it twice, yelling his pleasure at the top of his voice.

The only problem with the place, according to Mr. Hagopian, was the price. "Two-seventy-nine is more than we can afford," he said when the tour was finished. "Would the owner come down to two-fifty, do you think?"

"He might," Cecca said. "You wouldn't insult him by offering at that price, I can tell you that."

"Well, let us think about it overnight, to make sure it's the home we want. I'll be honest with you: We have an appointment to view another house tonight. It may not be what we're after, but we should look at it."

"I understand. Take as much time as you like, Mr. Hagopian."

But as they got back into the car she felt certain she would hear from them again tomorrow, and that they would make an offer right away. If Elliot was at all reasonable, and she thought he would be, they ought to have a firm deal by the end of the week. You got so you could gauge buyers, some buyers, with reasonable accuracy. Not the Agbergs variety, who waffled and argued over minute details and drove everybody crazy until they made up their minds; people like the Hagopians, who knew what they wanted and acted immediately when they saw it.

Months of frustration, lean months in which she'd sold just two properties, and now, in what amounted to a single day, she was about to make a pair of fairly substantial sales. For a real estate agent, it was like winning the lottery. But there was no pleasure for her in the sudden turnaround. The irony, in fact, was bitter. What good was business success, a measure of financial security, when your life was in jeopardy?

"It looks like you were wrong about Louise Kanvitz, Mr. Mallory."

"What the hell do you mean, wrong?"

"I spoke to her at length this afternoon. She denies any knowledge of your wife's lover. Says she didn't even know your wife might have been having an affair until Ms. Bellini brought up the subject last week."

"She's lying. Of course she'd deny it at first."

"She also denies any wrongdoing in the sale of your wife's last two paintings. And she has proof to back that up."

"Proof? What proof?"

"She identified the person who bought them."

"Who is he?"

"It isn't a 'he.' The buyer is a woman, an artist in Bodega Bay named Janet Rice."

"Did you talk to this Janet Rice?"

"On the phone. She confirms it."

"And you believe her."

"She was pretty convincing."

"I'll bet she was. You ask her why she paid so much for paintings by an unknown artist?"

"She agrees with Louise Kanvitz that they'll be worth a lot more someday."

"My wife was an undiscovered genius, is that it?"

"You don't think that's possible?"

"No, I don't. She was good but not that good. Get an art expert in to look at her work, he'll tell you the same thing. Kanvitz and Rice are both lying."

"Why would Ms. Rice lie?"

"Is Kanvitz a friend of hers?"

"Evidently. That was where she spent the weekend—at Ms. Rice's home in Bodega Bay."

"Well, for Christ's sake, there you are. Kanvitz is lying to protect her blackmail scheme and Rice is lying to protect Kanvitz."

"A conspiracy?"

"I'm not saying Rice is a blackmailer or knows that Kanvitz is one. I'm saying Kanvitz asked her to lie and she's doing it. Work on the two of them, break them down—one or the other will admit the truth."

"How do you propose I do that without violating their constitutional rights?"

"Fuck their constitutional rights! What about *my* constitutional rights? What about my wife's and Francesca Bellini's constitutional rights?"

"Calm down, Mr. Mallory. Flying off the handle isn't going to accomplish anything."

"All right. All right."

"I'm not telling you I think you're wrong. It's entirely possible that Janet Rice *is* lying."

"Then what are you telling me?"

"The same thing I told you yesterday. That I have to work within the boundaries of the law. I'm checking on Ms. Rice and I plan to talk to her again, in person. I've also ordered the increased patrols in your neighborhood and Ms. Bellini's, and I'll keep trying to convince Judge Canaday to issue a court order for the telephone wiretaps—"

"Keep trying? You mean you asked and he turned you down?"

"I'm afraid so. Insufficient cause."

"Fine, terrific."

"These things take time, like it or not."

"Time we might not have."

"I don't like suggesting this, but . . . have you and Ms. Bellini considered leaving town for a while?"

"Running away, hiding out? Oh, we've considered it. But we're not going to do it. Suppose he discovers where we've gone and follows us? Or you never identify him and he hunts us down or waits until we turn up again? We're not about to spend the rest of our lives hiding, living in fear. This thing has got to end soon, St. John, one way or another."

"What does that mean, 'one way or another'?"

"It doesn't *mean* anything. It was a statement of fact."

"You're not considering something foolish, are you? Taking the law into your own hands?"

"How would I do that? I don't know who he is either, remember?"

"I'll warn you anyway, just in case. Don't do anything outside the law or you'll regret it. Let us handle this—it's the only way. Do you understand?"

"All too well, Lieutenant. All too goddamn well."

When Cecca arrived home at five, there was a message from Eileen's brother waiting on the machine: Eileen was well enough to be moved and had been flown from Lakeport to Los Alegres Valley Hospital earlier in the afternoon. Thank God, she thought. Immediately she called the hospital and spoke to an admissions nurse.

"Yes, Mrs. Harrell is here," the nurse said. "But she's not ready to have visitors."

"When will she be ready? Tomorrow?"

"Perhaps. Call again in the morning."

"How is she? Is she able to talk?"

"Her condition is stable."

Cecca thought as she hung up: I wish I could say the same for mine.

SIXTEEN

The room was very white. Too white. White walls, white ceiling, white woodwork, white metal table and chairs and bedframe and sheets. Even the blind eye of the wall-mounted TV set seemed a pale gleaming white. Sterile. Familiar. One of the private rooms in Los Alegres Valley's intensive care unit: She'd know it anywhere, as often as she'd been in and out of this one and others like it over the years.

They really ought to put a little color into these rooms, Eileen thought. She'd brought it up more than once at staff meetings, but nobody would listen to her. Proper atmosphere, they kept saying, as if that meant anything. As if you couldn't maintain a proper hospital atmosphere by adding a little color to all that white. Not that there was anything wrong with white; white was very soothing and comforting. It was just that a little color here and there would make the rooms more cheerful. More hopeful, too. White was comforting, color was hopeful—couldn't you always find hope in bright colors? The curtains on the windows, for instance . . . yellow, or light blue. Or a wall decoration of some kind, a vivid painting of some kind, maybe a seascape or fruit in a bowl. Just a *little* color.

Of course there was color in this room now, but it wasn't permanent. Flowers. Let's see . . . roses, carnations, peonies, azaleas, African violets. Very pretty. Lots of different arrangements and plants, on the table and on the floor. Somebody was a very popular patient.

I shouldn't be lying here like this, she thought then. Why am I lying here? I should be up, making my rounds.

153

But she was so *tired*. So tired. Couldn't seem to think clearly about anything either. Every time she tried to think about something other than the room, something she wanted to remember ... no, didn't want to but had to ... it was as if she were being yanked away from it. Funny. She felt drifty and lost, not like herself at all. Almost a stoned feeling, like the time in college, such a long time ago, when she and Ted ... Ted ... they had eaten half a trayful of hash brownies. Oh, Lord, had she been stoned that night! But it had been a happy, giggly kind of stoned, and this was different. This wasn't happy, this was sad. This was *really* lost. This was sad and lost and—

The door opened and somebody came into the room.

Somebody said, "Eileen? Honey, are you awake?"

Familiar voice, as familiar as the white room. Her eyes had closed and the lids felt as heavy as if they had weights attached to them; she had to work very hard to get them open. Cecca. Oh, it was Cecca. Wearing a sculptured blue blouse and a pale blue skirt. Pretty combination. Pretty shades of blue. Blue was definitely her color. It went so well with her dark skin tones. And it looked so cheerful in the midst of all this damn white.

Cecca came to the bed, leaned over, and kissed her cheek. Sat down and took one of her hands. Cecca's fingers were like ice.

"Cold," Eileen said.

"What?"

"Cold fingers."

"Oh, honey, I'm sorry, I didn't realize—"

Cecca started to take her hand away. Eileen clung to it. It was good to hold on to Cecca's hand, even if it was as cold as ice. She seemed to need to hold on to something, but she wasn't sure why.

"Pretty blouse," she said.

Cecca didn't seem to understand her. Tongue wasn't working any better than her brain. Such an effort to get words out, as if she were having to push them up through some sort of blockage in her trachea. She really did feel stoned, sad stoned, bad stoned. Whoo. Shit. All right, who spiked the brownies *this* time?

"Your blouse," she said. "New?"

"Oh. No. You've seen it before."

"Pretty color," Eileen said sleepily.

"How do you feel, honey?"

"Tired. Stoned. Sad and lost."

"Poor Eileen."

"Spiked the brownies, Teddy boy?"

"It's Cecca. You do know it's me?"

Well, of course I do, Eileen thought. Nobody else looks that good in blue. Cecca. Cecca, Cecca . . . something she had to tell Cecca, wasn't there? Yes, but what was it? Something . . . trophy, that was it. Trophy and the accident.

"Accident," she said.

"Shh, don't think about that now."

"Tell you something."

"Not now. You'd better rest. I'll go away and let you rest, okay?"

Now why was Cecca crying? Tears on her cheeks, tears in her voice, definitely crying. Don't cry for me, Argentina. She felt a giggle forming, but it didn't seem right to giggle somehow. What, you think I have a striped pecker? *Ted.* No. *Kevin.* No. Get up off this bed, Harrell, what's the matter with you, lying down on the job? Lie in the sack, they'll give you the sack. Right? Right. Get up, make your rounds, you're a nurse, not a patient.

"Eileen?"

"Mmm?"

"I'm going now. Do you want the nurse to come in?"

"I'm a nurse."

"Yes, honey, I know, but I thought—"

"Crying for, Cecca?"

"I'm not crying." Wiped her eyes, smiled all bright and sunny. Not a Cecca smile, though—a Cheshire cat smile, big and bright, teeth in the dark with nothing behind them. "I'll come back later and we'll talk some more. Maybe you won't be so tired then."

"So *damn* tired . . ."

"I know. You rest now. Sleep."

"Accident," she said. "Cecca, the accident."

Cecca took her hand away—oh, Cecca, don't—and stood up and then kissed her again. Chanel No. 5, by golly. Wonder why she put on her best? Dix, maybe. Cecca and Dix. Cute couple, so much cuter than . . . Katy. Katy. The trophy, the accident . . .

She tried to say the words, but now they wouldn't come out at all. Mouthful of mush. What's the matter, cat got your tongue?

"Sleep," Cecca said, and went away crying behind her Cheshire cat smile.

But Eileen didn't sleep. She lay there feeling bad-stoned and trying

to think. Why couldn't she think? Why couldn't she remember what
it was she had to remember? It hurt not to think and not to remember.
It hurt, it hurt, it hurt . . .

Now she was crying, too.

It hurt and she was crying and she didn't even know why.

Charles Czernecki taught general biology and molecular biology
at Balboa State. He'd been on the faculty six years longer than Dix,
held a master's degree, and would probably have been appointed
Biology Department chair long ago if he'd been willing to keep his
personal opinions to himself and to play academic politics. He was
in his late fifties, a nondescript little man who favored bow ties and
affected an air of bored disdain, as if he considered himself not only
intellectually superior to his students and fellow professors but to
most of mankind. If you'd just met him, you might think from his
appearance and manner that he was apolitical, read scientific journals
and books on vascular plant morphology and vertebrate embryology
for pleasure, and collected butterflies or specimens of obscure marine
life as a hobby. You'd have been wrong on all counts.

Czernecki was an outspoken, radical right-wing gun nut. Belonged
to the NRA, wrote articles for *Gun Digest* and *Soldier of Fortune,*
ardently believed the country was headed for a class and/or racial
civil war, and was rumored to own a large collection of handguns,
rifles, and illegal semiautomatic weapons.

Dix couldn't stand him, an antipathy that was certainly reciprocated. He'd had an angry verbal run-in with Czernecki at a faculty
party years ago, and they'd barely spoken to each other since. He
hated the idea of going begging to the man, but he didn't see any
other reasonable alternative. At nine forty-five Wednesday morning
he entered the Hall of Sciences, where he found Czernecki alone in
his office, preparing for his ten o'clock class. Dix shut the door,
gritted his teeth, and asked his question—straight out, without pream-
ble or explanation.

The little bugger's surprise was well contained. His only visible
reaction was a cold, sardonic smile. That was all right; the one response Dix couldn't have stomached was derisive laughter. He stood
stiffly, poker-faced, meeting Czernecki's Daedalian eyes without
blinking.

"And what makes you think I'd sell you a handgun, Mallory?"

"I've heard you have a large collection. I thought you might be willing to part with one at the right price."

"I'm not licensed to sell firearms."

Dix was silent, waiting.

Czernecki said, "You can buy a handgun at any gunsmith's shop or sporting goods store. Even you must know that."

"I know it. But there's a waiting period before I could take possession."

"So there is. Two weeks for a valid permit."

"And the permit would be for premises only. I wouldn't qualify for a carry permit."

"No, I expect you wouldn't."

"So," Dix said.

Czernecki said, "Guns are dangerous. And too easy to obtain as it is; only qualified law enforcement personnel should be allowed to own a handgun, much less carry one on his person. Seems to me I recall you making those statements once, in no uncertain terms."

Again, Dix was silent.

"They're particularly dangerous in the hands of someone who doesn't know how to use them. We both agree on that."

"I know how to use a handgun. I was in the army."

"Yes, during the Vietnam War. You rode a desk on one of the East Coast training bases, if I remember correctly. Never got off U.S. soil."

"You say that as if I manipulated it that way. I was drafted, I served my two years, I went where and did what I was told. I didn't run to Canada."

"But I'm sure you thought about running. Gave it careful and serious consideration."

The hell with this, Dix thought. He said, "I didn't come here to argue politics with you, Czernecki. I told you what I want. If you won't sell me a handgun, say so and I'll go somewhere else."

"If you had anywhere else to go, you wouldn't have come to me. Frankly, I find this request of yours fascinating. A liberal peacenik and strong advocate of gun control suddenly wants the privilege of carrying a concealed weapon. Is it that you've had a philosophical change of mind on the gun control issue?"

"No. I still believe there need to be controls."

"In theory, but not where you're concerned."

"If you want to put it that way."

"Tell me, then: Why do you want a handgun?"

"For protection."

"Really? Protection from what?"

"That's my business."

"It's mine, too, if I'm to be your supplier."

Dix hesitated. Then he said, "I have reason to believe that my life is in danger, that I'm being stalked. That's as much as I'm willing to tell you."

"Why would anyone stalk a man like you?"

"I don't know."

"You do know the stalker's identity?"

"No, I don't."

"Invisible enemy, Mallory?"

"Yes."

"That sounds paranoid to me. In fact, it sounds suspiciously like the paranoia you liberals are always ascribing to men who hold my beliefs. Gun nuts, the so-called lunatic fringe."

Dix said carefully, "I'm sure you're enjoying the hell out of this, Czernecki. But spare me the irony. I wouldn't be here, compromising my beliefs, begging favors, if I weren't hurting and desperate. You must realize that."

"Of course."

"Will you help me, then?"

"I haven't decided. I want to think about it for a while."

"How long?"

"I live near the campus," Czernecki said, "and I generally go home for lunch. I'm going today at one. If I do decide to help you, I'll have a package for you when I return at two o'clock."

"All right, fair enough. How much?"

"We'll discuss that if and when. Any preference as to type and caliber?"

"Something small and not too heavy."

"Small-caliber weapons don't have much stopping power."

"I wouldn't feel comfortable with anything larger than a thirty-eight."

"Of course you wouldn't."

The air in the cramped space was stagnant, too-warm, tainted with the sweet smell of Czernecki's cologne. Dix felt a little sick to his stomach. He said, "Two o'clock, then," and made motions to leave.

"No, don't go yet," Czernecki said. "I have a few more questions for you."

"I'd rather not answer any more questions—"

"I'd rather you did."

"All right. Ask them."

"This stalking business. Is it related to your wife's death?"

Damn you! Dix thought. "No," he lied.

"And her death *was* an accident?"

"Yes."

"My condolences, by the way."

"Thanks so much."

"Under the circumstances, after such a tragic loss, I don't blame you for taking an aggressive position with this new trouble. I would do the same if I were in your shoes."

Dix said nothing.

"The police, I suppose, haven't been much help?"

"There isn't much they can do in a case like this."

"No. And self-protection is a constitutional as well as a God-given right. You agree with that, in theory at least?"

"I agree with it."

"But to what length? To the death?"

"I'm not sure what—"

"If I sell you a handgun, and you have occasion to use it against an enemy, would you shoot to kill? Could you take a human life?"

"If I had no other choice."

"Cold-bloodedly, if that was the only choice?"

"Yes."

"You're certain of that? Absolutely certain?"

"I'm certain."

"Then welcome to the real world, Mallory," Czernecki said. "Guns don't kill people—people kill people. And sometimes fighting violence with violence is the only solution. Now maybe you see the distinctions."

Dix saw them, all right. He saw them all too well. But what Czernecki didn't understand was that there had been no fundamental adjustment in his way of thinking. He believed as passionately as ever that if Charles Czernecki and his ilk had their way, they would help turn the real world into a nightmare place of ruptured freedom, atavistic violence as an accepted societal norm. The decision he'd made applied to him alone. He was scared, trapped by circumstances beyond his comprehension and control, driven to do what he felt he had to to survive, and these things made him weak, made him sell out on a personal level. But, by God, it didn't put him in Czernecki's camp. It didn't make what he was doing *right*.

The brief visit with Eileen left Cecca bleak and depressed. She'd been prepared for the worst, had tried to erect defenses to guard her own tender feelings, but imagining what Eileen would look, act, and sound like didn't match the reality of seeing her, listening to her. So pale, lying there; the stunned eyes and minimal awareness; the slurred voice and disjointed speech patterns. *Tired. Stoned. Sad and lost.* It had been a shock and it had shaken her. Even through an effort of will she hadn't been able to hold back the tears.

"Mrs. Harrell's mind is bruised," her attending physician, Dr. Mulford, had told Cecca beforehand. He'd insisted on seeing her first, to warn her that under no circumstances was she to mention the explosion, or what had happened to Ted and Bobby and Kevin. "She's in a great deal of emotional pain. She doesn't remember anything about that night, won't allow herself to even though at a deeper level she knows she has to eventually. She's afraid to face the enormity of it. But I don't think she'll let herself suffer that way for long. The wife and mother parts of her are too strong; she'll have to face the tragedy in order to find out what happened to her family. That's when the healing process can begin. But the decision to face it must be hers, must come from within."

"You couldn't even tell her that Kevin is out of danger?" Cecca had found that out from Eileen's brother earlier. And thank God for that much, at least.

"No. Not until she's ready to accept the rest of it."

Cecca drove from the hospital to Better Lands. Work, the universal panacea. The Hagopians, minus their two children, were waiting for her—willing and eager to make a $250,000 offer on the Messner property in Brookside Park, just as she'd anticipated.

She cared and she didn't care; mainly it gave her something involving to do. She took longer than usual preparing the offer sheet, going over the disclosure statement and other documents with them. Their credit appeared to be very good. And they intended to make a down payment of $135,000, thanks to the sale of a home they'd owned in Salina and to a cash loan from Mrs. Hagopian's father;

financing for the balance shouldn't be a problem. If Elliot cooperated, it ought to be a done deal.

She reached Elliot at the university right after the Hagopians left. He seemed delighted; and he wasn't bothered by the size of the offer. "I was afraid I had an albatross on my neck," he said. "Of course I'd like a little more than two-fifty. I don't suppose these people would go two-sixty-five?"

"I doubt it," Cecca said. "Two fifty seemed to be about their maximum."

"Well, let me think about it for a couple of hours. I have a one o'clock class, but I can cut it short. I could be at your office around two."

"Fine."

"You're a wizard, Francesca. Nobody else could have sold that pile of mine so quickly."

Right. A backward ten-year-old could have sold that pile to the Hagopians. But she said, "It was a pleasure. I'll see you at two."

Elliot arrived at five minutes past. The first thing he did was to grab her by the shoulders and hug her. She endured it stiffly; casual hugs, casual touching—especially by men—had always turned her off. When he let go of her and stepped back, grinning in his bearish way, she could see the heat in his eyes. It annoyed her—more than it would have under better circumstances. It wasn't exactly sexual harassment, but this was a business office and theirs was a business relationship, and it was plain that he was thinking of her as a woman, how her body had felt fitted against his. Did he leer at his students that way? Try to seduce girls almost as young as Amy? Probably. He was the type. Earthy as hell, in spite of his intelligence. To the Elliot Messners of the world, there was never a question of mind over hard-on.

She led him back to her office, leaving the door open after they entered. She was cool to him, but he didn't seem to notice. He kept grinning at her, flirting with his eyes, trying to touch her hand now and then as he spoke.

He'd decided on the way in, he said, to counter at $257,500 firm. "It's not as much as I'd like, but I can live with it. If the Hagopians can afford two-fifty, they can afford two-fifty-seven-five. Right?"

"I would think so. I'll write up the counteroffer and present it to them tonight."

"Will they decide right away, do you think?"

"They might. I'll let you know either way. Will you be home all evening?"

"No plans," he said. "If they accept the counter, why don't you come by instead of calling? We'll have a drink or two to celebrate."

"I don't think so," she said.

"I'm really not bad company, once you get to know me."

"I'm sure you aren't. But I'm not interested, Elliot. I told you that at least twice."

"Women don't always mean what they say. Or say what they mean."

"I do. And I'd rather not have to say it again. Now, can we please get on with the business at hand?"

He shrugged and said, "Sure thing."

She had been holding herself in check with an effort; it was a good thing he'd relented. If she blew up at him—and she might well have if he'd kept pushing—it would likely blow the deal, too, and the dubious satisfaction of telling him off wasn't worth that. He was carnal and irritating, but he wasn't the worst Mr. Macho around. Good God no, he wasn't. Besides, he seemed finally to have gotten the message. He left her alone as she wrote up the counteroffer. And when he signed it and stood to leave, his handshake was brief and formal, even if his smile wasn't totally impersonal. Good-bye, Francesca, thanks again. Good-bye, Elliot, I'll talk to you again tonight. And he was gone.

She poured herself a cup of coffee and sat sipping it at her desk. Tom came in and congratulated her on the evident sale. But what he really wanted to talk about was Eileen and what had happened at Blue Lake. She let him do most of the talking. Tom Birnam, friend, employer, confidant for more than fifteen years—and she no longer felt at ease with him, no longer quite trusted him. Was even a little afraid of him at moments like this, when they were alone together.

It was a relief when the phone rang and he left her alone to answer it. "Francesca Bellini," she said into the receiver.

"Hello, Francesca. This is Louise Kanvitz." The chilly voice had warmth in it today, the crackly warmth of anger. "I think it's time you and I had another talk."

SEVENTEEN

When she heard Kimberley yell, "Hey, look out!" Amy instinctively brought her foot down on the brake pedal. She saw the red light then, the cars starting to scream across the intersection in front of her, and braked hard. There was the screech of tires; the Honda tried to stand on its nose as it slid halfway through the crosswalk.

"God, Amy, wake up."

"Sorry." She put the transmission in reverse, backed up a few feet. Her heart was pounding.

"What's the matter with you?"

"I said I was sorry."

"Where were you anyway? Mars?"

"Just thinking too hard."

Kim sighed. "About Bobby Harrell, I'll bet."

She hadn't been, but she said, "Yes."

"I keep thinking about him, too. It's just such a *shitty* thing."

The light changed. Amy eased down on the accelerator, paying attention to her driving now. Going slow.

"You hear anything more about his brother?" Kim asked.

"Kevin's out of danger. But still critical."

"Burned like that, sixty percent of his body . . . jeez. You think he'll have scars?"

"I don't know."

"Can they fix burn scars with plastic surgery?"

"It depends on how bad they are."

"What if they're really gross? What if he ends up looking like Freddy Krueger or something?"

163

"Kim, for God's sake."

"Well, it could happen. He was so cute for his age. Better looking than Bobby, even. Jeez."

Amy didn't say anything.

"How's Mrs. Harrell?" Kim asked.

"Still the same. My mom went to see her yesterday."

"I'll bet it was a bitch for her."

"It was."

"Are you going?"

"Yeah. Up to see Kevin, too, when he can have visitors."

"I couldn't stand it," Kimberley said. "I hate hospitals. I mean, they just totally gross me out."

"They're better than cemeteries."

"*Anything's* better than cemeteries."

Amy turned into Kim's street, pulled up in front of her house. Kim said, "You want to hang out later, after you get off work?"

"I don't think so. Not tonight."

"Well, call me if you change your mind. And take it easy, okay? Driving, I mean. Bobby Harrell dying is, like, awful enough. I don't want to lose my best friend, too."

If you lose me, Amy thought, it won't be in a car accident. She waved, drove away slowly. Still paying attention to her driving, but she couldn't keep the thoughts from running around again inside her head.

For the hundredth time: He can't be the one.

Not *him*.

It was so hard to imagine any of Mom's male friends, anybody they knew, as a stalker. The whole thing was just totally nuts. But Mom believed it, and after all that had happened, she believed it, too. Crazy things went down all the time. People killed people just to steal their car, or for no reason at all. It could happen to them the same as anybody else. It *was* happening to them.

"Be very careful, Amy," Mom had warned her. "Promise me that. Until we know who's doing this and why, don't trust anybody. No matter how well you think you know him."

Not even him. Especially not him, because what if he weren't really attracted to her the way she was to him? What if it were all a trick to win her confidence, get her alone somewhere so he could kill her like he'd killed three people already?

It wasn't. But it could be.

Cool it for now, then. What choice did she have? She didn't want to die. Cool it until they found out who the stalker really was, and then—

Then.

She was downtown now. She turned into Water Street, the narrow alley that bisected the block behind Hallam's Bookshop. There was a little parking area back there for employees; she parked in the space closest to Hallam's back entrance, locked the car, and hurried inside even though there was nobody around in the alley.

Mr. Hallam had her work the front counter until four o'clock. Then UPS brought in several boxes of books, both new and used, and he asked her if she'd mind unpacking them, checking the contents against the packing slips, and shelving the books. She did mind; that was the part of working in a bookstore she disliked, being a box person and stock clerk. But Mr. Hallam didn't like you to argue with him, so she said okay.

She did the used books first. There weren't many of those and they were mostly nonfiction trade paperbacks from a bookseller in the Midwest that Mr. Hallam traded with from time to time. There was a big box from Sunset—new gardening and home improvement books. Easy. She separated them by subject, checked the packing slip, then lifted an armload of titles to take out front.

When she turned around, *he* was standing there in the stockroom doorway, smiling at her.

Seeing him like that, unexpectedly, startled her; her step faltered and she almost dropped the Sunsets. He jumped forward and steadied the load, his fingers brushing her bare arm and wrist. Most of what the contact made her feel was like before, a kind of tingly excitement, but there was something else, too, this time: fear. His touch made her a little afraid.

"Let me help you with those," he said.

"No, I can manage. You're not supposed to be back here."

"Well, you weren't in front. I thought this was where I'd find you. Sure I can't help?"

"It's my job," she said. She tried to smile at him, but the stretching of her mouth felt crooked and thin. "Um . . . excuse me, okay?"

"Sure," he said, and stood aside.

She carried the Sunsets out to the gardening section. It was at the rear of the shop, not far from the stockroom; there was nobody else close by, just Mr. Hallam and one customer up by the register. She put the books down on the floor and began to shelve them.

He came up next to her. Not too close, but still close. She could smell his cologne, the musky heat of his body.

"I finished the Talese book," he said.

". . . What?"

"*Thy Neighbor's Wife.* That's why I stopped by—to tell you I finished it last night."

"Oh."

"Remember when I bought it? Our plans to find someplace quiet where we can talk?"

"I remember."

"You haven't changed your mind?"

"Well . . ."

"It's all right if you have. I'll understand."

Such a terrific smile, so sweet and sexy. How could there be evil behind it? "No, I haven't changed my mind," she said without quite meeting his eyes. "It's just . . . you know, everything that's happened. It isn't a good time."

His smile vanished; he nodded solemnly. "The Harrells."

"Yeah. Bobby and his dad . . . I knew them all my life."

"I know you did."

"So I think I'd like to wait a while, okay?"

"Of course, Amy. It really was a terrible accident. It's going to take me a while to come to terms with it, too."

"I guess everybody feels that way."

"Those propane heaters are so dangerous," he said. "Your dad doesn't use that kind at his cottage, does he?"

"My dad?"

"He does still have the beach cottage?"

"Oh . . . sure. He wanted me to spend last weekend with him and his lady up there."

"Why didn't you?"

"I don't like her. Besides, I had to work."

"*Does* he use propane appliances?"

"I don't know."

"Well, you might want to ask him. I'm sure he's careful, even if he does; contractors don't usually make those kinds of mistakes. Still, it's always a good idea to be safety conscious."

"Next time we talk," Amy said. "I'll ask him then."

"Is he still at the cottage?"

"No, they came back Monday night."

"Going up again this coming weekend?"

"I don't think so. He never goes two weekends in a row. Megan doesn't really like it there, and she gets bitchy when he goes without her."

"It must be a nice place," he said. "Right near a big beach, isn't it?"

"Manchester State Beach."

"I love the ocean, walking on the beach."

"Me, too."

"I had a feeling that was another thing we shared."

She didn't say anything.

"Maybe you could show it to me sometime, Amy."

Oh God, she thought. She still couldn't look into his eyes. A day, a night, maybe even a whole weekend together at the Dunes, just the two of them. Walk on the beach, find out all about each other, make love in front of the fire ... it put an ache in her chest just thinking about it. She wanted so much to say yes, I'll show you *this* weekend, I'll tell Mom I'm staying at Kimberley's and then we'll drive up and I'll show you everything. Everything.

Be very careful, Amy.

Dry-mouthed, she said, "Maybe. Sometime."

"Whenever you say. But not too long?"

"Not too long."

"And it'll be our secret until then."

She nodded, thinking: Please don't let him be the one.

He smiled at her again, that incredible sexy smile. But he didn't touch her, and that was good because she might have weakened if he had, she might have done something not very smart. He said, "Be good, Amy," and left her alone.

She trudged back to the storeroom. She'd always been so sure of herself, of what she wanted in her life; confident that the decisions she was making about college, career, love, and sex were the right ones for her. Mature beyond her years. A woman at seventeen. But now ... now all of a sudden she was confused and uncertain. Everything had been turned upside down; her choices were no longer simple or clearly defined. And worst of all, she had begun to feel like the dorky little kid she'd once been, the kid who'd been afraid to sleep alone in the dark. She hated that. She hated being small and helpless and frightened. She hated not being an adult.

The gun, which Dix had accepted wrapped and bound and therefore sight unseen from Czernecki in exchange for one hundred dollars cash, turned out to be a small, flat .25-caliber Beretta five-shot automatic. It was no larger than Dix's hand; if his fingers had been any thicker, he would not have been able to slide his index finger through the trigger guard.

A woman's weapon. The kind a woman could carry comfortably in her purse, shoot with not much recoil and reasonable accuracy at close range.

Czernecki's little joke.

Dix waited until he got home to unwrap the package, and by then it was too late. Too late, probably, even if he'd insisted on examining the gun in Czernecki's office. The little bastard might have let him have his money back, but he wouldn't sell him another, larger caliber weapon. A one-shot deal—almost literally. If Czernecki was into lousy puns as well as slick irony, he was laughing his head off right this minute.

Dix should have been angry, but he wasn't. His only emotion was a kind of dark, weary determination. Make do with what he had, do what had to be done. There was nothing to be gained in wasting his rage on anyone but the tormentor.

The Beretta's clip was fully loaded. Czernecki had provided one spare clip, also maximum full. Dix checked the action, then field-stripped the piece. The barrel was clean and all the parts were oiled and seemed to work smoothly. Well, why shouldn't they? One thing you could say about gun nuts: They took pride in their firearms, kept them in perfect condition, and wouldn't dream of turning one over to somebody else unless it functioned properly.

He'd hung his gabardine sport jacket in the closet; he put the reassembled Beretta into the right side pocket. It was so small and lightweight that it made no discernible bulge, didn't even alter the hang of the jacket. Then he took the package wrappings into the kitchen, wadded them into the garbage bag. It was just four-thirty when he was done. Louise Kanvitz, according to her ad in the Los Alegres telephone book, closed Bright Winds Gallery at five o'clock. She lived out on Buckram Street, beyond the cemetery—less than a fifteen-minute drive from the Mill, even in traffic. If he left here at five-fifteen he'd be at her house by five-thirty. That ought to be just about right.

He considered calling Cecca, telling her what he intended to do. No, better not. She'd want to go along, and if there was trouble over this—and there probably would be—he deserved to bear the full brunt of it. She had enough grief as it was. Just Kanvitz and him ... and the Beretta. And God help her if she refused to tell him what she knew.

He made himself a light Scotch and water. Not for Dutch courage; just to help pass the time. He didn't need any chemical assistance for this task. He was on his way to the living room with the drink when the doorbell sounded.

Damn poor timing, whoever it was. He went and opened the door. Owen Gregory. Wearing a rumpled expression to go with his rumpled suit: a man with things on his mind.

Dix's first thought was that he should have kept his jacket on, so the Beretta would be close at hand if he needed it. Then he thought: For Christ's sake! He said, "Well, Owen. What brings you here?"

"Have you got a few minutes? I'd like to talk to you."

"I have to go out pretty soon. An appointment."

"This won't take long."

"All right. Come on in."

Owen declined the offer of a drink, went to perch on the edge of a chair in the living room—stiff-backed, his big hands gripping his knees. Dix occupied the sofa across from him.

"What's on your mind, Owen?"

"Cecca. She's always on my mind, it seems."

". . . Yes?"

"You know how I feel about her. It's no secret."

"Yes?" Dix said again.

"I have to know this, Dix: Is there something between you and her? Are you . . . involved?"

"What makes you think that?"

"The way the two of you acted at Jerry's Saturday night, for one thing. And the way she's been toward me lately—cold, distant. That's not like her, not at all."

"She has a lot of things on her mind," Dix said.

"What things?"

"Losing one close friend and half the family of another in less than a month. You're not that insensitive, are you, Owen?"

"Of course not. It's been a terrible time for all of us. But that isn't what I mean. I'm talking about her personal attitude toward me, as if I'd done something to her. As if she'd be glad if she never laid eyes on me again."

"I'm sorry if that's how you feel, but—"

"It's not just how I feel," Owen said, "it's the way things are. And you haven't answered my question. *Are* you and Cecca involved?"

"No. Not the way you mean."

"What other way is there?"

"You don't have to sleep with a woman to have a rapport with her."

"Is that all it is with you two? A rapport?"

"That's all it is."

"You swear to that?"

"If it's what it takes to convince you, yes, I do solemnly swear I am not having an affair with Cecca Bellini."

"Then it's something else," Owen said. "Or somebody else."

"I don't think she's romantically involved with anyone. In fact, I'm sure she's not."

"Would she have told you if she was?"

"I think so, yes."

"What *is* it, then? Why has she turned against me?"

"Maybe you're misinterpreting her actions—"

"I'm not."

"All right, then maybe it's that you're coming on too strong. Hanging around her all the time, calling her, dropping over at her house uninvited. Back off a little. The last thing she needs right now is to be pressured."

"I can't help it," Owen said miserably. "I think about her all the time, I dream about her, I can't stand not being near her. Dix, what am I going to do?"

His expression was even more rumpled; he looked like a big, gangly kid getting ready to bawl. Dix had always regarded him as something of an Inadequate Personality—likable, but emotionally underdeveloped. (And wasn't that a joke, him sitting in judgment of another man's inadequacies? In some ways he was an IP himself. Too many ways.) In the past he'd viewed Owen with compassion; you made allowances for your friends. But sitting here now, he could no longer work up any sympathy for the man. No feelings other than wariness, a lingering mistrust, and a vague dislike.

All of this an act, part of some sly ploy? Owen the tormentor, a cunning madman laughing behind his poor, fumbling, IP façade? It was possible. Anything was possible, no matter how bizarre; that was one lesson Dix Mallory had learned well in recent weeks. And even if Owen were as harmless as he'd always believed, his weakness was much less tolerable than it had been in the past. He sat diminished in Dix's eyes. Maybe, Dix thought harshly, because he himself sat diminished in his own eyes.

He said, "I don't have any advice for you, Owen." He meant to keep his voice neutral, but the words came out sounding cold. "Except what I said before. Back off, give Cecca some breathing room."

"I don't know if I can."

"If you care about her, you will."

It took him a few more minutes to pry Owen off the chair and out of the house. Five-ten by then: almost time to leave. He'd been calm enough before Owen's arrival; now he was keyed up, restless. The little scene they'd just played bothered him, and not only because he was uncertain of Owen's motives or his discovery that in any case he no longer cared for the man. Owen's questions had made him face something he'd been avoiding: his own feelings for Cecca.

He had told the truth about their relationship, but it was less than the complete truth. They were not involved, and yet they were. Bound by more than just their shared torment—a growing closeness, stirrings and yearnings that he sensed in her as he felt them in himself. Neither was yet ready or willing to bring it out into the open, to add another complication to their lives; and he wasn't sure he could handle a deeper relationship so soon after Katy's death. But the feelings, the capacity, were there, want them or not. Owen, whatever his motives, had cut straight through to the heart of the matter.

EIGHTEEN

Buckram Street was two blocks long and ran up the side of a hill at a steep slant. The houses in the lower block were small bungalows and ranch-style homes, on quarter-acre lots; the houses in the upper block were fewer and larger, mostly white frame and brick over stucco, built on half- to one-acre lots. Louise Kanvitz's property was one of the two biggest parcels, at the top on the east side—a two-story frame house with a partially enclosed front porch, surrounded by trees and shrubbery. The front yard was a cactus garden littered with exotic, and not very tasteful, wrought-iron, wood, and cement sculptures. A Jeep Wrangler was parked in the driveway. But what caught and held Dix's attention was the Ford station wagon drawn up at the curb in front.

The wagon was Cecca's.

He drove on past, made a tight loop where the street dead-ended at a patch of woods that crowned the hill, and braked to a stop behind the Ford. What was she doing here? On the same mission he was, probably. But she shouldn't have come alone, without telling him and without bringing along anything that had the persuasive power of the Beretta. She was inordinately afraid of guns; she'd made Chet sell two handguns and his hunting rifles after they were married. That was another reason Dix had wanted to confront Kanvitz alone.

He hurried through the garden, up onto the porch. There was an old-fashioned doorbell, the kind with a button inside a recessed circle like a nipple on a miniature breast; he pushed it. Chimes, not very

173

melodious. He waited, but the front door stayed shut. He pushed the button again, and when that also didn't bring anybody, he moved over to a nearby window. Drawn shade behind chintz curtains; he couldn't see inside. He worked the bell a third time. Still no response.

The restlessness in him had given way to a formless unease. He left the porch, followed a path through the cactus garden and along the side of the house, paralleling the driveway. At the rear the path right-angled toward a set of steps that led to a porch entrance. He climbed up there and knocked on the screen door. Listened to silence, knocked again, listened to more silence.

On impulse he opened the screen and tried the inner door. It was unlocked. He pushed it open, took a cautious step inside. Service porch, an archway on his left opening into the kitchen. Both the porch and the kitchen were empty. The house was still except for the faint hum of a refrigerator.

"Hello," he called. "Hello?"

Silence.

"Cecca? Louise? It's Dix Mallory."

He thought he heard something this time, movement somewhere toward the front. Footsteps? He couldn't be sure because the sound wasn't repeated. His unease deepened. He slid his hand into his jacket pocket, closed fingers around the Beretta, then walked all the way inside, letting the screen door bang behind him.

"Cecca? Are you in here?"

Movement again, the creak of a floorboard—definitely footsteps, hurrying. He went ahead to the archway. Just as he stepped into it, a swing door on the far side of the kitchen opened partway, cautiously, and Cecca's head appeared. There was a frozen moment as they stared across at each other. The look of her changed his edginess to alarm: Her face was milk white, her eyes wide and dark with fright.

"Oh, Dix!"

He went to her, yanked the door all the way open. She came up hard against him, put her arms around his waist and her head tight to his chest. There was a thin quivering in her body, like a wire vibrating in a high wind. He held her for a few seconds, then took her arms and moved her back away from him. Her skin was cold, and when he glanced down he saw that her arms were rough with gooseflesh.

"Cecca, what is it, what's happened?"

"*God*," she said.

"Where's Louise? Why didn't you answer the bell?"

"I was on the phone to the police. I didn't know it was you. I thought . . . I was afraid he'd come back."

"The police? What—?"

"The front hall," she said, "the stairs . . ."

He started to turn her so she could show him. She balked. "No, I'm not going back in there."

"All right. Wait here."

He crossed a formal dining room to the hallway beyond. The palms of his hands were moist; his mind seemed to be working in stuttering fashion, thoughts coming too fast and then not at all. The hall led him past a staircase to the upper floor. Two paces into the front foyer, he came to an abrupt standstill. There was no surprise in what he saw there, only a sick feeling of helplessness. His gorge rose; he swallowed to keep it down.

Louise Kanvitz lay crumpled at the bottom of the stairs, hips and legs twisted upward over the first three risers, veined and mottled flesh showing where her skirt had hiked up. Her head and shoulders were on the carpeted floor, head twisted at an impossible angle. Blood from a smashed nose streaked the lower half of her face. One eye, wide open, bulging goiterlike, stared sightlessly up at him.

Fell down the stairs, he thought. Tripped somehow . . . an accident . . .

But it wasn't. He knew that as unequivocally as he knew her neck was broken.

He retreated until he could no longer see her, then turned and ran back into the dining room. Cecca wasn't at the swing door; he found her in the kitchen, splashing her face with handfuls of cold tap water. He tore off a long section of paper towel from a hanging roll, gave it to her so she could dry off. There was a little color in her cheeks now. She seemed to have a better grip on herself.

She said, "He killed her, Dix. He killed her to keep her from telling who he is."

Dix nodded grimly. "How long have you been here?"

"Not long. A few minutes before you rang the bell."

"Why did you come alone?"

"She called me at the office this afternoon. She said she wanted to talk, she had something to tell me."

"About Katy's lover?"

"She wouldn't say. But it's obvious, isn't it?"

"You should have let me know."

"I tried to. You'd already left the university, so I called you at home, left a message on your machine.... You didn't get the message?"

"No. I didn't think to check the machine."

"Then why are *you* here? You weren't going to try to force the truth out of Louise—?"

"That's just what I was going to do."

"You can't admit that to St. John," she said. "We'll tell him you did get the message, you drove over to meet me—"

"St. John. Jesus, he'll be here any second."

"Dix, did you hear what I— Dix!"

He was already running. Out through the front of the house because it was faster that way, even though it took him a few seconds to fumble the door open. He could hear the sirens then—close, very close. Off the porch, across the yard, into the Buick. He had just enough time to lock the Beretta inside the glove compartment before the first police car turned into Buckram Street and came racing uphill.

St. John was angry. "I told you people to stay away from Louise Kanvitz. Didn't I tell you that?"

"And I keep telling you," Cecca said, "she called and said she wanted to see me. What was I supposed to do?"

"You should have notified me."

"If she'd wanted to talk to you, wouldn't she have called you instead? I was afraid she wouldn't talk at all if the police were here."

"You notified Mr. Mallory. Or claim you did."

"I *did*."

Dix said, "The message is still on my machine. We can go up to my house and listen to it if you like."

"You could have faked it."

"Faked it? Why in bloody hell would we do that?"

"I didn't say you did. I said you could have."

"You don't think we had anything to do with Kanvitz's death?"

"Did you, Mr. Mallory?"

"No! Cecca told you the woman was dead when she got here."

"Can anybody else corroborate the fact?"

"There was nobody else here! Dammit, St. John—"

They were sitting at a Formica-topped table in the kitchen; St.

John slapped it with the palm of his hand, a pistol-shot sound that made Cecca jump. "Don't come on hard to me, mister," he said to Dix. "You're on shaky ground as it is. The woman who owns this house is dead in the front hall—maybe an accident, maybe not. You two have no good reason to be here, especially after I warned you against it. At best you're guilty of trespassing—"

"And at worst we're murderers, is that it?"

"I'm going to tell you one more time in a polite way: Answer my questions truthfully and don't give me any more crap. Otherwise you'd better call your lawyer. Understood?"

Dix struggled to put a leash on his emotions. There was the harsh taste of frustration in his mouth. "Understood," he said thinly.

"Good." St. John took a cigarette from his shirt pocket, began his rolling routine on the tabletop. "Let's go through it again, Ms. Bellini," he said to Cecca. "What time did Louise Kanvitz call you?"

"About three-thirty."

"Was she calling from here or her gallery?"

"I don't know. She didn't say."

"What did she say, exactly?"

"That it was time we had another talk."

"Talk about what?"

"Katy Mallory."

"What specifically, concerning Mrs. Mallory?"

"I asked her that, but all she said was that I should come here after five-thirty. Then she hung up."

"What did you think she had in mind?"

"I wasn't sure at the time. But she sounded angry."

"At you?"

"I don't think so. At the man she was shielding, blackmailing, whatever. They must have had some sort of falling out."

"Over what?"

"Money. She wanted more to keep quiet . . . something like that. That's why he killed her."

"If he killed her. If anybody killed her."

"Have it your way."

"What time did you arrive here?"

"A little before five-thirty. Five minutes or so."

"And Mr. Mallory wasn't here yet."

"No, he wasn't."

"Why didn't you wait for him?"

"I don't know. I . . . I was nervous, I wanted to get it over with, to find out what she knew."

"Why did you go inside the house?"

"The front door was ajar and her car is in the driveway. I thought she must be here, that she hadn't heard the bell for some reason. I stepped into the foyer; I was going to call out her name."

"And that's when you saw the body."

"Yes."

"Did you touch her, touch anything in the foyer or on the stairs?"

"No. Just the door. I think I shut it."

"Why?"

"I'm not sure. I wasn't thinking too clearly."

"How long was it before you called us?"

"Almost immediately. A minute or two."

"And when did Mr. Mallory arrive?"

"Just as I finished talking to you."

St. John turned his vulpine gaze on Dix. After a few seconds he put the cigarette in his mouth, as if he were thinking about lighting it, changed his mind, and began thumb-rolling it on the table again. Floorboards creaked overhead: other officers moving around upstairs. Finding anything? This whole process was maddening in its mechanical slowness.

"It's your turn, Mr. Mallory," St. John said. "What did you do when you arrived?"

Dix told him. All of it, leaving out nothing except details of his conversation with Cecca and the Beretta.

"Did you touch the body?"

"No, I did not."

"We found Ms. Kanvitz's purse in the living room. Did either of you touch that?"

"No." But we damned well would have if we'd seen it. "I don't suppose there was anything in it that might help identify the man?"

"If there had been, I'd have told you. Did you touch anything on this floor? Open drawers, cabinets?"

"No," Dix said. "All we touched were doorknobs and the sink tap over there."

"Go upstairs?"

"No."

"Why were you outside when we arrived?"

"... What?"

"Simple question. You were out on the street next to your car when we arrived. Why?"

"Waiting for you. Why do you think?"

"You left Ms. Bellini in here alone while you went out front to wait? As upset as she was, in the house alone with a dead woman?"

"I didn't stay in the house," Cecca said. "I went into the backyard. I was there until I heard you come in through the front."

"Why the backyard?"

"I needed some air and I wasn't ready to face anybody yet. Are all of these questions necessary?"

"I think they are, yes—"

"Lieutenant." Another cop had opened the swing door and poked his head through. "See you for a minute?"

St. John went away with him. Dix reached over to take Cecca's hand; her fingers were still icy. She said, "He doesn't believe us."

"About why we came here, no."

"What do you think he'll do?"

"Nothing. What can he do? We've been cooperative and we haven't really broken any laws."

The swing door squeaked and St. John reappeared, alone. He stood behind his chair and looked down at each of them in turn—long, searching looks—before he said, "Did you know Louise Kanvitz owned a handgun?"

Dix said, "No," and Cecca shook her head.

"Thirty-two–caliber Iver Johnson revolver. Legally registered; officer found the permit upstairs. Box of ammunition for it, too. But not the weapon itself. It's nowhere in the house."

"Maybe she kept it at the gallery."

"Maybe. But her permit is for home premises."

"Well, we don't know anything about it," Dix said. "What difference does it make if her gun's missing? She wasn't shot; her neck was broken."

"It's a loose end. I don't like loose ends."

"Is that how you look at us? As loose ends?"

St. John was silent.

"Your men find anything else upstairs?" Dix asked.

"Nothing that would interest you."

"How about something that interests *you*?"

Again St. John didn't answer. He sat down. His cigarette was still on the table; he picked it up, looked at it, and then broke it in half between his thumb and forefinger, showering the table with shreds of tobacco.

"All right," he said flatly. "Let's go over your stories again one more time."

NINETEEN

Cecca could not seem to get warm.

She sat on the couch in the living room with a double Scotch, the furnace turned up to seventy-five. It was dark outside, nearly half past eight. St. John had detained them to the last to make a none-too-subtle point. And having made it, he hadn't bothered to issue any more warnings when he released them. All he'd said was "You'll hear from me, Mr. Mallory. You, too, Ms. Bellini."

She was alone now; Amy had gone upstairs to her room. So quiet in there she could hear the erratic thump of her heart. And every time she closed her eyes, every time she focused inward instead of outward, she could see Louise Kanvitz lying broken and bloody at the bottom of the stairs. She thought she would see that lifeless, bulging eye of Louise's for the rest of her life—a Cyclops to haunt her dreams.

Amy had taken the news well enough, as well as could be expected. She was afraid but just how deeply Cecca couldn't tell; most of the fear was locked within. She'd always been that way: emotions bottled up, not much outward display except in sudden sharp, brief outbursts when she was provoked beyond her limits. As a baby she hadn't cried much; as a little girl she had rarely thrown a tantrum. In fact, Cecca could remember seeing her cry only once since she'd passed the toddler stage—the day she'd told her Chet had moved out and she was filing for divorce.

Resilient at seventeen, yes, self-contained, but Amy couldn't handle this kind of psychological fear-pressure indefinitely. Neither

181

of them could. It would damage Amy just as it was damaging her. Survival was still the primary issue, and they would survive—Cecca refused to let herself think otherwise. But survival at what cost?

She started to lift the glass to her mouth, and almost dropped it. The fingers on her left hand had gone partially numb. They had a dead-white look, as if they'd been frostbitten. The ice in the glass radiating cold; and bad circulation on top of everything else. She went into the kitchen, ran hot water over her hand until the fingers began to tingle and turn a splotchy red. She was drying them with a dishtowel when the telephone rang.

Cecca stood rigidly, waiting for the machine to open the line. But it was only Laura Flores. She'd just heard about Louise Kanvitz, she said, and oh you poor dear, it must have been awful for you and Dix. What were you doing at Louise's house anyway? A nightmare, what's been going on lately—one hideous tragedy after another. Why are all these terrible things happening *here*? It makes you want to lock all your doors and windows and not ever go out anywhere again. Call me as soon as you can, Cecca, okay? I'm worried about you.

When the machine clicked off, Cecca finished her drink in one long swallow. News travels fast in a small town; she should have remembered that. And bad news travels fastest of all. Laura's call wouldn't be the last tonight. The phone would keep right on ringing, and then somebody would stop by—Owen, he would surely come— and she couldn't deal with it. She could not deal with any of it tonight.

Well? she thought.

There was no hesitation in the answer she gave herself. Admit it, Francesca: It's been there in the back of your mind all along.

She went upstairs, quickly, to have another talk with Amy.

Dix wasn't surprised to see her. He didn't ask why she'd driven up; it was almost as if he'd been expecting her.

"You okay?" he asked when she was inside.

"Not really. Hanging in there."

"Me, too. Take your jacket?"

"No, I'll leave it on. I'm cold."

"A drink might help."

"I don't think so. I've had enough liquor."

"Coffee?"

"Not that either. Have you had any calls?"

"Three so far," he said. "Laura and Jerry and that damn *Herald* reporter that tried to buttonhole us outside Kanvitz's house. I didn't talk to any of them."

"Laura called me, too. The first of many. I didn't think I could stand it alone."

"Did you tell Amy what happened?"

"Yes. She took it well enough."

"Sure it's a good idea to leave her home by herself?"

"I didn't," Cecca said. "I asked her to stay with my folks for a while, starting tonight. He can get to her there, too, of course, but ... I don't know, I just thought it would be best."

"I think so, too. She give you any argument?"

"A little. But she went. I want to call my dad, make sure she got there all right."

She made the call from the kitchen. Yes, Pop said, Amy was there and everything was fine. He hadn't asked any questions when she'd called before leaving home and he didn't ask any now. She wished she could confide in him. But there was no telling what he might do; he was unpredictable these days. And Ma's health was fragile enough as it was. At least they were accepting people, never prying or poking into her private life. There when she needed them; left her alone otherwise.

She said she'd talk to him again tomorrow, and that she loved him, then rang off. When she turned from the counter, Dix was standing a few feet away. He said, "Okay?"

"For now."

She was conscious again of her heartbeat. Its rhythm was rapid but less erratic than it had been earlier. She closed the gap between them, put her hands flat against his chest. They seemed very small to her at that moment, like a child's hands. Through his shirt she could feel the throb of his heart—quick, too, and as steady as her own. Her eyes held his, and when his arms came up she moved into their fold and fitted her body to his. She'd hugged him before ... earlier at Louise's ... but never like this. It was a good feeling. It felt right.

Against his chest she said, "Do you want to be alone tonight?"

"No."

Trust him now, this way, or she never would. You had to have complete trust in somebody at a time of crisis, above all other times. If you didn't, you were lost—you'd be trapped by suspicion forever.

"Neither do I," she said.

They undressed in the bedroom, by the pale light from the bedside lamp. She was unhurried and neither embarrassed nor shy, and this made him the same. Naked, her small body was firm, almost girlish, where Katy's had been long and ripe and soft; her breasts were half the size of Katy's, the nipples dark and hard rather than pale and plump; her pubic hair was as thick and black and curly as poodle fur, where Katy's had been sparse, blond, downy—

Angry at himself, he yanked down the mental curtain. Cecca, this is Cecca. No more comparisons. Cecca.

He drew her into his arms. Her flesh was cold and she was shivering. He kissed her tenderly, and when they lay down together he pulled the covers up over their bodies. He stroked her until the trembling eased, until there was warmth instead of chill under his hands; the skin of her breasts and hips was satiny once the gooseflesh disappeared. They kissed deeply then, and he continued to caress her, heard her breathing quicken, felt her begin to knead his flanks with mounting urgency and then take hold of him with her small fingers. Long minutes of this, sweet minutes.

But none of it had any effect.

There was not even a stir of arousal in his loins. It was as if he'd gone dead from the waist down.

"I can't," he said after a while. "It's no use, I just . . . can't."

"It's all right," she said.

"It's not all right."

"We'll just hold each other."

"I'm sorry, Cecca . . ."

"Shh. Lie still. Rest."

"I can't rest."

She reached behind her. The room went moonlit dark.

"Yes you can. Sleep. We'll both sleep."

"I can't sleep," he said.

And slept.

Sometime toward morning, he awoke with a hard-on.

That was the proper term for it. A great, throbbing, painful thing such as he hadn't experienced in more than fifteen years, since the early days of his marriage. A swelling pressure, a blood balloon that felt as though it would burst at any second. When he moved, the light friction from the sheet covering him was excruciating. He lay still, waiting for it to diminish. It didn't. If anything, the pressure and the hurt intensified. Finally, almost in desperation, he turned toward Cecca sleeping beside him.

She moved when his body touched hers, came half awake, murmuring something; then, when she felt the heat and bone-hardness, she said, "Oh!" and woke fully. "Oh, Dix."

"Do you still want to?" he whispered.

"Yes. Yes."

Their joining was awkward, fumbling, and when he filled her completely, they both gasped. For him, as they moved together, it was mostly painful, with very little pleasure and faint random twitches of guilt. His climax was sudden and fiery, and it brought no relief. He was just as hard and swollen afterward as before. He knew that it had not been good for her either, and immediately he tried to withdraw; but she held him tightly with her arms and legs.

"Stay with me," she said against his ear. "I like you there, I like the way you feel."

He stayed, and still he did not diminish. For a while they were motionless; then Cecca began to nuzzle his neck, to pet him with her fingertips. He held her fiercely, and soon the rhythms started again, now slow, now gentle, now synchronized. And this time it *was* good for both of them, relieving and searching. This time he felt mostly pleasure, with very little pain and no twitches at all.

"Dix?"

"Mmm?"

"Any regrets?"

"No. You?"

"No, but I keep thinking I should have."

"Why?"

"Katy. Katy's house, Katy's bed, Katy's husband . . ."

"Not anymore. 'That was in another country, and besides, the wench is dead.' "

". . . I know she hurt you, but that sounds cold."

"I didn't mean it like that. I just meant that she's gone. So is the man she was married to, in a way."

"Gone? What way?"

"I'm not the same person I was before Katy died. I've changed and I'm still changing and that's probably a good thing."

"Why do you think it's good?"

"I don't particularly like the old Dix Mallory."

"Why not?"

"He isn't much of a man."

"I always had the opposite view. I still do."

"You're not looking at him from in here."

"What don't you like about yourself?"

"Mostly it's what I've done with my life, the way I've . . . thrown a lot of it away."

"How do you mean, thrown it away?"

"Too many compromises, large and small. Self-delusion. Contentment with mediocrity."

"You think you're mediocre?"

". . . Yes."

"If you are, then so am I. So are most people."

"But we don't have to be. We don't have to settle for it."

"No, that's true. We don't."

"Let's talk about you. You don't really consider yourself ordinary?"

"I'm not that self-analytical. But if I were . . . yes, I'm ordinary."

"You must have taken a good look at yourself a time or two."

"A time or two."

"And what did you see? Who is Cecca Bellini?"

"An unfulfilled woman."

"You said that without missing a beat. Why unfulfilled? Not because of Chet."

"God, no. You can't think all a woman needs for fulfillment is the right kind of man?"

"No. That was a statement, not a question. Sexism, at least, isn't one of my failings."

"Well, it has nothing to do with Chet. It's . . . expectations, I suppose. I always expected a lot of myself. I don't mean I had visions of becoming somebody important or famous, being a mover and shaker. Or that I had any specific goals I haven't met. It's just that I expected more of myself, more out of life. And it's my fault I haven't gotten it."

"Settled for less when you didn't have to? Opted for what was easy, safe? Accepted and never questioned unless you were forced to?"

"Essentially, yes."

"So did I. It's the same feeling I have about myself, exactly the same. You call it unfulfillment, I call it mediocrity."

"Birds of a feather."

"Well? Aren't we?"

"I guess we are. And I guess I've changed, too."

"Grown more self-aware."

"Yes."

"And maybe found out some things about yourself that you don't like?"

"That, too."

"Things you want to change, if you can?"

"If I can."

". . . Funny."

"What is?"

"I feel closer to you than I've felt to anyone in a long time. Closer than I was to Katy for the last dozen years of our marriage."

"That makes me want to cry. And I'm not sure why."

"Do you feel close to me?"

"Yes. But I don't know how much of it is comfort, a reaction to what's ripping both our lives apart."

"Neither do I. But we'll find out."

"Yes. We'll find out."

Cecca left at seven. They had coffee together first, in the kitchen, and there was no awkwardness between them, no daylight doubts—as if they were old lovers rather than new ones. Dix still felt as close to her as he had in bed, in the dark. It was true, what he'd said to her, painfully true: He was closer to Cecca than he had been to Katy at any time except in the beginning. He could not have talked to Katy as he had to her, even in the dark. He could not have told Katy about his feelings of mediocrity.

After Cecca was gone he shaved and dressed—they'd showered together earlier—and then called the university and told the registrar's office he wouldn't be in today. The flu, he said. Two seconds after he disconnected, the phone bell went off. And as soon as it did, as if it were giving off some sort of negative energy that stimulated his brain synapses, he knew it was the tormentor and he knew what the son of a bitch was going to say.

The good feeling the night and Cecca had instilled in him vanished even before he heard the smarmy filtered voice. "How was it last night, Dix? Was it worth waiting for?"

He tried to walk away from the rest, out into the hall, out of the house. But the volume on the machine was turned up and he heard most of it before he completed his escape.

"Was Francesca better than Katy? What do you think, Dix? *I* think Katy was better, myself. All things considered, I think your wife was a much better fuck than Cecca. . . ."

TWENTY

Jerry Whittington's office was in a hundred-year-old High Victorian Italianate downtown that had once housed the Eagles Lodge. Twenty years earlier it had been chopped up into office space for a clutch of lawyers, CPAs, and financial consultants. Jerry wasn't the workaholic Tom Birnam had turned into, but he believed in putting in a full day; he was available for business before nine-thirty on most weekday mornings. Both he and Margaret Allen were on the premises and busy when Dix walked in at twenty past nine.

"I'm glad you stopped by," Jerry said when they were alone in his private office. Away from his business he dressed casually and stylishly, but here he favored his clients with conservative suits and ties. Dark blue silk today. "What the hell happened last night? There're rumors flying all over town."

"Not much to tell," Dix said. "Louise Kanvitz had a couple of paintings of Katy's. Cecca found out she sold them for a high price to some mystery buyer. I wanted to find out who bought them and why he'd pay such a price. I asked Cecca to come with me; she knew Kanvitz better than I did."

"Did you find out who the buyer was?"

"No. She was dead when we got there."

"Broken neck, wasn't it? From a fall downstairs?"

"Evidently."

"Accident?"

"What else would it be, Jerry?"

"Hey, don't get defensive. I told you rumors were flying."

189

"I suppose because the police kept us for a long time."

"They did, didn't they?"

"They asked a lot of questions," Dix said. "They always do in situations like that. The only thing Cecca and I are guilty of is being in the wrong place at the wrong time."

"I never thought any different. Lord, what a rotten few weeks for you. For all of us, but you especially. You must feel as if the gods have it in for you."

"Somebody has it in for me, all right."

Jerry didn't react. Just sat there behind his desk with an expression of grave concern on his handsome face.

Dix said, "Just when I think things can't possibly get any worse, I find out they can. First Katy's death, then her infidelity, and then Louise Kanvitz last night."

"Katy's . . . infidelity, did you say?"

"She was having an affair before she died. Three months or more."

Jerry's gaze shifted, turned into one of his lopsided squints. "I don't believe that," he said. "Are you sure?"

"I'm sure. And the hell you don't believe it."

"What do you mean?"

"I mean you knew she was cheating. You as much as admitted to Cecca last week that you knew. Why didn't you tell me?"

"Oh, shit, Dix . . ."

"Why didn't you tell me?"

"I *didn't* know, that's why. Not for sure."

"Who's the man, Jerry?"

"I wish I knew."

"You must have some idea."

"But I don't, that's the hell of it."

"All right, then what made you suspicious of Katy?"

"I saw her and a man together one afternoon about six weeks ago. In her car."

"Where was this?"

"East Valley Road," Jerry said. "I was coming back from seeing a client out that way and I passed her. Neither of us was going fast— forty, forty-five. It was Katy's Dodge and she was at the wheel; I'm positive of that. In fact, I waved. She . . . pretended not to see me. Looked away."

"You didn't get a good look at the man?"

"No. He had his head down. I didn't even get an idea of his age."

"So far it sounds innocent enough. She may not have recognized you."

"I asked her about it," Jerry said. "The next day—the swim party at Sid's, remember?"

"Sid's party was on a Saturday. So the day you saw her was a Friday."

"A Friday, right."

"What did she say?"

"Well, I wasn't trying to catch her out or anything. Just kidding around with her. You know, 'Who was the man I saw you with on East Valley Road yesterday?' "

"And?"

"She denied it. It wasn't her, it wasn't her car. Said I must have been imagining things."

"Is that all she said?"

"It was the way she said it, Dix. Nervous, flustered—guilty look on her face. And she told me not to say anything to you or anybody else about it because she didn't want rumors getting started. Practically warned me to keep my mouth shut."

"Did you?"

"Yes and no." Jerry tugged at the knot in his tie, as if it had grown too tight. "I asked around here and there—you know, discreetly. To see if there was anything to find out."

"Was there?"

"No. Hell, Dix, don't blame me for that. You're one of my best friends; I figured I had an obligation."

"So you'd have told me if you'd verified it, learned the name of her lover."

"Before the accident, I might have. After she was dead I couldn't have hurt you any more than you already were. That's why I kept quiet when you hinted around about it on the phone last week."

"You let it slip to Cecca."

"She's the only one. I was worried about you. I thought maybe you were taking Katy's death so hard because you'd found out somehow that she was having an affair. And you had."

"Not then. Just recently."

"You have any idea who the man is?"

"Not yet. Soon, though."

"How'd you find out she had a lover? If you don't mind my asking."

"I do mind, Jerry. I'd rather not talk about it."

"Sure, if that's the way you feel. But if you decide you want to hash it out, a sympathetic ear—I'm available. Anytime, day or night. I really am on your side."

Are you? Dix thought.

Can I trust you even if you *aren't* the tormentor?

Everything was all right at her house. No new packages, no damages, no nocturnal intrusion. Cecca went through every room, checked each door and window, to make sure.

When she was done she took another quick shower and changed clothes. Blouse and a pair of tailored slacks rather than the suits or dresses she usually wore on weekdays. She could not bring herself to go to Better Lands today. Face Tom, face a normal workday . . . no. There was one piece of business she did have to take care of this morning, though: deliver Elliot Messner's counteroffer to the Hagopians. She'd been too upset and too needy to do it last night.

The family was living temporarily in a one-bedroom apartment on the east side, near the river; she drove there first thing. Mr. Hagopian had already left for work, but his wife and children were home. Cecca gave Mrs. Hagopian the written counteroffer, went over it with her, and then asked her to leave a message at Better Lands when she and her husband had reviewed it and made a decision. The impression Mrs. Hagopian gave was that the response would be quick and favorable. Seventy-five hundred dollars really wasn't much when you were already prepared to spend a quarter of a million.

From there Cecca took the freeway north to Santa Rosa. On the way she allowed herself to think about last night—analytically, for the first time. On a purely physical level sex with Chet had been better, more exciting; he had almost always been able to make her climax, one way or another. But to him sex was an Olympic marathon event, with all sorts of wild experimentation, and he had worn her out in bed. Dix was much gentler, much more considerate. With him it was controlled, adult—and on a deeper level, more satisfying. If sexual boredom or dissatisfaction was what had driven Katy to another man, she must have suffered from some sort of biological deficiency. One that Cecca Bellini didn't have. After only one night with Dix Mallory, she felt she could be physically satisfied with and by him for the rest of her life.

Which opened up the larger question: Was she in love with him?

She thought she might be. But it was too soon to commit herself to it. The intense connection, the closeness, might well fade without the mortal danger they shared to enhance it. When their lives were normal again, if they ever were, then she would be better able to judge. Her feelings and his. How they interacted, how they communicated. Then she'd know for sure. Meanwhile—

Meanwhile, don't even think about the future. Hold on to Dix and let him hold on to her because neither of them could get through this alone.

Lieutenant St. John was "unavailable," according to the desk sergeant at the police station. The sergeant wouldn't elaborate on that, nor would he give Dix any information on developments in the Louise Kanvitz investigation. "You'll have to ask the lieutenant," he said. When would he be available? "I can't tell you that because I don't know."

The old runaround.

The law didn't care what they were going through. All the law cared about was the law—the goddamn cold, sanctified letter of the law.

At Santa Rosa Memorial they wouldn't let her see Kevin Harrell. Still in ICU; still not allowed visitors. His condition? No change: critical but stable.

She didn't know what to do with herself when she left the hospital. At loose ends . . . maybe she *should* have gone to Better Lands. No, she'd made the right decision there; better alone today than dealing with Tom and office work. She drove out of town to the west, as far as Forestville in the Gravenstein apple country. There was a place just outside the village that sold homemade apple butter; she stopped and bought three jars. Then she drove back through Sebastopol to Santa Rosa, and without thinking about it, headed out to the Codding Town shopping center. It was after twelve by then. She went into one of the restaurants in the mall and ate a sandwich. Macy's and the Emporium and half a dozen other stores after that. She bought two slips, a blouse, a vest, a set of towels, none of which she needed or even wanted. Mindless shopping spree, and she didn't know why she was doing it until it was over and she was back in the car. It was a groping for normalcy. Drive in the country, apple butter, lunch at the mall, clothing and household items ... activities, things, that represented the sane, mundane way of life—her life—she'd always taken for granted.

Who is Cecca Bellini? Dix had asked last night, and she'd said "an unfulfilled woman." Yes. A woman whose expectations had never quite been realized. Yes. But at this moment, on this bright sunny September afternoon, she would have given anything to be the old accepting, secure, unfulfilled Cecca Bellini again and for the rest of her life.

The woman in the hospital bed looked like a caricature of Eileen. The plump cheeks were sunken, as if some of the tissue in them had collapsed. The apple-rosy skin tone had bleached out to a chalky white. The mischievous eyes were dull, withdrawn. The big, competent nurse's hands lay on the blanket at her sides, unmoving, fingers cramped, like the arthritic appendages of an old lady.

She was aware of him, though, in a remote kind of way. As soon as he entered the room and spoke her name, she said, "Dix. What're you doing here?"

"Came to see you."

"That's nice. Everything okay?"

"Yes. How about you?"

"Wish they'd let me get up. I'm not sick."

"No, of course you're not."

"They tell me I need rest," Eileen said. "But I just had a vacation—" Abruptly her face twisted and she made a thin sound in her throat, as if a terrible memory had just struck her. But it must have been a fragment, a kind of subliminal blip; her face smoothed almost immediately and she smiled at him with cracked, bloodless lips. "Dix?"

"Yes, honey."

"Honey? Why, you flirt."

He could feel her pain; it seemed to flow out of her and into him, as if by osmosis. It hurt him and it made him feel all the more helpless. "I always flirt with attractive women," he said.

"Flatterer. I'll tell Cecca."

"She won't mind."

Eileen shifted her hips and upper body, wincing. Then she frowned and said again, "Tell Cecca. Dix . . . tell Cecca."

"Tell her what? That I flirted with you?"

"No. The accident."

"What accident."

"Katy . . . the accident."

"Katy's accident? What about it?"

"Pellagrin day."

That was what it sounded like. Her pronunciation was indistinct, as if the words were sticky in her mouth. He leaned closer. "I don't understand, honey. Say it again."

"Tell Cecca."

"I'll tell her. Pellagrin day. What does it mean?"

"God, my mouth is die . . . dry. Water?"

"On the table. I'll pour some for you."

"Big glass. Thirsty. Don't know why . . . so damn thirsty."

She seemed to like having company, despite the fact that she wasn't tracking very well. The hospital sounds and smells and the cloying scent of her get-well flowers had begun to dredge up memories of his mother's lingering death, but he would have forced himself to stay with her a while longer if Helen Garstein and Beth Birnam hadn't walked in. He tried then to make a quick exit, but they followed him out into the hall and pestered him to explain about Louise Kanvitz. It was just as well; give them what they wanted and maybe they would leave Cecca and him alone. He repeated the story he'd told Jerry earlier, fended off questions, and finally made his escape. He couldn't tell whether or not they were satisfied. He didn't care either way.

Pellagrin day, he thought as he rode the elevator down to the main floor. Didn't make any sense. A pellagrin was a person who was afflicted with pellagra, a protein-deficiency disease that attacked the central nervous system. He didn't know anybody who suffered from pellagra. Another word instead . . . pelican? Pelican day. That didn't make sense either. How about Pelagian? he thought wryly. A Pelagian was one of the heretical followers of the British monk Pelagius, who denied the doctrine of original sin and held that man has perfect freedom to do right or wrong.

Babble phrase, he decided. Meaningless non sequitur. What could "pellagrin day" possibly have to do with Katy's "accident"?

*   *   *

On the way back from Santa Rosa Cecca detoured by Los Alegres Valley Hospital. And for the second time today she was refused visiting privileges. Bad timing: Eileen had had several callers and Dr. Mulford had decided not to allow any more. She'd been given a sedative.

Uptown Cecca stopped at Hallam's Bookshop to see if Amy was all right. Amy was fine. Uncommunicative but fine.

As she drove to Shady Court, she agonized again over the wisdom of letting Amy stay with her folks. Suppose the tormentor went after her there, did something to all three of them, blew up the house as he'd blown up the Harrells' cabin? The thought was chilling, and no more unlikely than anything else that had happened. But Amy wasn't safe in her own home, and there was nowhere out of town to send her—or Ma and Pop—that was safe either. No safe place for any of them.

The house was as she'd left it that morning. She called Better Lands to check her voice-mail. Nothing from the Hagopians yet; it was too early. Two messages from Elliot Messner, wanting an appointment "to take another squint" at the Andersen farm—that was all. She played back the first four messages on her own machine, none of which she cared to return. The fifth message was from the tormentor. As soon as she heard his voice saying her name, she shut off the machine and then rewound the tape.

In her bedroom she packed a small overnight case. Then she locked the house and got back into the car and went the only place she had left to go—the only place, really, she wanted to be. Up to the Ridge. To Dix's house. To Dix.

He sat up in bed, listening.

The dark in the room was heavy, clotted. Cecca was asleep beside him; he could hear the steady rhythm of her breathing. He glanced at the bedside clock. The red digital numerals read 3:04.

The last foggy remnants of sleep dissipated; he was fully alert now. He didn't know what it was that had brought him up out of a deep sleep. A sound? A psychic awareness of danger? Whatever it was, it had accelerated his pulse rate, put a clutch of tension across his shoulder blades.

A wallboard cracked somewhere; otherwise the house was still. Something outside? He swung his legs out of bed, stood up. An early-morning chill had penetrated the bedroom and he was conscious of it on his naked body; he'd meant to put on pajamas after he and Cecca made love, but a warm lassitude had kept him burrowed under the covers and eventually carried him off to sleep. Shivering a little, he peered through the window in the front wall. The sky was black, coated with a high overcast that blocked out moonshine and starlight. There was a wind, thin, gusty, rustling and flexing the branches of the heritage oak. Through the branches he had a view of streetlights and night-lights winking on the flat part of town below. Beneath the angle of the roof, the near corner of the garage was visible; its back door was shut, as was the gate nearby that led to the front yard.

Dix moved to the windows overlooking the side garden. Compressed shadows and vague shapes, all of them motionless except for the stir of the wind. The hillside with its tall, dry grass, rising beyond the boundary fence, seemed to harbor the same empty shadows. False alarm, he thought. He couldn't remember dreaming, but maybe he had been; maybe the feeling of menace had come out of a gathering nightmare—

Movement on the far side of the garage, where a low cement retaining wall separated it from the hillside.

A faint carrying sound—brittle, as of something breaking.

There was a clenching sensation in his groin; he leaned closer to the glass. The movement wasn't repeated and he couldn't penetrate the darkness. An animal? The Ridge was crawling with raccoons, possums, skunks, deer. No reason for a man to be prowling over there. Nothing on that side of the garage except bags of rotting leaves he'd intended to use as mulch in the vegetable garden, some discarded pieces of lumber, a stack of dried-out prunings from the oak tree that he'd meant to haul to the dump—

Sudden flare of light, down low to the ground.

And behind it, for just an instant, the silhouette of a man crouched or kneeling.

Almost immediately there was another flare, and this time it didn't wink out. It wavered, steadied—and began to blossom.

Oh Jesus!

He'd been frozen; now he whirled to the nightstand, bumped the drawer open, dragged out the little Beretta he'd brought in from the car on Wednesday night. The sounds he made woke Cecca. She sat up as he fumbled feet into slippers.

"Dix, what's the matter?"

"The son of a bitch is outside setting a fire."

"*Fire?* The house—?"

"Garage." He ran around the foot of the bed, yanked his robe off the door hook. "Quick, get down to the yard . . . garden hose beside the door. I'm going after him."

Dix rushed downstairs in the dark, pulling the robe around him with one hand. Unlocked the side door and ran outside. The wind had caught the fire in the prunings and decaying leaves, was fanning it out low along the garage wall. If it got into the tinder-dry grass on the hillside . . .

He pounded up the cutout steps to the flagstone terrace built around the oak's massive truck. The fireglow lit up a small portion of the hill behind the garage: empty as far as he could tell. He pushed through a nest of ferns, climbed over the grapestake fence onto the slope, and ran parallel to the fence until he could see the front section of his property. The asphalt parking area, the driveway, were empty; so was the lower sweep of Rosemont Lane. He swung his head to peer up the hillside. Nothing moved up there except the wind-ruffled grass.

Which way? He stood shivering, aware but uncaring that his robe hung open and the breeze blew frigid against his bare skin. The rage in him was murderous, the gun cold and clammy in his fingers. Which way, goddammit?

He went ahead a few more yards. Trampled grass appeared on his left, an irregular trail of it leading at an angle uphill past the darkened bulk of the Bradford house, his nearest neighbors a hundred and fifty yards to the north. He started to run upward along the swath. Too late, too late—he knew that even before he heard the car engine throb into life in the distance. The tormentor had driven his car to the top of the dead-end street that ran up the west side of the hill, parked it just below the crest. From there it had been an easy walk over and down this side.

In frustration Dix slapped the flat surface of the Beretta against his leg. Part of him wanted to keep going, all the way to the top, even though the sound of the car was already diminishing. Reason and the crackle and smoke smell of the fire kept him from doing it. He turned back toward the garage.

The wind was blowing down from the west, pressing the fire in against the garage wall. Flames licked along the base of the wall, but they hadn't taken hold on it. Like the walls of the house, it was made of heavy cedar sheets treated with a fire-retardant chemical.

The roof, too, was fire-resistant—a lightweight composition material that resembled shakes. There was enough time to get the blaze under control before it did serious damage to the garage. The only real danger, particularly if the wind shifted, lay in sparks jumping the retaining wall and setting off the dry grass.

Dix ran on a long slant down to the fence. The yard lights and the kitchen lights were on, he realized then. And Cecca was out in the yard, wearing one of his old robes, dragging the garden hose toward the garage. She'd already turned the water on; as soon as she reached the building she lifted the spray nozzle, squeezed out a jet that made a thin hissing noise when it struck the burning debris. He climbed back over the fence, remembered the gun, and pocketed it before he reached her side.

"Don't aim at the fire," he told her. "The grass above the retaining wall—soak that first. There's another hose out front for me."

She nodded and he rushed away from her, around the garage to the far front corner. The second hose lay coiled near the stairs to the vegetable garden. He turned the bib on, took the hose atop the retaining wall. Cecca, he saw, was soaking the grass as he'd instructed her. He directed his stream of water onto the prunings and lumber and bags of leaves, most of which had been deliberately clumped together to form a pyre. The fire was still contained there; it hadn't had enough time or fuel to burn hot. Between them, working with the two hoses, they kept it contained and had it out in less than three minutes.

He was amazed to find, then, that none of the neighbors had been aroused. The Bradfords' house was still dark and nobody had come up from below. It had been a frantic few minutes, but his own heightened senses to the contrary, it had all happened without sufficient noise to raise an alarm. The fire had burned in a place where it couldn't be seen except by someone close by and uphill. And the Bradfords' bedroom faced another direction.

He listened for sirens. No sirens. Then he threw the hose down, went back to shut off the bib, scuffed around among the sodden debris to make sure there were no hot spots, and finally joined Cecca.

"Damn lucky the bastard's not an accomplished arsonist," he said. "Did you call the fire department?"

"I thought about it, but it seemed more urgent to try to keep the fire from spreading."

"Glad you didn't. I'm not sure my nerves could stand any more upheaval tonight."

"Shouldn't we report it? To St. John, at least?"

"In the morning."

"You didn't get a look at him up there, did you?"

"No, dammit. Not even a glimpse. He had his car parked on High Street, on the back side of the hill."

She hugged herself. "It's freezing out here. Let's go inside."

He left his wet and blackened slippers on the mat, padded into the hall to turn on the heat. Upstairs, he donned a pair of slipper socks and a warmer robe. When he came back down, Cecca was making coffee in the kitchen.

"Dix . . . where did you get the gun?"

The question caught him off guard. "Gun?"

"I saw it in your hand when you climbed over the fence. Where did you get it?"

"I bought it."

"Why?"

"Why? Why do you think?"

"I hate firearms," she said. "You know how much I hate firearms."

"I'm not crazy about them either. But this is different. Like it or or not, we have to have some way to protect ourselves."

"Is that the only reason you bought the gun, for protection?"

"Of course. What kind of question is that?"

"If you'd caught him on the hill, what would you have done? Would you have shot him?"

"Not unless he attacked me. I'd have brought him back here and held him for St. John."

"Are you sure you wouldn't have just shot him down in cold blood, after all he's done to us? Absolutely sure?"

"Absolutely sure," he said.

But he wasn't. He wasn't sure at all.

TWENTY-ONE

The buildings that made up the Andersen farm—sixty-year-old one-story house, barn, chicken coop, pumphouse—looked fine from a distance. And from certain angles closer in, too, as in Owen's photographs. The setting was attractive: wooded hill behind the house and barn, eucalyptus-flanked access drive, fields of alfalfa and corn, a ten-tree apple orchard. It was only when you got up close to the buildings that you realized how much repair work needed to be done. The farmhouse wanted paint, a new roof, a new front porch; the barn had gapped and missing boards in two walls and its doors hung crooked from a sagging lintel. The wire on the coop was badly rusted and would have to be replaced, and the coop itself needed shoring up. The fences around the yard and those that bounded the fields and orchard were tumbledown. The fields hadn't been plowed or cultivated in four years, since old Frank Andersen had been diagnosed with cancer. Weeds and grass grew thigh-high under the apple trees.

From a real estate agent's point of view, it had seemed like a white elephant. Tom Birnam had taken on the listing as a favor to Andersen's widow and two daughters, and he'd asked Cecca to handle it as a favor to him. The first time she'd viewed it, ten days ago, she'd thought it was the kind of property that might well take up a lot of her time and effort and never make her a dime's worth of commission—one that would be looked at but not bought by dozens of straightforward clients and bargain hunters, all the while deteriorating more and more from lack of upkeep. One day in the far future, somebody would finally decide to take it on spec at a rock-bottom price, but it might not be her listing anymore—or Better Lands'—when that happened.

So then here came Elliot Messner, the very first prospect she'd shown it to, and it was beginning to look like a quick sale after all. As with the Hagopians, she'd sensed his positive reaction on the first showing; obviously he saw something in the place—a reclamation challenge, maybe—that she didn't and any number of others wouldn't. The fact that he'd asked for this second look was even more encouraging. He was hooked; she was fairly sure of it. If he didn't see anything today to change his mind, she thought he would make an offer as soon as the escrow closed on his Brookside Park property.

She wished she cared.

She didn't seem to care about much of anything today, including the fact that the Hagopians had come in first thing to accept Elliot's counteroffer and sign a purchase agreement. There was an apathy in her that she couldn't seem to shake. On the one hand, it had allowed her to function at the office and to keep her appointment with Elliot that afternoon. On the other hand, she knew how dangerous that sort of feeling could be if she allowed it to continue. Prelude to a breakdown, the inability to function at all. Underneath the layer of indifference, her nerves were like sparking wires: Fray them any more and they would short-circuit.

The dusty yard was deserted when she drove in. She was on time; Elliot was late. She parked near the picket fence fronting the farmhouse, sat there for a minute or two, and then decided to get out. Although she could see the buildings of a neighboring farm less than half a mile away, the place had a desolate, lonely feel. A family's home once, teeming with vitality—now dormant, waiting for somebody to breathe new life into it or else to die. Freda Andersen had moved out as soon as her husband passed away, into the home of one of her daughters in town; the other married daughter lived in Texas. Two goats and the chickens had been sold off. There was nothing left but ghosts.

The wind was strong out of a partly overcast sky; Cecca buttoned her beige linen blazer. Clouds running overhead made irregular shadow patterns on the fields and nearby hills. The only audible sound was the ratchety turning of the blades in a rusted windmill behind the pumphouse. To her, its rhythm was like the beating of a weak heart.

She glanced at her watch, then out toward Hamlin Valley Road. Still no sign of Elliot. This was the reason she preferred to pick up clients and bring them to a property. But Elliot had had some sort of meeting in San Francisco and insisted on coming here directly from that. Not that it mattered, really, if he was late. She had nothing else she needed or wanted to be doing.

When the wind began to chill her, she slid back inside the station wagon. Sat there with the apathy wrapped around her like a shawl. And yet in her mind's eye she could see again the image of Dix climbing over the fence last night with the gun in his hand. The image made her even colder.

Her fear and loathing of firearms was almost pathological. Why, she didn't know; some phobias even a psychiatrist couldn't explain. She had never been shot at or threatened with a gun; never seen anyone hurt with one; never even touched one. Yet the first time she'd been confronted with a real handgun, her grandfather's target pistol at the age of six, she had reacted with shrieking terror, as if it were a snake coiled to strike at her. Ever since, she couldn't bear anything to do with them. She even shied away from watching make-believe shootouts in films.

She'd urged Dix to get rid of the gun he'd bought; his refusal had led to a brief and futile argument. She could see his point: They had to have some sort of protection. But what if he'd lied to her, or at best evaded her, when he'd said he would not have committed cold-blooded murder last night? What if the opportunity arose again and he *did* shoot down the tormentor? He would never be the same to her again; she could not love him, be with him. Irrational or not, and no matter what the circumstances, a man who pointed a gun at another human being and pulled the trigger would always be a source of revulsion for her.

The sound of a car laboring in low gear penetrated her awareness. She glanced into the rearview mirror, saw Elliot's dark-blue Lexus jouncing through the ruts toward the farmyard. She waited until he drew up behind the wagon before she stepped out.

"Sorry I'm late, Francesca," he said. "Meeting took a little longer than I expected." His smile, boyishly lopsided, went at odds with his professional outfit of a tan corduroy suit and a black pullover sweater. Appropriate. As far as she could tell, that was exactly the way he was—a clashing mixture of the intelligent adult college professor and the irrepressibly horny kid. He and Chet would have got along famously, she thought, at least on the subject of women.

"No problem," she said.

"Been waiting long?"

"Ten minutes or so."

"You look tired. Rough night?"

"I didn't sleep very well."

"Sleeping alone does have its drawbacks."

He said that offhandedly, through his crooked smile, but his eyes were steady on hers; he wanted a reaction. She didn't give him one. She said, "Where would you like to start? The house?"

"Fine by me."

He followed her onto the porch and she keyed them in. Cobwebs and dust. Musty smells of old wood, old wallpaper. All of the Andersens' furnishings had been taken away except for oddments here and there that the widow and her daughters hadn't wanted: a couple of chairs, a catchall table, some knickknack shelves, a carpet runner in the front hall. For Cecca, at least, there was a sadness in the leavings, in the dark squares and ovals on the walls where pictures had once hung. Elliot didn't seem affected. He took notice only of what interested him.

In the living room he said, "Look at that fireplace. I'll bet you don't see decorative tile inlays very often anymore."

"No, you don't."

In the parlor he said, "I could use this as my study. Plenty of light, view of the hills, no direct sun to fade book jacket spines. What do you think, Francesca?"

"I think it would make a fine study."

And in the largest of the rooms at the rear he said, "This ought to be big enough for my bed. It's a California king."

"Uh-huh."

"Water bed. I wouldn't own anything else."

"Uh-huh."

"You have a water bed, Francesca?"

"No."

"Ever slept in one?"

"A couple of times. I don't care for them."

"Some aren't very good. Mine's the best they make."

"I'm sure you wouldn't have settled for less."

"You ever make love in a water bed?" he asked.

Grinning, looking for a reaction again. This time she gave him one. "That's none of your business, Elliot."

"No, probably not," he said cheerfully. "*Have* you made love in a water bed?"

She turned toward the doorway without answering.

"There's nothing like it," he said behind her. "It's more comfortable, for one thing. And the motion of the water heightens the pleasure. No kidding, it really does."

He had succeeded in doing what she hadn't been able to all day: chip through the shell of her apathy. She was angry now; she bit back a sharp rebuke. I do not need this crap, she thought. Today of all days, I do not need to be sexually harassed.

She walked into the kitchen. Half-dinette table, one rickety chair, and on the windowsill over the sink, a Mason jar filled with the dessicated remains of flowers so long dead they were unidentifiable. Elliot was close behind her, like a dog at heel. She turned at the sink to face him.

"The kitchen," she said flatly. "Is there anything else you'd care to see?"

The boyish leer. "Yes. But not in here."

"Then we'll go outside—"

He leaned past her to look briefly out the window. When he straightened again he was close to her, too close. She tried to slide away; he caught hold of her arms, turning her so that her hips were against the drainboard.

"Dammit, Elliot, what do you think you're—"

He kissed her. Not roughly or violently, not for long and not using his tongue, but the kiss was far from being gentle. For an instant she was shocked. Then her anger flared into outrage. She would have slapped him except that he still gripped her arms, still had her body pinned.

"Let me go," she said between clenched teeth.

He was grinning again. "Come on, Francesca, it wasn't that bad, was it? Suppose we try it again."

"No! Let me go or you'll regret it."

"You don't mean that. Let's not play any more games."

"If you think I'm playing a game—"

"We've both been playing games," he said. "That's over now. It's time to stop playing. Time for it to happen, Francesca."

Time for it to happen ...

He's the one!

The thought was like an eruption in her mind. She recoiled from it, immediately sought to drive it away. It couldn't be Elliot, how could it? He wasn't one of their friends ... but he knew Katy, he could have been Katy's lover ... but he didn't know Eileen ... but he knew Ted, she'd run into him once in Ted's office ... but he'd never been inside her house, no one had broken in, how could he have stolen her bra and Amy's panties ... key, key, the spare key she'd given Katy long ago, he could have got the key from Katy....

She looked into his eyes, his leering face—and felt a surge of sick, raw terror.

He's the tormentor!

Dix had just two Friday classes, both in the morning. He thought he could get through them, as tired as he was; Cecca had said she was going to work today, so why shouldn't he? It proved to be the right decision. The campus activity and the routine of teaching distracted him, kept him from brooding.

When he returned to his office after his eleven o'clock, there was a message waiting from St. John. Would he call or stop by sometime today? That was all, so it was nothing urgent. Questions about the fire, probably. He'd reported it before leaving home that morning, not to St. John directly—he hadn't been in—but to the sergeant who'd taken the call.

Face-to-face, St. John had a way of getting under his skin and making him lose his composure. Dix called him instead. The first thing St. John said when he came on the line was that he'd just returned from investigating "the alleged arson attempt last night at your home."

"Alleged arson attempt. That means you don't find any evidence that the fire was deliberately set."

"None. But I don't doubt your version of the incident."

"Uh-huh. If only I'd gotten a look at him or his car, right?"

St. John let that pass. "Have there been any other harassments?"

Dix saw no point in telling him about the tormentor's call yesterday morning. His relationship with Cecca was none of St. John's business. He said, "No."

"Well, I do have a little positive news for you. Just so you know I'm doing my job. I spoke to Janet Rice again this morning. Louise

Kanvitz's artist friend in Bodega Bay. More than a friend, actually; turns out they were lovers. She admitted lying about buying those last two paintings of your wife's. Ms. Kanvintz asked her to say she had.''

"Did Kanvitz tell her why? Or who did buy the paintings?"

"She says no on both counts. Claims Ms. Kanvitz was secretive about her motives. That lends credence to your blackmail theory."

Credence, Dix thought. "I don't suppose there was anything at the gallery or among her effects that points to the man?"

"No."

"And of course there's nothing new on her murder."

"We still don't know that it was murder."

"All right, her death."

"Her nose was broken and there was a bruise on her jaw," St. John said. "She could have been knocked out first and then thrown down the stairs. Then again, she might have gotten those injuries in an accidental fall. We did find a fingerprint that isn't hers on the newel post. Might be significant; we're running computer checks on it."

Dix admitted, "That's encouraging." But not very. "None of the neighbors saw or heard anything?"

"Apparently not. If she was murdered, her killer may have parked his car on the other side of the hill and walked to her house through the trees up there. There's a path kids use from the school over on Highland. It leads right past her backyard."

Same damn method the bastard had used last night. Crazy but cunning.

"Did her missing handgun turn up?"

"Not yet."

"So the upshot of all this is, you're still reserving judgment. You're inclined to believe Francesca Bellini and her daughter and I are in danger, but there's nothing much you can do about it."

"You may see it that way, Mr. Mallory, but the fact is we're doing everything that can be done and we are making progress."

"Right," Dix said.

Status fucking quo, he thought.

It's him, it's Elliot!

Fear pushed Cecca toward the edge of panic. She couldn't get free of his clutching hands, his body pinning hers. He was half aroused; she could feel his burgeoning erection hot against her thigh.

He murmured, "Francesca," and tried to kiss her again.

She managed to tear her right arm loose. In the next second she spat in his face, brought her knee up, and swept the Mason jar off the windowsill and slammed it against the side of his head.

Her knee missed his groin, but the jar connected solidly, part of the glass fragmenting on impact, a shard of it cutting her palm. He grunted in pain, released her and stumbled away to one side. She had a brief impression of glazed eyes, blood streaming down from his temple. Then her back was to him and she was running.

She ran through the parlor, across the hall, dragged the front door open. Get inside the car, lock the doors! She plunged through, hitting the screen door with her shoulder; took two steps and then was violently yanked back and half around, a sharp wrenching in her left shoulder. She thought in that first confused moment that he'd caught her. But it was her purse, the strap of her purse had caught on the screen-door handle. In her panic she heaved backward, trying to free it—and the strap broke and she backpedaled off balance into the porch railing, the purse flying past her head. She twisted around as it hit the front walk and burst open, spilling its contents in a wide fan.

The car keys!

She stumbled down the steps. Didn't see the keys, bent to scoop up the purse, pulled it wide open so she could look inside, and the keys weren't there either—

Thudding footfalls. Her head jerked up; he appeared in the doorway. Holding his head with one hand, the left side of his beard glistening with blood. Saying dazedly, "Francesca, for Christ's sake," saying something else she didn't hear.

She took flight again.

Out through the gate, past the station wagon, across the empty yard. The barn was straight ahead, its sagging doors drawn shut but not locked, a gap like a skinny mouth yawning between them. She raced toward the doors, looking back over her shoulder.

He was behind her, chasing her in a lurching run, still clutching his head, still calling her name.

Just as she reached the doors, her foot slid on dry, loose earth and she went down hard on her left hip. The jarring pain was one of several; she barely noticed it. She lunged upward, grasped the latch on one door, dragged herself upright, and then scraped the door back and squeezed her body inside.

A half-darkness enveloped her, broken and thinned by fingers of dusty sunlight poking in through gaps in the walls and roof. The air was close, thick with the smells of hay and manure and harness leather; it clogged her nostrils, her throat, wouldn't let her catch her breath. She looked around wildly, trying to penetrate the gloom. Empty floor, empty stalls, loft above with remnants of moldy hay and nothing else—

Pitchfork.

It was propped against one of the vertical support beams for the loft. She hobbled over and caught it up. Rusted and crooked tines, a cracked handle that immediately became slick and sticky with blood from her cut palm. She whirled around with it, facing the door as it creaked open wide.

Elliot stood silhouetted there, backlit by the daylight outside. Looking for her, seeing her. Coming inside.

Instead of backing up, she went toward him. Now that she had the pitchfork, a weapon, some of her terror had been submerged by an adrenaline rush of fury. She jabbed the tines in his direction, belly high.

"Stay away from me," she said. "Don't come near me, you son of a bitch."

Elliot stopped, swaying a little, as if he were still dizzy from the blow with the Mason jar. He was in one of the shafts of incoming sunshine; she could see his red-stained face clearly enough to tell that the dazed expression was mostly gone, that in its place was an emotion that surprised her. What she'd expected was a fury to match her own, an implacable hatred. What she saw was fear.

He touched his temple again, stared at the blood smears on his fingers. "Jesus, Francesca," he said shakily, "you almost broke my skull."

"I wish I had."

"Why? I didn't mean . . . I misread the signals . . ."

"What signals? What're you talking about?"

He took another step forward, his hand held out to her as if in supplication. She reacted by advancing on him, closing the distance between them to ten feet, jabbing again with the pitchfork. "I'll put this all the way through you, I mean it."

He stopped, spread his arms. "I wasn't trying to attack you. Is that what you thought? Rape?"

"Rape?"

"It wasn't like that, I swear to God. I thought you wanted me as much as I wanted you. Playing games, being coy."

His apparent confusion had infected her, but not enough to make her relax her guard. She was sweating, a thick, oily sweat, and that smell combined with the barn stench was making her nauseated. "Turn around," she said. "Walk outside and keep walking."

"Francesca—"

"Do it, goddamn you, or I swear I'll stick you."

He turned, hunching his shoulders. And walked and continued to walk without looking back. She followed at a cautious distance, blinking when she came out of the dark barn into the sun-glare. He went halfway across the yard before his step faltered and his head swiveled toward her.

"Keep going. All the way to your car."

No argument; he did as he was told. His obedience had built an odd, grim sense of power in her. Now she was in control. Now he was the one scared and cringing. She hated the feeling—and relished it at the same time.

When he reached the Lexus she told him to stop. He stopped. "Francesca, what are you going to do?"

"Never mind what I'm going to do. Your car keys—where are they?"

"Jacket pocket."

"Take them out, put them on the hood. Then back up. Keep backing up until I tell you to stop again."

Once more he obeyed. When he was far enough away she moved forward and picked up the keys and put them in her blazer pocket.

"I wasn't going to force myself on you," he said. "You have to believe me. If you go to the police . . . the university, my tenure . . . I'm sorry I came on so strong, I mean it, I'm sorry . . ."

"Stay where you are. Don't move."

She backed up between the cars, not taking her eyes off him; backed through the gate to where her purse and its spilled contents lay spread over the walk. Elliot hadn't moved except to take out a handkerchief; he was dabbing blood off his temple, rubbing it out of his beard. She got down on one knee, the pitchfork in her right hand, and used her left hand to pick up wallet, change purse, compact, lipstick, comb, pen . . . key case. The case was partially hidden under a summer-dead bush; that was why she'd missed seeing it earlier. When she had everything in the purse she straightened and walked out to the station wagon.

Elliot made the supplicating gesture again. "*Please* don't report this to the police. I'll never bother you again, I'll never come near you, I'll buy this place and insist you have the commission . . . all right? Francesca? Just believe that I'm sorry, I never meant to hurt you, I made a mistake . . ."

"Shut up," she said.

He shut up.

"Walk away farther. Over by the chicken coop."

"Please," he said, and walked away.

The feeling of power was gone now; so was most of her anger. She felt . . . empty. She opened the car door, threw the pitchfork down, slid inside, and immediately locked all the doors. Now she was aware of the dull throbbing pain in her palm, of the blood that was dripping from the cut onto her clothing. Handkerchief in one of the blazer pockets . . . she found it, wrapped it around the hand.

Elliot was standing in front of the chicken coop, arms out slightly from his sides—a forlorn figure, like a poorly made scarecrow. Cecca started the engine, ran her window partway down. "I'll leave your keys in the mailbox," she called to him.

He called something back that had the word "please" in it.

She made a fast U-turn, drove fast out of the farmyard. Once she cleared the gate, she ran her gaze up to the rearview mirror. He was still standing by the chicken coop, fumbling with cigarettes and matches—diminished and diminishing.

At the end of the lane she stopped long enough to throw his car keys into the mailbox. Then she turned east on Hamlin Valley Road, drove straight to town, and straight home. In her driveway she shut off the engine and set the brake. But she didn't get out. She just sat there.

I'm sorry, I never meant to hurt you, I made a mistake.

Truth.

She'd been wrong.

Elliot Messner wasn't the tormentor.

Misread him as he'd misread her. Overreacted. He was a macho asshole who didn't really like or respect women, who until today had been secure in the belief that he could seduce—not rape, seduce—any woman he wanted because she must in turn want him. But that was all he was. Not dangerous; just a pig. Report him to the police? No, she wasn't that vindictive. She'd punished him enough out there— punched a huge hole in his ego and given him a scare that he wouldn't shake for days. He might not learn a lasting lesson from what had happened, but he would never forget this afternoon.

Neither would she.

She rested her forehead against the steering wheel. This is what living on the edge has done to me, she thought. Before, she would have been able to handle Elliot; she wouldn't have panicked, she wouldn't have resorted to violence. As it was, she had almost allowed herself to become the sort of person she despised. She'd worried that Dix was a potential killer. Well, so was she. If Elliot had come at her in the barn, she would have stuck him. She would have run that pitchfork all the way through him and killed him dead.

She kept on sitting there. Very calm now, still very much in control. Except that she couldn't seem to make herself get out of the car.

TWENTY-TWO

She was about to remember something.

Eileen knew it, felt it in every bone and fiber. The memory was like thunderclouds massing thickly on the edge of her mind. Ugly, terrifying . . . she kept wanting to run away from the coming storm. But she couldn't, not anymore. She was so tired. All she could do was lie here, helpless, and wait for it to overwhelm her.

The stream of people going in and out made it even worse. Doctors, nurses, visitors—so many people. They wouldn't tell her why she was there. They kept smiling at her, touching her, poking and prodding and taking her temperature and making her eat food she didn't want and walking her to the toilet to pee and saying things designed to cheer up patients. *Her* job, wasn't it? She knew all the tricks . . . except this one, what was going on with her. She wasn't sick, she was just so tired and discombobulated all the time. She shouldn't be lying in a hospital bed. Why wasn't she home in her own bed? Why wasn't she with her—

Maybe I am sick, she thought. Maybe that's what I don't want to remember, how sick I am.

"Amy," she said, "am I sick?"

"No. You'll be okay, really."

"Why can't I go home?"

"Um, your doctor says you have to stay here for a while."

"Doctors. What do they know?"

Amy laughed. She had a nice laugh, sweet. Such a pretty girl, almost as pretty as her mother, but with Chet's features. I wish I'd

213

had a little girl, Eileen thought. Not that I'd trade the boys, but . . . the boys . . .

Cecca. So many people visiting but not Cecca. Why hadn't she come back?

"Where's your mom, Amy?"

"Right now? I don't know."

"She was here but she didn't come back."

"Yes, she did. Yesterday. But you were asleep."

"Did Dix tell her?"

"Tell her what?"

"The accident. The trophy."

"I don't know what you mean, Mrs. Harrell."

"The trophy Katy saw."

"Katy Mallory?"

"But she wouldn't say where."

"What kind of trophy?"

"I told Dix about the accident. Did I tell him about the trophy?"

"What accident? You mean his wife's?"

"Pelican Bay."

"Pelican Bay? Where's that?"

"Oregon. Oregon coast."

"Oh, right. Isn't that where you and Mom almost . . . *that's* the accident you mean. Does that have something to do with what happened to Mrs. Mallory?"

"Tell your mom. Amy? Tell your mom."

"I will. Right away."

Eileen closed her eyes. It was only for a few seconds, didn't seem like any longer, and yet when she opened them Amy was gone and the blinds were closed again—somebody had come in and closed the blinds. She'd been asleep. But she wasn't rested. She was even more tired. Her mouth was sandy and her head ached and she was all twitchy. No, worse than that. Frightened. Terrified.

The memory clouds were still massing. And now they were huge, bloated. She could feel the expanding pressure inside her head, as if they would burst any second . . . *like the horror in her mind that had burst at the lake* . . . get away, get away! But it was too late. She couldn't move, couldn't hide, there was nothing to do but lie there, whimpering, afraid, and wait for the deluge.

She was about to remember something monstrous.

*   *   *

Mom wasn't at Better Lands. Amy found her at home, in her bathroom upstairs, wearing a robe and combing out her damp hair. There was a big bandage over the palm of her right hand. And the bathroom was steamy and hot, almost like a sauna; she must have been in the tub for hours.

"What'd you do to your hand?"

"Cut it. It's not serious."

"So I guess you're getting ready to go to Dix's again."

"Yes." Mom stopped brushing, gave her one of those searching looks. "Does it bother you, Amy?"

"Does what bother me?"

"That I've been spending so much time with Dix Mallory."

"Why should it? He's got the same crap to deal with that we have—more, on account of Katy. Besides, you think I don't know adults. get horny?"

"Amy, my sex life is none of your business."

Right, Amy thought. Just like mine is none of *your* business.

"Is it serious?" she asked.

"My relationship with Dix? It could be. That's why I asked if it bothered you, my seeing so much of him lately."

All of him, you mean. "I told you it doesn't. It's been a long time since you and Dad got divorced. You need somebody and he needs somebody. Everybody needs somebody."

"You like Dix, don't you?"

"He's okay."

But *boring*. Mom's speed. Boy, am I bitchy today, she thought. Bitchy and snotty to everybody. That's what happens when your life turns to shit. *You* get shitty, too.

Mom asked, "Why are you here anyway? Clean clothes?"

"No. I've been looking for you."

"Why?"

"I saw Eileen. I went to the hospital after work."

"That was good of you, baby. How is she?"

"Still pretty much out of it. She said some stuff . . . I don't know, maybe it's important. She wanted me to tell you."

Amy had worked to develop the skills she would need as an investigative reporter; she repeated the conversation with Eileen word for word. Mom was frowning when she was done.

"You're sure Eileen said Pelican Bay?"

"Positive. That's where you almost had the accident, right? You and Eileen and Katy?"

"Yes. But that was four years ago . . ."

"What did she mean about Katy seeing a trophy?"

"I don't know."

"Well, it must be what Eileen remembered last Sunday. The reason she called from Blue Lake."

"It must be, but—" Mom put her brush down, hurried into the bedroom. From the doorway Amy watched her take off her robe and start getting dressed. "I need to think about this. Talk to Dix about it."

"I'll go with you."

"To Dix's? No, I want you to go straight to Gran and Gramps's and stay there. I'll call you later."

"Why? I'm part of this, too."

"I know, baby, I know."

"Then why do you want to shut me out of it?"

"I don't. It's just that—"

"Just that you think I'm too young."

"No, it isn't that."

"Sure it is," Amy said cuttingly. "You think I'm too young, I'm not responsible enough, I can't help make adult decisions. That's bullshit, Mom."

"Amy, please. I haven't kept anything from you, have I? I haven't tried to shield you from the truth. Doesn't that tell you I think you're adult enough to handle it?"

"Then why do you keep trying to shove me off on Gran and Gramps?"

"For your own good, that's why. Will you please just do as I ask? No more arguments? We'll talk later, after I get this sorted out."

"After you and Dix get it sorted out, you mean."

"That's enough. Go. Straight to Gran and Gramps's. Promise me."

"Cross my heart and hope to die."

Downstairs, Amy saw that her mother had left her purse and car keys on the front hall table. She just hated being treated like a kid, pushed aside, left out; it made her wild. She was an adult—an adult! She took the pencil and notepad out of the drawer, wrote *Mom: In case you run out,* and set the pad next to the keys. On top of it she put the unopened package of rubbers from her own purse.

*　　*　　*

Pelican Bay, Cecca thought as she drove, the accident in Pelican Bay. *Is* there a connection? Such a long time ago, more than four years . . . God, that awful rainy night . . . three people dead, maybe four . . .

Fire. Burning. They hadn't just died in the crash . . . there'd been a fire, hadn't there? An explosion and a fire?

Soon, Francesca. But not too soon. The hottest fires burn slow. One fire burns out another's burning, one pain is lessen'd by another's anguish.

But it wasn't our fault. We weren't even directly involved. It was the driver of the van, not Katy. We never saw the victims, I don't even remember their names. The highway patrol up there never contacted any of us afterward. We never heard from anybody in Oregon. Who'd want to harm us because of that?

Dix said, "I don't have any idea either. But it's the first possibility that makes any sense at all." He began to pace the living room in quick, agitated strides. Watching him, Cecca had the unsettling sensation that Katy's "Blue Time" painting was watching him, too, from the wall above. That somehow Katy herself was in the room with them.

"Pelican Bay," he said. "So that's what Eileen meant."

"Meant when?"

"When I saw her yesterday. She mumbled something that sounded like 'pellagrin day.' Tell Cecca, she said. But I dismissed it, forgot about it; I thought it was a babble phrase. Christ, I should have remembered it was the name of that town."

"How could you, after four years? Katy didn't talk about that night, did she?"

"Not after she told me what happened when she first got back, no."

"None of us talked about it," Cecca said. "We wanted to forget it—everything about that night."

"I still should have made the connection."

"So should I, and much sooner, if you want to play that game. When I first heard about Katy, I thought, God, how awful she should die in a car accident after avoiding the one in Oregon. Eileen mentioned it, too, more than once. But the fact is, it happened four years ago, hundreds of miles from here, and we were only peripherally involved. Until now there was nothing to make either of us connect that with what's been going on here. The only reason Eileen did was whatever Katy said to her.''

''You're right.'' He scrubbed at his face with a heavy hand. ''Trophy,'' he said then, ''some kind of trophy. What kind?''

''I don't have a clue.''

''And what would a trophy have to do with Pelican Bay?''

She shook her head.

Dix stopped pacing, came back to where she stood. ''Can you remember the details of the accident up there? I mean everything before, during, and after.''

''Most of them, if I have to.''

''You have to. Katy's account was sketchy.''

''Let me sit down first.''

She curled up on a corner of the couch, her legs tucked under her. Her mind didn't want to open up to that June night four years before. She had to make an effort of will to force the memories into clear focus.

''All right,'' she said, and took a breath, and said, ''We were well up the Oregon coast, taking our time, playing tourist. I was in pretty rough shape when we left here, all wrung out over Chet, but by then—five or six days into the trip—I'd regained some perspective and I was actually having a good time. That day, a Tuesday or maybe a Wednesday, we spent shopping in Lincoln City. Katy and I wanted to stay the night there, but somebody in one of the shops told Eileen Pelican Bay had more atmosphere . . . you know, it's a little fishing village. And it was only a few more miles up the coast. So we drove up and took rooms in a beachside motel. The woman at the motel said the best place to eat was a restaurant a mile or so north of town . . . Crabpot, I think it was called. We were hungry, so we decided on an early dinner. Thank God we didn't drink much. One glass of wine apiece was all.''

''The accident happened as you were leaving the parking lot?''

''That's right.''

''And Katy was driving.''

''Yes. I was in the front seat with her and Eileen was in back. It was raining, one of those thick, misty rains, and just dark. Visibility was practically zero. You could see bright lights—headlights—at a distance but not much else. There were headlights approaching in both lanes, far enough away for Katy to safely make the turn across into the southbound lane. It just didn't look like there was a closer car in that lane. A car was behind us, people leaving the restaurant like we were, and the driver said he thought the lane was clear, too, that he'd have pulled out just as Katy did if he'd been ahead of us."

"But it wasn't clear," Dix said.

"No. Just a few seconds after she made the turn—she was still accelerating—she cried out, something like 'Oh my God!' and swung over hard to the right. We were just beyond a turnout on the ocean side; we almost went off the road. The other car, the van came roaring up . . . only its fog lights on and they were dim. He must have been doing at least sixty."

"Almost hit you, Katy said."

"Almost. If the northbound lane had been clear, he might have been able to veer around us without going out of control. But by then the lights we'd seen coming that way—two cars—were too close. The only things he could do were to plow into us at full speed or veer into the turnout."

"Not much of a choice."

"No choice at all. We talked about it afterward. Each of us would've done just what he did."

The cut on her palm had started to burn and itch; she rubbed it through the bandage. Dix hadn't asked about the bandage. Even if he had, she wouldn't have told him about the incident with Elliot. Someday she would, but not now. It was no longer important.

She said, "The turnout was fairly wide, fifty or sixty yards. It overlooked a place called Pelican Point. Steep cliffs, a rocky beach. But he was going too fast. And the highway was too slick and the surface . . . gravel, but there was mud under it, and deep rain puddles. He couldn't stop, couldn't even slow down. The van kept sliding, fishtailing. The rear end hit the guardrail first and then it . . . sailed through and dropped out of sight. The crash was awful. We could hear it above the storm, even closed up inside the car."

"Did it explode, burn?"

"It burned, yes; I remember the fireglow. I don't remember an explosion . . . it was all so confused . . ."

"There must have been one," Dix said grimly. "Gasoline igniting—that would have been what caused the fire."

"I guess so."

"What did the three of you do?"

"Just sat there in the car," Cecca said. "We were all petrified, in a state of shock. It happened so fast. Eileen . . . she said, 'I think I wet myself.' She wasn't kidding. She really did wet herself.''

"Then what happened?"

"Two or three other cars stopped. The driver of the one that had been behind us in the parking lot got out and ran over there, too. There wasn't anything they could do. Somebody at the restaurant called the highway patrol. The three of us stayed where we were, waiting, until the officers got there."

"There were four people in the van?"

"An entire family. Two young children."

"But they weren't all killed outright."

"Three were. The fourth—the driver, I think—was thrown clear. He hadn't been wearing his seat belt. They found him in some rocks partway down the cliff."

"Alive?"

"Yes. Badly injured."

"How badly?"

"I don't know. We never found out. They were still trying to get down to him when the officers let us go back to our motel. We couldn't bear to stay there any longer than we had to."

"You said 'him.' The father?"

"Yes."

"Katy told me she called the hospital the next morning, before the three of you left Pelican Bay. He was still alive then?"

"In serious condition. That was all they'd tell her." Cecca licked dry lips. "One of us should have checked back again later, to find out how he was. But we didn't."

"You can't blame yourself for that. You didn't know him and the accident was his fault."

"Still, we were responsible. If we hadn't been there, if Katy hadn't pulled out when she did . . .''

Dix said slowly, "It could be somebody else thought the same thing. Blamed you, the three of you, for the accident."

"Revenge after all this time?"

"It's possible. There could be a valid reason for the four-year time lapse . . . an incapacitating injury that took that long to heal, for instance."

". . . The father?"

"If he lived. Or someone connected to the family. Do you remember their name?"

"No, it's gone. Completely gone."

"Well, we've got to find out. The family name, if the father survived, and what happened to him if he did. There's only one way I can see to do that quickly, and it doesn't involve St. John. We'd have to convince him it was worthwhile and then he'd insist on going through official channels. That could take days."

"You mean go to Oregon ourselves."

"That's right," Dix said. "Fly to Portland, rent a car, drive over to the coast. And don't tell anybody we're going. It's a gamble, sure, but it's better than waiting around for the tormentor to make his next move. What do we have to lose except a day and a few hundred dollars?"

"When? Tonight?"

"The sooner the better. It's early enough; we ought to be able to drive to SFO in time to catch one of the last flights out. Stay at a motel near the Portland airport, get an early start in the morning. Are you up to it?"

"I'll call United while you pack a bag."

TWENTY-THREE

It was raining on the Oregon coast.

There had been overcast and scattered showers in the Portland area, more of the same on the drive west on Highway 6 in the rented Datsun. The heavy rain started near Tillamook and hammered them in gusty streamers as they headed south on Highway 101. The storm had a wintry feel; its chill penetrated the car, even with the heater on, and numbed Cecca's feet. Neither she nor Dix had thought to check the Oregon weather before leaving Los Alegres, and they were both dressed according to California conditions. The suede jacket and thin sweater and slacks she wore weren't nearly adequate.

They hadn't said much since leaving the airport motel shortly before nine. There was nothing left to say; they'd picked and probed at it last night on the drive to SFO and throughout the flight, until they had reduced it to raw, bleeding tissue like a wound with the scab torn off.

The digital dashboard clock read ten-forty when they passed through Neskowin, the little village north of Pelican Bay. The sea was close on their right here, partially obscured by low-hanging clouds and mist: slate-gray, heavy-swelled, the waves throwing up dirty white spume when they battered against the rocky shore. Visibility was poor; most of the daylight had been consumed by the storm, and what light there was had a dusky, nebulous quality. Dix had long ago turned on the headlights, but the beams seemed to deflect off the wall of wetness ahead rather than penetrate it.

Cecca said, "This is the way it was that night."

223

"Raining like this?"

"Yes. Clouds down low over the road."

"Miserable driving conditions, especially after dark."

She nodded. "Even if he'd had his headlights on . . ."

"Katy might not have seen them. But the accident would still have been his fault for driving too fast. How much farther to Pelican Point?"

"It can't be more than a few miles now."

It was about four miles. The Crabpot restaurant's big blue and white neon sign, unlit at this early hour, swam up out of the mist ahead; Cecca sat forward as soon as she saw it. "There," she said, but Dix had seen it, too, and was already tapping the brakes.

The restaurant and its front and side parking lots looked the same to her as they had four years earlier. The turnout across the highway also looked the same, except that the new guardrail rimming the cliff's edge was larger, sturdier. Slowly, Dix swung in off the highway. The turnout was empty except for them, a flat expanse of rain-puddled gravel glistening blackly where the headlight beams traced over it. He pulled up near the guardrail, at an angle to it. Left the engine running and the lights on, but set the hand brake.

"I'm getting out for a minute," he said.

"Why?"

He shook his head, as if he wasn't sure himself. Through the rain-streaked glass Cecca watched him walk to the guardrail, lean forward cautiously to peer down the cliff wall. Without making a conscious decision she opened her door and joined him. The wind was abrasively cold, the rain it flung into her face as stinging as thrown sand. She had to squint and shield her eyes to see what lay below.

The ocean seemed to be boiling. Surf lashed over huge offshore rocks coated with seaweed, over the base of the curving promontory to the south, sliming them all with white froth; inundated smaller inshore rocks and a tiny rind of beach. Jets of spray burst fifteen, twenty feet into the air when big waves surged in. The violence of it made Cecca cringe inside. She shivered and backed up a step.

Dix put his arm around her shoulders, said something that the wind tore away from her ears. She tugged at his jacket to draw him back to the car. Inside, she turned the heater up as high as it would go; sat hugging her breasts, her hands tucked inside her jacket and under her arms to try to warm them.

"You should have stayed in the car," Dix said.

"I wish I had. What did you say out there?"

"I said it must be more than a hundred-foot drop. It's a miracle the father wasn't killed, too."

She shivered again. "Miracle?" she said.

He was waiting when Amy came out through Hallam's rear entrance. Sitting on the passenger seat of her car: She must have forgotten to lock that door.

As soon as he saw her he got out quickly and came toward her, smiling. His car wasn't anywhere around; he must have walked over. There was nobody else in the alley, just the two of them. She almost turned back inside. Instead, she stood nibbling her lower lip, waiting for him. She was glad to see him and yet she wasn't. No matter how desperately she wanted to believe in his innocence, he scared her now almost as much as he attracted her.

"Hi," he said. "I was beginning to think old man Hallam was working you overtime."

"Um . . . overtime?"

"It's quarter past one. Half day on Saturdays, right?"

"Right. I had some things to finish up."

"Well, now you're free for the rest of the weekend. Any plans?"

"No. No plans."

"Not going anywhere with your mom?"

"No."

"Where is she, anyway?"

"At home, I guess. Or at Better Lands. I don't know."

"She isn't either place. Dix Mallory's nowhere to be found either. They go someplace together?"

"Beats me."

"Come on now, Amy. You can tell me."

"I really don't know."

Which was the truth. Mom had kept her promise to call last night, but she wouldn't say much about Pelican Bay or what she and Dix had decided to do. She'd sounded distracted and in a hurry; she hadn't even mentioned the condoms. "I won't be here tomorrow"— that was all she'd said. It didn't take a genius to figure out they'd gone up to Oregon, to Pelican Bay. Amy was still pissed at being left out, but not pissed enough to do something defiant.

He said, "You've been staying with your grandparents the past few nights. Why is that, Amy?"

"They wanted me to," she lied.

"It wasn't your mom's idea? So she could be with Dix?"

"No."

He watched her silently. It was like the other day: She couldn't quite meet his eyes. She looked at his mouth instead. His smile had a little quirk in it and she could see the tip of his tongue in one corner.

When she started to imagine his tongue in *her* mouth she shook herself and said, "Well, I guess I'd better get going . . ."

"Are you in a hurry?"

"Um, I've got some errands to run."

"Errands aren't urgent. How about going for a ride first?"

"A ride? With you?"

He laughed. "Of course with me."

"Your car's not here."

"You don't mind driving, do you?"

"No, but— Where?"

"Not far and not long. We'll be back inside of half an hour."

She wanted to; she didn't want to. It was like being pulled from two sides at once, as if she were a rope in a tug-of-war game. She made herself say, "I'd better not."

He touched her cheek, stroked it with his knuckles. "Come on, honey," he said. "Just a short ride. What do you say?"

Honey. That and his touch almost made her give in. She took a breath and said, "No, I really can't," and tried to move past him to her car.

He stopped her with his body and tight fingers on her arm. He was still smiling, but now it was just a mouth smile. His eyes . . . they'd changed. They'd gotten cold and hard.

Oh no, she thought, oh no!

"Give me your keys, Amy. Then get in the car on the passenger side. I'll drive."

Sudden fear held her rooted. Behind him Water Street was still empty—there was *never* anybody around back there. She could hear the hum of traffic on the cross streets, somebody talking loud in one of the adjacent stores, but it was as if the two of them were alone in the middle of a wilderness.

"Let me go," she said. "I'll scream," she said.

"No you won't," He unbuttoned the front of his suit coat, pulled one flap aside. "You won't scream and you won't argue."

She stared at the gun tucked into the waistband of his slacks.

"Give me your keys and then get in the car," he said. "Now there's a good girl."

Pelican Bay was like most Oregon coastal towns, loaded with picturesque cottages and beachfront condos and motels and seafood restaurants and native craft shops. The inlet that gave it its name extended under an arched highway bridge, forming a sheltered harbor for a fleet of fishing boats and a handful of weathered fish-processing companies. In the height of the summer season, with the sun shining and tourists swarming around, it probably had a certain charm. Now, seen through the bleak curtain of rain, its streets empty and some of its shops already closed, it had a remote and unwelcoming aspect.

Dix pulled into a service station and spoke briefly to the attendant on duty. Pelican Bay was too small to have a library, the man said; the nearest one was in Lincoln City, down the coast a few miles. That was where the nearest newspaper was published, too—the weekly Lincoln City *News Guard*.

Back in the car, he relayed this information to Cecca, who sat huddled against the passenger door. Then he asked her, "Want to get some coffee before we go on? Warm up a little?"

"No. Let's just get it over with."

The rain was easing a little when they reached Lincoln City. This was the center of the north-coast resort area, an exceptionally long, narrow town—actually a collection of tiny hamlets strung together—that spread out for several miles along Highway 101. Dix stopped at another service station there to ask directions. Driftwood Library was only a few blocks away, as it turned out. And it was open, Dix saw with relief as he pulled up in front. In these hard times you never knew about library hours.

They had a microfilm file of issues of the *News Guard* dating back several years. A librarian showed them to the microfilm room, brought the tapes containing the issues for June and July of 1989, and left them alone.

Dix threaded June into the magnifier, cranked it rapidly through to the issue for Wednesday, June 25. The accident was bound to have been front-page news, but there was nothing in that issue about it. "It must have been that Wednesday night that it happened," Cecca said. She was right. The following week's issue had the account.

Three-column headline and photo on the lower half of the front page. The photo was of a crane lifting a wrecked and fire-ravaged van up the side of the cliff at Pelican Point; two uniformed highway patrol officers stood in the foreground, and visible in the background was a splintered section of guardrail. The headline read:

FIERY CRASH CLAIMS 3 LIVES

The screen on the magnifier was scratched and the newsprint on the accompanying story was small and smeary. Dix worked the focus knob to sharpen the image.

A fiery highway accident last Wednesday evening claimed the lives of three members of a prominent Pelican Bay family. Cheryl Cotter, 36, and her two children, Angela, 5, and Donald, 6, of 289 Barksfield Road, died instantly when the van in which they were riding plunged 120 feet to the rocks at Pelican Point and burst into flames. The driver, Gordon Cotter, a tax accountant with offices in Lincoln City, was thrown clear. He suffered a broken leg and minor injuries and is listed in stable condition at North Lincoln Hospital.

According to highway patrol officer Edmund Deane, Cotter was driving southbound on Highway 101 shortly past nightfall, at an excessive speed and without headlights. He swerved to avoid a rear-end collision with a car that had just exited the parking lot at the Crabpot restaurant, and lost control on the rain-slick highway. The driver of the other car, Kathleen Mallory, of Los Alegres, California, stated that rain and darkness prevented her from seeing the oncoming van. Several witnesses corroborated her account. She was not cited.

There was more, continued on an inside page. Gordon Cotter was a native of McMinnville, had met and married his wife in Pelican Bay, and had lived there for nine years. He belonged to civic and social groups in Pelican Bay and Lincoln City; the head of the Lincoln City Lions Club was quoted as saying, "It's a terrible tragedy. Gordon was totally devoted to his family." There were no photographs of any of the victims.

A thin excitement pulsed in Dix. They were on the right track; he was convinced of it now. Cecca's expression said that she felt the same way.

He cranked ahead to the next week's issue. One small follow-up story giving funeral information and stating that Gordon Cotter was soon to be released from the hospital. That was all.

Cecca said, "Why didn't they publish a photo of him?"

"Local policy, maybe."

"Would the McMinnville paper have run one?"

"It's possible. We'll see if the library keeps a McMinnville file."

But the library didn't.

He kept talking at her. Talking, talking. Amy didn't hear it all; she didn't want to listen. She sat slumped on the seat beside him, the seat belt tight around her—he'd made sure she put it on and kept it on—and told herself over and over to stay cool. He hadn't hurt her yet and he wasn't going to, not if she could help it.

"... Didn't want to do it this way, Amy, I really didn't. I wanted so much for us to get to know each other first, to be close. But you're not ready and there isn't enough time to wait. I thought there'd be, but there isn't. Your mother and Dix ... I wish I knew where they went. You really don't know, do you? No. I don't think they suspect me yet, but they may be getting close. Now I'll have to hurry with them, too. ..."

Him him *him*! All the time she'd been fooling herself; all the time it was him. Katy Mallory, Mr. Harrell, Bobby ... *he'd* killed them. What if she'd actually let him have sex with her? She felt awful enough as it was, sick and shamed, but if she'd let him do it to her, she'd have hated herself for the rest of her life.

How could she have thought he loved her?

How could she have thought she loved him?

How could she have been so *stupid*!

"... Pick you up like that, with a gun in broad daylight. Somebody might have seen us together. I don't think anybody did, but what other choice did I have? I've got to finish it. That's the only thing that matters. Why couldn't you have made it easy for me? Making me use a gun ... I don't like guns any more than your mom does. This one isn't mine, I'd never own a gun. It belonged to Louise Kanvitz. I didn't want to hurt her, but she forced me with her gun and her demands. Greedy bitch. Her fault, not mine. Hers and Katy's. Katy shouldn't have let it slip about us. I warned her to be careful. Didn't I warn her? They never listen, they never listen ..."

Why?

Amy still didn't know that. He had hardly stopped talking since they'd left Hallam's ten or fifteen minutes earlier, but he hadn't said—she couldn't remember him saying—anything about *why*.

"Why?" The word just popped out of her.

At first she didn't think he'd heard. Then his head jerked toward her and he said, "Why what?"

"Why are you doing this? Why do you want to hurt Mom, me, everybody we know?"

"Not everybody, Amy. Just the ones who deserve it."

"I never did anything to you. Neither did Mom."

"Yes, she did. She hurt me worse than you could ever know. Her and Katy and Eileen."

"What did they do?"

"They killed me," he said. "They destroyed my life."

"That doesn't make any sense . . ."

"Never mind now. I don't want to talk about that now. We'll have a nice long talk when we get there. There'll be a little time for us to get to know each other better."

"Get where? Where're you taking me?"

"Don't you know, Amy? Haven't you guessed?"

She hadn't been paying attention to where they were. She peered through the windshield, saw that they'd left town, were traveling through rolling brown farmland. Familiar landmarks told her they were on outer Bodega Avenue. Heading west, toward the coast.

She knew then, even before he said it.

"Up to your dad's cottage. Up to the Dunes."

Barksfield Road was on the northeast side of Pelican Bay, a snaky street that extended inland through pine woods. The houses that lined it were a mix of old and new architectural styles on large lots, well built and well maintained. Number 289 turned out to be a newish ranch-style home, ell-shaped, at least four bedrooms, with a detached garage. It was nearly one o'clock and raining heavily again when Dix pulled into the driveway. No cars were visible on the property and no lights showed in any of the facing windows.

"Nobody home," he said.

"Now what?"

"We'll try the neighbors."

The nearest was across the road, a hundred yards away—a big frame house with firelight dancing behind its partially draped front window. Dix swung the car in along a crushed-rock drive, stopped next to a deep porch. The wind was gusting, driving the rain in near-horizontal sheets; they ran from the car onto the porch.

The man who answered the bell was in his seventies, stooped but sharp-eyed, wearing a heavy wool sweater over baggy trousers. He frowned when he saw that they were strangers, but it wasn't a frown of displeasure; if anything, he seemed glad to be having unexpected visitors. He cocked the left side of his head toward them. Behind his ear on that side was a flesh-toned hearing aid.

"Do something for you folks?"

"We're looking for Gordon Cotter," Dix said.

"Cotter, did you say?"

"Gordon Cotter, yes. We understand that he—"

"Wait a minute. Can't hear you with that rain rattling down. Damn hearing aid don't work good in weather like this. Come in so I can shut the door."

It was warm in the house, smoky from a blazing wood fire. The old man said his name was Delaney, Martin Delaney, and invited them to sit down.

Dix said, "We can't stay, Mr. Delaney. We'd just like to know about Gordon Cotter, if he still owns the house across the road."

"Not anymore. Family named Elroy owns it now. Baptists, holy rollers. You friends of his?"

"Cotter's? No. We have business with him."

"What kind of business?"

"It's personal."

"None of *my* business, eh?" Delaney laughed; his false teeth made a clacking sound. "You know what happened to his family?"

"Yes, we know."

"His fault. Driving too fast in the rain, didn't have his headlights on. He always did drive too fast and loose. But he wouldn't admit it."

"Wouldn't admit the accident was his fault?"

"That's right. Talked to him once, after he come home from the hospital. He said it was the people in the other car's fault, the one that pulled out from the restaurant."

Dix glanced at Cecca. She moved closer to him, either for warmth or support.

"Oh, he took it hard," Delaney said. "Real hard. One thing you can say for Cotter, he loved his wife and those two kids. Cute kids, too. My wife was alive then—she used to say they were a perfect family. Blessed, she said. Terrible thing to lose them like that, all at once. Just the opposite of blessed.''

Cecca asked, "How long ago did he sell the house, Mr. Delaney?"

"Three, four months after it happened. Sat over there all that time, didn't go to work, wouldn't hardly leave the house. Grieved longer and harder than any man I ever knew. Then one morning he was gone and the place was up for sale. Just up and left."

"Do you know where he went?"

"No idea," Delaney said. "Haven't seen nor heard from him since. Nobody around here has. Didn't take his furniture, wherever he went. Left it all right there in the house. Sold the house with the furniture included. Hell of a deal for the holy rollers."

"Would you please tell us what he looks like?"

"Looks like? I thought you knew him."

"We think we know him," Dix said. "We need to be sure."

"Well, I'm not too good at that sort of thing . . ."

"Please try."

"Gordon Cotter, eh? Man about forty, now. Tall, good shape— played a lot of tennis and golf. Blond hair, blue eyes like mine used to be—real bright blue. Handsome. Handsome as the devil."

Jerry.

Jerry Whittington was Gordon Cotter.

And Gordon Cotter was the tormentor.

TWENTY-FOUR

By the time they passed through Point Arena, late in the afternoon, Amy was no longer afraid of him. She'd gotten her head totally together. She felt the way she'd always imagined she would when she was a working reporter and found herself in a dangerous situation: cool, crafty, determined. You didn't get your ass out of trouble by panicking or wimping out. You used your head, waited for the right opportunity, and then did what you had to do. *Whatever* you had to do.

Meanwhile, she'd pretended to be scared out of her skull. Meek and obedient, too. Let him think he could do anything he wanted to her and she wouldn't fight back. Let him think she was going to be an easy victim.

She studied him out of the corner of her eye. Sitting over there all smug, his hands dirtying the wheel of her car, probably thinking he could put his hands on *her* if he felt like it and she'd just turn to jelly. Once he could have; once she would have. She couldn't stand to think how willing, how stupid, she'd been just a short while ago. Well, she'd learned her lesson. Hatred was all she felt for him now. The attraction was totally gone, as if it had never existed. He wasn't handsome or sexy, he was repulsive. He was Freddy Krueger with a hunk's mask on.

His eyes were steady on the road; they didn't seem to blink much anymore. He looked relaxed, not even a little tired or cramped from all the driving. Super cool or bat-shit crazy? She couldn't tell. He didn't show much of what was going on inside him—and it was

probably just as well he didn't. Amy shifted position again. Her buns
were sore from sitting in one place for almost three hours. They
hadn't stopped once, not even for gas because she'd filled the tank
that morning. Down around Fort Ross she'd tried to get him to stop
at a gas station so she could use the bathroom—a trick that might
give her a chance to slip away from him or at least to write a
message on the mirror with her lipstick. But he hadn't fallen for it.
"I really have to pee," she'd lied, and he'd said, "You'll just have
to hold it. Either that, or go ahead and wet yourself."

That was about all he'd said to her since way back at Bodega
Bay. Talk, talk, talk nonstop for half an hour—and then nothing, as
if a faucet inside him, turned on for a while, had suddenly been
turned off. It was all right with her. The silence was a lot easier
to take.

The long ride was almost over. They were passing the turnoff for
the Point Arena Light Station; that meant the one for Manchester
State Beach and the Dunes was only a couple of miles farther on.
He knew it, too—must have read a map or something, because he
began to slow down even before she spotted the half-hidden sign for
Stoneboro Road. He didn't come close to missing the turn either,
something even she'd done once.

Stoneboro Road wound in for more than a mile, through open
fields and cattle graze, before you could see the sand dunes and the
abandoned development. At that point you could also see miles and
miles of the curving beach, and inland across a long valley dotted
with dairy ranches to the mountains of the Coast Range. It was
lonesome and windswept and beautiful. Even today, with *him* beside
her, she was aware of its beauty.

The weather was pretty good, windy and mostly sunny, and there
were a half dozen cars parked at the entrance to the beach. None of
the people was in sight though. He turned off on the road that ran
through what was left of the development. Narrow, carpeted in blown
sand, it paralleled the outer sweep of the dunes and took them past
signs and paved streets that led nowhere: Barnegat Drive, Duxbury
Road, Coventry Lane. No cars here, just sawgrass and gorse and
cypress and scrub pine. And the high dunes covered with thick tufts
of tule grass that had always made her think of a vast herd of hairy
creatures watching the sea with hidden eyes.

Another mile ... and when they came around a bend in the road,
the Dunes appeared. Gray, salt-weathered, set seventy or eighty yards

off the road on high ground, built on pilings so that blowing sand could drift underneath. The unpaved lane that led up to it was half gravel and half weeds, so it was barely visible until you were right on top of it, but he seemed to know where it was. He turned, and they jounced along and finally stopped on the flat-topped rise, behind the cottage. He shut off the engine, but he didn't move to get out right away. He rolled down the window a little and sniffed the air with a little smile on his mouth.

"Nice here," he said. "I love the coast, the ocean."

Amy didn't say anything.

"It reminds me of where I used to live."

Pelican Bay, I'll bet, she thought. She almost said it, caught herself in time. If she made a slip like that and he *had* lived in Pelican Bay, he'd know they were on to him, that that was where Mom and Dix must have gone. There was no telling what he might do then.

"You've been a good girl," he said. "Keep on being good and everything will be fine."

"I will," she said.

"I'm going to get out now. You sit there until I come around and open your door. When you get out, don't try to run away. If you do, I'll shoot you. I won't like doing it, but I will."

"I won't try to run."

When he opened the door, she took her time unkinking her body. He stood back a few paces, his hand on the gun in his belt. No, she wouldn't try to run. Even if he didn't shoot her, he could probably chase her down; he wasn't that old and he was in such good shape. Stay cool, she told herself. There'll be a time when he forgets to be careful.

He made her climb the outside stairs ahead of him, one hand on her arm. His touch was no longer silky or electric; it made her skin crawl. The wind was chilly on her face, sharp with the salt tang of the ocean. It would be cold later, when the sun—already falling and starting to turn red around the edges—dropped below the horizon. How long would he keep her here? All night? She'd have to try to find out about that right away.

On the narrow landing at the top she said, "How are we going to get in?"

"With the key your father gave you." He jangled her key ring, then held it out to her. "One of these. Find the right one and use it."

As soon as she had the door open, he took the key ring back and put it into his pants pocket. The right-hand pocket. When they were both inside, he turned the deadbolt lock, put the chain on. The only other ways out were off the balcony or through one of the windows. He knows that, too, Amy thought. He knows everything about the Dunes.

The big front room smelled of sea-damp and old smoke from the cigarettes Megan sucked on constantly and the joints she and Dad smoked when they were alone. It was a mess, too. Papers and crap on the floor, tables littered with dirty glasses and ashtrays, even a plate with sandwich crumbs on it. If she hadn't known better, she'd think kids or homeless people had gotten in despite regular patrols by the county sheriff and the park rangers. But it was just that Dad was sloppy and Megan and that dickhead son of hers were total slobs.

He didn't seem to notice. He'd pulled the drapes open over the sliding door to the balcony, letting sunlight pour in, and he was peering out with that little smile on his mouth again. Admiring the view. "You can see for miles from up here," he said. "All the way from the lighthouse to Irish Beach. Come take a look, Amy."

"I've seen it before. I still have to go to the bathroom." It wasn't a lie this time. She really did have to pee now.

"All right. Go ahead."

For a couple of seconds she thought he was going to make the mistake of letting her go by herself. But no, he followed her down the hall. And when she went into the tiny bathroom he stood leaning against the wall right outside.

"Leave the door open," he said. "And come right out again when you're done."

"Are you going to watch me?"

"I wouldn't do that. I'll look away."

Useless to argue with him. She moved to the toilet, made sure he wasn't looking before she hiked up her skirt and slid her panties down. But she had trouble going with him out there, even if he wasn't watching. The embarrassment of it made her hate him even more.

She didn't come right out afterward. She stepped over to the sink, and when he didn't object, she washed her hands, taking her time, thinking that there might be something in the medicine cabinet she could use as a weapon, a packet of Dad's razor blades or something. Could she reach up and open it without him seeing? No. Shit. The bathroom was too small and she could see him in the mirror, which meant that he could see her, too. And his eyes were on her again.

Back in the living room she said, "It's cold in here. There's plenty of wood—I could make a fire."

"No, no fire."

"We'll freeze once the sun goes down."

"Isn't there some kind of heater?"

"There's a space heater, but it's old and it doesn't work too well. We always just make a fire."

"Well, we'll just have to find other ways of keeping warm."

Oh-oh, she thought. "How long are we going to be here?"

"A while," he said.

"All night?"

"A while. Several hours at least."

"Doing what all that time?"

"Getting to know each other better," he said. "Isn't that what we talked about, Amy? What we planned?"

A little fear wiggled back into her. But mostly what she felt was determination. And the hate, like a wad of something in her throat, choking her. "When do you want to start? Now or later?"

"There's no point in waiting."

"Whatever you want." In her mind were pictures of things she would do to his private parts, if she just had the chance. She could endure anything for that chance. "You won't have to rape me," she said, and began to unbutton her blouse.

They were in the rented car again, moving through the wet afternoon toward Highway 101. Freezing in there after the warmth of Martin Delaney's house; Cecca reached out automatically to turn the heater up. It was already on as high as it would go. She pressed her hands between her thighs.

"Jerry," she said. "My God."

"You didn't look surprised when Delaney described him."

"No. I thought at the library it had to be Jerry."

Dix nodded and said bitterly, "Mr. Congeniality. The guy who'd do anything for you, give you the shirt off his back. All an act contrived to win our friendship and trust."

"I can't imagine a mind that could conceive of such a . . . a hideous revenge."

"I can, at least up to a point. What I can't imagine is that much hate. He killed someone I loved—in cold blood, not by accident—but I don't hate him nearly as much as he must hate us. Do you?''

"No," she said, ''not that much.''

"Ironic as hell, isn't it? Before the accident, he wasn't much different from you, me, any of us—a more or less normal person with a family, a job, an average middle-class life. It was the hate that pushed him over the edge.''

"But the accident was *his* fault.''

"Transference," Dix said. ''If he'd accepted culpability, he'd have been a monster in his own eyes. He couldn't bear that. So he made you three the monsters instead.''

"How could he live so close to us for so long and never let any of it show?''

"Force of will. Four years is a long time to us, but not to a man like him. His family was his whole life; without them he has nothing left except revenge. Just killing each of you wasn't enough for him. It would've been over too fast and then he'd have no more reason to live. He had to savor his revenge, make it last. Get to know you first, get as close to you as he could. Katy was the driver that night, Katy was his primary target. He set out to seduce her and he probably didn't care how long it took. You can't get any closer to a woman than inside her body.''

I almost let him inside my body, too, Cecca thought. Came nearer than I ever want to admit.

Dix said, "Hard to tell if he murdered Katy on some sort of timetable or if something happened—the trophy business, maybe—to make him do it before he wanted to. Once he committed himself, though, he was driven to go after the rest of us.''

"Our families . . . we took his, he'd take ours.''

'' 'One's pain is lessen'd by another's anguish.' Yeah, that was part of his plan all along.''

"But why go after you once Katy was gone?''

"Maybe he meant to kill me first, and blames me because he couldn't do it that way. Or his hate for Katy was so great, it included me: guilt by association. Or he'd decided all family members have to die no matter what. One thing I'm fairly sure of: Ted and his sons were the targets at Blue Lake, not Eileen. He knew about her evening walks, counted on her being away from the cabin when the timer set off the propane. The whole idea was for her to see her family destroyed by explosion and fire, as his was.''

"Sick, so sick . . ."

"He had it all planned like that, in detail. To him it must all make perfect sense, fit some kind of pattern of retribution. His mind has to be deteriorating though. The things he's done since Katy have been progressively more bizarre and disconnected."

Cecca watched the rain slant against the side window. After a time she said, "He must have loved his own children. How could he justify harming Bobby, Kevin, Amy? Innocent young lives."

"They're not innocent young lives to him. None of us is even human to him anymore, if we ever were. This is a grim analogy, but I'll bet it's reasonably accurate: In his mind we're like germs, the source of all his torment. You don't look at germs as individuals. Don't think twice about killing germs that have infected you."

"Germs," she said.

"Prevalent psychology today. Gang wars, freeway shootings, mass murders . . . the ones who commit those atrocities are exterminators of objects, bugs, germs, not people. Get in their way, hurt them somehow, and they feel they have every right to destroy you."

Again Cecca watched the rain form its teardrop patterns on the window glass. "It makes me feel so damned helpless," she said. "The idea of a man none of us ever met or saw, a man we barely knew existed, plotting our deaths from hundreds of miles away—and then moving to our town, making friends with us and a whole new life for himself just so he could destroy us from within. If that kind of thing can happen . . ."

"I know," Dix said.

An uneasy silence built between them. Hiss of tires, clacking of the wipers, rush of wind and water as trucks and cars passed—all external sounds. Then Cecca realized they were approaching a town. A roadside sign materialized through the misty rain: Neskowin.

She sat up. "Where are we going?"

"Back to Portland. We ought to be able to make the five o'clock flight to SFO."

"We should've stopped in Pelican Bay," she said. "We'd better stop here."

"What for?"

"To call St. John."

"You think he'd listen? Act without proof? All we have to give him are sketchy facts and supposition. We can't even prove to him quickly that Jerry Whittington and Gordon Cotter are the same man, and even if we could, there's no evidence to link Jerry with Katy's death, the explosion—any of it.''

"There has to be something at his house."

"Yes, but St. John can't get at it without a search warrant. And he can't get a search warrant without probable cause."

"He could *talk* to Jerry, couldn't he? Let him know we're on to him. And least that might stop him from doing anything else."

"Would it? I don't think so," Dix said. "I think it would have the opposite effect. He doesn't care what happens to him, Cecca. His whole focus is revenge—finishing what he started."

". . . You want to go after him yourself, don't you?"

"I don't *want* to, no. I don't see any other choice."

"Use that gun you bought? Shoot him down like a dog?"

"No. My God, I'm not a murderer."

"Do what, then?"

"Force him to admit the truth, get it down on tape. It won't be admissible in court, but it'll damned well get St. John's attention. Then search his house for evidence and make a citizen's arrest. There'll be legal repercussions, but I don't care about that now. All I care about is saving our lives."

"If you're right about his mental state, he won't let you search his house or arrest him. He'll make you use the gun, he'll make you kill him."

"I won't let that happen."

"You may not have a choice." She was thinking about yesterday afternoon, Elliot Messner, the pitchfork. How close she'd come to an act of deadly violence herself—a sudden step, a menacing gesture, was all it would have taken. And how she'd felt afterward.

"Cecca? You know there's no other way."

"If you use that gun," she said, "no matter what the reason, you and I will suffer for it—and I don't just mean legally. We'll suffer and Gordon Cotter will have his revenge on both of us, too. He'll have won."

"How can you say that? We'll be alive, won't we? Safe?"

"He'll have won," she said.

"*Rape* you? Lord, Amy, is that what you think?"

"Well? You want to fuck me, don't you?"

He winced. "No. Not like this."

"But you said we should get to know each other better . . ."

"I didn't mean that way."

"I don't ... what did you mean?"

"For us to talk. About you, things that matter to you."

"You never wanted to have sex with me?"

"Yes, I did. Very much. But that was before, when it was part of the equation. It would have been right then. It isn't right now. It's too late. It wouldn't have any meaning."

"I don't understand ..."

"I know you don't. It's all right. Button up your blouse and we'll talk. Go on, button your blouse."

She buttoned it. She was confused, relieved, frustrated, all at the same time. Confused because she didn't know where he was coming from, he was so crazy and weird; relieved because he didn't want her body after all; frustrated because as much as she would have hated having him inside her, she could have hurt him—oh, could she have hurt him!—and then gotten away.

"Let's go out on the balcony," he said.

"Why?"

"I like to look at the ocean, smell the sea air. Don't you?"

"I guess."

"It should be warm enough. There's still plenty of sun."

It wasn't warm out there; it was almost cold. He didn't seem to notice. He made her sit on one of the canvas deck chairs and then leaned on the railing and took several deep breaths. At first he was smiling that little smile, but it went away and all of a sudden, when he turned toward her again, he looked sad—sad and lonely and kind of lost.

"I miss it," he said, but he wasn't really talking to her. Or even to himself. It was as if there were somebody else on the balcony with them. "I miss home. I miss you."

"Who?"

He didn't hear her or just ignored her. Gulls, a whole flock of them, came swooping in over the dunes, screeching and scolding each other; he turned his head to watch them. After a couple of minutes they scattered and quit making so much racket, and he sighed and sat down on one of the other chairs.

"Fascinating birds," he said. "I used to watch them for hours. Grebes and terns and pelicans, too."

She said, "I hate them."

"Do you? Why, Amy?"

"Scavengers. Always screaming and fighting and pecking at dead things. Not like the swans."

"Swans?"

"They come in the winter sometimes, drifts of them. Whistling swans. They nest or something down at the mouth of the Garcia River."

"I didn't know that," he said. Now he looked sad again. "I'd like to see them sometime. But I never will."

"Why not?"

"There isn't enough time. I won't be here next winter."

"Where will you be?"

"With my family."

"I didn't know you had a family."

"I don't anymore," he said.

For a few seconds it looked like he was going to cry. Then his face smoothed and the mouth smile came back. Creepy . . . God, had he always been this creepy and she somehow hadn't noticed? No. Underneath, probably, but not out where you could see it. He just wasn't bothering to hide it anymore.

"Tell me some more about yourself, Amy."

". . . Like what?"

"Things that I don't know about you."

"Personal things?"

"Personal, private, special."

"Like whether or not I'm still a virgin?"

"Well. Are you?"

She thought about lying but she didn't. "No."

"I didn't think you were. But that's good."

"Why is it good?"

"Sex is healthy. There's nothing wrong with sex between consenting people. Consenting, Amy. That's the key."

"It was consenting with me. You want to know his name and how many times and what we did?"

"No. Don't be nasty. You're not a nasty person at heart."

The wind kicked up and blew fine particles of sand from the dunes below. One of them got into her eye and made it sting and water. She sat there, chilled, rubbing her eye until she got the grit out. He didn't seem to notice how cold and uncomfortable she was. It was as if he saw her only when he wanted to, when there was something he wanted to know or she did or said something that made him aware of her. The rest of the time, she might have been invisible.

She said, "Why do you care that I'm not still a virgin if you don't want to have sex with me anymore? Why do you want to know so much about me?"

"I just do. It's important to me."

"Why? Will it be easier to kill me if you know me better?"

"Oh, Amy . . ."

"Well? That's what you're going to do, isn't it?"

"You don't understand."

"You keep saying that. I understand you want me dead."

"It's not a question of wanting."

"No? Then why?"

"You're part of her, that's why."

"Who? My mother?"

"Yes."

"What did my mother ever do to you?"

"She helped destroy me."

"You said that before, too. It's a lie, she never hurt you or anybody else—"

"The hell she didn't!" He was suddenly angry. His face got red; veins bulged on his forehead. "She killed them! Three beautiful lives! Her and those other bitches. An eye for an eye. One bad burn deserves another."

Jesus, she thought.

He was quiet again for a while, staring out toward where the white finger of the lighthouse stuck up from the southern headland. The sun was edging down toward the horizon; the clouds around it looked like spilled red wine. The beach was deserted now. Just her and him and the gulls for miles and miles . . .

When he spoke to her again, his voice was soft and sad and his face was the same—as if he'd never been angry at all. "Do I look alive to you, Amy?" he asked.

". . . What?"

"Alive. I look alive to you, don't I?"

"You *are* alive."

"No, you're wrong. I'm not. Do you know what a zombie is?"

"I saw *Night of the Living Dead*."

"Well, that's what I am. A zombie. I walk, I talk, I eat, I work, I go through all the motions, but I'm not alive. Inside I'm dead. Oh, there are sparks now and then. Sparks. When I do what I have to for them, Cheryl and Angie and Donnie, I remember what it was like to be alive. But that's all, just sparks. I'll never be alive again. The important pieces are gone. The three important pieces are gone. Three parts to the whole, and only one part is left, and that part can't survive alone. It can function until it finishes what has to be done, but it's already dead. It simply hasn't gone to its grave yet. But it will soon. Zombies can't walk for long. I won't be walking when the whistling swans come next winter."

He smiled at her, almost a tender smile. "Tell me more, Amy. Help me to know you. What else do you like besides the swans?"

TWENTY-FIVE

It was after nine when they reached Los Alegres. Dix drove straight up to the Ridge. The first order of business was to arm himself with the Beretta—it was still in the drawer of the nightstand next to the bed—and his tape recorder. Then . . . Jerry Gordon Whittington Cotter.

Beside him, Cecca sat huddled and silent. She'd hardly moved or spoken since they'd picked up the car at the airport parking lot. Still brooding over what he intended to do, even though she knew—had to know—it was the only course of action that made any real sense. Hated guns, hated the idea of him using one. Did she think *he* liked it? The mere thought of having to shoot a man, any man, roped his stomach into knots. She'd refused to go with him to Jerry's house, which was just as well; he could handle it better alone, without her to worry about, too. An hour and a half. That was as much time as she'd been willing to give him. If he didn't contact her within that time limit, she would notify the police. Reasonable enough. If he couldn't accomplish his mission and make a telephone call within ninety minutes, he would need police assistance. Or a doctor. Or a priest.

He turned off Rosemont into his driveway, turned again at the top of the hill. The house looked all right from the outside; he hadn't expected any different. Jerry would not have made another arson attempt. His actions were erratic, but they didn't seem to run in repeat patterns.

Dix parked alongside Cecca's station wagon, hurried into the

245

house. He put on lights; everything looked all right inside as well. Upstairs for the Beretta, which went into his jacket pocket. His voice-actuated cassette recorder was in the study downstairs; he made sure the battery was functioning before he pocketed it, too. He didn't bother to lock the front door again on the way out. Locked doors meant nothing now, one way or another.

Cecca had taken her overnight bag out of the Buick and was putting it into the wagon. He joined her. She faced him, but she wouldn't meet his eyes. Her cheeks had a talcum-powder whiteness in the light from the rising moon.

"You're sure you don't want to wait here?"

"I'm sure," she said.

He read the luminous digits on his watch. "It's nine thirty-five. I'll call you or come to your place no later than eleven-fifteen."

She didn't respond.

"It'll be all right," he said.

"Will it?"

"He won't kill me and I won't kill him. I promise you that—"

"Don't. I don't want to hear any promises."

He kissed her. Her mouth was cold and unresponsive, her body rigid. Neither of them had any more words; he left her and got into the Buick and backed it up and turned down the hill. A few seconds later the station wagon's headlights appeared in his rearview mirror. They stayed close behind him until he reached the bottom of Rosemont, then they veered off and he was alone.

His body felt cramped, achy, as he drove across town. Stress. But his mind was free of it, his thoughts clear and sharp. He was almost anticipating the confrontation with Jerry. Citizen's arrest, no violence. *I don't want to hear any promises.* Okay. Okay, then I won't make any.

Walnut Street. Dark, quiet. Jerry's house. And that was lightless and quiet, too. No sign of his car in the driveway or on the street. He wasn't home.

Dix parked across the street, doused his lights. His first reaction was disappointment. Where the hell was he? Saturday night, and Jerry Gordon Whittington Cotter was a popular guy, lots of dates, lots of social activities. Either that, or he was in his psycho mode, off somewhere making more torment. Better not be that, God damn him.

Then he thought: No, maybe it's better this way. Now there's time to search the house. Evidence . . . more leverage to force a confession out of him.

He left the car, crossed the street. Lights showed in both neighboring houses, people home, people alert . . . but he might not have to break in. One thing about their bogus friendship: It had been close enough for him to know where Jerry kept his spare key. Jerry'd used it once when they were together after a golf date, when he had forgotten his regular set of keys.

On the front porch Dix lifted the decorative iron frog that crouched among half a dozen fern planters. The spare key was still there underneath. He let himself in. Heavy silence, broken only by the ticking of a mantel clock. He found the light switch, flipped it. He couldn't search in the dark, and if he'd brought the flashlight from the car, he would only have been inviting attention from the neighbors or a passing police patrol. If Jerry came home while he was hunting, let him come.

There wouldn't be anything in the common rooms, the ones Jerry let visitors into. His bedroom, then. And the spare bedroom that he'd mentioned having turned into a home office. The third possibility was the garage. Dix crossed to the center hall, switched off the living room light, and put on the hall light. The door to Jerry's bedroom was open. He went in, fumbled around until he located the wall switch.

The room was almost monastic. Standard double bed, nightstand, dresser; no photographs, no pictures or wall coverings of any kind. All neat, dusted and vacuumed, the bed made and the coverlet smoothed out to a military tautness: Jerry was as fastidious about his surroundings as he was about his personal appearance. Dix opened the nightstand and dresser drawers, found nothing to hold his attention, and moved to the closet. It was deep and wide, not quite a walk-in closet. Clothing carefully arranged on hangers, half a dozen pairs of shoes on a shoe tree, a few small storage boxes. And on one of the shelves, in a back corner—

A trophy.

Thin-lipped, Dix dragged it off the shelf. Tennis trophy, figure of a player—a woman player—mounted on top. Heavy wood and brass, not pot metal like most trophies of the type. The brass plate on the front bore an etched inscription: *Cheryl Adams. Singles Champion. Oregon Coast Invitational Tournament. Pelican Bay, 1979.*

Dix stood holding the trophy. Jerry had kept it because it had probably belonged to his wife: Cheryl Adams, her maiden name, won before their marriage. A memento tucked away in his closet, where nobody was likely to see it. Nobody but Katy. Most of their assignations had been at La Quinta Inn or up on Lone Mountain Road, but at least once he'd made the mistake of going to bed with her here. Katy had been snoopy; while he was in the can or else-where, she'd poked around in the closet and found the trophy. Asked him about it then or later—probably later. What did he have to do with Pelican Bay, when he supposedly came from Washington State? Who was Cheryl Adams? That was why he'd killed her when he had. Only she'd already said something to Eileen. Something oblique, but the fact that she'd mentioned it at all meant that she'd been worried about the possible connection. But not worried enough to keep from meeting Jerry on Lone Mountain Road on the night of August 6. Not worried enough to save her life.

He was gripping the trophy so hard, its edge cut painfully into the pads of his fingers. He relaxed his grip, put the thing back on the shelf, and turned to the storage boxes. Nothing in any of them but sweaters and other winter clothing. He got down on his hands and knees and looked under the bed. Not even dust.

The spare bedroom/office was across the hall. Small desk, Apple pc, chair, catchall table, not much else. On the desk, spread partway open, was a map. Dix picked it up. Topographical map of Mendocino County. The open part was of the coastline; and the intersection of Highway One and Stoneboro Road, a secondary road that led to the southern end of Manchester State Beach, had been circled by a red felt-tip pen. A series of red dashes had been drawn along Highway One from the intersection, as far north as a short distance beyond the hamlet of Manchester, and as far south as Point Arena. Two sets of inked numbers in Jerry's precise handwriting were bracketed next to the dashes: 0.3 and 1.1 on the north, 2.3 and 4.7 on the south. Mileage, evidently. One set could be the distances from the intersec-tion to Manchester and Point Arena. But what did the other set indicate?

Manchester State Beach. Wasn't that where Cecca and Chet Bracco had had their summer cottage? Yes, sure—the Dunes. He and Katy had gone there with them one weekend seven or eight years before. Chet had gotten the cottage as part of their divorce settlement; he remembered Cecca telling him that. Did he still own it? Probably. Chet never let go of anything unless he was forced to.

What the hell could Jerry have been planning for the Dunes? Nothing involving Cecca; she couldn't be manipulated into going there, not the way she felt about Chet and anything they'd once shared. Nothing to do with Dix Mallory. Chet? Did Jerry's mania extend to an ex-husband Cecca had been in the process of divorcing when the accident happened in Pelican Bay? Possible. Amy? More likely. Lure her to the cottage, blow it up the way he'd blown up the Harrells' cabin?

Dix rummaged quickly through the desk. Nothing else that concerned Mendocino County or Manchester State Beach, and nothing pertaining to the Dunes. But he did find one thing in a drawer: a small, round piece of electronic equipment that would fit over the mouthpiece of a telephone, that had a mouthpiece of its own and a control gizmo on one side. The phone filter Jerry had used to disguise his voice. Dix left it where it was without touching it. Not conclusive evidence in its own right, but evidence just the same.

He opened the door to the office closet. Two heavy coats on hangers, some pc discs and other supplies on the shelves, and on the floor, a pile of blankets. He started to shut the door, paused, and looked again at the blankets. Why would they be on the floor like that, as neat as Jerry was? He knelt, tugged at them. And uncovered what was hidden underneath.

Two small oil paintings.

Katy's paintings, the ones Louise Kanvitz had sold for a thousand dollars apiece.

More evidence. Hard evidence.

He didn't touch the paintings either; recovered them with the blankets. Straightening, he checked his watch. Ten-twenty. Still plenty of time before he was due to call Cecca. Kanvitz's missing .32—that was the final piece of evidence that would condemn Jerry. He must have kept the weapon for some reason; otherwise, why take it from her house. Where? Not on his person, not Jerry. In his car, maybe. Or somewhere else in the house. Or out in the garage. His office downtown was also a possibility; he had a safe there, Dix remembered.

All right. Search the rest of the house, then the garage. After that . . . call Cecca, convince her to give him more time if he needed it. He was willing to sit there all night in the dark, waiting for Jerry to come home, and she should be willing to let him. Whatever it took to finish it.

He returned to the living room, put on the ceiling globe in there.

He was opening a drawer in an old maple sideboard when he heard
the noise out front. Somebody running up onto the porch, not being
quiet about it. He took the Beretta out of his pocket, stood tensely
listening.

The doorbell rang, a shrill ripping of the stillness.

Jerry wouldn't ring the bell. Who—?

The knob rattled, but he'd thought to reset the lock. The bell
clamored again. And an agitated voice called out, "Dix? For God's
sake, Dix, let me in!"

Cecca.

A fragmentary confusion gripped him. He put the gun away,
crossed to the window nearest the door to peer past the shade. She
was alone out there, pounding on the panel now with her fist. When
he unlocked the door and pulled it open, she rushed in past him,
stayed close as he pushed it shut again. In the ceiling light her face
was bloodless, her eyes wide and frantic.

"What're you doing here? What happened to—"

"Amy, it's Amy. She isn't at my folks', they haven't seen or
heard from her since this morning."

"Calm down. It doesn't have to mean what you think. You know
how kids are, she may be with friends—"

"No, it's him, it's Jerry. She was supposed to meet Kimberley at
two, but she didn't show up. Dix, he's got her, I can *feel* it. He may
have already . . . she may be . . ."

"Stop that, don't panic."

"I prayed he'd have her here, that you'd found them and she was
all right, but when I didn't see his car . . . Where would he have
taken her? *Where?*"

The map, the red marks on the map.

Chet's cottage on the Mendocino coast?

Now that it was dark, the cottage was drafty and cold. He'd let
her have a blanket and she sat wrapped up in it in Dad's old recliner,
her feet pulled under her, but she still couldn't get warm. She'd
practically begged him to let her put on the space heater, at least,
but he wouldn't. They really didn't need it, he said, which had made
her think they weren't going to stay much longer. But that had been
hours ago and they were still there.

The cold didn't seem to bother him. Or if it did, he didn't let on
about it. He hadn't even taken a blanket for himself. He was sitting

over by the balcony doors, nothing on but his suit coat and slacks.
She could see him in the pale moonlight that came in through the
glass, a black, lumpy shape like a huge bird with its wings folded.
For a long time now he hadn't said anything to her, not one word.
He wasn't asleep though. She knew that if she tried to get out of
the chair, he'd be on her in about two seconds flat.

What was he thinking about over there? What was he planning to
do to her?

She was afraid again. A little, anyway, because of the way he kept
sitting in the dark without moving. How much longer before he told
her what he was going to do? Or went ahead and tried to do it? The
worst part was the waiting. Not knowing was bad enough, but the
waiting . . .

Her stomach hurt, too. That cold chicken soup . . . it was like a
big greasy puddle sloshing around under her breastbone. He'd eaten
some and told her to eat the rest and wouldn't take no for an answer,
so what else could she do? Last supper, she thought. She pulled the
blanket tighter under her chin.

At first, when he'd said he was hungry, she'd thought he might
let *her* fix something to eat. The drawer with the kitchen knives in
it—that had flashed into her mind right away. But no, he wouldn't
let her near any of the cupboards or drawers. He'd found the soup
and opened it and made her eat her share with a dinky little teaspoon.
He was so smart, so smart. But he wasn't perfect. He'd make some
kind of mistake, and then she—

His chair scraped. Amy sat up convulsively. Getting up? No . . .
he'd just shifted position for the first time in a long time. Now he
was motionless again.

How much *longer*?

She settled back and went over again in her mind all the things
he'd said when they were out on the balcony. All the personal questions, all the crazy crap about one bad burn deserving another and
sparks and being a zombie. And all the stuff later, after he'd run out
of questions to ask her, that must have to do with what he was
planning. But what, exactly?

That had been right after sunset. He'd been quiet for a while,
watching the sky darken and the lighthouse beacon begin to revolve
down on the headland; then he'd said he was hungry and finally let
her come inside out of the freezing wind; and then he'd turned on
the table lamp and sat down next to it and took a notebook out of

his pocket and started reading whatever was written in it. It was one of those times he seemed to forget she was there, because when he started talking, it wasn't to her. He'd talked the whole time he was reading, more than five minutes, in that turned-on-faucet way he had in the car. She hadn't heard all of it—part of the time he mumbled—but what she had heard was still pretty clear in her mind.

"Point Arena or Manchester, Point Arena or Manchester. Longer walk to Point Arena, two point three miles compared to one point one ... motel there ... bus service but not on Sunday. Lose a full day if I stay over anyway." Mumble. "Margaret? Only fast way to get back. Then it might as well be Manchester, phone at the general store. She'll come, no problem there, but what about the risk?" Mumble. "So little time. Does it really matter?" Mumble. "All right, Manchester. Good, settled. And Dix and Cecca tomorrow, if they're back by then." Mumble. "Move the timetable up, no choice now. Both at once. But how? Equation for her won't work for him, too. Equation for him maybe. Think about it, adapt it. Doesn't matter if it's foolproof, just as long as they both die." Mumble. "Mathematics, same as always. Numbers, numbers." Mumble, mumble.

She understood what some of it meant. The stuff about Mom and Dix all too well. And Margaret had to be Margaret Allen, the woman who worked in his office. She had a thing for him; it seemed like half the poor females in Los Alegres had a thing for him. He was going to call Margaret and have her drive up and get him tonight, after he ... afterward. Amy bit her lip, trying to work out the rest of it. Was he going to leave the Honda here or somewhere nearby with her in it, dead? But why not just leave *her* and drive the car back to Los Alegres and abandon it there? That would be less of a risk than calling Margaret, wouldn't it?

Walking to Point Arena or Manchester ... that didn't make sense either. It was farther than 2.3 miles from here to Point Arena; it was almost five miles. And less than 1.1 miles to Manchester. What was 2.3 miles south and 1.1 miles north of here? Nothing that she could remember. Nothing but empty coastline—

And cliffs. High, steep dropoffs from the road to the ocean below.

Oh God—cliffs like the one near Pelican Bay!

Dix said, "We can't waste any more time." They were at the cars, hers parked behind his Buick across the dark street from Jerry's house. "You have to decide one way or the other. Right now."

"I still can't think straight—"

"I'm going to the Dunes; that's my decision. But Amy's not my daughter. You do what you think is best for her. If it's the police, all I ask is that you don't tell them where I am or what I'm doing."

Common sense, all her conditioned reflexes, said the police—of course the police. Dix didn't *know* Jerry had taken Amy to the Dunes, the map didn't have to mean that. Guesswork, desperate hoping. Long way to the Mendocino coast, nearly three hours of driving, and what if they weren't there or hadn't been there? Another three hours to drive back, a total of six or seven hours until the authorities were finally notified.

But he'd had Amy six or seven hours already, enough time to do any number of unspeakable things to her. If she was still alive, why not at the Dunes? Where else was there to look for her? And the police were so skeptical and disapproving, so maddeningly slow to act . . . it might take three hours to convince them to do anything at all. St. John would be furious that she and Dix had withheld information, broken the law—he might not even believe her. She had no proof Amy had been abducted, couldn't even file a missing-person report after only a few hours. No proof that Jerry was a murderer; without a search warrant St. John couldn't, wouldn't, go into his house. And she was so tired, so strung out . . . she wasn't sure she could endure the endless questions, the awful passive waiting—

"I'm leaving," Dix said heavily. He had the Buick's door open, was sliding in under the wheel. "Come with me or go to the police. Which is it going to be?"

She didn't reply with words. Her answer was to run around between the cars and thrust her body onto the seat beside him.

TWENTY-SIX

"Amy. Wake up, Amy."

Voice in her ear, hand shaking her shoulder. She came up jerkily out of a thin, cold sleep, groggy for a second, then amazed at herself for having fallen asleep, then frightened and pulling away from his touch as her eyes slitted open and she saw him leaning over her. There was light in the room—he'd turned the table lamp on again. His blond hair was all mussed from the wind, his eyes as shiny as blue glass. The skin over his cheekbones and around his mouth looked like wax in the lampglow.

He straightened. "It's time," he said.

"Time for what?"

"Time to go."

"What time is it?"

"Time to go, Amy."

She shook her head; it was like Alice and the White Rabbit talking nonsense. I'm late, I'm late, for a very important date. Instinctively she tried to burrow back under the blanket. He didn't like that. He yanked it off her, wadded it, and threw it on the floor behind him.

"I said it's time. Stand up, young lady."

The cliffs . . .

Her body didn't want to move. And her right leg, caught under her left, was partly numb. "All right," he said. He clamped onto her arm, lifted her out of the chair with hardly any effort.

As soon as she put weight on the numb leg, it buckled. She said, "Ow," and wrenched loose and sat down again.

255

"What's the matter?"

"My leg . . . it's asleep."

"It won't do you any good to lie to me."

"I swear to God. It's asleep."

"Rub it, then. Keep rubbing until the feeling comes back."

She leaned over and rubbed with both hands, thinking about the cliffs waiting in the darkness. *I don't want to die.* The leg started to tingle, to burn a little the way legs and arms did when the blood was flowing again. She'd be able to stand now. But she didn't get up. She kept rubbing, rubbing.

"Hurry up, Amy."

"It's still numb. I don't think I can walk."

"I'll help you. Give me your hand."

She extended her left hand; his fingers closed hot and sticky around hers. Once more, standing at the front side of the recliner, his body slanted toward her, he lifted her strongly to her feet. And this time, turned as he was, turning as she did, she was right up in his face.

She stepped down hard on his instep, shifted her weight, and drove her right knee into his crotch.

Ballbuster! He jackknifed at the waist, yelled, let go of her hand, and staggered backward, moaning deep in his throat. A wild elation flooded her. But he didn't fall and the direction he went put him between her and the front door. There was no way to get past him quickly and no time to unbolt and unchain the door. The elation died as quickly as it had been born. No time to run to the kitchen for a knife either; he was already starting to unbend, one hand clutching himself and the other fumbling at his belt for the gun, his face all pulled out of shape, his eyes popped so wide it was as if they were coming right out of their sockets.

"Damn . . . little . . . bitch!"

She ran for the balcony door.

He hadn't flipped the lock; she got it open wide enough to squeeze through, slid it partway shut behind her. The wind, strong and chill, almost took her breath away. She fled across the balcony to the outer railing, peered over and down. It looked like a long way to the shadowy sand and grass below. Ten feet, maybe more. She threw a look over her shoulder at the sliding door.

It was opening—he was coming through.

She caught the railing, swung her legs and hips over it, and let go.

*   *   *

Mile after mile of dark, twisting roads, yellow-white headlights, red taillights, wind moaning at the windows, tires humming, the hiss and rumble of passing cars. After a while it began to have a hypnotic effect on Cecca, creating a feeling of detachment and suspension in time. The same feeling induced by the muscle relaxers Dr. Peavey had prescribed to help her sleep after the breakup with Chet.

But it was an illusory calm, a surface detachment as thin as an ice glaze over roiling water. It could be shattered easily, in an instant. She was no different from Eileen in that respect. The black currents and whirlpools were the same, and it was possible that she, too, could be sucked down into them. Once already she'd imagined she could hear the currents, like voices whispering to her: *If Amy dies, it's your fault. You shouldn't have left her alone. You should have sent her away, hidden her someplace safe. It'll be your fault ...*

For the countless time she looked at the dashboard clock: 12:58. And while her eyes were still on it: 12:59. On the road for more than two hours now. They ought to be nearing Gualala, *must* be close to Sea Ranch, but thick forest crowded in on both sides of the car here and the road was so sharp-winding it was almost switch-backed. The ocean seemed far away.

At least the long, treacherous section of highway that hugged the cliffs between Jenner and Fort Ross was behind them. She'd never liked that section—what her father called "white-knuckle territory." Tonight it had seemed even more frightening. Bright moonlight made the sheer rock walls and the foaming ocean far below stand out in sharp relief. It had been too easy to imagine Amy at the bottom of one of the cliffs, broken, lifeless—or worse, a smoldering charcoal ruin. Shutting her eyes had only sharpened the images. She'd endured the stretch of road with her eyes open.

The dashboard clock now read 1:03.

She shifted her gaze to Dix. He sat bow-backed over the wheel, pinching grit out of his eyes with thumb and forefinger. As tired as she was, but alert. He didn't seem to need conversation to help him maintain his concentration. And she didn't want it to intrude on the thin surface of her calm.

The woods thinned out and the road straightened into a long line of white-striped black. There were no lights on it except theirs, but she could see house lights off on both sides ahead. And the ocean

again, too, wind-whitened in the distance. Sea Ranch, the wealthy
retirement enclave just south of Gualala.

Dix said, "It won't be much longer. Another half hour."

"Yes."

"You holding up all right?"

"Yes."

"Sure?"

"Yes." As if it were the only word left in her vocabulary.

We'll find Amy. We'll find her alive.

Yes. Yes.

But he didn't say his lines. And she didn't say hers.

The drifted sand cushioned Amy's fall. But she landed flat-footed,
with not enough bend in her knees, and the force of impact drove
pain up both legs, pitched her forward onto her face. Grimacing, she
gathered herself onto her knees. She didn't turn her head to look
upward; she could hear him at the railing, his voice rising furiously
above the wind.

"Don't run, Amy! You can't get away!"

She was already on her feet, already running.

"I'll shoot you, I'll blow your head off, I won't let you do this
to me . . ."

She hunched her shoulders, but she didn't stop or slow her hobbled
pace. One of her shoes had come off in the fall; the other had filled
with sand after only a few steps and she'd kicked it off. Fragments
of shell and wood dug into the soles of her bare feet as she dodged
into the shadows behind one of the scrub pines. That and the hurt
in her legs and the clinging sand made it seem as if she were
hardly moving.

Any second he would fire the gun . . . but he didn't. She dodged
again, so she could look back to the cottage past the branches of the
pine. He wasn't on the balcony anymore. He wasn't anywhere that
she could see.

Coming after her.

The Honda was off to her right, a thick, boxy shape at the edge
of her vision. Why hadn't she listened to Mom and put a spare key in
a magnetic holder under the bumper! She ran, and the grit underfoot
deepened, grew less firm . . . it was like being in heavy syrup up to
your ankles, having it tangle up every step. The muscles in her legs
were already burning from the strain. But she was nearing the dunes,

almost to where the loose sand gave way to a mat of sawgrass and weeds that would make running a little easier.

The dunes bulked high and round against the sky, their coarse grass coats swaying and rustling in the wind. The dips between them were deep-shadowed, like the craters in pictures of the moon landing. She plowed ahead, gaining speed as the footing improved, and finally reached the first of the cratered areas. But then her left foot came down on something hard and sharp; the sudden stinging threw her off stride, almost toppled her. She said, "Shit!" under her breath and looked back again. She could still see the upper part of the cottage, the lamp burning behind the door glass, but the sand hills and scrub cut off her view of the car and the road and the flats.

If she couldn't see him, then he couldn't see her either.

The thought rekindled the elation she'd felt when she kneed him. All she had to do was to keep moving, get deep in the maze of dunes, and then find a place where she could cover herself with sand and grass and anything else she could find. He'd never find her then, not even if he kept hunting until after daybreak. The dune area was at least two hundred yards wide and a mile or two long, and some of the hills were thirty feet high. He'd have to be able to fly to spot her hiding place.

Her foot throbbed. Cut, probably, by whatever she'd stepped on. She limped and slogged to her left, around a small dune, and then to her right around a higher one. There was a scatter of driftwood at that one's base. She poked quickly among the wood, found a slender, crooked piece about three feet long: a crutch to help her walk, and a weapon just in case.

She was out of breath and her thighs were quivering. She had to rest for a couple of minutes or she'd collapse. The slope there was as good a place as any; she sank onto the sand and grass still warm from the day's sun. Down low like this, she was sheltered from the wind, but it was still cold. Her bare legs were icy to the touch. She'd have to find a place where she could burrow pretty soon—for warmth as well as for safety.

She listened to the night around her. Small sounds: the wind skimming over the tops of the dunes, the seagrass whispering, the breakers making their hissing rumble in the distance. That was all. Not that he'd be out there shouting her name. And you couldn't hear anybody walking in sand anyway.

Amy pulled her left leg over her right, twisting her foot so she could probe at the sole with her fingers. Cut, all right. Sticky with blood and caked grit. But it didn't feel deep and it didn't hurt the way her hand had the time she'd sliced it with the can lid and had to have stitches. A cut foot was the least of her troubles. She dismissed it from her mind.

Her breathing was back under control and the quivery feeling was gone from her thighs. Better get moving. She used the driftwood crutch to lift herself upright. The cottage was to her right and behind her; she looked up at the moon and what stars were visible among the clouds to make sure. Straight ahead, then, or at an angle to the left—toward the beat of the surf. In a little while she could veer north or south, to put even more distance between her and the Dunes.

The moon threw her shadow out alongside her, an extended goblin shape on the whitewashed sand and grass, as she struggled between two smaller hills. Big tufts grew thickly in the lower places here, and walking was easier than it had been. Along the flank of another drift, to where a burned-out log was half buried in the sand: the remains of somebody's cookout fire. She skirted that, rounded another dune—

Something made her stop. All at once there was a tingling on her neck, a clenching in her stomach. One of the more massive dunes reared up on her left, its hairy sides wind-sculpted into ridges. Her gaze crawled up along it.

He was standing on the matted grass at the top, legs spread, outlined blackly against the sky.

She stood in frozen disbelief.

No! He couldn't have found her, it wasn't fair, she'd done everything right, she was safe, he *couldn't* have found her—

"I told you you couldn't get away, Amy."

Voice booming above the thrum of the wind, the words like a lash that broke her paralysis. She stumbled away, but now it was like running in one of those mixed-up dreams: somebody chasing you and you ran and ran and got nowhere at all. And at the same time he was flying down the dune's side, long, sliding steps that tore the grass and kicked up spurts of sand.

He caught her before she could get clear of the cratered area. Grabbed her arm, jerked her around. She hissed at him like a cat, a sound she'd never made before, and swung the length of driftwood with all her strength. Hit him with it—low on his body, bringing a grunt but not doing any damage. Off balance, she tried to club his head. It was a weak blow without leverage and he fended it off with his arm. Then he clutched at the wood, caught a grip on it, wrenched it out of her fingers, and hurled it away.

She fought him, still hissing—hands, feet, knees. But she was mired in loose sand and he was too strong for her. He twined his fingers in her hair, whipped her head back with such force that cartilage cracked in her neck.

"Bad girl," he said.

The whole left side of her face erupted in pain. But only for an instant.

The abandoned development near Manchester State Beach was a wasteland at this hour: lifeless, no lights except at a distant dairy ranch, not even a parked car. The grassy dunes stretched ghostly pale along the left flank of the road. Wind spurts blew sand that ticked against the surfaces of the Buick, fluttered in the headlight beams like will-o'-the-wisps.

Dix's head ached. The strain of driving, pain radiating upward through his neck from knotted shoulder muscles. The last twenty miles had been the hardest, with the urge strong in him to increase his already excessive speed. Only the winding road and the possibility of encountering a highway patrolman or deputy sheriff kept him from giving in to the impulse. Now, finally, the long drive was almost over. And at the end of it, at the cottage, what would they find?

Please let her be there, he thought, please let her be all right.

It was the closest he'd come to praying since his altar-boy days at Old Saint Thomas.

Cecca had been leaning forward, her hands gripping the dash, since they'd turned off Highway One. She said, "The Dunes is on the other side of that sharp bend ahead."

"Visible from the road?" he asked. He didn't remember.

"Yes. All by itself on higher ground."

They were halfway through the bend when he saw it, insubstantial-looking on its pilings, like a black cardboard cutout propped up with sticks. Not wholly black, though. Lampglow made a pale rectangle of one of the fronting windows.

Cecca sucked in her breath. He said warningly, "Easy. Maybe Chet's spending the weekend here."

"No, he was here last weekend, he invited Amy. He wouldn't come again the week after a long holiday—"

Brighter lights seemed to jump out of the darkness, under or behind the cottage. Moving lights—arcing around the building, then
separating into two eyelike beams. Car headlamps.

"Dix!"

He gunned the engine. Now the other headlights were making
erratic vertical jumps as the car bounced downhill toward the road.
It was on a weedy access lane; Dix saw the intersection materialize
in the glare of his lights. Saw, too, that they were closer to the
junction than the other car. Block it off, he thought, and veered over
to the left side of the road. His brights slid over the car's small,
lumpish shape, gave him a brief glimpse of the driver.

Cecca cried, "That's Amy's Honda!"

But it wasn't Amy behind the wheel.

The Honda was twenty yards away when Dix skidded the Buick
to an angled stop across the foot of the lane. Jerry Gordon Whittington Cotter kept coming without slackening speed. At first Dix thought
he would try to ram them out of the way; he yelled, "Brace yourself!" to Cecca. But with only a few feet to spare, the Honda sheered
off the lane onto the grass and packed sand that bordered it—Jerry
gambling on enough traction to slide him around the Buick and onto
the road.

He made it a little farther than halfway before the tires began to
slip and spin. The Honda slowed, settled, the engine roaring. Dix
threw his door open, fumbling to free the Beretta, and ran to the
compact and ripped at the door handle on the driver's side. Locked.
Through the glass, in the glow of the dashlights, he could see Amy
slumped in the passenger seat. Unconscious? Dead?

No, she was moving one of her arms . . .

Cecca had pushed up close beside him, was trying to peer inside.
She screamed at Jerry, "What have you done to her, you son of
a bitch!"

Jerry's strained white face had turned toward them. Astonishment
was written on it, and dismay; he couldn't comprehend how they'd
known to come here. He mouthed something that Dix couldn't hear
over the howl of the engine and the sand-churn of the tires. Dix
moved Cecca back to give himself more room, then hammered on
the window with the butt of the gun. The glass wouldn't break. He
backed off a step, thinking to take aim, thinking: I'll shot you through
the window if that's what it takes.

The tires, spinning deeper, caught traction.

The Honda jerked, gained a firmer bite, and slewed ahead out of the soft grit onto the asphalt. It fishtailed violently on the sand film there, seemed on the verge of going out of control. Then it straightened and shot away.

Dix ran back to the Buick. The engine was still running; as soon as Cecca was inside, he snapped the transmission into gear, cut into a sliding turn in the Honda's wake.

Cecca said in a voice caught midway between relief and panic, "Amy . . . she was in there with him. Could you tell if she—?"

"Alive," he said, "she's alive."

But for how much longer? Ahead of them Jerry was already driving faster than Dix dared to, at a deadly, reckless speed.

Amy clung to the hand-bar with her right hand, the edge of the seat with her left, her feet braced hard against the floorboards. Outside, the highway and the few scattered buildings of Manchester hurtled past. He'd been going faster and faster since she'd regained her senses, realized where she was and that they were turning out of Stoneboro Road onto Highway One. Why so fast? Headlights bobbed behind them, not traveling quite as fast but staying pretty close. Was he trying to get away from whoever was in the car back there? The police . . . was it the police?

She was still woozy and she couldn't think clearly. And the whole lower left side of her face felt as if it were on fire. She could hardly move her jaw. Broken? As hard as he must have hit her, it might be. She couldn't remember the blow or anything until she'd woken up in the car. He must have carried her all the way in from the dunes.

He was saying something, but not to her. Babbling to himself again. Hunched over the wheel, hair all wind-tangled, eyes not blinking—throwing up words into the light-spattered dark.

"How could they have found us? Showing up like that, spoiling, spoiling, always spoiling. Damn their souls! Too late to burn them now. Too late. Only one thing left to do. Cheryl, I'm sorry. Donnie, Angie, I'm so sorry. I should have done a better job of it, I shouldn't have waited so long . . ."

They were going so fast now, the night was a blur around them. As fast as the Honda would go; it shimmied and groaned and rattled, as if it were getting ready to fly apart at the seams. The road had been string-straight, but now it was starting to wind a little again.

"Forgive me," he said. "O God, forgive me."

Turn coming up—sharp right-hand turn. Beyond where the road bent, Amy could see the ocean shining a silvery black in the distance. And closer in, a narrow parking area with a guardrail along its outer border. Guardrail . . . dropoff, cliff . . .

" 'Yea, though I walk through the valley of the shadow of death, I will fear no evil. Thy rod and thy staff they comfort me . . .' "

Chills chased each other along her back. She tried to yell *No!* at him, but her jaw hurt so much she couldn't form the word. She clawed at him, clawed at the wheel; couldn't break his grip. It was as if his fingers had fused with the wheel's hard composition plastic.

" 'He leadeth me beside still waters. He maketh me to lie down in green pastures . . .' "

And they were off the road, rumbling over the rough surface of the parking area. Amy's head cracked into the window glass. Instinctively she clutched at the dash, at the hand-bar again, to hold her body in place.

The white horizontal lines of the guardrail rushed at them.

Heaving impact. And then they were airborne.

As soon as Dix saw the Honda careen off the road, he knew it was deliberate: no skidding, no flash of taillights. The mad final act he'd been dreading. He jammed his foot down harder on the accelerator—but it was a reflex action, nothing more. They were still three hundred yards behind the Honda when it crashed through the guardrail.

"Amy!"

Cecca's anguished cry sawed at his nerves. A hundred yards from the turnout he began to pump the brakes, but they were still going a little too fast when the Buick came off the road onto the gravel. The front end tried to break loose into a skid. He fought the wheel, maneuvered the car under control and to a rocking stop halfway across. Cecca was already out and running by the time he yanked at the hand brake.

He expected to hear crash sounds or their afterechoes; he expected to see a burst of flame and smoke from below the rim. He heard and saw neither. Far-off clatterings, that was all. Cecca reached the splintered guardrail first, half turned as he came up and gestured frantically, shouting something that the sea wind shredded. He looked past her—and the despair in him gave way under a rush of hope.

The ground below the turnout, rocky and covered with thick grass and gorse bushes and scrub pine, fell away in a long, gradual slope—nearly a hundred square yards of it—before the land sliced off in a vertical drop to the ocean. The Honda was still on the slope, its erratic downhill path marked by dislodged rocks and torn-up vegetation that had slowed its momentum. What had finally stopped and held it was a pair of boulder-size outcroppings near the cliff's edge. It was canted up on its side, the two upthrust tires spinning like pinwheels in the wind, lodged in a notch between the outcrops. There was enough moonlight for Dix to make out that the sides and front end were caved in but that the top was uncrushed. The car had somehow managed to stay upright after it landed. If it had flipped and rolled, there would be little chance that Amy was alive down there. As it was . . .

Cecca said something else that the wind tore away, jumped down onto the slope. He was right behind her, then moving past her. The angle of descent wasn't steep enough to require handholds to maintain his footing, and he could see well enough to avoid obstacles in his path. The thing that impeded his and Cecca's progress was the wind. It was strong here with nothing to deflect it, gusting straight into their faces, the force of it like hands trying to push them back. It numbed him, filled his ears with moans and shrieks and the sullen wash-and-thunder of the surf below the cliff. The nearer he got to the edge, the harder he had to struggle through the heaving blow.

When he finally reached the Honda he saw that it wasn't anchored as solidly between the outcrops as it had looked from above. The wind had it and was shaking it like a dog with a toy. The passenger side was the one tilted skyward, at little more than a fifteen-degree angle. He was able to look through the spiderwebbed window glass without much of a stretch.

The interior was thick-shadowed: the crash and slide had knocked out the car's electrical system. He thought he detected movement, but he couldn't be sure. The cracked glass distorted the shapes inside.

Cecca crowded in next to him as he tugged at the door handle, added her strength to his. At first the door wouldn't budge. It was badly dented and he was afraid it was frozen shut. Together they wrenched and pulled at it, the wind burning Dix's eyes, watering them so he was nearly blind. The door gave a little, a little more, and then the latch tore free and they were able to wedge it open. She held it as he wiped his eyes clear, leaned in to feel for Amy in the darkness.

She was twisted down against the driver's seat, half on top of her abductor. Jerry wasn't moving, but she was, struggling feebly to free herself.

Dix grasped her arm. She stiffened, crying out in pain when he tugged on it. He could feel the car quivering under and around him as the wind gusted; he couldn't afford to be gentle. He slid his other hand under her armpit, then braced himself and lifted her. The strain on his arms almost broke his grip, would have if she hadn't been able to help by pushing upward with her feet. Another few seconds and he had her out, safely cradled in his arms.

With Cecca's help he carried Amy upslope, shielding her with his body. The blow at their backs made the climb up easier than the one going down. Still, Amy's weight and the uneven ground surface had his legs trembling by the time they reached the Buick.

It was the only car there. And they were the only people. Highway One stretched black and empty in both directions. As late as it was, nobody had driven along this lonely section in the past few minutes; or if anybody had, they'd either failed to notice what had happened or ignored it. He thought sardonically: Still nobody to help us but ourselves.

He laid Amy gently on the backseat. She was conscious and she seemed alert. Black streaks of blood, a swollen and discolored mouth and jaw, made a Halloween mask of her face. None of her limbs seemed to be broken or dislocated. He stood aside to let Cecca get in and minister to her, question her. There was a blanket in the trunk; he went and got it, shook it out, reached in to drape it over the girl's body.

He asked tersely, "Internal injuries?"

"No, thank God," Cecca said. "Glass cuts . . . and I think her jaw is broken."

"Nothing more serious?"

"Doesn't look like it."

Urgent to get her medical attention, but not so urgent that a few more minutes would be crucial. He said, "Make her as comfortable as you can. I'm going back down to get Jerry."

"Get him? Dear God, you're not going to—?"

"Don't worry. I won't be long."

"Just leave him in the car!"

"I can't."

The wind had pushed the Honda over a little, so that its two tilted-up tires almost touched the ground. When it was upright again, it would be free of the notch and then it would slide or be wind-prodded over the edge. The passenger door had blown shut; he popped it open, managed to jam it back on its sprung hinges. He leaned in. Jerry Gordon Whittington Cotter was a still-unmoving mass in the driver's seat, the seat belt buckled across his middle. Dix fumbled with the buckle release, then took fingerholds on cloth-ing slick with blood and hauled him up across the passenger seat. When he had Jerry's inert weight on the ground, he half carried and half dragged him a short way upslope. He was exhausted by then. All the muscles in his body seemed to be vibrating with fatigue.

He lowered himself to one knee long enough to cleanse his hands on a tuft of grass, then to put fingers to Jerry's neck. Faint irregular pulse. All right.

Dix stood. One more thing to do before he climbed up to Cecca and Amy. He took the Beretta from his pocket, hefted it on his palm as he looked down at Jerry. And then he hurled it into the teeth of the wind, with just enough strength to get it out over the cliff's edge.

He had learned a lesson tonight. One of those hard lessons that ought to be easy but seldom are.

Guns and revenge were the tools of mediocre men.

And Dix Mallory didn't have to be mediocre anymore.

EPILOGUE

Ashes

Dix sat on the terrace alongside the pool, the sun hot on his bare chest and legs, his head and shoulders shaded by the beach umbrella canted next to his chair. It was a warm day, the temperature in the high seventies—the probable final day of a brief Indian summer. Unseasonable weather for early October, and the reason he hadn't kept to his usual schedule of shutting the pool equipment down on the first of the month. Might as well get the last bit of use out of it before fall took a firmer grip. The forecasters had promised fog tonight, cooler temperatures tomorrow, and a slight chance of showers by Monday night.

Cecca had gone into the house to use the bathroom. Amy was in the pool swimming laps. He felt drowsy sitting there alone in the quiet. Almost relaxed for the first time in a long while. Birds chittering, the faint sounds Amy made as she stroked back and forth, the faraway pulse of Los Alegres—horns, car engines, kids' voices—filtering up from below. There was a sense of peace in his surroundings, at least, if little enough in him.

He watched Amy swimming. She was graceful in the water, long arms and legs making very little splash. Her underwater turns were particularly smooth. He was a good swimmer himself, but that kind of turn was something he'd never been able to master. Maybe he could still learn. A minor project for next summer.

If he was still here next summer.

The sun had gotten under the lip of the umbrella and was toasting his chin. The skin on his belly and legs was hot, too. He moved his chair back beyond the umbrella, into the dappled shade under one of the liquidambar trees. Better. Direct sunlight was supposed to be bad for you anyway: skin cancer from the UV rays. His mouth quirked wryly. A lot of things were supposed to be bad for you these days. Most foods, many activities, the water you drank, the air you breathed, the sun that warmed you. But nothing could be worse for you ... nothing ... than your fellow man.

Amy had finished her laps and was at the side ladder near where he sat. When she climbed out he asked her, "How many did you do?"

"Fifty."

"I'm impressed. It took me weeks to get up to fifty."

"Well," she said seriously, "I'm younger than you are."

Physically, anyway, he thought. She'd done a lot of growing up in the past several weeks. Cecca: "Amy used to think she was mature for her age, already an adult. Now she really is." She'd paid a hell of a price for her maturity, though. Was still paying it. Under the harsh sun, as she stood drying off, he could see the tiny scars on her face where flying glass had cut her. Most would fade in time; one or two might remain as outward reminders of what she'd been through. At least she hadn't had to suffer through the lengthy, wired-up healing process of a fractured jaw. Hers had been bruised and dislocated, not broken, that night four weeks ago today.

A great deal had happened in those four weeks, much of it unpleasant. The suffering hadn't ended on the Mendocino coast; only the cause of it had been neutralized. It wouldn't be over for anybody involved for a long time to come. And for some, it would never be over.

Jerry Gordon Whittington Cotter. Survived his second cliffside smashup in about the same condition as he had the first; was still hospitalized in the prison ward at Santa Rosa Memorial with half a dozen broken bones, a punctured lung, other injuries. As a precaution he'd been put on antipsychotic medication, even though he'd exhibited no outward leanings toward violence. During his lucid periods he continually begged for forgiveness—from his wife, his children, his God. But not from his victims. A small but vocal segment of the media conveniently overlooked this, portraying him as a pathetic figure, a victim even more tragic than those he had hurt and killed.

Eileen. Out of the hospital now, being cared for by her brother in Fairfax. Slowly coming to terms with her loss. But she would never be completely whole again. How could she, with her husband and one of her sons dead, and her other son facing years, perhaps a lifetime, of skin grafts and plastic surgery?

Cecca and himself. Under official siege for the laws they'd broken, charged with willful obstruction of justice and illegal trespass. That much was tolerable, if just barely. You were responsible for your actions, right or wrong, and you had to be willing to accept the consequences. Even when you held on to the conviction that you'd been justified in all you'd done. Even when you knew you'd do most of the same things, if not in precisely the same way, if you had to live through it all again.

What wasn't tolerable was punishment for being victims. Official or otherwise. From strangers like the county district attorney and the media people who made allowances for Cotter. And most galling of all, from those you considered to be your friends . . .

Cecca was on her way back from the house. He smiled at her as she dragged her chair over beside him and sat down. "You were in there a long time," he said. "I was beginning to worry."

"There was a call. I thought I'd better answer it."

"Let me guess. Drummond."

"The very same."

"What now?"

"He wants to go over a few more things with us."

"Today? Can't it wait until Monday?"

"He insisted. The hearing date is close and he wants our case to be tightly scripted. That was the phrase he used—'tightly scripted.' "

"Christ. What did you tell him?"

"That we'd have dinner with him tonight."

"In Santa Rosa?"

"Brookside Park. Scannell's. Do you mind?"

"I guess not. Necessary evil."

Michael Drummond was their lawyer. From Santa Rosa, and a good one—up to a point. He believed in them, and that the charges were an unreasonable—"unconscionable" was the word he liked to use—political backlash, the product of an upstaged Los Alegres Police Department and the county D.A.'s overzealousness in trying to make an example of them as a deterrent to the concept of "vigilante justice." Drummond hadn't been able to get the charges dropped, but he was confident that there wasn't a jury that would convict under the circumstances. The problem was, he was as big a publicity hound as the D.A., with political axes of his own to grind, and over their protests he insisted on fighting the case in the media. Currying public favor was smart strategy, he claimed. Dix had twice come close to firing him. But where were they going to find a better lawyer at this late date, and at an equally affordable fee?

When the charges were first brought, he'd asked George Flores to represent them. George had hemmed and hawed and finally declined, on the grounds that he was too close to the principals and might not be able to provide adequate counsel. Which was bullshit. The truth was, George felt uncomfortable with the whole sorry business. He wanted to forget it had ever happened, that he'd walked arm in arm for four years with a homicidal lunatic. And to do that he had to disassociate himself from the lunatic's primary victims.

George wasn't alone.

Laura, Tom and Beth, Sid and Helen . . . all cut from the same cloth, all scrambling to avoid the taint of evil. Solicitous at first, then backing away as more facts came out and the publicity heated up, and now mostly invisible. Using the excuse that they felt betrayed— Dix had made the mistake of admitting that he and Cecca had been suspicious of all their male friends—when in fact *they* were the betrayers. Owen, at least, was honest enough to have shunned them all along: too hurt by Cecca's relationship with Dix to make even a pretense of caring. Friends for years, these people, some for nearly a lifetime, all of whom he'd forgiven time and again for their sins and shortcomings—and one by one they'd gone away.

It was the same sort of thing elsewhere in the community. When Amy returned to school, she'd found herself a social misfit; even her best friend, Kimberley, had begun to avoid her. At Better Lands, Tom had taken to giving newer agents listings that should have gone to Cecca. She wouldn't be surprised, she said, if he found an excuse to fire her before long. At the university, the president and the dean of faculty affairs had been supportive in the beginning, before the criminal charges were pressed; now Dix sensed that if he were convicted, he might well be asked to resign—or at least to relinquish his tenure—in the best interest of the state university system. He could fight that with Drummond or an ACLU attorney, and he'd probably win, but it would be a hollow victory.

At the university, too, he had been treated like a freak in a sideshow: stares, whispers, avoidances, even a few tactless and infuriating questions. The one time he'd encountered Charles Czernecki, the smug little bastard had laughed in his face. Elliot, embarrassed and self-protective—Cecca had told Dix about the episode at the Andersen farm—would have nothing to do with him, communicating on faculty business through memos. If he were squeezed out, Elliot would be relieved. Might even go so far as to actively lobby for his dismissal. For all of these reasons he'd considered resigning immediately, to make sure he kept his tenure, and then finding a position at another school. But he wouldn't do it any more than he would sell his house and voluntarily leave Los Alegres. It would be running away, and he was all through running—from people, things, phantoms, and himself.

So there you had it. The law punishes the victims; society punishes the victims. Fair? Hey, nobody ever said life was fair. But there were moments when he would have liked to get into the faces of all the self-righteous people, friends and strangers alike, and say to them: "What would *you* have done if it had been you? Look inside yourself and tell me honestly that you could have handled it any better than we did."

Cecca stirred in the chair beside him. "Amy," she called, "you shouldn't lie in the sun like that. You'll burn."

"It's not that hot out here."

"At least put some sunblock on your back and shoulders."

"Oh, all right. Where is it?"

"Stay there, I'll get it."

He watched her fetch the sun creme, take it to where Amy was stretched out on a towel, begin to apply it to the girl's shoulders. Average middle-class domestic scene: family at poolside on the last day of Indian summer. False illusion. They weren't average, not anymore. They were a cluster of three little islands cut off from the mainstream, alone and vulnerable. And he felt a fierce protectiveness toward each of them, himself included.

Surviving victims. People damaged and set apart by circumstances beyond their control. People no one could truly understand or empathize with except others like themselves.